CONVERGENCE
THE ZOMBIE WAR CHRONICLES

BOOK TWO

BY

DAMON NOVAK

CONVERGENCE
The Zombie War Chronicles

IS A WORK OF FICTION BY

Damon Novak

All characters contained herein are fictional and all similarities to actual persons, living or dead, are purely coincidental.

©2018 Dolphin Moon Publishing

ISBN **978-1721127689**

Edited by Seven Editing

Cover Art By Jeffrey Kosh

Damon Novak

ACKNOWLEDGEMENTS

First, let me thank everyone out there who decided to pick up my first book and read it. It's more than an amazing feeling to know that some of you are enjoying what I've created.

If you're reading this, then you liked it enough to grab the second one, so double thanks to you.

Next, let me thank the beta readers. (Who even knew what a beta reader was?) They are the ones who get first eyes on a book – at least in the indy world – and their input is really, REALLY important. If I've confused them, or messed up a timeline or a storyline along the way, they'll often catch it. So, Giles Batchelor, Lana Sibley, Nick Wisniewski, Laurie Mault, Connie Nealy, and Tammy Sue Hooper-Hubbard … THANKS.

Finally, thanks to Ramona Martine, proprietor of Seven Editing, and to Eric A. Shelman, my mentor, publisher, and friend.

Ramona's excellent work made the beta readers' job much easier, and Eric's support and input along the way has been invaluable.

Now – on with *Convergence: The Zombie War Chronicles, Vol. 2.* Enjoy.

PROLOGUE

CLIMBING FOX WATTANA

Sixty-seven days before the black rain.

The Henomawi Tribe had always been determined, despite their predicament. They had survived – but hardly thrived – on the postage stamp-sized piece of land to which they had been relegated years ago by the United States government.

Many of the younger members of the tribe had fled, seeking prosperity elsewhere. The tribe was aging, and without some drastic action being taken, would die away.

Almost as if they never existed.

Climbing Fox Wattana was their Shaman, their *medicine man*, as the white people called him. To the Henomawi Tribe, he was Mundunugu. The One Who Speaks to the Spirits; their mystical leader.

He was not supposed to have ever been the tribe's leader; that had been Standing Rock's honor. No, Wattana was knowledgeable in the tribe's ancient ways of healing and held an undying faith in the spirits who held power over the earth, the sun, the moon, and the stars.

His time was best spent in the presence of the spirits, not at a tribal council or sitting before American government officials, fighting for scraps.

The Chief had been adept at that. Even so, he gained little for the Henomawi Tribe.

Chief Standing Rock had died a month earlier, the victim of an attack just outside of the Henomawi Reservation. He had gone to meet with a local congressman in his efforts to gain approval to expand the reservation by over a hundred square miles.

The meeting did not yield fruit; nobody believed it would. But Standing Rock's disappointing news was never delivered.

Not by him, anyway.

The Grove County Police, whom Wattana had never trusted, said their chief was found battered and beaten, lying in the dirt outside of his pickup truck, just a short walk from the entrance to the reservation.

It was a blow to a community already in deep decline, and ravaged by alcoholism and hopelessness.

The chief's son, Yellowfoot, had been one of those youths who had abandoned the tribe. He would not become Chief.

Everyone had looked to Wattana. They had been without leadership for three weeks, and since Standing Rock's death, Wattana had received dozens of tribe members, appealing to him – practically begging him – to become their new Chief.

He had refused until the night of Dancing Rain's visit, believing a younger man may find more success in negotiations with the outside world.

That was his opinion before taking possession of the ancient texts.

Climbing Fox was one of only a dozen or fewer who could still read the old language; there were some words with which he was unfamiliar, but he could usually use the context to understand the meaning.

When the knock came at his door, he had been settling down for the night. Irritated, he looked at the door and considered letting it go unanswered.

They rely on you, he thought. He stood and went to the door, pulling it open. A young woman stood there.

"Dancing Rain," he said. It was the late chief's daughter.

The girl smiled. She was twenty-three years old, a beauty whose beaming face was the exact duplicate of her mother's, who had died two years before of breast cancer.

"Mundunugu, I am sorry to disturb you at such a late hour."

Mundunugu was the name many of the tribe members used when addressing Wattana. It translated roughly to *Medicine Man* but had ancient origins.

Clutched in Dancing Rain's arms was a tattered, leather knapsack. She looked down at it and asked, "May I come in?"

"Yes, yes, of course," said Wattana, stepping aside to grant her entry. He waved his hand toward the kitchen table and chairs.

Dancing Rain hurried in and he closed the door behind her. "Sit, sit," he said. "I'll light a fire. It is cold tonight."

She pulled out a chair and took a seat at the table, placing the satchel in the center. Climbing Fox stirred the dying embers until a flame appeared, then added two small logs to the fire.

He pulled the screen closed and turned, approaching the table. "What have we got here?" he asked, as the fire crackled to life behind them.

Her hands atop the worn, leather satchel, she said, "This was found in my father's possessions, but not in his filing cabinets with the other tribe records. It was in a secret place beneath his bed."

Wattana reached for it, sliding it toward him. "Beneath his bed? How did you discover it?" He lifted the flap and peered inside.

"The carpet was badly worn, and I intended to remove it and finish and polish the wood beneath. Shining Eyes was going to help me. When we moved the furniture out, we found a cut in the carpet. The panel was beneath it, just a dirt hole, really. The satchel is all that was inside. They appear to be ancient texts."

Wattana slid an old book from inside the pouch, its cover fashioned of timeworn animal hide, likely deer. The hair was nearly worn away over most of it. The book wasn't thick, perhaps only a half-inch. He opened the powdering cover to find brittle and yellowed paper inside, with handwritten words scribed on them.

Wattana carefully inspected the pages. "These appear to be Henomawi texts. Very old. Have you read any?"

"I do not read the language, Mundunugu. Some, but not enough to know the meaning. There are too many words with which I am unfamiliar."

Wattana carefully turned the pages, reading only a sentence or two from each page. By the time he had reached the fourth page, his heart was beating noticeably faster. He put his open palm over his heart, trying to control his breathing, which had grown shallow.

"You must go. Leave the bag with me."

"Is everything alright?" asked Dancing Rain.

Wattana nodded. "It will be. I must study these pages. Much can be learned from our ancestors."

"You're pale, Mundunugu. I hope I didn't –"

"I'm a healer, Dancing Rain. If I need help, I shall heal myself."

The girl smiled and nodded. "Of course. I'm sorry." She stood. "Please, stay seated. Thank you for seeing me, and I'm very sorry for the interruption."

Wattana waved a hand at her, turning back to the first page as she closed the door behind her.

His thoughts were filled with fear.

And hope.

Ω

Wattana stayed awake reading the contents of the old book until the yellow glow of the morning sunlight dissolved the night. His fingers continually played on the two words scrawled in the center of the book's cover.

Giga Artleiste.

Blood Revenge.

This practice had been known for centuries, and it was taken seriously by elders in the Henomawi Tribe. In ancient, and even more recent times, when hunters returned with deer or other game, it was believed the ghosts of the animals would follow the hunters back to their village to take blood revenge. The Henomawi feared that the ghost could retaliate by infecting the hunter and his family with disease, or misfortune. Native hunters performed special incantations over the game they killed to pacify these spirits.

Wattana's mind drifted through their history as he sifted through the texts. He referred to some of his other books to decipher the exact meaning of the words before him, and the implications of it all.

To him, it was earth-shattering. World-changing.

The consequences ran through his mind. If he were to carry out the curse detailed on the pages, would the ghosts of millions and millions of dead retaliate against him and his tribe?

It may not matter. He and his people were doomed to slowly die away and vacate the world if nothing changed. Nobody had answers, and the outside world seemed to have closed their eyes and ears to their pleas.

Wattana closed the cover. He would go to sleep and see what the gods told him in his dreams.

He would know the answer upon awakening.

Ω

Climbing Fox awakened at noon. He was hungry but did not take the time to eat; his mind kept returning – as it had all night – to a passage describing the aftermath of the ceremony he now considered performing.

The words were cryptic, even to him. He pored over many books, trying to find anything similar, but in the end, he gave up.

The words translated as follows:

After the moon and the sun cross the sky three times, an inky blackness will rain down over all creatures of the world. Only those with the blood of our land in their veins shall live; the others shall walk the earth, forever hungry, forever dead.

What was the inky blackness to which the words referred? Surely it could not be a literal description?

Often, the Henomawi elders used creative language to add a mystical air to their ceremonies. They believed it encouraged loyalty and dedication on the part of those in attendance.

These downtrodden tribe members, marginalized by the outside world for all their lives; left to live in poverty and squalor on an ill-suited, tiny patch of land.

Land granted by the white men who only wanted to shut them up. Shut them away.

They may as well be caged for the freedom they had.

The ancient words were, no doubt, meant to empower them; to give them a sense of privilege that their people had the power of magic at their disposal.

Climbing Fox had believed it for many years. His doubts had begun to settle in fully at Chief Standing Rock's death.

When it was only the two of them, it had been Henry and Jim. They would drink whiskey in moderation and discuss the fate of their tribe. Two men facing an uphill battle to save their people. Then Jim had been murdered outside their gates, and Wattana had been burdened with the weight of the world.

Of the entire Henomawi Nation. For all that nation was anymore.

His mind returned to the strange words, and what they might mean. *Walking the earth, forever hungry and forever dead?*

Surely this was also another way of saying that those affected would be filled with regret, and would change their way of thinking; more a reference to what men would feel in their souls. It could not mean to physically kill people. If that were the case, how, then, could they walk the earth forever hungry?

After meditating with this knowledge for a long while, Climbing Fox Wattana picked up his cell phone. He scrolled down the list to the name Atian Shining Eyes and pressed the button.

"Hello?" came the young man's voice.

"Atian? It is me, Climbing Fox. I'd like you to find Silver Bolt and Dancing Rain and join me here. At my home."

"Silver – oh, Magi. Yes, Mundunugu. When?"

"As soon as you can. I will eat now, so will be done by the time you arrive."

Ω

As he cleaned the dishes, the knock came on the door. "Come in!" he called.

The door opened, and Atian came in first. Behind him was Anjeni Dancing Rain and Magi Silver Bolt.

"Mundunugu," said Anjeni. "It smells like chicken soup."

"Your senses are finely tuned," said Climbing Fox. "Please, sit there on the sofa. You should be comfortable while we discuss my decision."

As they moved to the couches, Atian said, "So you have decided to become our Chief!"

"It is not about that. Your guesses will be wasted, so don't bother."

He finished drying the bowl and spoon and put the pot aside to dry in the rack. As he passed the kitchen table, he gathered up the text Dancing Rain had brought him the night before.

"Ah, the book," said Anjeni. "Did you find it interesting, Mundunugu?"

Wattana sat. "It is why you are here. I trust you. I believe you will be of vital importance as I carry out my duty."

"Your … duty?" asked Anjeni Dancing Rain. "From there?" She indicatcd toward the book.

He nodded. "It was the great spirits who caused you to find this book. They also directed you here."

"Are there answers in there, Mundunugu?" asked Anjeni.

Magi and Atian jerked their heads back and forth between Wattana and Anjeni, confusion on their faces.

Wattana leaned forward. "Anjeni, were you able to read any of this?"

She shook her head. "I recognized the words on the front. *Giga Artleiste.* I know those words translate to *Blood Revenge.*"

Wattana nodded and patted the worn, leather cover of the book. "Let me be clear. I do not yet know what the ceremony described here will do to help us. It is described as a way to take revenge against our enemies, so that means it is likely a curse. However you describe it, it is meant to affect others in a bad way, and to help our people."

"How?" asked Magi. "Has anyone ever performed it before?"

Wattana stared at him. He had asked him to come because he had been very interested in their people's history and heritage from the time he was a young boy.

"I do not know when it was written. Perhaps it was used, but did not work."

Magi stared, fascinated. "May I?" he asked. Wattana slid the book to him, and he opened it with reverence.

Magi could both speak and read the language of the Henomawi. He was born on the night of a great storm, and as his head pushed out of his mother, a great bolt of lightning had struck a mighty oak tree nearby. It lit up the sky like daylight, and the fire that had burned inside that enormous tree had smoldered for a week.

Magi had shoulder-length brown hair, almost black. His eyes were a deep brown, so black his pupils were almost non-existent. He was a serious young man who loved his people and would do anything for them.

Dancing Rain was Magi's fiancée. He was twenty-two years old when he asked for her hand in marriage two years prior, and the Chief had given the union his blessing.

Standing Rock died before the ceremony could even be scheduled.

It was one more reason; his future father-in-law and the chief of his tribe had been killed by those who would be the targets of the ceremony.

Wattana knew Magi would be all-in.

Part of the reason he knew that was because while the other young men and women respected him, they did not believe in the mystical ways of the spirits.

Magi did. He was Henomawan through and through, embracing all their beliefs and ceremonies.

Wattana could not blame the other young people for their lack of faith; they had seen little help come their way, and things seemed only to get worse from one year to the next.

The spirits were nothing more than stories and wishes to them, Wattana knew.

Still, he thought. That will make it easier for them to assist me. They will humor an old man – just an old man, not a shaman with extraordinary powers – to summon help from their gods.

Wattana carried on. With great patience and in fine detail, he explained what he intended to do; he told them why, and what he suspected would happen as a result. He told them to be patient afterward, for worthwhile things often took time to manifest.

Whatever this ceremony would achieve, it may take some time to realize it was working.

Then he asked for their help if things went wrong.

He didn't say it to his young visitors – soon to be his accomplices in his dark venture. He didn't really believe it. Still, the thought lingered:

What if the words were meant literally? What if it was dark magic contained on those timeworn pages?

It did not matter. The Henomawi people had nothing to lose.

Interim Chief Climbing Fox Wattana dismissed his guests. After they left, he began at the first yellowed page, and read the book over and over again.

He could make no mistakes.

Ω

August 28, 2017

The time had come. A month earlier, the tribe had unanimously deemed him to be their new Chief, despite his insistence that a younger man was needed.

Or a woman. It was the 21st century, after all. He would not have objected.

They would not have it. He was now Chief Climbing Fox Wattana of the Henomawi Tribe.

He felt no pride. He felt no sadness or joy. He merely accepted the title as the burden it was, with little hope of making a difference in any of their lives.

He stared at the book. It was time. So far, only Dancing Rain, Silver Bolt and Shining Eyes knew of his plan.

For it to work – if it had any chance at all – he must perform the ceremony before every member of his tribe. He could do nothing about those who had abandoned their home and families, but he did mandate that all who lived on the reservation be in attendance.

Ω

On that important night, with a silver, crescent moon hanging in the sky above them, the entire tribe gathered. No guards at the gate, no baby under the watchful eye of a sitter; all were present.

He wore his native dress; what the young people called a *costume*. They could not know that was an insult; it was ceremonial garb, worn only during momentous occasions when the spirits must look down on his people with great favor.

His headdress was worn from time, but still brightly colored. The sky above them blossomed with stars, the air cool enough for many in attendance to wear sweaters or wraps.

Some had brought lawn chairs, others blankets. As was typical, they arranged themselves in a large circle on the ceremonial field, where all such gatherings were held. A large bonfire was set up in the center, and Wattana stood between the unlit pyre and where the people of the Henomawi Tribe waited.

"I will not ask for proof that all are in attendance. Either what we do here tonight will work, or it will not. I believe it is our peoples' last hope."

He went to Dancing Rain and nodded. She held out the ancient text. He took it from her, bowed his head one time, and returned to stand before the crowd.

"This text was found in Chief Standing Rock's home, hidden away beneath a floorboard. I have come to believe the reason it was hidden away is that it was a last resort for him; something to which he would turn if all other efforts to expand our reservation and give us a chance to survive failed."

"Have they now failed, Mundunugu?" asked someone from the tribe.

"Is our time almost over?" another voice asked, almost sounding resigned to the fate of their people.

Ignoring their shouted questions, Wattana said, "This night will mark the beginning of a great battle. Things will be set in motion that will test our courage and resolve. I urge you all, do not be frightened, and understand that our people are the first people, and therefore should be the last people."

Quiet murmurs came from the crowd. Wattana knew why; his words were cryptic, yet powerful, and left little doubt that if the coming ceremony was successful, their world could change forever.

He nodded his head and began. In response, Magi carried a lit torch over and touched it to the base of the huge stack of wood. The flames quickly traveled the circumference of the pyre, and soon licked at the night sky. As it grew, the light from the massive bonfire bathed the faces of those watching in a dancing, yellow-orange glow.

Wattana spoke, his voice rising over the crackling fire behind him: "On the first day, as on the last day, we, the Henomawi people stand proud and free …."

$$\Omega$$

CHAPTER ONE

Present Day

I awoke to the sounds of gentle water lapping up against the side of the Sea Ray and stretched out in my bed. Checking the battery-powered clock on the nightstand, I saw it was just 6:10 AM. Turns out I wake up around the same time no matter where I am, or how many zombies enter the equation.

Sliding the curtains aside, I looked out on Key West in the distance. I couldn't see anything or anyone moving on shore, and I wished like hell we could just motor back over to the dock and go hang out at Margaritaville. Maybe do the Duval Crawl later on.

It struck me to wonder what rhymed with shuffle or shamble. Maybe there was a Cuffle or a Gamble street the zeds could play on, where they could get run over by a drunk in a golf cart or a scooter.

Eyes closed again, my mind turned to Lilly and Georgie. Then my thoughts immediately shifted to Roxy and her friend, Terry.

It was just a bit nerve-wracking, knowing I had four people relying on me. If there were gonna be four people, it would suit me just fine if Clay and Tanner were in the mix. They didn't deserve what they got. I didn't deserve to be the sole surviving brother. I still wondered why.

You may wonder why I didn't mention my Pa when I said that just now. The reason is, he wouldn't want to live in a world like this one. I think he's wanted to go home to Jesus and see Ma again since she checked out, so he's truly in a better place.

I got up and pulled on my boxer shorts. I like to sleep in the nude no matter the situation; just can't stand pajama pants bunching up in my ass crack at night.

I pulled my jeans on and a fresh tee shirt, and walked to the door of the master cabin, pulling it open. The boat was quiet, except for the sound of the water and my footsteps.

There were two other sleeping berths; one was set up with bunks, which is where we put Roxy and Terry. The other was just a tad smaller than this one, but with a queen-sized bed. Lilly and Georgie took that one.

I'm tall, so they graciously let me have the king-sized bed.

I climbed the six steps to the bow and moved over to the side rail to take a piss. We hadn't figured out how to get the head set up yet, and I didn't need our waste sloshing around for the entire trip. Shower water was one thing. Black water was another.

Black water, I thought. *I'd rather have it in a smelly tank than falling from the sky*. I unzipped my jeans and let it flow.

As my eyes scanned the shoreline, I saw a couple of fires burning, the smoke ebony and thick, telling me nobody was even trying to put 'em out. Who knew how they started; somebody crashing a car into a house, an ember from somebody's fire catching the building they were hiding in.

I was just tucking away when I heard soft footsteps and a voice behind me.

"I didn't think that was the bilge," said Georgie. "You presentable?"

I laughed, and the sound was foreign to me; it'd been a while, it felt like.

"Yep, all stowed and ready for next time. How'd you sleep?"

"Sleep?" she said, smiling. "I passed out."

"The zombie apocalypse'll do that to ya."

She stared at the city, her eyes tired. "I put coffee on. They have a bunch."

"I saw," I said. "It's a Keurig, right?"

She covered her mouth as she yawned and said, "Yes, which means it's done. Ready for a cup?"

"I'm ready to plot our course. This ain't the kinda boatin' I'm used to. You ever?"

"Only with someone else driving," she said. "Cole?"

I turned. "Yeah?"

"I can't even tell you how grateful I am you came to get Roxy and Terry. I know you lost your brothers and your father, but thank you for not shutting down and … well, if you were someone else, you might've made a different decision."

I looked at her. She looked like she'd just gotten out of the shower; her hair was wet, hanging down and soaking into the shoulders of her white top. She had on beige capris and white, canvas shoes.

If I didn't know better, I'd think she was just up and ready for a day on the water. Maybe a Bloody Mary first.

"Georgie, you let strangers into your house that day. I know you're a doctor, but you didn't need to put yourself at risk and let us in. So, it's me who owes you. Lilly, too. If you hadn't done what you did, Tanner or Clay might've eventually killed me."

She shook her head and took my hand. "I would never have turned you away. And now, I want you to promise me something."

"Name it."

"Stay with us. Please. I'll do whatever I can, and I'll make sure Roxy and Terry pull their weight. You and Lilly are the only two I can imagine going through this with. Meeting you was like getting straight 7s on a slot machine."

"Gamble much?" I smiled.

She smiled back and shook her head, her wet hair bouncing against her neck. "Oh, you have no idea how many weekends I spent cleaning up at the Indian casino in Immokalee. But that's neither here nor there. *You're* the bonus. *Our* jackpot. I'm just begging you not to be fool's gold. Be the real thing for us, Cole."

"I tell ya, I'm as real as that coffee that's gettin' cold," I said, pulling her by her hand to the galley. I smelled the brew immediately.

"How do you like it?" she asked, letting go of my hand and going to the machine.

I felt brief disappointment at the absence of her fingers squeezing mine. "Black, light sugar," I said.

She pulled out the old pod, put in the new one, and started a second cup. She doctored mine and carried it over. "Here. Let me know if I need to add anything."

"I'm thinkin' we need to hug the shoreline in case anything goes wrong. Definitely want to stay out of any shippin' lanes if we can figure out where they are."

"Why?"

"Unmanned ships that size? They plow into us, we're finished."

"Good point," she said. "What about fuel and necessities?"

"Checked out the food supply. Only non-perishables on the boat. Macaroni and cheese, canned soups and stuff. Plus what we brought. We'll have to stop eventually, but we can probably go a couple days."

"Maybe we'll find a boat adrift or something," she said. "Get some more food there."

"As long as nobody's on board," I said. "I'd really like to avoid runnin' headlong into anymore of those dead things. They scare the fuck outta me, if I'm bein' honest."

I was sitting at a soft-edged table shaped like a kidney, with bench seats curving all around it. Georgie carried her black coffee over to where I sat and slid into the bench seat across from me. She drank deeply from her steaming mug and put it in front of her.

"I can almost believe none of this happened if I close my eyes."

"You'll wanna keep 'em open these days," I said. "That said, I think a boat's the way to go. With those things out there, deep water all around you is the only way to have true peace of mind."

Georgie stared at me, her face morphing into concern.

"What is it?" I asked her.

"Us."

"Us?"

"All of us." She leaned forward and lowered her voice to a conspiratorial tone. "Cole, how sure are you that none of us can still – I don't know – change into them? In the middle of the night, then just get up and kill everyone else in their sleep?"

"Shit, like I needed to start worryin' about that!" I was frustrated. She was right, but damn. I didn't need to even consider that.

"I'm sorry," she said. "I guess in the abstract, I'm just worried about Terry."

22

I knew what she meant. She knew her daughter, Roxy. She had no doubt gone over her inch-by-inch and knew she didn't have any bites or scratches from those monsters out there.

None of us really felt good about having a young man strip for us – particularly me – and giving him a good once-over. I supposed I needed to, just to set our minds at ease.

"You already check out Roxy?"

"100% clean," she said, smiling. "You knew I'd do that, huh?"

"You're a doctor, number one, and a mother, too. No doubt in my mind you'd examine your daughter."

She slapped her hand on the table. "I don't know what I was thinking. Yes, I'm a doctor."

I stared at her. "And this comes as a surprise, why?"

She shook her head. "It's just that I don't think in those terms. Normally, patients are dressed or have already been prepped by our nursing staff before I perform surgery. I rarely examine grown, nude men, at least when they're awake. But Terry's gay, I'm a woman and I *am* a doctor."

"Match made in heaven?" I asked, still not sure what she was talking about. "You figure that out, or did he tell you?"

"Roxy told me when I was looking her over. She's funny. She said of all the guys to be stranded with, she picked the one she couldn't even have sex with."

"TMI, Georgie. So, I'm off the hook, is what you're sayin'."

"I know. I'm babbling. Anyway, yes, I was originally thinking it would be better for you to examine Terry, but he'd likely be more comfortable in front of me than you."

I breathed a sigh of relief. "Well, that's settled. Tell you what. If he's infected, I'll hoist him up and toss him overboard. That can be my contribution."

Georgie just stared at me, mouth open.

"Not because he's goddamned gay! Because he'll be a zombie!" I shook my head.

Georgie patted my hand and smiled. "I was just messing with you. Still, to be humane, you might be better to just have him look at the pretty water and put a bullet in the back of his skull."

"Mom?" said a voice.

We both jerked our heads toward the door. Roxy stood there, her face aghast. "Put a bullet in whose skull?" she asked.

"Terry's," I said, then took a sip of my coffee.

Georgie spit coffee through her nose, and Roxy stormed toward the table, her eyes blazing anger. "What?"

I laughed. "I'm kiddin', Roxy. We were just sayin' the doc here needs to check out your friend. Make sure he didn't get touched by those zombies out there."

"He didn't."

Georgie looked at her daughter. "He's worn long sleeves since we found you two. That doesn't strike you as —"

"He always wears long sleeves!" she said. "He has psoriasis on his elbows, and he's embarrassed by it."

Georgie held up her hands. "He needs to be checked out, just like you. Send him to me when he gets up and we'll do it in the big bathroom. Get it over with so we know we don't have to murderize him."

Roxy slapped her mother on the arm and laughed, despite herself. "Murderize?"

"Let me," I said, smiling at Georgie. "It's a Three Stooges reference. One of 'em was always gonna murderize one of the others."

"I wish they *would've* murderized each other," said Roxy. "My mom tortured me with their dumb movies when I was growing up."

I stood. "Careful what you say about my Stooges or I'll give you the old triple slap or a double eye-poke. Anyway, you guys hang out and have your coffee. See what you can find in the way of breakfast, and I'll check everything out and make sure we're good to cast off. If we're ever makin' it to Lebanon, we need to get movin'."

"Lebanon?" asked Roxy, her face contorted. "Why on earth would we go to the Middle East?"

Georgie laughed, and I shook my head. "We're not going to the Middle East, but when you find out where we are going, you might feel the same."

"You said Lebanon," said Roxy, looking back and forth between us.

"Lebanon, Kansas," I said. "The land of 7-night-a-week bingo and parties where the only booze is in flasks in the attendees' back pockets."

"Careful, Rox," said Georgie. "Your face might stay that way if you hold it too long."

The look tweaked but didn't go away.

Ω

By the time I figured out the valves and connectors for the black water and went over the entire boat for anything else I'd need, I had a manual and two sets of keys that were both in the same bag. Luckily, I hadn't destroyed the ignition switch when I hotwired it, so we were now good to start and stop at will.

To be honest, I was relieved, because I was scared of frying something when I was crossing the wires. I'm good, but I'm still human.

Turns out the almost-yacht was indeed a 40-footer. It was a Sea Ray 400 Fly, to be specific, which meant that it had a flying bridge where you could drive the boat from on top, rather than from the main cabin, where the galley and dining areas were. In weather, the inside helm would be the obvious choice, but on a nice, sunny day, or when you wanted excellent visibility due to a zombie apocalypse, the flybridge was the best option.

When I was all done, I went back into the galley and the attached dining area. Everyone was kicked back, and Terry was flipping through television channels.

"Gettin' anything?" I asked.

He looked over. "No, just black, with the channel number."

I walked over to it. Behind the 50-inch TV was a plate on the wall. It said SATELLITE. The switch was in the off position. I flipped it up. "There. Try now."

On about the fourth channel change, he was on 143 when we heard a blip of a voice.

"Stop!" I said. "Hear that?"

He'd already flipped to 144. "Go back," I said. "One."

The number changed, and I heard, "... ode ... our way ... zombie ... dogs."

"Zombie dogs?" asked Terry.

"We missed somethin' in between those two words, I'm sure. Listen."

We did, but apparently the broadcast was over.

"This may sound crazy but did that voice sound like that Micky Rode guy?" asked Georgie.

"I know Micky Rode!" said Roxy. "Well, sort of. He came to our school once. Talked about radio, or broadcasting or something."

"Seriously?" asked Georgie. "To your college?"

"No, way longer ago than that. High school. I was like, a junior."

"Did you meet him?" I asked. "Would he remember you?"

Nokosi trotted through the door and ran directly to Lilly, sitting beside her as she stood leaning on the counter.

"Nah, I wasn't near this hot then," said Roxy. "I'm sure he didn't even see me."

"Sexy confidence," said Terry, giving Roxy a slap on her arm.

"Learned that from you," she said, swatting at him.

"Well, I'm glad to see the walkin' dead haven't dampened your senses of humor," I said. "I want to pull anchor in ten. No sense in sittin' around when we can be underway."

"Should we keep the television on that station?" asked Lilly. "Don't know how we picked up the broadcast, but if it was Rode, we need to monitor it."

"True enough," I said. "There's a marine VHF radio in the wheelhouse, too. We'll see what that thing picks up, plus, we still have Pa's ham radio too."

"Terry?" said Georgie.

He looked at her. "Yeah, Mrs. Lake?"

"It's Doctor Lake, but you know that," she said. "Which is why I need to give you a once-over."

"Once over what?" he asked.

"Mom wants to make sure you haven't been bitten or scratched. And don't bother arguing. Claims to the contrary will not suffice."

I left before I saw the outcome, but I knew Georgie pretty well by then.

Terry would comply.

Ω

27

CHAPTER TWO

We set a north-northeasterly course, and while I was a boater, I wasn't this kind of boater. This was bigger'n any boat I'd ever driven before.

Maybe I already told you that. Either way. I was nervous.

The depth gauge was easy enough to figure out, and there were channel markers in the waters just off the Florida Keys, but reading nautical maps and just whipping around the Florida Everglades are two different things.

It was 8:15 in the morning by the time we scooted out of there. I thought about the owners of the boat, wondering if they'd been on their way to use it as their own escape, but I didn't dwell on it; there were plenty of other options at that marina, if they made it that far.

By the time we left, the two fires had burned together, creating one giant burn. As we headed out toward deeper water, we kept bumping into debris in the water. I had Lilly take the wheel while I went down to have a closer look.

It turns out it was human debris. Many of 'em still squirming around in the water. One man's body was bloated to probably four times its girth; he clawed at the water and screeched at us. The bloat had formed in such a way that he was destined to float on his back until something changed in either his position or his buoyancy.

Our hull bumped him easily out of the way, and he began his angular trip along the v-shaped wake, to the rear of the Sea Ray.

Other bodies, both men and women, dressed and nude, floated in the water, too. Some of 'em clawed at the foamy wake as they floated by, and even when I didn't see any body parts moving, I figured most of 'em were zombies. What that meant to me is they'd eventually wash ashore and use whatever mobility they had left to get to food.

Shellers beware.

I ran back up the steps to update my sis and take over at the wheel.

She turned green at the news of what we were plowing through, and we were both relieved when we got into deeper water where currents had taken the zombies out to sea.

"It's getting rough," said Lilly.

"Yeah, I know. I had some dumb idea I'd be doing about 25 miles an hour up, but with this shit, I can barely manage 20. If everything goes perfect, we're talking five plus hours to get up to Naples."

"We need to stop there?"

I guided the boat to the west to head directly into a growing swell. "Shit."

"Water doesn't do this in the Glades," said Lilly. "You okay?"

"I'll manage," I said. "It's a big enough boat. Good stabilizers."

We heard footsteps, and the smell of coffee hit me before I saw the top of Georgie's head.

"I smell that!" I said.

"You've had three cups already. This is for Lilly."

"Too late, I saw you had two cups before I turned around."

To my great surprise and disappointment, she sat down in the bench seat behind us and said, "It's for me."

I waited for the punchline that never came. Then I shrugged like I didn't give a rat's ass.

"I like her," said Lilly.

"I used to," I said.

Georgie got up and put the coffee cup in my cup holder. "How long until we hit land again?"

I picked up the cup and took a sip. "It's around a hundred miles. With this chop, we're lookin' at five, six hours."

"Terry's already seasick," said Georgie. "I checked the boat for Bonine or Dramamine, but nothing."

"Poor kid," said Lilly. "Nothing worse. At least while you're sick."

"There are worse things, as we all know," said Georgie. "Thankfully, not out here."

Her previously wet hair was now dry and shiny. I guess there was a blow dryer in the head. Anyway, she had it pulled up and tied, and she looked fresh as a daisy.

"We'll need to get together and talk strategy before we hit land," I said. "We're still runnin' a democracy here."

"Look," said Georgie. "You went against your sister's wishes to save Roxy and her friend. I appreciate that, and –"

"Wait a minute," said Lilly. "I never said I didn't want to go to Key West. I just … well, I didn't know you very well then, and I was afraid I'd either die or lose my only living brother to help a stranger."

Georgie nodded. "I understand that. You could've argued against it, and I saw in your eyes you wanted to. So, thank you, too."

Lilly was in the co-pilot's chair to the left of the captain's chair I sat in. She got up and went to sit on the seat in the back of the bridge cabin. I turned to see her take Georgie's hand.

"I *do* feel like I know you now. I suppose that process accelerates during a crisis. Thank you for saving CB. From what I know, he might've died without your help."

"We basically saved one another," said Georgie, leaning forward and hugging Lilly.

Almost everything seemed okay in our little corner of the world. At least the zombies were at bay.

For now.

Ω

There were different bands on the radio, and I don't know what he was doing or what kind of equipment he had, but as I drove the boat and Lilly sat in the co-pilot's seat, her feet up on the helm, she hit a station and we heard our old friend, Micky Rode's voice.

"… if you're heading out to find us, know we're just now in Benton, Illinois. I know that's not far from our last stop but let me tell you; over-the-road travel isn't easy now. The changed people are everywhere now, and if you're following these broadcasts and attempting to connect with us, stay off highways running through heavily populated areas."

"Lilly, call everyone up. I want them to hear this guy. They need to know who we're followin'."

"You got it," said Lilly, getting up and trotting down the steps. Less than a minute later, Georgie, Terry and Roxy sat on the curved, bench seat in the back of the bridge, all listening intently. Nokosi lay at their feet, her head up and her tongue flopping out as she panted.

"I have some new news," Rode continued. "First, and I'd guess most disturbing, is that it's not just people this happened to. From what we've seen, it killed most of the dogs and cats. Maybe other wildlife. We've run across several dead deer and some dead opossums and racoons."

"That's horrible," said Georgie. "I wonder how Nokosi survived it."

Micky Rode went on: "I've seen a couple of live dogs, but few. Maybe they were out of the black rain when it hit, which could mean there are a lot of people and animals in their homes now, safe."

"That's a good point," said Roxy. "We were inside the Hemingway house when the black rain hit. Terry and I had broken away from our tour group –"

"That was my idea," said Terry. "I don't like structure."

"Hold on, y'all," I said. "Pick that story up when this guy goes off the air. I want you to know who we're followin', and why."

I saw Georgina pat her daughter's leg to reassure her I wasn't an asshole, I guess. She was basically saying, 'He's right. Shut up for a sec.'

"In every population center, you'll find more of the dead people, and I've noticed they tend to migrate toward one another. I guess it's the movement of the others that draws them toward one another, and once they discover – if that's how it even works – the other isn't a food source, they just move along together."

I turned and everyone on the bridge was nodding along with Rode's assertions. So far, he hadn't said anything that I didn't also believe to be true.

"If any of you have been out on the streets, you know what these things are after. They want *you*, and they will attack you and tear you apart, like hyenas or jackals would.

"If you're housebound for any reason, and you haven't left your home in a long while, just know you won't be getting that Amazon.com package or that delivery from Blue Apron anytime soon. I recommend finding a friend who's not sick and getting in your car to join us in Lebanon, Kansas. I'll go over what I've shared before, because if you've just picked up this broadcast and you don't know anything, I'd recommend taking a good long look outside your window."

At that point, Rode recounted the video from Climbing Fox Wattana of the Henomawi Tribe. He also shared his thoughts on the faked suicide of the Indian shaman.

"So, that's it," he continued. "When you hit the road, I'd strongly recommend you avoid the main population centers. The GPS put us through St. Louis, but we're taking detours around it. You do the same when you hit a bit city, or even a larger town.

"If everything goes well, we should be in Lebanon in roughly six or seven hours. I'll try to set up and broadcast once we're there. Meanwhile, I hope you all have angels on your shoulders. Godspeed and good luck to you all. Micky Rode, signing off."

The radio went dead. "Keep it on that channel," I said. "I wasn't sure we'd find him again."

Everyone was quiet. I just stared out at the water, trying to gauge the oncoming swells and keep the boat heading into the bigger ones.

"I didn't really want to believe it," said Terry, his voice just barely audible over the sound of the Sea Ray's engine and the splashing of the wake on our bow. "I saw what was happening to everyone, but I believed it was just some sickness that the government would get under control."

"You saved our lives," said Roxy. "If you hadn't pulled me away from that tour of the grounds, we'd have been out in that rain. You're the only reason we were inside the house."

Terry turned and hugged Roxy, and both of 'em started to cry. Georgie rubbed their backs and did what she could to comfort the pair.

"Anyway," I began. "I'm real glad you two are safe. You know what we're doin' now and why we're doin' it. I don't know if it's the best idea, but we now know this mess is all over the country, and nobody seems to have a handle on how to stop it. I figure there's safety in numbers."

"And what do we do when we get to Lebanon, Kansas?" asked Roxy, breaking from the embrace and wiping her eyes.

I shrugged as I turned the yacht into an oncoming swell. The bow lifted up and splashed down again, and once more, I corrected our course.

I said, "All we can do is play everything by ear. React as situations present themselves, just like we've done up until now. I'm wide open for input and ideas from any one of y'all."

"Where's our first stop?" asked Georgie. "Still shooting for Naples?"

"There are marinas there where we may be able to fuel up," I said. "If we can get the pumps workin'." I looked down at the GPS. We still had sixty miles to go to reach Naples, Florida.

"That's a lot of guns down there," said Terry, out of the blue. "I've never shot a gun."

I figured it struck him to mention the guns and his lack of experience when I mentioned hitting land. I said, "Then a shotgun might be your best choice. Scatter shot, but deadly if you use the right gauge. Maybe I'll train you on the DP-12."

"How?"

"I know," I said. "I thought of that, believe me. We can't shoot at anything on the boat, and shootin' out at the open water's just a waste of ammo. We'll figure somethin' out. Roxy, you ever handle a gun?"

"She has," said Georgie. "Her father and I used to take her to the range. She's been shooting since she was around ten years old."

Terry turned toward her. "You never told me you were Annie Oakley!"

"Didn't want you to think I was a redneck, I guess," said Roxy. "I actually love shooting."

"I know your heart by now," said Terry. "Plus, most rednecks I've met love me. I've always thought they were mostly latent homosexuals."

"Excuse me," I said. "I like you fine, but I'm a dedicated breeder."

Georgie laughed, Lilly cringed, and Terry got up and came up behind me, wrapping his arms around my neck from behind. Next thing I knew, I felt his lips on my cheek and he gave me a little smack.

"I saw how you look at Dr. Lake." He turned to look at Georgie. "Don't' worry, Georgina. I won't steal him from you."

My face must've turned 18 shades of red. I shook my head and had to laugh with the others.

Lilly laughed hardest of 'em all. I was glad to see it. I knew she, like I, was hurting inside from the loss of our family. Distractions were rare and good for both of us.

Ω

35

We came across the boat, clearly adrift, about three hours into our trip. The second I saw it, I wished everyone else was asleep. Unfortunately, they all still sat behind me, quietly watching the open water ahead, all lost in their own thoughts.

I thought about distracting everyone by pointing out the gathering storm clouds again, but we'd already talked about the thunderheads building over the Atlantic, being pushed west by the same winds that were kicking up the chop we were cutting through.

Plus, it's an unspoken rule of boating; if someone is in distress, you come to their aid. You do that either by helping directly, or contacting the U.S. Coast Guard to assist.

I was pretty sure the Coast Guard wasn't an option, so it came down to us.

Like I mentioned, the weather had taken a turn, and the wind was out of the east, starting to blow real good.

The heavy chop was keeping me down to about 17 miles per hour, and I'm well aware a more experienced open water boater could've handled it without any issues.

Like I said, I'm an airboat swamp guy. This shit was outta my league.

"Guys, we have a boat off the port side. Cabin cruiser, looks like."

Lilly grabbed a pair of binoculars went to the port side window and slid the curtains open along the brass rods. "Looks buttoned up."

"No power," I said. "They're not movin' anyway, far as I can tell."

"They may need medical attention," said Georgie. "Or … they're those things."

"If we're lucky, someone already rescued them," said Lilly. "Or they had a smaller skiff. But CB's right. We have to check."

That's why I fucking hate it when I'm right. Most of the time. The wind was picking up, and I was getting less and less comfortable by the minute. I wouldn't say anything, because I know ignorance is bliss, and we all had enough to worry about.

I checked for oncoming swells and guided the boat over the chop, doing my best to go in my intended direction. The cabin cruiser was about seventy yards northwest of us, and I pushed the throttle forward to overcome the wind and just get it over with.

What should've been achieved in under a minute or two took nearly ten, jogging left and right to keep us from getting thrown sideways. By the time we reached it, I saw it was a Bayliner. Sure enough, like Lilly had said, it looked to have at least the side windows covered. That made me wonder whether it had just come loose from its moorings.

To be honest, I sure as hell hoped so.

The boat was now dead ahead, about fifteen yards off our bow. Lilly moved forward and raised the binoculars again. "Oh, shit," she said.

"Oh, shit, it's sinking? Or oh, shit, it's full of zombies?"

Lilly lowered the glasses and looked at me. "What qualifies as full?"

"More than one," I mumbled. "Are you serious?"

"There's one that I see. A woman." She handed over the binoculars. "On the stern. Looks like she's on her knees."

I raised the glasses and tried to keep them steady. It wasn't easy with both boats rising and falling with the ocean. Sure enough, I found her. She'd crawl forward, reaching toward the cabin door. Then when a swell came, she'd tumble backward and slam into the inside rail again.

We'd drawn a little closer now, and Terry, Georgina and her daughter were all standing at the window now, looking out.

"There has to be someone trapped in there," said Terry, swiping his long bangs away from his eyes. The rest of his hair looked like it was probably spiked or something, but he clearly didn't have any gel. "Maybe if you blow your horn, whoever's inside will hear."

"Damned good idea, Terry," I said, as I scanned the helm of the boat. My eyes fell on a small button marked HORN. I pressed my palm against it. The sound was like someone blowing a New Year's Eve noisemaker under a blanket.

I shook my head. "Why do they put the worst goddamned horns in the best boats?" I asked.

"Because nobody beeps the horns at boat shows," said Lilly. "They're figuring out how much booze the coolers will hold."

"Good point," I said.

"Do you have one of those boat horns?" asked Terry. "The cans? I know most boats have them in case they lose all their power."

I looked at him. "You have some depth of knowledge we don't know about?"

"My dad used to race sailboats. I've been part of his crew on a number of occasions, but mostly I just do what they tell me to."

Georgie and Roxy were already on their knees, opening panels and searching.

"Got it!" said Georgina, pulling out a red and white can with a bell-shaped horn on it.

"Go up top to do that," I said. "Give it a good long blast, unless there's some special code you use. Terry?"

He shrugged. "Just make noise. There are signals if you're going to pass them, but I don't know any to ask if they need help."

"Gotcha," I said.

He trotted up the steps behind Georgina. In another ten seconds, I heard a high, shrill chirp. She blew it five times.

Lilly had the binoculars up. "There!" she said. "Someone's pushing on the cover over the window there."

"Lemme see," I said. She gave over the binocs and I looked. On the lower left side of the window, the vinyl cover, which had been fully snapped down, now flapped in the wind. A second later, I saw a hand stick out and wave twice, then pull back in.

"See that?" I asked. "Someone stuck their hand out!"

"You have the glasses," said Roxy.

"Yeah," I muttered, still looking. "They're a little gun shy, but someone's definitely in there. Probably for good reason with that zombie chick out there. So, what's the plan?"

Georgina came down the steps and said, "Whoever it is, we have to save them, right? We can't leave them there to die."

I waggled my hand in the air. "Eventually the zombie'll probably get washed over the rail. Then they could –"

"Then they'll be stranded in the middle of the ocean, CB," said Lilly.

"I know, I know," I said, shaking my head. "I'm freaking kiddin'. Ideas, anyone?"

"There's two life rings hanging on the railing back there," said Roxy. "And dock lines. If you get close enough, can we toss it over there? Maybe tow them clear, and pull them to the boat?"

"I hope someone has a good arm," I said. "And Georgie, you've got a helluva shot, based on what you did to that tit-swingin' zombie outside your place. Wanna take her out?"

"There was a tit-swinging zombie?" asked Terry, a smirk on his face. "Somebody else's tits?"

I looked at him and nodded, my eyebrows doing a dance on my forehead. "Nasty ol' banana tits."

Terry crinkled his nose.

"Immature much?" asked Roxy. "Terry, seriously? From you?"

He shrugged as Georgina explained her acumen with a gun earlier. "I was on solid ground, and only about twenty-five feet away from her."

"Yeah, but you hit her right in the head with a pistol. Think you can hit her with a rifle?"

"If it has a scope, sure," said Georgina.

"I can get within about thirty feet comfortably," I said. "On a pass-by, I might be able to get closer. We can throw the life ring with the rope attached. Swing it from the rope, get more distance."

"I'll get the ring set up. Mom, you kill the zombie lady."

I looked from Terry to Lilly. "I love it when a plan comes together."

Lilly got up and walked out of the wheelhouse. Before she disappeared, she said, "You may be a smartass joker, but it really is nice to know some things never change."

I knew my sister, and she was telling me I was keeping her sane. I was still the brother she knew and loved, despite what had happened to the world.

I heard a slapping on the side. I slid the window open and stuck my head out. "Okay, closer!" shouted Georgina, gripping the rifle with one hand, and the railing with the other.

"Roxy all set?" I asked.

"She's gettin the rope tied to the ring. Hurry."

I looked around us out of habit, and pushed the throttle forward a good amount. The props pushed the Sea Ray closer to the Bayliner. Now that I was serious and we had a plan, I got us into position fast.

I was ready to throw it into reverse if things got hairy, mainly because I didn't know shit about thrusters, and I hadn't taken the time to learn how to use 'em.

I'd do it the old-fashioned way for now.

"Okay, good enough?" I asked.

"Roxy!" she yelled. "Come here, quick!"

I heard the footfalls on the deck, and Roxy came into view.

"Lean against the cabin and crouch down. Just wrap your arms around my knees and hold me," said Georgina.

It took Roxy only a second or two to get into position and grab hold of her mom. Once she was stable, Georgie raised the rifle to her eye.

She waited. I turned the wheel and gave it forward and reverse thrust, trying to keep the boat in position.

"Don't move," Georgie yelled, and I saw her steady, despite the movement of the boat beneath her.

I looked up. The zombie woman was on her knees now, her head and shoulders visible above the rail.

Boom! Boom!

The first shot missed. The second was a dead hit. No pun intended.

"Yes!" yelled Roxy, standing up and taking her mother by the hand as they moved back toward the stern. When they were out of view, I closed my window.

"Terry, go out there and have them blow the horn again. Tell 'em to do somethin' fun, you know, like shave and a haircut, two bits."

Terry looked at me like I was a zombie with two heads. "Shave and a *what*?"

I did the knock on the wall. His face lit up.

"Got it," he said, rushing out. A moment later, I heard the familiar pattern squeaked out on the boat horn.

Ten seconds after that, I saw the vinyl cover move aside again, only this time it lifted higher and I saw a kid's face. I couldn't tell his age, but I'm thinking pre-pubescent.

I stuck my arm out the window and waved, as though telling him to come on over.

His head moved quickly from side to side, and next thing I know, he's pointing toward the back of the boat.

I responded the best way I knew how. I drew my finger across my throat and stuck out my tongue. Then I waved him over again.

We waited about thirty seconds after the flap closed again. The rear door of the cabin eased outward, and the kid appeared.

He stared at the motionless body on the deck.

"Blow that horn again, Georgie!" I yelled out the window.

She did, and he looked over. I was right about his age; he was probably thirteen or fourteen, but I was shit at estimating ages anymore. I'm guessing that was his mama out there on the deck. That didn't give me much confidence in his mindset right then.

I didn't know what was happening up top, but Roxy must've held up the swim ring, 'cause he pointed to us, then at his deck, nodding. I saw him keep glancing down to the deck, and though I couldn't see the dead zombie, I pretty much knew why.

He moved to the rail, holding on.

Terry ran back in. "Okay, your sister said she'll throw it. They said for you to get as close as you can."

"Got it," I said, taking a deep breath. "Tell her to be ready."

He trotted off again, and I pushed the throttle forward and steered to the left, angling toward the boat.

Just then, a huge gust came out of nowhere, and I found myself fighting the wind as well as the choppy swells that tossed both boats around like toys in a two-year-old's bathtub.

The kid teetered to the side, holding onto the rail with one hand. His feet apparently slipped, and he went down, out of sight for a few seconds. My bow was now pointed straight at the Bayliner, and I was getting so close I worried I couldn't make the turn in time.

The gust subsided, and I cranked it hard right, bringing us into a parallel position. I pushed the throttle again and knew we wouldn't be able to get any closer.

Lilly was smart; she must've known it, too, because I saw that life ring fly, the rope whipping in the wind behind it.

The wind gusted again, blowing the ring sideways. It hit the outboard on the Bayliner and drifted away from the boat. Lilly immediately started reeling it back toward the Sea Ray.

"Shit!" I yelled and leaned out the window. "Hold on!"

I didn't know whether they heard me or not, but I didn't have a choice with the weather and surf building up. I pushed that throttle forward again and guided the Sea

Ray around the front of the Bayliner, rounding the boat until I was facing south, now on the port side of our target.

The wind was now blowing me away from the Bayliner. I felt better about that, but it required me to turn into the wind to keep from moving too far away for Lilly to hit it.

Just as I was sure I'd drifted too far west, the ring went out again. We were only fifteen feet off the other boat's rail, and this time, despite the fact Lilly was throwing into the wind, she hit it. The ring just made it over the portside rail.

I stuck my arm out the window and jabbed my finger at the ring, and saw the boy run across, hesitate when he reached the body on the deck, and move around to grab the life ring.

"Go! Go!" I screamed. "Jump!"

The boy stared at me for a second, then stuck the ring over his head and leapt over the rail.

He hit the water and disappeared beneath the heavy surf. I saw the edge of the ring, but I had no idea whether he had a hold on it.

Lilly ran back inside. "CB, you need to go down and haul him in!"

"Has he got it?" I asked, staring toward where I'd last seen him. His head popped up, his arm curled around the life ring. "There!"

I jumped up and ran toward the steps leading down toward the rear deck. "Hold the boat steady south, as best you can!"

Lilly came over and dropped down into the captain's chair. "I got it," she said, with more confidence than I felt.

I said a quick prayer and jammed down the steps two at a time. I hit the deck and ran to the rail. Lilly had tied it off to the rail. I reached out and pulled it in to give me some slack and untied it.

Looking out, I saw the boy still had a good grip on it. I ran to the rear step and planted my feet, leaning back as I hauled that dock line in with everything I had.

Twenty feet. Fifteen. Ten. I could see the boy's eyes now, scared as hell, his face white as a ghost.

I gotta be honest with you; when that boy was out there, in that churning water, my mind went right back to the gators. How they'd changed. Yeah, I know they're reptiles, but what I knew about the transformation of the world could fit inside a thimble.

I feared something would come leaping outta the water and rip that boy right off that swim ring, dragging him down into the depths of the Gulf of Mexico.

With that in mind, I leaned back and pulled, hand over hand, coiling the dock line up on the swim step behind me.

With a thunderous crash, the clouds that had moved above us let loose a torrential downpour, the drops so big and heavy that I felt like someone was dumping a bag of grain on my head from twenty feet up.

I squinted my eyes against the blowing rain and saltwater as I continued to muscle the kid to the boat.

I was almost working blind, but next thing I knew, he was at my feet, his chest resting on the swim platform.

Reaching down, I grabbed the swim ring with one hand, and wrapped my other fist in the material of his shirt, yanking him up and into the boat. I followed right behind, and dropped down to my ass, exhausted.

Georgie and Roxy were both standing at the door to the lower cabin, waving at me to bring him in.

I'd have yelled for them to give me a sec, but I couldn't breathe yet. I was shaking pretty good from the exertion.

I looked around; the Sea Ray was a good distance from the Bayliner now, so Lilly had open water in which to maneuver. She took full advantage, and now had the boat pulling away, heading back toward the southern tip of the Florida mainland.

The emergency past, I just waved the girls off, breathed and looked at the kid. "You okay?" I huffed between gasps. The rain dumped buckets down on us.

Thank God the water wasn't black.

He didn't answer me. He stared at his feet, his hands pressed flat on the boat's fiberglass deck. His hair was red, and it hung down over his face, water cascading off it. I saw his arms were heavily freckled; the kind of freckles that go on forever on some gingers.

"Kid, you alright?" I yelled over the roar of the storm. "Better answer me or I'll throw you on your back on this deck and do CPR. I don't know my own strength, so I'm bound to break some ribs"

He looked at me, his face and his voice obscured by the pouring rain. "You only do CPR when someone's not breathing!" he yelled over the torrent. "You see me breathing, don't you?"

Great. I'd caught us a smartass. I wondered if I shouldn't throw him back. Instead, I laughed and called back, "C'mon! Let's get inside! It's shit out here!"

I actually kinda figured me and that smartass kid might get along fine.

He nodded and tried to stand up, but the boat was tossing us all over the place, and he stumbled right into me.

"Grab hold of my elbow," I said. He didn't hesitate. I guided him up into Georgie's and Roxy's open, waiting arms.

$$\Omega$$

CHAPTER THREE

In the torrential rain, the flybridge was no longer feasible. It was necessary when I needed a higher perspective to maneuver around the Bayliner, but that was done.

We all retreated down into the main cabin where I toweled off, managing to put on a shirt and a pair of dark blue cargo shorts in between turning the boat into the oncoming swells. Georgina had found the clothes in the master cabin dresser, and it was good to be dry again.

I used my towel to dry off Nokosi, who'd been laying with us up in the weather, I guess more comfortable in our company, no matter the conditions. She let me, and never growled once.

The only shirts in the dresser were ultra-thin, V-neck undershirts, so thin my modest areolas showed through. Guess the former owner always brought the newest, most fashionable button-down shirts when he went out on his mini-yacht.

Lilly threw all my stuff and the wet towels in the dryer after giving everything a quick wash in the sink using dishwashing soap. We didn't find any Tide Pods. Probably the owners' kids ate 'em all.

Lilly and Georgina took the kid into the master suite cabin and made him strip down to his birthday suit.

Georgie had the boy sit on the closed lid of the master bathroom toilet, and looked him over, inspecting for signs of bites or scratches.

Lilly had given his clothes a quick washing, too, and they were in the dryer with the rest of the stuff.

When the door to the master cabin slid open and they reappeared, Georgina said, "Well, Liam here says that *was* his mommy out there on the deck of the other boat. She didn't bite or scratch him, nor did anyone else. I gave him a quick rundown of what caused her to change."

"*And* my dad, *and* my brother and sister," he said, sitting on the curved bench seat that ran along the starboard side. "Why didn't I get sick?"

His eyes were as green as some of my favorite marbles when I was a kid; the ones that looked almost like cat eyes. He was inquisitive, but not necessarily sad. I figured he was in some kinda shock, and all this would catch up with him eventually. We'd try to be ready if it did.

"Luck of the draw will have to do for now," I called back to him. "Seems pretty random right now."

"That was a dumb answer," he mumbled.

"And *that* was rude," said Georgina. "You had better respect your elders if you intend to remain with us."

"Yeah?" he challenged. "What're you gonna do? Kick a kid off the boat into the ocean?"

I had to bite my lip. What I wanted to do was go grab that kid by the ankles, hang him upside down as I carried him back into the rain and dangle his ass over the railing. I imagined it would straighten him out fast, but in reality, it might scar him further – or more accurately, erase any chance we had at establishing trust between us.

I didn't want his good behavior based on fear. Not a healthy way to start. Of course the kid was upset; he'd just lost his family. I could relate.

He sat there wearing a burgundy-colored robe with the Sea Ray logo embroidered on the lapel. It hung almost all the way to the floor on him.

"What's your last name, Liam? Cool name, by the way," said Terry.

"Are you a gay?" asked the boy, staring at Terry.

Terry was nonplussed, which I'll grant you, is a word I don't use much.

Terry said, "Yes, as a matter of fact, I am gay, which is how that word is used. You're not 'a gay', you're just 'gay'. I feel like using it the way you did is ... well, making fun of gay people in a way."

Liam began fiddling with the belt on his robe. "My Uncle Michael calls them bone smokers."

Keeping a straight face, Terry said, "And when you hear that term, *bone smoker*, how do you think it relates to gay men?"

Liam's face turned all shades of red. He shook his head and averted his eyes, but never answered.

Terry looked around the room at us. I was trying to hold my laughter and failed. When I let it out, so did everyone else.

Terry shook his head and began to laugh, too. "There's the ever-popular rump rangers, too," he said, which further sent us all into a tizzy.

The kid laughed now, too, but I'm not sure he even knew why. I never would've believed using gay slurs would cheer him up, but whatever it took. If he kept it up after, we'd set him straight as necessary.

Terry settled in and started asking him questions, and Liam told what he could of his story, seeming to warm to him.

Anyway, I started to think it was good that Terry didn't take offense at Liam's comments. He was still young and psychologically pliable, and maybe they were just words to the boy.

Turns out he was only twelve years old. He looked older, but maybe that was because his red hair was pretty long, down just past his shoulders, and his eyes were haunted and sunken.

Liam told Terry his last name was Murphy, and he'd been out on the rental boat with his brother, Finn, his sister, Fiona, his mother, Grace, and his stepfather, Declan. His mother had married Declan when Liam was just two years old, taking on his four and six-year old kids as her own. Liam said his real father had passed away in an accident.

They'd been visiting Key West from Vermont, just sightseeing and doing fishing charters and stuff. The whole family'd been out on some rented golf carts, driving around town when the black rain started.

Being in open carts, they all got soaked. He said it was just hours later when his brother, who was fourteen years old, and his sister, sixteen, started to get sick.

"How did you get the boat then?" asked Lilly.

"Dad rented it and picked up the keys from the rental place the morning we got the carts to ride around in. We were going to leave the next day for Cuba. Dad always wanted to go to Havana and buy cigars. It's all he talked about from the time we got there."

I figured his dad must've had decent boating experience to take that trip. With the hope of giving the kid an out so he wouldn't have to say what happened to his brother and sister, I asked, "How'd you guys manage to get to the boat with everything goin' on?"

He didn't take the bait. Maybe he needed to get it out.

"It was so weird. When that weird rain was pouring down, we just drove the carts back to our Airbnb house and parked them in the driveway, even though we were supposed to return the carts in a couple of hours. When we got inside, mom made us all take showers. It was really stinky, so we wanted to."

"Did your parents get sick?" asked Georgie.

"My mom was fine for the longest time. She got sick later," said Liam. "After dad kinda … I don't know …." He didn't finish, but let his words just disappear.

Terry leaned forward and touched the kid's hand. He didn't pull away. I wondered if he even realized it had happened.

Terry said, "Liam, you don't need to talk about it now. Later, if you want. The important part is, you're safe. And you aren't showing any signs of the sickness."

He raised his eyes and looked around. "None of you are sick. Do you have medicine?"

I shook my head, but Georgina said, "No, which either points to some immunity within us, or different gestation periods for the disease. If anyone – and I mean anyone – begins to feel out of the ordinary, you must let one of us know. For the good of everyone. Understood?"

Everyone, including Liam, nodded.

"Fiona and Finn both got really weird," said Liam, his voice almost reflective. "Like monsters. I saw a movie once where people came back from the dead and turned into zombies. They growled and bit people and then those people –"

"Liam, you don't need to go through –" started Terry.

"I tried to kill her!" he shouted. "She was always so skinny I could wrestle her and always win, but she was strong then! She was scaring everyone, and I thought I could … I tried to smother her with a pillow, but daddy came in and pulled me off her!"

Liam was hyperventilating, and Georgie had moved in next to him and had an arm over his trembling shoulder. "Sweetheart, you don't have to go on," she whispered.

He pulled away and looked between us all. "It's all I thought about the whole time I was on that boat!" he blubbered through his tears. "She was too strong! If I'd have done it right, she wouldn't have bit daddy, and she wouldn't have bit mommy! I let it happen!"

He broke down into tears, the kind of sobs that shake your whole body. We let him cry. He needed it. I figured when he was all done, he'd collapse and sleep for a few hours. I didn't envy him his nightmares.

The German Shepherd must've sensed his fear. Nokosi got up, walked over to where he sat and put a paw on the boy's knee.

"It's okay, Liam," I said. "She's a good girl. A police dog." He tentatively reached out and scratched her head between the ears.

Roxy found a cold Coke in the galley refrigerator and gave it to the kid. He drank a quarter of the can before he settled in, and once he got started – either from the caffeine in the pop or just unable to stop – he told us the whole story, right up until we found him.

Liam Murphy shared how his daddy, pale and beginning to stumble, had carried Fiona from the small bedroom with this hand over her mouth, pressing her body to his chest, her head resting – by force – on his shoulder. At least it looked to Liam as though he held her there by force, because she wasn't relaxing.

As he watched his mom on the phone trying to call 911, and his dad pacing back and forth with his stepsister, a screech came from the bedroom again.

Liam said he knew right away it was Finn. He stayed in his chair, a throw pillow clutched to his chest. His mother looked more worried than ever, and she and his father, whose eyes were dark and sunken by then, hurried with Fiona still in his arms back to the bedroom.

By this time, Liam's curiosity had gotten the better of him, scared or not, and he got up and followed. Just as his parents were ready to turn into the bedroom, his father screamed and practically threw Fiona to the ground.

Blood poured down his father's shoulder, and when Fiona sat up, her face finally looked excited. Thick blood ran down her chin and neck, dripping onto the floor.

At that point, Liam explained that his father looked into the bedroom, yelled something, and slammed that door. He ran into another one of the bedrooms and grabbed a blanket off the bed. He spread it on the floor of the living room, and when Fiona came staggering down the hall toward all of them, he scooped her up.

She tried to bite him again, but he held her away and put her in the middle of the blanket. Then he folded it over her, and tied the corners together, pulling it so tight that his sister couldn't move inside.

Finn was no different from his sister. Liam said his father did the same with his brother, explaining it was the only way to immobilize them and keep them from attacking them more.

Afterward, Liam's mother cleaned and bandaged up his shoulder as best she could, and he carried both the bundled kids down to the car.

When they were on their way to the hospital, there were crashed cars everywhere, doors open and people staggering around like they were drunk. They'd wander, as if with no direction, then all of a sudden, they'd take off stumbling after someone and attack 'em.

I listened to the kid, amazed at his power of recall, especially after a nightmare like that. It reminded me of bad things that happened to me as a kid; they were the most detailed memories I had.

The bad stuff sticks, is the point I'm gettin' at. That stuff leaves a mark, and you don't forget it.

Liam said he knew his stepdad wasn't going where he really wanted to; he was driving to keep away from all the bad people everywhere, turning when he found an open piece of road. He kept asking him where they were going, but after a while, he just screamed at him, telling him to shut up and let him concentrate.

"I wasn't sure how, but next thing we knew, we were down at the place where dad had rented the boat you found me on. He said he already had the key, and then he pointed to it and told us he was going over to get it started. He said he'd come back for us once he was ready to … cast off, I think he said."

"Liam, you can stop, baby," said Lilly. "I mean, if this makes you feel bad, you don't have to go through it."

The kid looked at Lilly, his brows furrowed over green eyes. "I don't wanna forget," he said. "I need to remember it, so I learn from it. My dad always told me that. He said I need to learn from everything that happens, and he said history is important. Like him not being my real dad, but still *really* being my dad in his heart and in my heart. So, I wanna tell you before I forget, so in case I do, you'll remember."

He looked between all of us; Terry had his knees pulled up to his chest, his arms wrapped around 'em. Roxy was beside him, her arms folded, and her brows nearly as furrowed as the boy's.

I'm sure hers and Terry's minds were running over what they'd gone through at the Hemmingway place. There were no easy stories in the apocalypse.

"Go on then, sweetheart," said Lilly. "Stop when you feel like it."

Liam nodded, absentmindedly petting Nokosi, whose eyes were closed, her tongue lolling from her mouth. "After a few minutes, he ran back to the car and jumped in. We had a case of water in the car and some other snacks and stuff. Like cheese crackers and Twizzlers and candy and junk. He said grab everything, and I got all the candy. Mom got the water, but before she did, she … I don't know, I guess she forgot! She opened the door to see Fiona, and when she pulled open the blanket, she bit mommy on the hand!

"Dad didn't see it, but I did. He was checking for other people outside, then he told us to run down to the boat and stay inside while he got Finn and Fiona."

"So he brought them in the boat with you?" asked Roxy, her eyes fixed on the kid.

Liam shook his head, and his eyes started to well up. I figured we were getting to the next bad part of his story.

Through his tears, he said, "Daddy watched us to make sure we got there okay. There were some of the crazy people coming toward the car from the street, but it wasn't far, so I knew my dad could make it.

"Me and mom got to the boat, and she told me to follow her down a little ladder into a room, and that's where we dumped the stuff we carried. When we got back outside, we saw my dad. He had the blanket with Finn in his arms, and just as he was about to run to us, two people just jumped on him. One of them grabbed him by the head and yanked him back, and he fell down, dropping Finn.

"My mom started screaming, but it got worse, because when Finn hit the ground, his blanket came open. I could see from all the way at the boat that he was just like he was at the house, just like Fiona was. He grabbed my dad by the leg and started biting him. My mom was just screaming and screaming, and I was so scared I didn't know what to do.

"By the time my dad fell down, there were so many people on top of him I couldn't even see him anymore. I didn't see Finn, either. I don't know what happened to Fiona."

"Your mom know how to drive a boat?" I asked. "Is that how you ended up on the water?"

He nodded. "We used to go out all the time, and mom drove a lot. Our boat was kinda like the one he rented."

I nodded and got down on a knee in front of the kid, who was draining the last of his Coke. "Liam, I don't know if you need to hear this, but we both know what became of your mom, and I'm sure you're about to tell us that part. Before you do, let me tell you somethin' you might not know."

He nodded, so I went on. "The sickness out there. It changes people, so they don't know what you are anymore. So they don't know who you are. Your mama didn't know you were her boy on that boat. Not after she got sick."

"Did she have rabies? Dad told me bats and stuff with rabies will bite people, even if they don't normally do that."

I supposed rabies was enough to tell the kid for now, but at the same time, I didn't want to lie to him. I fudged somewhere in the middle.

"Somethin' like rabies, yeah. There was a book I read when I was a kid called Ol' Yeller. There was a good dog that loved his family. Then he was bit by a rabid animal, and he turned mean. That's basically what happened. Not only to your mom, but to your brother and sister."

"I never saw a bat," said the boy.

"My point is, they never meant to hurt one another, and they never meant to hurt you."

He nodded. "You want me to tell you the rest?"

I nodded back. "If you want to, yeah. I can wait if you don't feel like it."

"I'm not tired," he said. "I can finish."

He nodded and went on. Liam told us how his mother waited on the stern of the boat with him for another few minutes, a paper towel wrapped around her bleeding hand, until Finn and the crazy people saw them. Once they noticed them, they left his dad lying there and started heading for the two of them down the dock ramp.

"Mom told me to untie the dock lines, and I'm really good at that because they're only wrapped around those metal thingies like the number eight. When I jumped back in the boat, mom just took off, crying the whole time."

"Where were you planning to go?" asked Roxy.

"Honey, I imagine they were just getting away," said Georgina.

"Mom didn't say," said Liam. "She was starting to look funny, too."

He suddenly turned to me. "Fiona changed my mom, right? Was it just the rain that changed everyone else?"

"Seems so, sweetheart," said Georgina. "Something in it made a lot of those people sick. It's what caused them to bite people."

His confused eyes told us all that he had zero concept of immunity. If it happened to one, it should – or would – happen to all. I'm sure it wasn't comforting to believe that, especially after what he'd seen.

He took in Georgina's explanation without further questions and continued with his story.

"Anyway, we were on the water for a long time and it got dark. Mom was still talking then, and she told me to go find the anchor and throw it out. I ran out and found it on the back of the boat, and I threw it into the water, but I guess I messed up, because the motor started making weird noises, then it just stopped all of a sudden."

"I'm guessin' it got tangled in the prop," I said.

"I don't know, but mom was yelling at me and crying and talking to herself, too. She finally quit yelling and went inside and laid down. I sat in the driver's chair and I guess I fell asleep, too."

"How did you get locked in the cabin by yourself?" asked Terry.

I held up a hand to Terry, but when he looked at me, his expression told me he already knew he'd been wrong to interrupt the kid. I figured it was good to let Liam tell it in his own way and time, mainly because I was so surprised he had the composure to tell it at all.

"Like I said, I guess I fell asleep. Something woke me up – a noise or something – and I went into where the bed was. My mom wasn't there, so I thought she must be feeling better."

Liam went on with his story, and I could pinpoint the moment it transformed from just a very scary story to a terrifying one.

He told us how he climbed those steps up to the deck, hoping to see his mom sitting in a chair, taking in the sunshine, feeling better. How he saw her standing against the rail, facing the water, and how he called her.

He said he was just about a yard behind her when she turned around. He looked into her eyes.

"They were dead-like, and they were twitching all funny. They didn't move like normal eyes do. And they were all cloudy. She started coming at me right away, but she couldn't walk very good and she wouldn't answer me, no matter how much I called her. Then she started growling, and it didn't sound anything like my mom."

Liam was staring off into space now, as he told the story. It was like he was reliving everything. I fully expected either Roxy, Lilly, or Georgie to try to stop him, but none did. I kinda wish they woulda, but maybe they knew something I didn't about psychology.

"I ran back to the cabin and climbed down the steps, and she came after me. Once I got in I turned around to see where she was. She was coming to get me! I know it was my mom, you know? I didn't think she'd hurt me, but I'd never seen her like that, and I saw what those other people who were sick did to my dad."

"Honey –" started Georgina, but he charged on, full speed ahead.

"When I saw she was coming after me, I got scared, and I ran up and grabbed the door and slammed it in her face! I barely got it closed, because her hand was on it, and her fingers got caught. I was holding the door closed and trying to pull her fingers off it, and finally I got it closed."

"I'm so sorry, Liam," whispered Terry.

"She kept scratching on the door the rest of the day, and then all night," the boy explained. "She would go around the sides and scratch and just when I'd think she was done, maybe sleeping or something, she'd start again."

"How long were you on the boat?" asked Lilly. "Do you know?"

"No," he said. "I don't even know what the date was when we got to Key West. Kids aren't supposed to worry about stuff like that."

"That's right, Liam," I said. "Leave the schedulin' to the big folks. I have a question, though."

"Yeah?"

"Water. I take it there was a head in the bedroom down there?"

"A head? Like a … human head?"

I laughed out loud, but it surprised me as much as everyone else. I think everyone jumped. "No, man. A bathroom."

Just as I said the words, a gust of wind turned my bow west, and I fought it as I got it straight again, then pushed the throttle forward to crest another swell.

"Hold on!" I shouted, and I assumed everyone braced. The bow came splashing back down and popped back up.

I just wanted to get my ass back to the mainland. We'd figure out which mode of transportation was best once we scoped out the number of dead there.

The kid must've been numb to the roiling waves, because he just continued with his story. "Yeah, that's where I got the water. In the bathroom. There was a shower in there, and you pumped this thing and it came out. I drank that. It never ran out. There were the Twizzlers and cookies and stuff, too. That's what I ate."

My mind was running over and over what we'd done to the kid's mother. Georgie'd lined that zombie babe's head up in her scope and shot her dead. Not once did Liam ever ask us why or accuse us of killing her.

I didn't think I could let that go without some kind of explanation. Maybe I'm a dumbass, but I wanted to address it before he had a chance to really think about it, maybe start to hold a grudge.

"Hey, Liam. How's that Coke?"

He nodded. "Good. It's cold."

"Good," I said. "I need to tell you somethin'. It's stuff you're gonna need to know, and it's kinda hard to hear. You want it now, or you wanna sleep on it tonight?"

"Sleep on what?"

"Let it go for now, CB," said Lilly.

"I agree," said Roxy. "He's been through an ordeal."

I stood up and arched my back, working out the kinks. "Yeah, probably for the best. But you and I are gonna have a talk tomorrow, okay? Man talk. Just you and me."

"I still qualify for man talk," said Terry, smiling at me.

His smile was kinda infectious. I found myself smiling, too. "Fair enough," I said. "Just the three of us, then."

Ω

CHAPTER FOUR

The weather was grinding on my nerves. What was worse, I couldn't see shit with my eyes, and had to rely on the GPS map to guide myself toward the southern tip of Florida.

The track line said we'd made it about halfway. That depressed me, because I felt like I'd been driving that boat for a full day. I checked my watch, keeping one eye on my depth gauge.

It was only 11:45 AM. Hell, it felt like closer to 3:00.

I was down to about 18 miles an hour, and at that rate, it'd take me another three hours at best to get to the marina in Marco Island, on the Gulf Coast.

I knew that marina pretty well, 'cause me and my childhood best friend, Danny Williams, used to go out on his dad's center console out of there, and fish for anything that was biting.

I admit, it was more about picking up chicks than fishing. Danny, a handsome black dude who's about six-foot-four inches tall and all muscle, could buy beer from the time he was sixteen. I think it was just because nobody had the balls to ask him for his ID.

By the time another hour had passed, the wind died down, and I started to see blue skies north of us. That was good; I was grinding my jaws together and gripping that wheel like I was on a roller coaster.

"Easing up out there it looks like," said Georgie, sitting down in the curved couch just behind me. Nokosi was right behind her, and she plopped down on the floor at her feet. She'd really taken to Georgina Lake after Sonya was killed. She was real good with everyone else, but she followed Georgie like she was her owner.

"That coffee?" I asked. I knew it was, but I was looking for an offer.

"It is, would you like a cup?" asked Georgie.

Worked like a charm. "Oh, yeah. Where's Roxy and Terry at?"

I knew Lilly was taking a nap. So was Liam, who had to be wiped out.

"They're out on the stern. They zipped the enclosure up, so it's dry out there."

"They're not gonna need it in about twenty minutes or so. You're right. The weather's almost past us."

"God, that's a relief," she said. "I'm sure it is for you."

"How does Roxy seem?" I asked. "I don't know her, so …."

"Really good, actually. I was afraid she'd be traumatized. Terry's funny. I think he kept her sane with his jokes."

"Priceless," I said. "Sometimes laughin' at the absurd situation you're in is what keeps you from goin' nuts."

"Is the plan still to head to Kansas?" she asked.

I thought about it for a few seconds before answering. It seemed foolish, even to me, to follow a classic rock DJ across the country.

"Georgie, if we hadn't seen the video he was talkin' about, I'd really be strugglin' with the idea. But that rain was fallin' behind Wattana, and he clearly set up his camera and stuff before it started. You were asleep, I guess, but the black rain didn't go on all that long. Maybe twenty minutes. He'd have had to know it was comin' ahead of time to get everything in place."

"I didn't consider that," she said. "But it doesn't tell us anything about Micky Rode."

"I judged your character pretty well. And you judged mine. What do you think of him, based on what we've heard?"

She got up and went to the Keurig coffee maker, and I heard her lift the lid up and pop in one of the little plastic pods. A second later I heard it heating the water. "He sounds clear-headed to me, but even Charles Manson could sound sane when he wanted to."

"Nah, he couldn't."

She laughed. "Okay, bad example. Let's use Ted Bundy."

I whistled. "Yeah, now I agree. Slick son-of-a-bitch. So, you think Rode's a serial killer?"

"I'm not saying that," she said. "Just that we have no way of checking his backstory. Had you ever heard of him before all this?"

"I listen to country, mostly," I said. "I coulda passed his station a dozen times, maybe only caught a snippet."

The coffee maker started sputtering, and I heard the beautiful sound of coffee pissing into a ceramic cup.

"You never know," she said. "We might get to Marco and find the police or the National Guard is back in control."

"I, for one, will cling to that hope. We'll know in a few hours if I don't get us stuck on a sand bar."

I smiled as she scooped sugar into my coffee without asking and stirred it. Not sure why the thought of her remembering how I liked my coffee made me happy, but it did. Georgie handed me the cup as she said, "If you do get us stranded out here, we have those water scooters you grabbed. They're in back. We could get to shore that way."

I took the cup she held out and turned to look at her. "You know how freaked out I was when Liam was in the water? I just kept thinking about those gators, wondering what else was swimming around out there changed. Bull sharks were on my mind, for sure."

Georgina visibly shuddered. "Too much to worry about. At least my daughter's off that list. I don't even know how to thank you for that. She's so skinny."

"I was gonna say," I said. "Thought she might be anorexic."

"No, no. I'd guess she lost ten pounds or more in that house. Maybe fifteen. I need to fatten her back up."

"Where's your ex? Is Doctor Richard Lake her dad?"

"Yes, and the alimony checks have been coming from an address in Orlando, so I assume he's there. Believe me, I'm not giving him a thought."

"Good," I said. "That's on the other side of the state. Is Roxy givin' him a thought?"

Now she was quiet again. "Shit. Now I feel selfish. She didn't ask about him, but he's got to be on her mind. She was still mad at him for what he did to me, but that doesn't negate the fact that he's her father."

I was still reeling from the fact she'd said 'shit'. I hadn't heard her cuss since I met her. She stood.

"Leavin' so soon?" I asked.

"This won't wait," she said. "I should talk to her about it. I didn't ask, but she might have been texting him, too."

"But he didn't go rescue her."

"Maybe he's on his way there now. Or dead. I'll talk to you in a little while."

"Good luck," I said.

Ω

Lilly kept me company over the next couple hours. She said Liam was still sleeping, and Georgie was having a conversation with Roxy.

"Georgina asked Terry if he wouldn't mind giving them some privacy," said Lilly. "Roxy told her it was fine if he stayed. She said Terry knew all about her parents and what they'd gone through."

"Yeah, he cheated on her," I said. "Can you believe that?"

"Doctors have big egos," said Lilly. "I dated a couple boys who planned to become doctors. They were already well on their way to thinking they were God's gift to women."

"And?"

"One of them was a master with his tongue."

"Jeez, Lilly! I hope you're talkin' about what an orator he was."

Lilly smiled, and I saw it go away as quickly as it came. I knew she was glad I was still around, but it would be a long time before she got over her dead brothers and father. Just like me.

"Land!" said Lilly, jumping to her feet.

"Yeah!" I yelled. "Fuel gauge is still good, but I can't tell you how good it feels to see that!"

"What's the plan? Docking in Marco?"

66

"It depends, right? We need to scope it out. Georgina said maybe the cops or the Guard's got it back under control."

"In a day?" asked Lilly. "Doubtful."

"Fuck, it's only been a damned day since we left there? Why does time move like molasses in this mess?"

Lilly stood beside me, her arm over my shoulder. "CB, you don't know how I've hoped I'd wake up. Find out this is all just the weirdest dream ever."

"I nodded off a couple times, drivin'," I said. "I'm not tired, so I don't even know why. But yeah, I was hopin' the same thing. Damned if every time I opened my eyes, I was still drivin' somebody else's McYacht."

"McYacht?"

"Well, it ain't quite a yacht, is it? Kinda short."

"How long to get there?"

Pushing the throttle forward, the Sea Ray's bow lifted up. I trimmed the motors and it came back down. Now we were gliding over the water, doing the twenty-eight miles per hour I'd planned on. Smooth as silk.

"Probably about an hour," I said. "Now that I can run at a decent speed."

"Don't fall asleep," she said. She started to walk away, but stopped. She plopped down on the seat behind me. "On second thought, I'll stay with you."

"Like I said, where else you gonna go on a McYacht?"

"Stop it, CB, or I'll McSlap you."

Ω

By the time the mainland of Florida was on our starboard side, I'd moved back up to the flybridge, and everyone else was up there, too. Even Liam.

"Can you cruise close to the shore?" asked Terry. "Maybe we can see something. Get an idea if things are bad."

I pointed. "See all that black smoke? That means fires are burnin' and nobody's tryin' to put 'em out. You can tell when they start hittin' it with water, 'cause it turns white."

"Not a good sign," said Roxy.

"Not at all," said Georgie.

"But to answer your question, the marked channels are deep, but on the Gulf side of the state, you really have to watch, 'cause the water gets real shallow pretty far from shore."

"That sucks," said Terry.

"You and I agree. Remember the song *It's Five o'clock Somewhere*? Alan Jackson said, 'keep it between the navigational beacons.' That's what he was talkin' about. *Red-Right-Return*. We'll be lookin' for the green markers to be on the left, and the red on the right, which means return to harbor."

"For someone who mostly drives airboats in the Everglades, you know your nautical law," said Georgina.

"It was the time out with Danny taught me that," I said. "He could thread a needle with a boat. This thing would be like child's play for him."

I wondered where my friend was now. I hadn't heard from him since this whole mess started. We'd been best friends since forever, and although life sometimes caused us to go longer than we'd like without talking, our friendship was still strong. I hoped he was alive, out there somewhere really giving it to the rotters.

I didn't have that much hope, but I didn't have my phone, either, so he'd have no way of getting hold of me. I shoved it to the back of my mind. I had people to keep safe.

We continued north, with me about a mile offshore. In some cases we were seeing flames, but mostly it was smoke. I hoped like hell the marina wasn't either of two things: outta gas, or on fire. Both would be bad.

I didn't know yet whether we'd need to keep the boat or grab another vehicle or two on shore. I figured it might be good to talk it out.

"Lil, you wanna drive a bit?"

"Sure," she said.

I got out of the seat and stretched my legs, then arched my back, hands on my hips. "Damn. Stiff," I grunted.

"Tension will do that," said Georgina. I went over and sat down beside her on the couch. Roxy and Terry were on the same side, heads craned toward the shore, and Liam was on the other side, apparently uninterested in watching the shore.

Somehow, through it all, Nokosi slept, long, deep snores breaking any silence we might allow.

"Lil, be lookin' for channel markers headin' in toward Marco. I got no idea what the numbers are."

"There's the Cape Marco building right there," she said. "Marina's just past that, right?"

I moved up and looked. "Where's the binoculars?"

"Right here," said Liam. He had 'em around his neck. "Sorry."

"It's okay, man. You can have 'em back when I'm done." I looked out ahead of us. "Yeah, Lil. About half a mile more. Go real slow once you get in the channel. I don't see any other boats on the water, which is weird. You'd think that would be a popular way out of the state."

"Unless nobody's leaving," said Roxy. "Maybe the government did get things under control."

I cleared my throat. "Fires. Burnin' outta control. Y'all hear any sirens?"

Everyone stopped and listened. The boat motor might've drowned out faint noises, but I didn't hear anything.

"We'll be observers until we know it's safe," said Georgie. "Right, Cole?"

"Until I don't wanna watch anymore," I said. "Might be a good time to say your prayers, if you believe in that sort of thing."

The red-headed boy put his hands together and started reciting the Lord's Prayer.

Guess his family was Irish Catholic.

Ω

We were about a hundred yards from the mouth of the harbor when I said, "Pull back, Lil. Coast to a stop. I think I wanna anchor for a bit before we go in. Just eyeball stuff, get the lay of the land, so-to-speak."

"Anyone hungry?" asked Georgina.

"What do we got?" I asked.

"Well, I'm guessing whoever owns this boat has a penchant for two things. Smoked oysters and pork-n-beans."

"I'll have a can of beans," I said. "And my apologies up front."

"CB," moaned Lilly. "Eat the oysters."

"Nope. That'd just come out the same hole it went into. Beans, please."

"Who else wants beans?" she asked.

Liam, Roxy, and I raised our hands.

"So, oysters for everyone else? They have Saltines."

Everyone started heading down but me and Lilly. "Go on and get 'em hot," I called. "We'll anchor and come down in a few minutes."

Ω

We got a little closer than we planned, just so we could see the shore clearly without the binoculars. When we were sure the anchor was set, we headed down to eat.

When I was about halfway through my bowl of beans, which tasted like a gourmet meal for some reason, Roxy asked, "So what's the plan?"

Easier question to ask than answer.

I shrugged. "Y'all already know we planned to head to Lebanon, Kansas. I say we just keep movin' in that direction until somethin' happens to change that."

"I'll feel better if we keep picking up broadcasts," said Lilly. "That'll at least let us know what he's put in motion is still happening."

"I know, and believe me when I tell you, I'm questioning everything," I said. "I'm not blindly followin' the guy, but have you heard anything else comin' across the radio?"

Everyone shook their heads.

"Yep. So now we're close enough to shore and whatever cell towers might be workin', call anyone you know and see if you can reach anyone. Who's still got workin' cell phones?"

"I charged mine," said Roxy. "So did Terry."

"Terry, you got any friends over this way?"

"Some in Fort Myers," he said. "I texted everyone when we were at the Hemingway house. Nobody answered."

71

We were all quiet for a few moments, letting that sink in. I parted the curtains and looked out at the distant fires burning. "I'm assumin' your friends are reliable answerers of texts?"

"Oh, yes. I text, they text back. Maybe some lost their phones, but nobody's answering."

"Hold on to that hope," said Georgina. "Lilly, are those two-way radios on board?"

Lilly's head bobbed. "Yeah, they were in one of the ammo bags. On top."

"I'm assuming we're not all leaving the boat," said Georgina. "Whoever goes should take one of the radios. So whoever's here knows what's going on."

"I'm goin'," I said. "Call me a caveman if you want, but I'm puttin' gender equality on hold. Just in case any of y'all had different ideas."

Terry held up his hands, palms out. "I'm chill. Rox and I can stay here and monitor both radios."

I nodded. "Good. Lil, you wanna come with? We may need shootin' skills out there."

"That was my plan all along," said Lilly. "Did you try Danny? Textin' him?"

I shook my head. "I don't text, Lil. Plus, Tan didn't have Danny's number in his phone, and I rely on technology, so I don't remember it."

"Oh, shit," said Lil. "I might still have it."

My eyebrows went sky high. "Why would you have it?"

She fiddled with her phone and looked up at me with a sly smile. "We dated a little while. You know we both went to college in Miami. Plus, we went out on his dad's boat a few times."

I looked at her. "His dad's boat ain't in Miami."

"Okay, so we dated longer than a little while."

I shook my head and laughed. "And y'all didn't tell me because?"

"I thought you'd be jealous," she said. "Me stealing your boyfriend."

Shaking my head, I said, "He never said anything, either. It never went anywhere?"

"Not yet."

"Not *yet*?"

"Our last date was two weeks before all this started. I tried calling him from our shop a few times. Never texted him, though. Didn't think it would go through."

I leaned back and folded my arms across my chest. "You two were *still* datin'? Now I feel like a dumbass."

"CB, it was only because Danny thought you might be pissed he was dating your sister. I told him I didn't care, but it was his idea, so I respected it. If it went on, I'm sure he'd have told you eventually."

"When? At the wedding? Maybe the baby shower?"

"You wouldn't have been invited to the baby shower, silly. Are we going or what?" asked Lilly. "I'll text him now, if it makes you feel any better."

I nodded down toward her phone. "Hell yeah, I want you to text him. We're in his home town."

Down her head went, thumbs flashing across the keys. She looked up. "Okay. Done."

"What'd you say?" I asked.

She looked at her phone. "Me and CB are down at the marina. Are you okay?"

I stood. "You brought some clothes, right? Jeans?"

"Yes, why?"

"Put 'em on. This isn't a time for exposed skin. And I hope you brought somethin' besides those skimpy canvas shoes."

"I got jeans and my swamp boots."

73

"Okay, get changed and let's go. Be sure to bring your phone with you in case Danny texts back."

"Always."

"Okay, I'll motor in," I said. "Hope there's somewhere to dock this beast."

Ω

While Lilly got changed, we pulled anchor and I guided the Sea Ray through the channel leading into Marco Bay. I knew Danny's dad's boat was docked at Rose Marina, so that's where I was headed first. They had fuel there, too.

Georgina went down, Nokosi right on her heels, and came back with the two-ways from the ammo bag. She gave one to Lilly. "I checked the batteries," she said. "Both good."

"Thanks," said Lilly, now looking a bit more protected in the jeans and boots. She still wore a pullover tee, but it was still hovering around 80 degrees, so I got it.

Because of the bigger boats all the rich folks in Marco Island owned, they'd dredged all the canals and waterways leading into the marina to a minimum depth of nine feet. Some spots were even deeper, and in the summer, you'd see mature tarpon swimming right near the docks.

I wanted to pull it right up to the fuel pumps, but there was another boat docked there. I didn't spot anyone on it at first glance, and there weren't any lights on through the windows.

"Can't get to the fuel dock right now," I said, searching for another available section of dock.

"Right there!" said Lilly, pointing.

"Perfect. We'll move that other boat if nobody's around. Lil, go on down with someone else and get those bumpers over the side, and get the dock lines ready. Try to tie us tight to the dock."

"Not before we check it for those things," she said.

I nodded my head. "Right. Be damned careful." I grabbed the binoculars from the helm and held 'em up. "Nobody right there, but the motor might draw 'em."

"Can you cut it and coast in?" she asked.

"This ain't an airboat, Lil," I said. "Coast this thing, and I'll take out the whole dock."

"Let's hurry, then," she said, running down the steps. "Georgie, follow me!"

Georgina ran after her. I saw 'em down on the starboard rail a couple seconds after. Lilly helped Georgina tie the big bumpers to the railside boat cleats and drop 'em over the side.

I scanned the helm controls and saw a small light switch-sized panel that said, THRUSTERS. It had two joysticks, one marked BOW and the other marked STERN. Arrows to either side were red and green. I needed green.

I keyed the radio. "Lil, let me know when you're ready. Is it still clear?"

A second later, she came back. "Still clear so far. Can you get us up to the dock?"

We were still a good fifteen feet away, but parallel to it. "Gonna try," I said. "Hold on. I don't know how strong these thrusters are."

I leaned out and saw both women hanging onto the rail, their eyes on the dock. Georgie was down at the stern, and Lil was up near the bow.

I hit the toggle switch to the ON position and pushed both joysticks over toward the green arrows.

A low hum sounded, and next thing I knew, the Sea Ray was rumbling to the right, easing closer to the dock. It was so smooth, I was amazed. I'd seen people use thrusters, but damn … it made docking this big beauty a breeze.

"Back off, CB!" said Lilly through the radio. I let off the joysticks and the boat floated gently to the dock.

Seeing Lilly ready to open the side hatch and jump to the dock, I pushed the button on the radio and said, "Hold on, Lil! One last check."

She didn't answer, but I saw her pause and scan the dock, like I was doing. I still didn't see anything or anyone.

"Okay, go!"

"CB!" she said.

"What, Lil? Go, before we drift off!"

"I just got a text from Danny!"

I can't tell you the feeling that came over me right then. Just knowing my buddy was alive somewhere. As I watched my sister stuff the phone back into her pocket, I realized we'd already drifted too far for her to jump to the dock.

I keyed the radio. "That's great news. Hold on a sec, and I'll move you in tighter." I bumped the joysticks, and the boat jarred starboard, again coming up against the dock.

Lilly threw the bowline out and swung open the rail door. She took a small hop down to the dock and ran to grab the line, which she expertly wrapped in a figure-eight pattern around the cleat.

"Toss that line!" she shouted to Georgina, and she did. Lilly caught it and tied it to the aft cleat. When she was done, she gave me a thumbs-up.

By the time I shut off the engine and came down, Georgina had her 9mm out as she scanned the dock behind my sister. I knew she didn't see me coming, so I tried to walk louder and put a hand on her shoulder. "Okay, we're good. Y'all go inside so you don't draw anything to the boat. We'll keep in touch."

"Be careful, Cole," she said. "Watch out for one another, and for God's sake, come back safe."

"If I'm lucky, I'll have another friend with me. Lilly got an answer from Danny."

Her eyes brightened. "That's wonderful!"

I shrugged. "Good to know he's alive, but where is he? He texted, so he could be in Georgia for all we know."

She squeezed my arm. "He's alive, Cole." She turned back toward the cabin. When she was halfway there, she turned and called back, "Hold on one minute. Don't go anywhere."

I watched her walk away, confused. One minute passed. Then two. I started in when she came back out, the DP-12 in her hands. "Sorry, I had to figure out how to load the shells. I saw Richard do it once, so I got it. You've got 14 shots. I guess it's supposed to take 16, but I couldn't get any more in. Don't waste them."

"You gotta chamber a couple to get full capacity," I said. "I'm hopin' I don't even need one round, but yeah. This is the puppy I'll feel best with. Thanks."

"Have to take care of my … what do the rappers call them? My crew."

"I'm gonna take your word for it," I said. "Now get inside and y'all stay there. You get eaten you'll have me to answer to."

"Keep your radio on or I'll sic Nokosi on you."

I was thinking that dog might just follow her orders.

Ω

CHAPTER FIVE

"Going elephant hunting?" asked Lilly, as I jumped down onto the dock.

"If I see a zombie elephant, sure. I know you saw Georgie give it to me. Helluva gun, but I have this, too." I pulled the .45 from the back of my pants. "For smaller game."

Lilly looked around. "Still pretty cloudy," she said.. "Wish it was dark. I feel exposed out here."

"It's a natural feelin'," I said. "'Cause we're all alone. Eerie as shit. It'll be dark in an hour or so."

"I'd rather stay alone."

"If the only company's zombies, yeah. You text Danny back?"

"Let's get somewhere first. What exactly are we looking for?"

"Job one is to make sure we don't get surprised. While we're doin' that, we need to move that boat over there off the fuel dock, so we can pull in. It'll be easier now that I figured out how to use those thrusters. Then we gotta hope there's power, and if there isn't, we need to figure out their generator."

"First things first, then." Lilly pulled out a gun I recognized from Georgina's safe. It was a custom-engraved Sig Sauer P226; a 9mm semi-automatic. It had gold accents in the form of a skull on top of the slide, and pointing skeleton hands on the sides.

"Georgina said I could have it. Her ex bought it for her, and she hates him." She looked at me and winked. "Hey, maybe she'll hate you like that someday."

"If she does, don't think she'll be givin' you free shit then," I said. "Let's go."

We walked over to the fuel dock. When we got there, Lilly tucked the gun away and pulled out the filler nozzle. She flipped up the lever on the pump. "Nothing. The pump's got power, though. See the LED readout?"

"Okay, one less thing we have to worry about. The boat."

We walked over to it. It was about a 30-footer, and the name on it said it was an Albin. I'd never heard of that boatmaker before, but she was pretty.

Lilly stopped suddenly, pulling out her Sig. "You hear that?"

"No. Water slappin' the side of the boat? Tide's comin' in."

"Maybe," she said, giving the area a good once-over before tucking her gun away again.

"You take the bow, I got the stern line. We'll untie it and just push it out into the canal."

"Owner's going to be steamed," said Lil.

"They'll probably eat him raw," I said, as I walked over and knelt down, putting the DP-12 down on the dock. Whoever'd tied the boat up had no idea what they were doing. It was wrapped around like thirty times and tied off right to the end of the rope.

"How you makin' out with yours? Some idiot must've –" Right then I looked up to see a half-dressed man staggering across the bow of the boat toward the rail, right where Lilly knelt, untying her line.

"Lilly, look out!" I yelled.

Right then he hit the rail and flipped over.

Lilly had time to put up her hands and fall backward, onto her ass. Both her feet went into the air as she tried to stop her backward momentum, and the rotten bastard dropped right down on her legs.

I watched, feeling the blood drain from my face as her gun slid across the dock, landing right near the edge of the planks. Grabbing the DP-12, I ran toward them, Lilly now trying to scramble backward in a spider crawl while the infected man's jaws stretched wide to take a bite out of her leg.

Halfway to her, I knew there was no using the shotgun. I dropped it to the dock and took two more leaping steps to reach the pair, just as the sick bastard clamped his teeth on her left leg and jerked his head back and forth.

Screaming, Lilly drew her right leg back and planted her boot on the top of his head. His mouth came away from her leg and I charged toward her and grabbed her arms, dragging her ten feet back like she weighed only ounces.

Just then, as I pulled her to her feet, another figure appeared on the boat beside us; it was a ragged woman, the front of her peasant blouse stained with dark brown gore.

I grabbed my gun from the back of my pants and spun around, pulling the trigger twice in quick succession.

She flew backward into the gel coat cabin of the boat, black goo running down behind her. Then she staggered forward again and fell to the deck, rolling off into the water.

The second she hit the water, it was like a baitfish boil; the water started churning like goddamned sea monsters were under there, ready to bust through the dock and send us into the water, just like in a B horror flick.

The man-freak had gotten his bearings again and made it back onto his feet, stumbling toward us. He paid no mind to the churning water beside him, but I did. As I jerked the barrel of my .45 up to put a couple in his face, something began to churn the water beside him, just under the bow of the boat we'd been trying to move.

I instinctively threw my arm around Lilly and dragged her backward again, her petite frame no match for my size. Behind us was maybe twenty more feet of dock, but nothing but water beyond.

The crazy wasn't distracted by the disturbance, but right then, the roiling water became an eruption as something broke the surface, shot high out of the water, its toothy mouth open as it hissed.

"Jesus!" I shouted. It was a massive saltwater croc – the first I'd ever seen – and its jaws snapped closed on that rotter's head and shoulders before dropping back down to the surface of the dock, causing the old timber to shake under our feet.

Already halfway out, it slammed its massive jaws down on the screeching zombie again and again, before clawing the rest of the way out of the marina water.

"CB, fire!" cried Lilly.

Just as the words left her lips, the crocodile, now fully on the dock, whipped its head sideways and released the freak, throwing his body against the hull of the boat beside us. The deadhead hit with a loud thud and splashed into the water below, a black-red streak running down the side of the gel coat. The croc's head turned toward us, and it raised up on its stubby claws and started forward.

I glanced between the dropped DP-12 on the dock, and the croc, gauging the distance. It would be a butt puckerer, but I didn't have a choice. My .45 wouldn't do shit against the beast headed our way.

Screw it. I ran to the shotgun, snatched it up, and hauled my ass back to where Lilly sat stunned on the dock. I'd never even fired a DP-12 before. I knew what a 12-gauge could do, but not against a gator, much less a croc.

"CB," Lilly whispered now, and I saw her eyeing her gun, still there on the edge of the dock.

"I got it," I whispered. I lowered the barrel and cocked the shotgun. I felt resistance as two shells slid into the chamber.

I pulled the triggers and fired. *BOOM!*

The monster croc's snout exploded in raining chunks of meat, but even with its jaws destroyed, it let out a screeching hiss and I swear I could smell its foul breath.

"Again!" shouted Lilly, as it advanced.

I fired again and ejected the spent shells, loading two more in as the empties clattered away.

I didn't need the other two. The croc's body seemed to deflate into the dock, now laying still. The black oozed down its head, draining between the dock slats down into the water below.

The water was still bubbling and churning to the left of us, and I said, "Come on!"

We ran to the T in the dock and I handed the shotgun to Lilly. "Keep it pointed at the water! I gotta push this boat out!"

She took it and held it, double barrels aimed down at the water. I grabbed the dockline and unwound it from the cleat that Lilly'd been struggling with.

Once it was free, I double-wrapped it around my fist and trudged back toward the end of the dock, pulling that boat slowly behind me. As something broke the surface of the water again, I heard the DP-12's throaty report.

BOOM!

Whatever it was sank back into the depths, and I said a silent prayer as the boat gained momentum and slid out into the canal beyond.

When I was sure it had enough steam to keep going, I let go of the dockline and ran back toward Lilly, taking the big shotgun from her. She ran back and retrieved her Sig from the dock, and we charged back to the Sea Ray.

I heard Nokosi barking up a storm as we reached the boat. Everyone had apparently heard the shots. Don't know how they couldn't have. Georgie leaned over the rail, her hand out. Lilly took it and jumped back aboard, me right on her tail. I leapt up in one motion and dropped the shotgun onto one of the bench seats.

"*Stille!*" commanded Georgina, and Nokosi immediately stopped barking. "Are you okay?" she asked us, her voice tinged with fear.

"Now we are," I said, as Lilly went into the main cabin and I ran up the stairs to the flybridge. Georgie stayed right behind me, paced by the dog.

"Goddamned saltwater crocs! Came right outta the water after us!"

"We have those here?" she asked, her breathing shallow and fast.

"Yeah, but you never see 'em. I guess the infection has 'em out searchin' for food where they don't usually go."

I dropped into the captain's chair and tuned the key, glad I didn't have to touch the starter wires together anymore. The boat motor turned, and the RPM meter pegged, then settled at idle speed. I pulled it backward, engaging reverse with a typical, mild grinding sound.

Lilly came in then, and dropped down onto the curved couch on the port side of the bridge. I pulled the throttle back all the way and the motor ground, but we didn't go anywhere. The boat just drifted side to side.

Confused for a second, I tried to calm myself, checking my senses as I ran a mental checklist. "Damnit!" I shouted. "The fuckin' dock lines!"

"I'll get them," said Lilly, who was squeezing her leg through her jeans where the thing had clamped down on her with its teeth.

I stared at her, worried. "No! I got it. Georgie, check her leg, would you? One of those rotten bastards bit her."

As though she understood, Nokosi's ears went on alert.

Georgina looked panicked, too. "A crocodile?" she said, her eyes wide.

"No, no, sorry. One of the zombie fuckers. Look her over. I'll be right back in."

She knelt down as I ran down the steps and hit the deck. I scanned the dock and didn't see anything. I was tempted to grab a knife and just cut the lines, but we'd need 'em again to tie up at the fuel dock.

We were several docks away from where the altercation happened, so I figured it was safe enough. All the noise that might attract anything had come from where we'd been, not where we were.

I took the chance and dropped down to the dock, making quick work of the lines – properly tied for a change.

I tossed both lines back up over the railing and jumped back on board. Running back to the steps, I took 'em two at a time and dropped back into the captain's chair.

"CB, Danny's on his boat!" said Lilly.

"Are his mom and dad with him?"

"He hates texting like you do, so his answers are hardly more than a word." Her eyes did a funny thing they do when she's holding back on me.

"What?" I asked. "What'd he say?"

She blushed. Actually full-face blushed. "He said he loved me."

My eyebrows went up. "Man, this relationship is developin' fast," I said. "You love him?"

She nodded quickly. "Jesus, I think so, CB. He's coming back." Her smile said all I needed to know. I hugged my sister then. "That's great, Lil."

"I didn't think I'd ever see him again," she said, breaking the embrace and squeezing my arm.

"How far out is he?"

"Just off Naples. So, within an hour."

I was really happy to hear my old buddy was okay, but I had other concerns. "Fantastic," I said. "How's your leg?"

"It didn't break the skin," said Georgina. "Just red, but not even teeth marks."

"Thank God," I muttered, as the bow of the boat slipped out and I turned the wheel until we pointed west. I gave it throttle, and we motored toward the fuel dock.

As I reached the turn-in, I pulled the throttle back into neutral and waited for a few minutes. The water that had been moving like a boiling pot was back to its normal amount of chop. I didn't know how long that would remain true once we pulled in. I hoped those croc monsters had headed out to bloodier pastures.

The good part was, the pumps were on the left side of the dock, not the right side where we'd had all the turmoil before. I was glad, 'cause that big, dead croc wasn't going anywhere, and with those massive teeth hanging over its jaws, it was scary just sitting there.

"Is it clear?" asked Lilly. Now Terry, Liam, and Roxy all came in. None of them sat; they all stood, their eyes scanning all around our boat.

"What's going on?" asked Terry. "Did you get the fuel?"

I guessed he wasn't aware of the plan. "Nope. I'm gonna pull the boat right in there, use the thrusters to keep the boat left, and we'll figure out how to get the pumps goin'. Lilly, you said there's still power?"

"Yeah, the backlights were on inside the pump."

"Anyone got a credit card?" I asked.

"I do, if mom charged it up for me."

"It's a pre-paid," said Georgie. "And yes, when I got off work the day that black rain started, I went onto my bank's website and put $500 on it."

"So, there's still around $400," she said, pulling it from her bag.

I'm so used to seeing women with purses, I didn't even notice she was carrying it when we'd rescued her. It's crazy how women will cling to their purses in the biggest of disasters.

"I'm goin' in now," I said. "Lilly, Georgie, when I get us up against the dock, go down and move the lines to the port side cleats, then toss 'em to the dock. When you get it, radio me and I'll cut the motor and run down."

"Want me to jump out and tie it off?" asked Lilly.

"No!" I shouted, louder than I meant to.

"CB!" scolded Lilly.

Shaking my head, I said, "Sorry. It's just that I'll do it, is all. But Lilly, you handled that DP-12 already. Grab Roxy, Terry and Georgie and arm 'em with the other shotguns from our stock. While I'm down there tyin' us off, I want all of you at the rail, aimin' down at the water. Anything pops up, you kill it."

"What if it's a Navy Seal?" asked Liam, his expression serious. I had to check to be sure.

I shook my head, forcing a smile. "It won't be a Seal."

"How do you know?" he asked. "They're badass."

"Then we'll give over control to them and let someone else take care of all of us," I said. "Assumin' it don't involve a concentration camp or some kinda quarantine."

"What do you concentrate on?" asked Liam.

"Huh?"

"In concentration camps."

"I'll explain later, bud."

"So, just so we're clear," said Terry. "If it's a Navy Seal, don't shoot."

"I like a crew that listens," I said. "Go get your guns while I get us in position."

Ω

Once everyone had shotguns in hand, Lilly and the others went below, where she went over how to brace 'em on their shoulders, how to fire, and how to chamber a new shell. This was done without ammo. We didn't need to call every gator, croc, and rotten piece of humanity to come running to us before I even got out there.

When they all came out, they left Nokosi shut in the main cabin, 'cause we didn't need her barking like crazy if something went wrong.

They came back up top where I was just bumping the thruster joysticks to move the Sea Ray to the left side of the slip, near the fuel pumps. The dead croc was stinking to high Heaven on the opposite side.

"Okay, I'll hold it here. You two get those dock lines to the other side and toss 'em out. Just like we talked about."

"Now?" asked Roxy, seeming kinda nervous.

"You got that credit card?" I asked her.

"Oh, sorry," she said, reaching into her pocket and pulling it out. "It's not a debit, so when you need the zip code, just ask and I'll tell you."

"Tell me now."

"33124."

"Yeah, I won't remember that. Tell me when I'm down there. Everybody ready?"

They all raised their weapons.

"Okay, stay sharp. Liam, do me a favor and walk around the boat. Look for the fuel filler cap on the port side. Should look like a chrome circle, and it'll say fuel on it."

"Port?" he asked.

"Left," I said. He nodded and ran down.

"And it's a diesel, CB," said Lilly.

I looked at her. "Yeah?"

"Yeah. I've been smelling it since we got on board. So use the card on the green pump."

"Thanks."

I drifted forward a bit more and engaged the thrusters, still tickled at how easy they were to use, and how damned easy they made docking a big-ass boat.

"I'm set. Toss the lines," I said over the radio.

"They're out, CB. Hurry up and you've got it."

I ran down, and as my feet hit the deck, I heard Liam call, "Found it!"

"Good boy!" I said, heading right to the rail, opening the side hatch and jumping down to the dock. Three shotgun barrels aimed down at the water.

Georgie said, "Liam, stay in the middle of the boat or go up to the flybridge."

I quickly lashed the dock lines to the cleats, securing the boat. So far, nothing had come up from the water to attack.

"Hurry, CB," said Lilly.

I slid the card from my pocket and stuck the chip end into the diesel pump's card slot. It asked me for the zip code. "Zip?" I called, looking up at Roxy.

"33124," she said.

I punched the numbers in. LIFT HANDLE AND BEGIN FUELING came on the screen. I'm good at following instructions, so I did just that.

The pump was fast, like so many marina pumps are. The numbers were rolling by, and I didn't know if I'd be filling that boat up or not.

The diesel was $3.05 per gallon, and I was already up to 110 gallons by the time I started to worry. I didn't think the tank was halfway down yet, but it was starting to look like it.

"You almost done?" asked Georgie.

"I'm gonna max out the card before I fill it, it looks like."

Just then it clicked. I looked at the read out. $381.25. I'd gotten 125 gallons on the button. I pulled out the nozzle, put the cap back on, and hooked it back to the pump.

"CB, heads up," Lilly said, her voice a whisper.

I looked up at her and saw a man standing at the end of the dock, right where it hit the wider, main dock that led up to the marina stores and restaurants. He didn't move. He just looked at me.

I pulled my .45 from my pants and held it up, my heart rate increasing by the second.

"You alive?" the man called.

I let out my breath, closed my eyes and said a quiet thank you to the powers that kept me from pulling that trigger when I drew it.

"Yeah," I said. "Name's Cole."

"Saw you motor in," he said. "Sun's about to go down." He spoke with a Hispanic accent of some kind. Might've been Mexican, but possibly Cuban.

He started walking toward me and all four shotgun barrels swung his way. He stopped all of a sudden, saying, "I didn't see you folks 'til just now. I'm harmless." He held up his hands.

I motioned to the girls and Terry to lower the shotguns. "Keep 'em on the water, though. Any crocs come up, shoot first, ask questions … well, you know."

"Do you know what happened? Where did you come from?"

"Let's start with your name," I said, walking toward him. "You know mine already."

He walked forward and extended his hand. When we reached one another, we shook. "Oscar Santoyo," he said. "I live here, on my boat."

"You safe here?"

"Fishing has gotten a little risky," he said. "So I'm raiding boats for food. There's a restaurant up there," he said, pointing. "I haven't had the balls to check it out. Some of those crazy people come down here sometimes, but I just close myself in my boat and I'm okay."

"Any other food sources around?" I asked. "We're headin' north, so now that we've got fuel for the boat, we need more for us."

Oscar laughed, then stifled it and checked around him. "I tell you what," he said. "I'll make you a deal."

"I like to barter," I said, figuring he'd want us to take him with us. "What you got?"

"Food. Canned tamales. Hundreds of them."

"Hundreds? What kind?"

"Carne Asada, Pollo, some Carnitas, too."

"On your boat?"

He shook his head. "No. I found them when I was searching. They're stacked floor to ceiling inside the salon. I think he owns the company. Same name that's on the can is on the boat."

"And what's your bargain? What do you need?"

He nodded toward my guards on the boat. "A gun. I have no protection. All I found searching the boats is a couple of spearguns."

"The water workin' here?" I asked.

"Yes. The power has stayed on here, but on the radio, I heard it's out in many places."

"You get in that black rain shit?"

"No, I stayed inside my boat when it came. That doesn't help, though. So did many of my neighbors. Here, at the marina. They're dead now. They changed into those things and I had to kill them."

I looked the guy over. He'd have to stretch his neck to get to 5'6" tall, and his skin was droopy for a guy who didn't look to be much older than forty. I figured he'd lost some weight, despite the supply of tamales. Either way, he didn't look like much of a killer.

"With what?"

He turned and motioned toward a boat that looked like it'd been ridden hard and put away wet. "The fucking speargun and my baseball bat. It's what I normally use for protection when I stay on my boat."

"It's a good idea anyway," I said. "Bat's quiet. I'd use it whenever you can. Anyway, sure. I'll set you up with a … you prefer a shotgun or rifle?"

"Shotgun. I got lots of tequila, too. Easier shooting with a shotgun."

"Okay, we got a good selection. I'll get you a 12-gauge and a few boxes of shells. Deal?"

He shrugged. He wore black pants and a teal button-down shirt. "Take as much as you want. I have a lot of boats to go through yet. I'll probably find more food. The gun will make sure I'm here to eat it."

I went back to where Terry stood. "Hey, Ter. Hand me your shotgun, would ya?"

He did, lowering it down by the barrel. "Would you grab a sack or somethin' and throw him in about four boxes of the 12-gauge shells? In the main cabin there, on the seat."

While he did that, I ran over to where the hose was coiled. I pulled it over to the boat and found the water fill. Uncapping it, I stuck the hose in, and turned on the valve.

When I was done, Terry was back. "Here you go, as ordered."

"Perfect," I said, carrying both the gun and ammo over to Oscar. Before handing him the gun, I pumped it several times, emptying the ammo out. I put the ejected shells in the sack and gave both to him. "Here you go."

He smiled. "You're not dumb, are you?"

"Oh, hell yeah I am, just ask my sister. But the fact is, I don't know you, and there ain't a stranger in the world I'd hand a loaded gun to these days. Now, you got a cart or somethin' I can haul these tamales back to my boat with?"

He went right to one of the marina's dock carts and swung it around so the handle pointed toward me.

"Well, then. Show me this boat and I'll get 'er filled up."

Ω

CHAPTER SIX

When I was aboard the large cabin cruiser filled with stacks of various tamales – and the name on the boat was definitely the same as the name on the cans – I offered to let Oscar travel with us.

"No, amigo," he said. "I've got everything I need here. Now that I have this," he added, holding up the shotgun, "if I'm careful, I can get more. My boat is secure, and if things get very bad, I can take it off the dock."

"Your call," I said.

"Gracias. Take all you want of this. I already have twenty cans or so. I'll be sick of them by the time I'm done."

"Cole?" came Georgie's voice over the radio. "Everything okay over there?"

I unclipped it from my belt. "Yeah, Georgie. Oscar's helpin' me load up on canned tamales."

"I don't think that's going to be much better than the beans, as far as your sister's concerned."

She had a smile in her voice.

"I'll be back over pretty quick. Y'all get ready to take the cans when I hand 'em up."

"Oscar, you all alone? Got any family?"

We stepped out of the boat and I lifted the handle of the cart, stacked high with cans.

He nodded. "Si, many. They're all in Texas, though. I'm going to try to get to them when I see an opportunity." He waved his arm in a sweeping motion, indicating the boats around us. "There are many boats, so maybe I will try to take one across the Gulf."

"Get a weather radio," I said. "Just in case that robot voice is still broadcastin' somehow. Don't need to get caught in a squall out there."

"Gracias, amigo," said Oscar. "Vaya con Dios. Go with God."

"Well, gracias to you, Oscar. You do the same. Stay safe, man."

He retreated to his boat and I did the same, the heavy cart rolling smoothly on large wheels. When I got there, Terry hopped out and started hoisting cans up to the ladies.

"Appreciate it, Terry," I said. "You like tamales?"

"Mexican's my favorite. I could eat it every day."

"More work, less talk," said Roxy, winking at me. "That's what mom always said when I was doing homework."

"And lookie how smart you turned out," I said, winking back.

"And gorgeous, too," said Terry. "Like her mom."

I looked up, and even in the waning daylight, I could see Georgie blushing. "It's true," I said.

We handed the last four cans up to the women and I said, "Water full yet?"

"Oh, crap," said Terry. "I forgot you put the hose in!"

I walked over to the filler and saw water was running down the side of the boat. "Okay, it's overflowin'. That means we got fuel, food, and water. I'd say this was a good trip, aside from the zombie croc encounter."

Terry had climbed back aboard and now stood with the ladies. Lilly said, "So we're sticking with the boat for now, right? How far can we get on the fuel we have?"

"It's full up, so about 220 miles."

"You're going to hate me," said Lilly. "But since I don't care, I think we should find a skiff to tow behind. That way we can anchor offshore and take the skiff in."

"No need," I said, pulling myself up and onto the boat. I closed the hatch gate behind me. "Danny's center console will do just fine for that."

"Oh, that's right. He did say he wanted to keep his boat."

"I didn't even have to ask. He loves that boat."

"Can we go?" asked Roxy. "I really don't like being tied up here now that it's dark."

"I'm ready," I said. "Lil, think you can drive this thing outta here? Once you get 'er started, I'll untie us."

"Sure," she said. She went inside to the enclosed cabin's helm.

A moment later, I heard the motor crank, then settle into an idle. I opened the hatch, jumped out, and quickly untied the dock lines, throwing 'em over the rail. We'd never moved the bumpers over, because they didn't touch the dock anyway.

Jumping back on, I returned to the salon where everyone else sat. The boat was already sliding backward out of the slip.

Somebody, I'm guessing Lilly, had put a Waylon Jennings disc on, and when I walked in, *Good Hearted Woman* was playing. It was the version with Willie Nelson. One of my favorites.

Lilly didn't vacate the captain's chair. The sun had almost dropped below the horizon now, and I checked my watch. 8:23. I wasn't sure if running at night would be better or worse than in the day, or if it made any difference at all. The GPS would keep us on track, but anything floating out there – like Liam's boat – could become a dangerous obstacle we wouldn't see until it was too late.

I was about to voice my concern to Lilly, who now put the Sea Ray in forward and bumped the throttle. She guided the big boat around the small protective jetty and into the choppier water.

Seeing she had it under control, I went to sit beside Georgina, who had Nokosi sitting on her feet on the floor.

"You got it, sis?" I asked.

"There's beer," she said. "Settle in."

"I want tamales," I said, dropping down. No sooner had my buttcheeks hit the leather seat, I heard a shrill shriek.

I knew that sound; it was a canned boat horn. I knew right way it was Danny.

Ω

I ran out of the cabin and up the steps to the flybridge, waving my arms.

"CB!" he called, standing shirtless on the bow of the Sportsman center console. He started pointing down at the water, and I barely heard, "Drop anchor!"

I gave him a thumbs-up and trotted back down to the salon. "Lil, pull to neutral. I'm droppin' anchor. I'm guessin' he's going to tie up to us."

"Good," she said. "Okay, go."

I ran back up and pressed the anchor switch with my foot. I heard the chain feeding off the spindle. When it started to slack, I let out several more feet and stopped again, waiting.

The boat drifted, turned, then I felt a slight jerk as the anchor caught on the bottom.

I stood up again and waved at Danny, who began motoring toward us immediately. As he neared, he jumped out of the captain's chair and dropped his bumpers over his starboard side, tying both in place.

"Man, you don't know how glad I am to see you," I said as he pulled up beside us. Now Lilly ran up behind me, leaning against the railing.

"Y'all don't have any idea," he said.

Behind us, Terry, Roxy, and Georgie emerged from below. I turned to look at 'em, and I think I was just a tiny bit jealous when they all stared at Danny, standing in front of that steering wheel, his shirtless black body glistening with sweat, accentuating every goddamned muscle.

"He's … amazing," said Terry.

"No shit," said Lilly, a smile planted on her face now.

I was used to it. I remember in school, seeing Danny in the shower after gym class, all 6'2" of him at the time, making the rest of us boys look like 98-pound weaklings. He was a god at our school, a star of our basketball team and an amazing high jumper on our track and field crew.

Now he was 6'5" if he was a foot. Hell, I'm 6'3", 235 pounds, and believe me when I tell you, I don't like having to raise my head to look a man – or a woman – in the eye. I'm used to being the big guy in the room.

"Everybody take a cold shower," I said. "This ain't the time for gawkin'."

Lilly shook her head as she caught the first of the dock lines Danny threw over. "Do I hear jealousy?" she quipped.

"A shitload," I said. Laughing, I shook my head and ran down to grab the stern line. We pulled his Sportsman up against the bumpers and tied it off, leaving just enough slack to handle the rolling waves beneath us.

"Sight for sore eyes, brother," I said. "Get over here."

Danny laughed, his perfect teeth stark against his black skin. "I ain't never been happier to see somebody," he said, leapfrogging onto the Sea Ray. He looked over the boat. "CB, man, you steal this?" He pulled me into a hug.

I hugged him back. "Glad you're okay, man. Yeah, I stole it."

"Y'all know what's happenin', right?" he asked, pulling away, his hands on my shoulders. "You hear that crazy DJ dude?"

"Yeah," I said. "I'm glad *you* did. You heard his call to head to Lebanon, Kansas, right?"

"Yeah," he said, his eyes narrowed. "What do you think?"

I shrugged. "It's where we figured we'd go. He's the only one with any kinda plan we've heard about."

Danny nodded, but his eyes weren't on me. I guess Lilly was giving us time to say our hellos, because once his eyes left me, he turned, and she ran into his open arms.

As I watched, no words were exchanged between 'em. They just held one another, both their eyes closed.

This told me two things: first, they'd been dating longer than she'd said. Second, that it was way more serious than she'd let on.

I didn't care, but I might've felt a bit slighted.

Ω

We left the boat anchored for the time being, while we got caught up.

"My gas tank's full," said Danny. "It was almost on empty when this thing started, but I just hid out at the house for a few days. I tried to get out of Florida on the

98

highways, but it got too crazy. I got down to the marina and took off. So far, I've just been siphoning from boats. Cut a good piece of hose at my house before I left."

"I'm almost afraid to ask," said Lilly. "Where are your parents?"

Now Danny's face went slack. His lip started to quiver, and I realized I'd never seen him like that before, except once.

That was when he hadn't yet grown into the beast he is, and a bunch of racist pricks from our school were trying to force him to jump maybe twelve feet down from a tree.

He'd just moved to Everglades City from Shreveport, Louisiana, and there weren't many black kids in school then. All kids can be cruel, but introduce anyone different to a backwoods school, and trouble won't be far behind.

I was almost home from school when I saw 'em, just a block from where I lived. Danny had used a rope ladder that was always attached to the tree to climb up to a platform someone had built up there, but one of the assholes followed him and pulled the ladder up behind him.

Danny later told me the kid, Jimmy Waldrup, told him the only way he was getting down was the hard way.

I could hear Danny crying from where I was. He was wailing, his feet dangling over the edge while he tried to gauge whether he'd make it or not.

I didn't like any of those kids. I decided Danny wouldn't be jumping down – not that day.

I ran to my house and grabbed my .22. I remember sneaking around the bushes and getting real close. I aimed at the tree just above Jimmy's head, and fired. The bark exploded above him, and he dropped the rope ladder clutched in his hands. Then he lost his balance.

Jimmy fell out of the tree, landing face-down with his arm beneath him. When he finally sat up, I saw his lip bleeding and he was holding a broken arm. He was crying like a baby, and afterward, the four bullying bastards ran off and I went over to see if Danny was alright.

That was the first time we met. He'd been my best friend since.

"Danny, man, *are* your folks okay?" I asked.

He shook his head, his expression grim. He looked over at Liam and said, "It's bad. He okay?"

"Liam," said Georgie. "Why don't you go into the cabin there and close the door for a few minutes."

"Don't want to," he said shaking his head. "Don't you think if I saw what happened to my mom, my dad, and Fiona and Finn, that I can handle what happened to *his* mom and dad?"

"He's got a point," I said. "The kid has seen a lot. Talk about closin' the barn door after the horse got out."

Everyone nodded. "Your call," Roxy said to Liam. "If you feel uncomfortable, you can leave anytime."

"Okay," said Danny. "Anyway, I got a call from Dad about forty-five minutes after that weird rain stopped. I was on the internet trying to figure out what caused it. That's when I found the viral video from that crazy Indian medicine man.

"Dad said he and mom were out gardening, but dad admitted he was on the covered porch listening to a baseball game on his old-ass transistor radio. Mama was on her knees on a pad, tending to her tomatoes."

"Not that same old radio," I said.

He pointed at me. "Yep, same one. About the size of a brick, silver. Broken antenna. That it was still working was a source of pride for my dad. Had it since he was like seventeen. Philco Ford I think it was."

"Go on," I said.

Danny shifted in his seat. "I didn't wait long. When he called, he said mom was acting real strange. I told him to call 911, but he said he tried and couldn't get through. I hung up and tried myself. Then I understood. I got in my car and hauled ass to his house from work."

"When I got there, Mom was on the floor and dad was over her, pinning her arms to the floor, crying. She was snappin' her jaws at him."

"How horrible," Lilly whispered.

Danny nodded. "You know our family, guys. You know how tight we've always been. Horrible's the least of what it was. Anyway, Dad's fingers were all bandaged up, and he told me to get back, because she bit him once already. He shut himself in the bathroom to tend to it, and she just scratched at the door the whole time.

"When he came back out, she was just as crazy, and somehow he got her on the floor. That's how I found him. Anyway, you know I didn't know what the hell was happening yet. When I saw 'em, I took charge, I guess. I pulled my dad off the floor and made him sit on the sofa.

"By the time I got back to her, she was on her feet, comin' at me. I grabbed her by the arms and spun her around so her back was against my chest, and I muscled her to the bed. It wasn't easy, man! She was fightin' me like a wildcat."

He paused, his eyes seeing it all over again, his thoughts back in that room with his mother. As if talking to himself, he said, "The second I let her go, she was at me again … you've all seen them, right? How they are?"

I nodded. "Lilly had to put Pa down. I had to shoot Clay and Tan."

His eyes saddened even more. "I'm so sorry, you guys," he said, reaching out and taking Lilly's hand. "This shit makes me lose hope."

He waited for a few seconds before continuing with his story. "Anyway, I didn't know what to do, so I held her arms down, but she was bucking and snapping her jaws, never getting tired, never changin' at all. I had to have been there two hours. I know I'd have held her there all night if my dad hadn't come in."

"Did he offer to take over?" asked Roxy.

Danny shook his head. "He attacked me from behind."

Tears ran down Georgie's face. She whispered, "Danny, did he bite you?"

He shook his head. "No, thank God. I remember, my heart was pounding. I heard his jaws snap together right beside my ear, and for some reason, I thought he was joking or something. I know, not the time for that, but then I smelled his breath and it smelled … rotten. I let go of my mom and dove to the ground. Dad didn't try to attack her, he was focused on me, but the second I let my mom go, they both came after me."

"What the hell did you do?"

"I ran outside and shut the door. The rain had stopped a long time before, but that black shit was everywhere. The grass was black, trees, streets, benches, everything."

"Don't we know it," said Lilly. "Danny, you don't have to finish. We can guess."

He shook his head. "I haven't talked about it to anyone. I maybe need to."

I nodded, and he nodded back. "Anyway, I was outside, freakin' out, lookin' through the window at them. That was when I noticed Dad's bandage had come off. He was missing two fingers. It wasn't just a bite."

He wiped a tear from his cheek with his finger. "They both just wandered around for a while. Neither one was paying any attention to the other. He wasn't worried about her, and she wasn't worried, either. They just staggered around. Finally, after trying 911 again, I tapped on the window."

"Not good," I said.

"No," said Danny. "Not good at all. They both saw me and just came toward me. Both of them hit that window together, and it shattered. They fell through it and the glass cut them."

"And they didn't bleed," said Georgie.

"Some places they did, but not their faces. I remember seeing their blood was darker somehow. Their faces were cut by the glass, but it looked like a cadaver cut."

"How do you know what that's like?" asked Roxy.

"Pre-med," said Danny. "We did a dissection of a cadaver. Worst day of my life before Mom and Dad changed."

"Did you run?" asked Liam.

"No, because they were my folks and they were sick. I lured them back into the house, got them into a bedroom. First I ran in there and opened a window and closed the curtains. Figured I'd open a path for them to follow me and use my speed against them. I moved slow down the hall and turned into the bedroom, moving behind the door. Once they came in, I slammed the door and jumped on the bed to get to the window. They were both on the other side of the room when I jumped through and closed it again. With the curtains there, I guess they forgot it was a way out."

"What did you do then?" asked Terry, transfixed.

He shrugged. "I ran over to a neighbor's house. Tammy and Diane. Middle-aged, divorced roomies always tryin' to talk me into a threesome."

"Seriously," said Lilly.

Danny smiled. "Not my type, 'specially now. Nobody answered when I knocked, but I'm pretty sure they hit the inside of that door. I went to the window and saw them in there. They were both stained with that black shit and they looked just like my mom and dad and all the others."

"So that's when you first learned it was more than just your parents," said Georgie.

Danny nodded. "I watched them for a while. It was easier than watching my parents, but it told me all I needed to know about them, too. When I'd seen enough, I grabbed my keys and got out. I didn't drive very far before I figured out the roads were jammed. Then I worked my way back and went to get the boat keys, water, food, and other stuff like gas cans. I left and hit the marina."

"Why didn't you try to call us?" asked Lilly.

"I did," said Danny. "Tried your phone and CB's. Got circuits busy message or nothing. I didn't think to try texting. Figured it would be the same story."

"I'm so sorry about your mom and dad," said Georgie. "Did anything become of them?"

He shook his head, and in that simple gesture, I saw him begin to crack, just a little. I suppose being with us again kinda brought home how messed up everything else really was. He choked out the next words. "My parents are … still there as far as I know. This is a catastrophe, guys."

"You up for Kansas with us?" I asked. "I take it you're not plannin' on stickin' around?"

"I'm relieved as hell to be with you guys. And I know this is kinda out of the blue, but is the shower working on this boat? Can I take one?"

"Yeah," I said. "Go ahead but keep it short. We just filled the water, but we don't know what's ahead of us. You hungry?"

"For somethin' hot, yeah. Been eating room temperature, canned stuff."

"We have tamales comin' out of our asses."

Danny stared at me, a sly smile on his face. "Don't think I want any ass tamales."

"C'mon," said Lilly. "I'll show you where the shower is and get you a towel. I still need to check you over for any bites or scratches."

"Maybe Georgie should do that," I said. In the back of my mind, the minute the words left my lips I was thinking how I didn't necessarily want Georgie looking at the big stud's nude body. Lilly saved me.

"Oh, don't worry," she said. "I'll know if anything's out of place."

I shook my head and smiled as I watched 'em walk away. I was glad Danny was here. He had a good head on his shoulders, and we needed all the help we could get.

Ω

With Danny's boat tied off on ours, we stayed at anchor. Tide was high, and there was no danger of hitting any sand bars, especially with the depth-finder, but I didn't like boating in the 'Glades in the dark and I didn't dig doing it in the Gulf of Mexico, either.

Forty-five minutes after he headed to the shower, Danny came back into the salon with my sister in tow.

"Tamales!" he said. "Load me up." He plopped down on the bench seat behind the captain's chair, where I sat. I think everyone else was afraid to sit there for fear I'd have them drivin'.

"Lilly, you goin' with Danny on the Sportsman?"

"For a while, I think," she said. "That okay with you guys?"

Everyone nodded. That made me feel pretty good. If they didn't think I needed Lilly around me to keep me in check, it was a rare feeling indeed. She definitely kept me from doing a lot of stupid shit in my life.

"See you brought all your rods," I said.

"Can I fish?" asked Liam. "We were going to go fishing, but we never got the chance."

"Sure," said Danny. "Probably tomorrow, though. We'll need to cast my net for some baitfish."

Danny glanced at me, then threw a sideways glance at Liam. I knew the question. It was: *You mess up? He yours?*

Two old friends could say a lot with just a look and an eyebrow. I laughed out loud.

Everyone looked at me. "What's funny?" asked Georgie.

"I guess it ain't that funny, now that I think of it," I said. "Danny here thought Liam might be a gift from an old girlfriend. You know, from back when I was 19 or 20."

"Because CB's hair is so red?" asked Lilly, leaning over to smack Danny on the back of his head. "That boy right there is as Irish as the day is long."

"I don't know Irish from nothin', Lil," said Danny. "God, it's good to see y'all. Felt like I was just wanderin' until now. Crazy to think it's just been a couple weeks. Feels like months this has been goin' on."

"The only voice we've heard that seems to have any kind of plan is Micky the DJ," said Georgina. "Our classic rock pied piper."

"Y'all *see* them crazy zombie gators? Asked Danny. "Rode mighta sounded a little scared, but at least he was rational when I caught him for a while in my car. Any plan that gets us outta gator country's good enough for me."

106

"You don't have a ship-to-shore in that boat?" asked Roxy.

Danny smiled big, his white teeth gleaming against his black skin. "It ain't no 1950s fishin' trawler," he said. "I use my cell and my MP3 player. No CB radio, no … whatever the hell you asked about."

Roxy shrugged, and Terry said, "Seriously, Rox. Ship-to-shore? Where'd you even hear that?"

"Old movie, I guess," she said, blushing.

"I'd like to get up at the crack of dawn and get movin'," I said. "If that suits everyone. Like Danny said, maybe we can get some bait and catch some fish for lunch and dinner. We're gonna get awful tired of tamales."

Ω

That night, Lilly doubled up with Danny, which was just a bit weird for me. I had Liam on the other side of my bed, and the dude tossed and turned all night.

That kept me up.

The next morning, maybe twenty minutes before dawn, I snuck into the main cabin and found Lilly's smokes. I slid one from the pack and headed up to the flybridge and sat, lighting it with some waterproof matches I found in a dry box built into the helm.

On my second draw of the cigarette, I heard, "Still stealin' smokes from Lil, huh?"

I turned to see Danny ease into the bench seat behind me, stretching out his legs. He only had his swim trunks on, which was normal for him when he was on a boat.

"Yep," I said. "And it just occurred to me I didn't bring my trunks."

"Boxers'll do," said Danny. "How you doin', brother?"

107

"Better now you're here," I said, and I meant it. "Believe me when I tell you, there are some bright minds here on this boat. We can make all the plans we want, but if I run us aground, none of it's for shit."

"You can handle boats just fine."

I shook my head. "Nope. You're way better on big water. I got here by the skin of my teeth."

"You got here. That's a feat."

"Sorry about your folks, Danny. You doin' alright?"

He shrugged. "Best as can be expected. I haven't cornered the market on sorrow. So, your pa, and both Tanner and Clay?"

"Lilly dealt with Pa. I was with Clay and Tan when Tan got sick. Then Clay did. I didn't have a choice."

Danny stared at the smoke curling from my cigarette until I flicked it over the edge, out into the water. He sighed.

"Lilly told me about your dad. You both did what I shoulda done, man. I shouldn't have left mine like that."

"From what I can tell, they don't know. No idea what they are."

Danny nodded, but added, "I know. That's almost worse."

I stared at the shore. When I turned back, I saw Danny was, too. "Look how dark it is," he said. "Normally you can make out that shoreline like a line on a map."

"The things out there don't need lights," I said.

"CB, I just keep tryin' to wake up."

"You and me both. Remember you and me, after we saw 28 Days Later? What was that? Back in 2001? 2002?"

Danny nodded his head and flashed an embarrassed smile. "Yeah, somethin' like that. We were just kids. Remember, we thought we'd just get out there and knock heads. I remember, we both just thought we'd carry around baseball bats and whack our way through 'em."

I laughed, but the moment passed as reality set in again. "So, you wanna tell me I'm hallucinatin' or somethin'? Kick me to wake me up? 'Cause there's no way we're really havin' this conversation, right?"

Danny stared out at the blank shoreline. "It's real as shit, man. You know as well as I do we ain't crazy."

"You really wanna fish today?"

"Look. I'm up so I can motor off and get that bait. The kid wants to fish, and you guys will probably eat somethin' before we take off, so I got time. Maybe get us a snook or two, some trout or redfish or somethin'."

"Good plan. Take a radio with you."

He patted my shoulder. "No worries, CB. Give me maybe twenty minutes. I know a good bait spot."

He started to get up, but I grabbed his wrist. "Wait. Let's both go," I said. "I'll leave a note."

"Lilly's awake," he said. His face broke into a smile. "You cool? As for me, I'm glad it's finally out."

I winked. "Tell your girlfriend we're headin' out."

Ω

109

CHAPTER SEVEN

We grabbed a couple of bottled waters from the refrigerator inside, and pushed off in the Sportsman. When we'd drifted off about twenty feet, Danny lowered the trim until the motors were in the water and fired 'em up.

In the smooth way he operated that boat, he got up on plane quickly and motored east, to a spot even I was familiar with, just about a half-mile from the Sea Ray.

It was grassy, and the moment we reached it, I saw the familiar white-green flashes of the silvery fish we used for bait. The school was thick, darting back and forth like a magic carpet in a cartoon.

Danny threw the transmission into neutral and jumped back to pull his cast net from a 5-gallon bucket. He expertly draped it over his shoulder, picked several sections of the net up, holding them in his teeth. Then he half-pivoted right, and unwound his body, throwing that net in a perfect circle.

When he pulled it up, it shimmered with hundreds of baitfish.

"Jesus, man!" I shouted. "One cast, done!"

He laughed, and I saw a lot of the tension drain from his face, not to mention his body. He opened the live well and turned the net inside-out, dumping the catch in. He turned to me. "Let's do one more. Can't have enough, plus these greenbacks die easier than pinfish."

I nodded and stood back. "King of the Cast, proceed, sir."

He did his prep and windup again and tossed the net.

Just before it hit the water, I saw something move. All the baitfish darted away.

"What the hell?" asked Danny.

Suddenly, he was fighting with the net. He stumbled forward, his knees hitting the rail.

"CB, give me a hand!" he shouted.

I ran up beside him.

"Grab the net and pull!" he said. "Maybe have a grouper or somethin'."

It was on the bottom, I could tell, but now the water was clouded with silt, and visibility was zilch.

"Pull!" he yelled. "Even if it's a nurse shark, we can cut that bastard up and have some good shark steaks."

We both leaned back, pulling hand over hand, hooking our fingers into the net as it slowly rose from the depths.

"One more!" he said, and we leaned back, giving it everything in us.

"Shit!" I screamed, when the man's face came out of the water, his netted hand reaching straight up at us.

"Holy fuck!" shouted Danny, and we both let go of that net at the same time, both tumbling backward onto the Sportsman's deck.

We were back on our feet in an instant, pressing ourselves to the other side of the boat. I didn't have to reach into the back of my pants to remember I'd left my gun aboard the Sea Ray.

"It's caught on the cleat!" I yelled. "You got a knife?"

"I don't wanna cut that net!" said Danny. "It's the big one!"

"Danny, if you have a smaller one, cut it! Fucker's climbin' in!"

And he was. I don't have any idea *how* he was, but the second his hand clutched the rail through the net, his body started to come into view.

I knew we were both approaching panic. I heard screaming in the distance and looked up to see the Sea Ray. Lilly was on the deck with the binoculars to her eyes.

I'd never hear the fucking end of it. I could hear the questions about leaving my gun over and over.

"Wait, Danny! Get your gun! Shoot it!"

"Fuck, right," said Danny, and he turned toward the console and reached into a netted storage pouch.

He came back with a revolver of some kind; I'd never seen the gun before. It was big; maybe a .40 or a .45.

The struggling zombie dropped into the boat, hitting the deck on his back. He jammed his fingers through the webbing and pulled hard, tearing it like it was paper. Seaweed was wrapped around his body, and his hands and feet were torn up, probably from dragging across the sharp coral beds that trashed so many boat propellers.

I knew now, from how he pulled himself over that railing and how he tore that net away, just how goddamned strong they were. His face jutted through the webbing, and he opened his foul mouth to let out a throaty scream, when a crab crawled over his bottom teeth and skittered up over his shredded face, then to the deck of the boat.

I think that was too much for both of us. Danny fired the gun into his right eye, his hand shaking bad.

The thing's body went slack. I let out a big breath and fell back down to the deck. "Pull the rest of that net in so nothin' else can climb up it," I wheezed, barely able to make the words audible. "Fuck, Danny!"

"Net's fucked anyway," he said. "And who knows what the damned bait fish have been feedin' on. Come here. Give me a hand."

I sighed, pushed myself up, and went to him. "There," said Danny. "Get his ass. I got his arms."

"I get dibs on the arms next time," I said.

Together, we hoisted him over the edge. The net was still caught, but Danny took out a knife and cut it away. The dead zombie sank back to the depths of the deeper water we'd drifted into.

"On the bright side, we have bait," he said. "And no matter what they been feedin' on, the fish we catch with 'em won't have time to digest 'em."

"So, I got myself a glass half full motherfucker," I said.

"Damned straight."

"Good."

Ω

The net trashed and the livewell full enough, Danny fired up the Sportsman and motored back to the boat. Lilly was waiting for us by the time we pulled up.

I guess we woke up the whole boat, because everyone came out right behind her.

"Dumbasses!" shouted Lilly, as we pulled up alongside the Sea Ray. "What were you thinking?"

"Relax, Lil," I said. "We just went out to get some baitfish. Didn't seem like a risk."

"Until you pull up a damned zombie!" she said. "Are you alright?"

"Fine," said Danny, still visibly shaken. "Just another lesson learned."

"Deeper water," I said. "Definitely need deeper water."

"You both need bigger brains more like," said Lilly. "You about scared me half to death. What were we supposed to do if you both got yourselves killed? What if there were four or five of those things instead of just one?"

I finished tying off the bow, and Danny got the stern line. "I know, I know," he said. "Sorry Lil."

I smiled, knowing Lilly's face. She didn't wanna be mad at Danny. I was a different story. I think she liked being mad at me.

She took his hand as he climbed aboard. "You're okay, right? No scratches or bites?"

Danny shook his head. "Didn't let it get close enough. Damn. That freaked me out."

"The good news is the crabs survived," I said.

"Do I need to look you two over?" asked Georgie, from inside the salon door.

"We're fine, Georgie," I said. "Close call is all. It didn't touch us."

Liam pushed past Georgina and ran over to the rail. "Can we go fishing?"

"I got lots of bait, but I think we'd be better off heading up the coast a bit," said Danny. "Maybe have a bite and head out?"

"I'm not hungry," said Lilly. "I'd feel better if we were moving."

"Me, too," said Terry. His face was pale, and I realized the water was beginning to get choppy. The boat at anchor was gonna play hell with seasickness if I didn't get going.

"Okay. Danny, you wanna grab somethin' to eat on board, or you plan on trollin' for your breakfast?"

"I'll take whatever you got. Lil, you wanna ride with me?"

"I'm not letting you go alone. You'll have that net out again."

Danny shook his head. "That net's gone. Just got the small one now. Don't worry. I learned my lesson."

Lilly made a sound that told us both she wasn't so sure. I took my own advice and hurried into the main cabin and fired up the Sea Ray.

Danny settled on canned pears. I gave him a second can of peaches – Lilly's favorite – and they headed out to his boat.

"You sure you don't wanna ride in this, Lil?" I called out. "I'm sure Liam would go with him."

"That boy stays in this boat," shot Lilly. "Danny knows what he's doing. We'll have the radio, so just stay close behind us and keep your eyes open."

"I'll fuckin' tailgate you."

"Then I'll pray, too," she said, shaking her head.

"You'll pray," I mumbled. "Like I'm dangerous or somethin'."

"You're kind of dangerous," said Georgie. "And you're really big. How tall are you?"

I laughed. "My driver's license says 6'4" but I lied. I'm 6'3". Felt tall until Danny showed up."

"How long have you known one another?""

"Hold on a sec," I said. "Lilly will have my gizzard if I mess this up. Where's everyone else?"

"Down in the salon. You need help?"

"You wanna operate the windlass? I'll bump us forward and break the anchor loose, then you just hit the switch to bring it up."

"Got it," she said.

We got it done without help from anyone else. Georgie told me Roxy and Terry were playing Jenga or some shit like that. I couldn't figure out how that'd work once we got underway, but 'twern't my problem.

That's a mispronunciation of the English language, one among many we like to do in the south. Visit sometime. You'll get used to it.

"How was that?" asked Georgie.

"Did the anchor slide in the slot and snug up against the bow rail?" I asked.

"Snug," she nodded. "Whatever a bow rail is."

I smiled. "Ready for a boat ride?"

"Wish that's all it was. You and Danny going to need more time to hash things out?"

I shook my head. "Don't think so. You mean about him and Lilly, or about headin' to Kansas?"

"I was talking about Kansas."

Danny was idling around in circles, so I pushed the throttle forward and the motors kicked in. We slowly gained momentum, and he took off, leading the way. Once I got the trim set, I kept one eye on the depth gauge, which currently read 21 feet.

"What are those squiggly lines?" asked Georgie, sipping on a cup of coffee that I wished I had. Rather than ask for one, I held out my hand and she gave me the cup.

"Thanks." I took a sip and gave it back. "Those are past trips the owner of this boat took. Lookie right there. See that black line? Looks like it goes straight up to right around Beaumont, Texas. Not a bad spot to land."

"How many miles is that?" she asked.

"Just over 750 as the crow flies," I said. "Means a few refuels, but that also means we'd have to hug the coast, which means even more miles, more diesel and more stops."

"When did you work all this out?" she asked.

I laughed. "Had you thinkin' I was a nautical navigator extraordinaire, didn't I?"

"Actually, you did."

"After Lilly fell asleep, Danny came out. We had a couple beers and went over everything. Our mileage is around 220 miles per tank, give or take. With the wind at our stern, calm waters, and no bullcrap on the way, that might hold."

"How many gallons does it hold?"

"275, accordin' to the manual. No reason to doubt it."

"This gets less than one mile per gallon? That comes out to around .8 when I round the number."

"These boats ain't built for poor folks."

She shook her head. "Apparently not. Makes it easy, though. 750 miles times 0.8. That's over nine hundred gallons of fuel, Cole. Including what's in the tank."

I whistled. "We ain't doin' that with 5-gallon cans. We're gonna need a fillin' station, 'bout fourteen 55-gallon drums and a good drum dolly."

"And a bigger boat," said Terry, from behind us. We both spun around.

"And you know that how?" I asked.

"Oh, just some inane trivia my dad always filled my head with. The most useless stuff stuck, but now I'm thinking it wasn't as dumb as I thought at the time. A gallon of diesel weighs around six-and-a-half pounds. With as much fuel as we need, you'd be putting over 5,000 pounds on the boat. One big wave shifting those barrels and we roll over."

The kid was right, and I didn't even have to think about it. "Good point, Terry. No tellin' where we'd have put 'em all anyway."

"Sometimes it's better just knowing what you've got to do ahead of time. Rather than get to the fuel and realize it's not possible."

"Looks like we're cruisin' up the coast," I said. "We'll cut corners where we can, but this is gonna be a long-ass haul."

"Do you need to let Danny know?"

"He knew we'd need to dump his boat at some point. Might be smart to pick up a smaller skiff to tow behind and he can ride in here." I took a deep breath. "Where's the radio?"

Georgie got it from somewhere and gave it to me. I pushed the button. "Lilly, you read?"

"Yeah, what is it, CB?" The Sportsman's motor was loud in the background.

"We're gonna have to hug the shoreline all the way. Too many refuels, not enough weight capacity to handle all the fuel we'd need to carry."

"Well, that sucks," said Lilly. "How long are we looking at that way?"

"No idea," I said. "I'll have Georgie the Calculator Queen figure it out and get back to you. For now, I'll let you know if we need to fill up."

$$\Omega$$

We'd been underway about three hours when I spotted it. From the map on my GPS, it looked like we were just off Venice Beach.

At first I didn't know what I was seeing. The first thing that came to mind was iceberg, but that wasn't possible.

Georgina saw what caught my eye and picked up the binoculars, raising them to her eyes.

"I have 15/15 vision," said Terry, standing beside her. "That's a sunken cruise ship."

"Looks like it ran aground," said Georgie. "It's down on its starboard side. The funnel's almost in the water."

"Boating in southwest Florida's dangerous, the bigger the boat," I said. "Wonder what happened. All captains know how to navigate here."

"Not if the captain changed into one of those … those monsters," said Roxy.

"My mom wasn't a monster," came Liam's voice from behind all of us. We hadn't seen him come in, and I never heard his feet on the steps leading up to the fly bridge.

"Don't mean any slight on your mama, Liam," I said. "You know how Frankenstein's monster wasn't really all that mean? Just scary lookin'?"

Liam walked over and stared out through the window. "I guess. I think he's scary."

"Well, most people do, which is why everyone turned on him."

"So, my mom was like Frankenstein?"

I shook my head. "No, man. This is a little different. These things – like what your mom turned into when she got sick – they're brains aren't normal anymore, and they think they want to attack people who aren't sick, like them. What I'm sayin' is, it's not their fault."

"Liam, what Cole's trying to say is it's instinct, not hatred or any malice."

"Malice?"

"Ill-will."

"Huh?"

"They don't mean to harm us," she tried to clarify. "They're essentially out of their minds and aren't

119

responsible for their actions anymore. Your mother and all these others can't help themselves. They're sick."

I thought that was as good an explanation as any. I hoped the kid got it. He settled onto the couch behind me, looking lost in whatever thoughts swirled around in his head. I told myself I'd have a long talk with him later.

We moved closer, and I saw Danny angle to the northwest more to put more distance between us and the ship resting on the sandy bottom.

It was still a ways ahead, but it loomed larger on the horizon as we approached. My eyes went right to my depth gauge, just to be sure. I was only in fifteen feet of water, which wasn't deep enough for my comfort. I knew that could turn into eight, then six, then we'd be scraping propeller against coral and sand.

My radio burst to life. "CB! You on?"

It was Danny. I grabbed it and pushed the button. "Yeah, man. See that shit?"

"Cole," said Georgina. "Liam. You mind?"

I wasn't used to watching my language when I was off work, but I figured she was right. No sense in corrupting the kid. "Sorry," I said.

Danny came on again. "Current's really pullin' out here. Swirling pretty good."

"That normal?" I asked.

"Further on out in the Gulf, yeah," he said, his motor vibrating in the background. "Not this close to shore. It's tryin' to pull me toward the coastline."

"How's your fuel?" I asked. "Can we head farther out, try to get around it?"

"No way. I wouldn't make it back. I was ready to head in."

"I could tow you back, right?"

"Not with this current. It's … shit!"

I would've asked what interrupted his thought, but I could see it with my own eyes. I was about a hundred yards back from the Sportsman.

It started teetering from side to side, even as it continued its forward motion. I pushed the throttle forward.

"Danny! Danny!" I called into the radio. Nothing came back, and I could see him struggling with the steering wheel. Lilly was on her feet, holding onto the rail, trying to grab something out of our view.

Georgie, Liam, Roxy, and Terry ran up to stand beside me, everyone watching what was happening.

I was gaining on 'em now, fast, closing the distance. Now the Sportsman was turning, it's stern swinging to the west, the bow now pointed right toward shore. It kept going, the rotation now with the boat heading right toward me.

"Holy shit!" I shouted, no longer worrying about Liam or his delicate sensibilities. I cranked the wheel hard right to get out of Danny and Lilly's path, and saw my depth drop quickly down to 9-1/2 feet.

"What's happening?" called Roxy, her voice two octaves higher.

Suddenly our boat hit something. I didn't see it at first, but just then I saw the Sportsman ahead of us now listed port, then starboard, almost tilting to the rails on both sides.

My radio burst to life again. "Bodies! There's bodies everywhere! Under us!"

I stared at the radio in my hand. The Sportsman looked like it was high-centered on a sand bar, the bow moving from side-to-side, but not going anywhere.

We were close enough now; I saw hands reaching from the water trying to grab hold of the rails and the rear swim step.

We were plowing through, but whatever had affected that smaller boat was doing its level best to put us in the same position. I jammed that throttle to full ahead and felt the propellers shudder and strain.

"Look over the edge!" I shouted to anyone who'd listen. "See what it is!"

I jerked my head around to make sure somebody was doing what I asked, and saw Liam pressed up against Roxy on the bench seat, crying his heart out. She held him tight as Georgie and Terry charged out to the rails.

By the time I saw 'em leave, I didn't need any more confirmation. There were bodies all around the Sea Ray, churning in the swirling current that pulled us this way and that.

"Roxy, come here and take this wheel! Just keep it goin' straight as you can, but whatever you do, don't hit their boat!"

"I can't drive this boat!" she shouted.

"Just steer!" I shouted, grabbing the DP-12 from the floor beside the seat. "Liam! Go down into the main cabin and close the door!"

I was up, Liam in front of me. I guided him down the stairs. "It's okay, buddy. We'll be alright!"

I only wish I believed it.

Gunshots sounded as I ran down the steps. I hurried to the rear, feeling the boat lurching over the dozens of bodies that clustered on every side of the Sea Ray, arms reaching and heads, legs, and feet breaking through the water before disappearing again beneath the churning surf.

As I reached the stern, the motors beneath me rumbled and strained, and I prayed nothing got caught in the props and locked 'em up.

As I reached the back rail, I saw two figures had managed to climb onto the huge, flat step in the rear. I lowered the barrel of the DP-12 and fired. The head of a rotted man in a purple-flowered Hawaiian print shirt exploded in a burst of black-green blood. Because of the wind blowing in my face, I didn't smell it. His headless body rolled onto its back, then into the water.

The other was a woman, and she'd managed to crawl to the rail and had pulled herself halfway to her feet.

Just as I raised the shotgun again, the boat lurched to the left and I found myself going over. I reached for the rail as I held the gun, but my feet went out from under me.

We must've been running over body after body. I fought the up, down, side-to-side motion as I tried to right myself, but when I looked up again, that dead bitch was right over me.

I turned my head and got my eyes on the gun. Swinging the barrel back in a fast arc left, I got it into position just as her head came down, mouth open.

My barrels went right down her goddamned throat, and I thrust it forward and fired, sending her brains out through the back of her skull, and her entire body flying backward, into the foamy water behind us.

I scrambled to my feet and got back to see one more, the arm clutching at the slots on the step. I fired again, severing it at the elbow. I was spared seeing the rest of the zombie, and it disappeared into the Gulf waters.

"Georgie, Terry!" I screamed as I charged back up to the flybridge. "Get in the cabin with Liam!"

"Where's Roxy!" shouted Georgie.

"Drivin' the damned boat!" I yelled.

They both dodged past me. As I reached the helm, Roxy jumped up and gave me the chair. "They're going to sink!" she cried.

"Not if I can fuckin' help it! Get downstairs!"

The Sportsman was only forty yards or so away now, but it no longer had any forward momentum. It looked like a boat caught in a hurricane, moved not by the water or wind, but by what could be hundreds of dead-but-not-dead bodies all clamoring to get aboard.

Danny and Lilly both stood by the center console, holding the bimini support as they fired round after round into the water.

They wouldn't last much longer. I made a decision. I slapped my hand on the button marked HORN again and again, as I once more pushed the throttle full forward. I'd backed it off before giving over control to Georgie's daughter.

My plan was dangerous. I'd have to hit the Sportsman just right to keep from sinking us both.

Ω

CHAPTER EIGHT

I was close enough now to see the entire cluster of drifting bodies, the heads, torsos, arms, and legs breaking the surface of the water. The bright colors of their vacation clothes made it look like a churning rainbow of garbage as they surfaced and sank again, only to come up somewhere nearby.

Like Danny had said, they were clearly caught in a circular eddycurrent of some kind, 'cause I could almost spot the path of their progress through the turquoise water. I used this as my gauge. If I could get my boat in the middle of it, with my thrusters, I should be able to push sideways right up against the Sportsman.

I grabbed the radio and mashed the button. "Hold on! Keep shootin'!"

I didn't know if they heard me or not; whether the damned radio had gotten wet and no longer worked, but his motor was dead now, and if it was quiet enough, he'd hear me.

To my relief, I saw Danny wave at me between fired rounds. Then he threw a thumb up in the air.

I had my permission.

I cranked the wheel side to side, trying to use the big hull to split the bodies. Just as I got pretty far into the middle of the swirling current, I saw the Sportsman tilt 45 degrees to the port side.

My fucking heart nearly stopped when I saw Lilly teeter on one leg and just catch the bimini mount with her outstretched hand. Centrifugal force caused her to swing hard left, her body striking the steering wheel and Danny, who'd seen her lose her balance.

He caught her with one arm, steadying her. I swore they briefly embraced right then. If I'd have blinked, I'd have missed it.

I *know* why. They both thought they were gonna die. It was on my mind, too.

I had to hurry. With Danny's boat squarely off my port side, I hit the thruster switch and pushed both joysticks at once, hard to port.

The diesels strained right then; I knew my worst fear had happened. Some rotter's clothing got twisted onto the props, and I prayed what I knew was coming, wouldn't.

Either my prayers were too late, or they weren't good enough. Next thing I knew, the motor cut out completely.

Now I'd have to rely solely on the thrusters to keep us moving. I heard the electric motors humming, and I hoped to God there'd be enough force behind 'em to get me where I needed to be.

We were definitely getting closer – it *was* working. My hand was sore from pushing those joysticks, but no amount of pressure would make us go any faster. I honked that horn again and again, and finally saw Danny point at us and slap Lilly on the arm.

The boat had settled to mostly level again, and Danny and Lilly let go of the bimini mount and shuffled over to kneel down on the bench seat on the starboard side. They were ready, but both had to keep firing down at the zombies trying to crawl over the rail and get inside the boat to their fresh meat.

Suddenly an eastern swell rose up in the water, pushing me faster than I intended. Now we were fifteen feet apart, then ten feet, and the five-foot gap closed with a jarring thump as we banged into the smaller Sportsman. I couldn't see shit from where I was; the boat was so close the much taller Sea Ray blocked my view of everything but the fishing rods sticking up outta the holders and the small bimini over the center console.

We were slamming broadsides now, which caused both boats to teeter-totter from port to starboard and back again, over, and over. Each time we tilted to port, the Sportsman and all the zombies briefly came into view.

From the flybridge, I could look down and see a dozen bodies smashed between the two boats as we bounced off one another. I realized Danny's boat was once again sitting on a goddamned floating island of bodies, and there I was, pushing the whole kit-n-kaboodle to the west.

I slammed my feet on the floor and yelled, "Somebody get on the port rail, now!"

I stomped over and over, hoping they'd get my urgency in the cabin below. I heard the cabin door slam, and I knew they had.

"Help them!" I yelled, still mashing the thrusters.

I couldn't see anything now. Everything was behind me, all the action closer to the stern than the bow.

I heard a thud from somewhere behind me, and a few seconds later, Roxy ran up the steps.

"Lilly's aboard!"

I felt my heart settle, but only a little. "What about Danny!" I shouted.

She was already gone again. Good. I didn't need updates at the cost of my best friend.

I couldn't let go of the thrusters. If he was almost in and the boat drifted off, he could fall into the water and get torn to pieces by the waterlogged deadheads.

I heard a familiar voice cry, "Danny!" and I knew it was Lilly, despite the pitch and terror contained in that single word.

Fuck it. I let go of the thrusters and charged down the steps to the deck. Just as I reached it, Danny, soaking wet and chest heaving, landed on his back on the deck, his gun still clutched in his hand.

"You okay?" I called, seeing more of the dead people trying to climb onto the swim step.

He only had the wherewithal to nod quickly. I ran to the swim step and pulled out my .45, firing two bullets into the backs of the heads of the crawlers. They were face-down as they tried to mount the Sea Ray, and I was glad; I didn't need to see 'em. Their blood and black brains splattered over the swim step, and I watched 'em slide back into the water, waiting for more to surface.

There were plenty behind us, but none were close enough to grip the step now. I turned and ran back up to the flybridge, throwing the transmission into neutral. I turned the key and fired the engine again. It caught.

If I went forward, whatever was caught in the props would wind tighter. Instead, I threw it into full reverse.

The engines moaned at first, but after about four deep reverberations, the boat lurched backward as whatever had been wrapped around the propellers cleared, freeing them again.

This time I turned the wheel to the east and gave it a little throttle. I heard shots being fired from behind me, and I was glad. More deaders must've climbed on, and my crew was doing its part. Now I just had to get us out of there.

The motors immediately did a goddamned repeat of what they'd done earlier. No doubt wound up with clothing, hair, arms, legs, whatever, it had grabbed as it spun.

Thrusters. They were my only hope. I pulled the throttle into neutral again and hit the thrusters back over to port. This time I just let 'em run.

The Sportsman had drifted off now, and I was clear to the west, aside from the thrashing bodies all around us. I felt the boat pushing foot by foot, and I kept those joysticks full to port until Danny came plodding up the stairs.

"You got it, man," he said, hardly able to breathe. "Just water now. We're out of that current."

"Props are wound up again with God knows what. You okay? You and Lilly hurt?"

"None of them got us, if that's what you mean," he said. "You try reverse?"

"I did before. Make sure everyone's holdin' on."

He moved slowly toward the steps, and I could see his whole body shaking. My heart was still pounding in my ears.

I fired the motors again, and when I saw both RPM meters peg, I said a prayer of thanks. I pulled the throttle toward me, hitting reverse again.

The deep rumble came, and whitewater surged on our port and starboard rails around our stern. After a few seconds, and several stops and starts, it unwound whatever was caught. The minute we gained speed, I pushed it forward again and turned west, trimming down as the big boat got up on plane and leveled out.

Danny trotted back up the steps. "Looking good, brother."

I smiled at him. "I feel better."

"How are you doing on fuel?"

My eyes dropped to the gauge. "Still over half a tank. I'm good for another 180 miles or so. Where will that get us to?"

"We're about 30 miles north of that cruise ship, and that was at Venice Beach. CB, man, check your goddamned GPS. Don't you know how to use that thing?"

I smiled at him and shook my head. "The one in my car, yeah. This thing's got too much bullshit on it."

Danny got up and knelt down beside my chair. He punched the screen a few times and a clean map appeared.

"There we are," he said. "That's Amelia Island there. That point."

"Nice name," I said. "So, what'll 180 miles get us?"

"Looks like about to Steinhatchee. You'll see markers for Deadman Bay."

"Don't like the sound of that. Sounds like what we've been tryin' to avoid."

Danny laughed. "Well, I haven't been there, so it's whatever it turns out to be. Judging from all the markers on the GPS, there are lots of restaurants, and a couple marinas there. Symbol for propane, too. Got a need?"

"I'm sure everything down there runs on propane, so we'll fill as needed. Hell, if we find a boat we like more, we'll just swap it out."

Danny looked around. "This is a damned nice Sea Ray."

"Hell yes," I said. "But we can get a great deal on somethin' better."

"It's the only consolation. I can replace Dad's Sportsman with somethin' better, too. I'd trade it all to have my folks with us."

"Me too, man. No doubt," I said, reaching over to pat his shoulder. "Anyway, there are seven of us now. And you know that's my lucky number."

Danny pulled back and gave me his sly smile. I knew it because it came along with narrowed eyes. "So, if anyone else need rescuin', it's a big screw 'em?"

"My next lucky number's 35, so for a while, yeah. We'll need to come across a desperate group of 28 people to hit that one dead on."

"Smaller's better anyway," said Danny. "We need to stay fluid."

"Wanna drive a while? I'd like to go hang with Georgie a bit. Talk to Lilly."

Danny stretched, then checked his watch. "You're holdin' at 30 knots. Mind if I bump it up to 35?"

"Be my guest. You know your stuff."

"Okay," he said. "I say we keep runnin' 'til we're just off Deadman's Bay, then anchor for the night. We'll navigate the Steinhatchee River in the mornin'."

"Sounds good. I found a humidor down there, man. And Jack Daniel's Single Barrel."

"Once that anchor's planted," said Danny, "it's a fuckin' date. Get up."

I stood, and he slid into the seat.

"How's my sister doin' anyway?"

"She changed out of her wet clothes, so go on. I'm not as wet as she got."

I thanked him and plodded down the steps. I was feeling the exhaustion from our most recent ordeal. To be honest, I couldn't wait until we stopped and took a break.

When I went into the salon, Lilly was sitting in the captain's chair, watching the others set up some game or other on the dinette table. "Hey," she said, a slight smile on her face.

"Hey, sis. You doin' alright?"

She stood up and hurried toward me. I opened my arms and let her walk into me. It might've been the tightest hug I'd ever given her, and she was squeezing just the same in return.

"So glad you're okay," I said. "When I saw you almost fall, I thought you were toast."

"More like toast with all the fixins, as Ma used to say. I was scared, I won't lie."

I pulled back and looked at her freckled face. Wiping the hair from her face, I said, "You sure you're okay?"

Lilly nodded. "Yeah. Shakes are almost gone. Thanks for saving us."

I eased her away from the table where Liam, Terry, Roxy, and Georgie sat, lowering my voice. "I was just reactin' to my sister and my best friend about to become zombie food. Now. We need to make sure we're prepared before any of us hit shore again."

"I was thinking about that when Danny and I were driving. Liam, Roxy, Terry. Do we know their skills?"

"Terry's got a bit of boating knowledge. Already came in handy. I don't know if he's ever shot a gun, and I doubt Liam knows anything about 'em. I asked Georgie about Roxy, and it seems she's got some decent skill, like her mama."

"What's the plan?"

"We're tryin' to get as far as we can on this tank. Danny found a marina that'll have gas. Stein somethin'."

Lilly's eyes were kinda distant. "If we can stop while there's still daylight, I think we ought to give everyone the opportunity to do some basic gun safety and use training. If they don't know how to defend, they stay on the boat."

I shook my head. "Even stayin' here they need to know how to defend. Bandits, zombies. Never know what'll come along."

She scrunched up her face. "Bandits? You've been watching too many cartoons."

"Fuckin' love eatin' cereal and watchin' cartoons. You don't know what you're missin'."

Ω

After I sat down and jawed with the others for a little while, I went back up and offered to take over driving again, but Danny had settled in.

"I'm almost dry," he said. "She doin' alright?"

"Yep. She wants us to stop a bit before dark, so we can do some offshore weapons trainin' for anyone who needs it."

"She's smart," said Danny.

"She is."

We rode in silence for a while. I was surprised to find that an entire hour had passed since we got free of the cruise ship passengers. In that time, he'd navigated back closer to shore. We were running about a mile off the coast now.

We switched again, and Danny ran down to grab us a couple of brews. The refrigerator still kept everything real cold, even though we turned the temp down a bit to preserve propane.

The ladies, along with Terry and Liam, were apparently involved in a wild game of Uno, and I heard people yelling the word repeatedly, even from up top.

"How's the fuel?" asked Danny. "I was ready to fill up the Sportsman. Don't have to worry about that now."

"Man, that was sketchy. You just ended up right on top of 'em?" I asked.

Damon Novak

"Like running a jet ski onto the beach, man," said Danny. "All my shit's gone. Fishin' rods, stuff we could've used."

"I'm bettin' everything's available on a discount nowadays. We'll stock up on more gear."

He downed his beer. "I'm gonna go down and hang with them for a while. I'll maybe send the kid up. You can talk to him about training."

I waved at him and he thumped down the steps. About five minutes later, Liam came up and I offered to let him drive.

"Really?" he asked. "This thing?"

I looked around. "I don't see any other thing around here."

Nodding big, he moved toward me. I got up and he sat in the seat. He had to extend his arms all the way out to reach the steering wheel, but I'd tried earlier to slide the seat forward and it was stuck.

Sometimes it didn't matter whether you were on a yacht or a dinghy. Shit broke around saltwater.

"I got it set to a good speed. You see that swell out there?"

"That one?" he pointed to the distant ripple that would eventually turn into a substantial swell.

"Yep. As it gets closer, you just gently angle the bow – that's the front of the boat – right at it. Just turn the wheel ever-so-slightly. Once you get over it, you just turn the wheel bit by bit again until the compass here is showin' north. That's the direction we're goin'."

I showed him how to read the compass. From that point on, he drove in silence, never taking his eyes off the water and the controls.

"Can I talk while you drive?"

He didn't answer at first, just wiped the red hair from his eye, biting his lower lip, like Lilly. He finally said, "Sure. What about?"

"You ever shoot a gun?"

"Only a BB gun," he said. "My dad got me one with some paper targets. He only let me use them at our cabin in Maine."

I was thinking *'A cabin. You lucky shit, you,'* but then I remembered his stepdad was either deader'n dead or he was one of the walking dead. I knew what became of his mama. Not so lucky, I guess.

"Well, I got my first gun when I was a few years younger'n you. You got the muscle and the brains to handle it. You wanna learn how to shoot tonight? Before it gets dark?"

"On the boat?"

"Yep. I saw some junk out there you can shoot at. Good thing about bein' a mile offshore. No worries about collateral damage."

"Huh?"

"Never mind. Do me a favor, would ya? Run on back down and send Danny up. You tell Terry and Roxy what we're plannin', and find out if they wanna train with you."

The kid was up and out of his seat so fast I just stared after him as I dropped back into the captain's chair to take the helm.

Guess I figured out what sounds fun to a kid. Hell, not sure why I was surprised – I was the same way.

When Danny came back, he had another two beers.

I told him about our plan. "Lilly still doin' alright?" I asked.

"She went in the master cabin, took a nap. You know how freaked she gets of the Gulf. Anywhere real deep touches a nerve."

"Kinda out of our wheelhouse," I said. "We prefer open boats, shallow water. Reptiles that'll kill ya."

"Just gotta know your shit," said Danny.

"For all the good that does us now."

Ω

The rest of our trip north was uneventful, and we got to our destination with about an eighth of a tank of fuel left. That'd be plenty, so long as we got to that marina.

Danny'd lost a lot of ammo, but luckily, we'd brought enough with us that we had plenty to spare. In my gun collection I had a Henry Repeating Arms .22 rifle, called a Golden Boy.

It was similar to the guns I started shooting with, and reminded me a lot of the gun Mark used on an old black-and-white TV show I watched as a kid, *The Rifleman*.

The boat safely anchored, I went out to the stern and found some old, orange life preservers like the ones we strapped on our tourists at Baxter's. They had a pretty good flat surface, and the holes would be easy to see.

I found a black marker and drew several circles on it. Three up top, and four on the sides. I got 'em mounted as best I could on the outside edge of the swim step, using a couple boat hooks I found snapped into brackets along the inside rail. In the supply cabinet was a roll of duct tape, and that was all I needed. We'd stand about twelve feet back to practice.

Liam hung with me the whole time, and Terry joined us, joking with the kid about what a great shot he was, and how he'd teach the kid a thing or two.

I'd never asked Terry if he knew how to shoot, so I was pretty eager to see how he did.

"Okay, you guys hang here. I'll get the guns we're usin' for this exercise."

I ran into the salon where everyone else was hanging out.

"CB, don't let him shoot a hole in this thing and sink us," said Lilly. "You stay with him the whole time."

"He's only usin' a .22, Lil. Don't get your panties in a wad."

"Are you planning to let him use that on shore?" asked Georgina.

"Only if he shows some skill," I said. "Eye-hand coordination's all it's about. Shoot what you see."

"Don't forget the freak-out factor," said Danny. "When this thing first started, I was so freaked out I missed shots I could've hit with my eyes closed."

"You're still alive," I said. "Come on out if you want. You can work with Terry. Roxy, you want to come out? Do some shootin'?"

Roxy, ever the daughter, looked at her mom. "Should I?" she asked.

"You haven't been to the range since your dad was around. It might be a good idea."

She looked at me, and I saw reluctance there.

"Roxy, you know what's goin' on out there. I don't want anyone out there without a weapon, and right now, we don't have anything but guns. You prefer a machete?"

"Gross," she said. "I can't even imagine swinging one of those at somebody."

"They're not somebodys anymore," I said. "They're pretty much monsters now."

"They still look like people," she said.

137

I sat down next to her and she scooted over. "See this lady sittin' next to you?"

She looked at her mother. "Mom?"

"Yeah, that's the one. Anyway, she was worried as shit about you all the way down there. I don't think she really ever thought she'd see you alive again."

Her mother patted her leg, squeezing it. "He isn't lying."

"I know," said Roxy.

"So," I went on. "She wants you to stay alive, and with what's goin' on, you're gonna have to leap pretty far out of your comfort zone. This is the first jump."

"I hate this."

"We all do, sweetheart," said Georgie. "You feel better if I work with you?"

"I'm going to be terrible," she said.

"The gun I'll let you use is a .22," I said. "We got a couple of 'em. Nice long guns, easy to shoot, hardly any kick at all. You can get comfortable with that, and when you're ready, you can move up to a higher caliber."

Finally, she nodded. "Okay. But don't laugh at me."

"I'm thinkin' you might laugh on your own. Shootin' is fun, especially when you start to get better. We're all set up. You ready?"

She rolled her eyes and stood.

I said, "Good. We'll go through a couple boxes. Couple hundred rounds."

"That's a lot," she said.

"It'll go way faster than you think."

"If you say so," she said.

"I do."

Georgie stood, too. "I'll work with her a bit," she said. "And the only one I actually shot from a distance was the one at my house. I need to make sure that wasn't just a lucky shot."

"Come one, come all," I said. "We hit shore tomorrow, so now's the time. Couple hours of daylight left." We all went out.

We could chow down on tamales later.

Ω

CHAPTER NINE

The other .22 I had might be described as intimidating if you didn't know guns. It was a Ruger 22LR Charger, and I'd gotten a couple of high-capacity magazines for it.

It looked badass for a .22 long rifle, 'cause it had an A-2 style pistol grip and a 30-round mag that curved forward. Anyone who didn't know guns would take one look and call it an assault rifle.

"Okay, listen up," I said, as everyone sat on the bench seats along the port and starboard sides of the stern deck. "Barrels always pointed down, but not at your damned feet. Finger off the trigger unless you plan to shoot somebody, and that's rule number one. I'll warn you twice about all the other rules, but not that one. Even with the other rules, you blow it a third time, you're gettin' benched."

"No need to be a dick about it, CB," said Lilly. "I see why you never became a teacher."

"Tough love, sis," I said. "I want all of y'all to stay alive, so it's my way or the highway."

"Can I hold it now?" asked Liam, getting up.

"Danny and I are gonna split duty," I said. "I want you usin' the Henry for now, Liam. We'll use the Ruger a bit, then we can switch. You see there are two targets, so we'll take the one on the left. Danny, y'all take the one on the right."

"Right on," said Danny. He took the Henry and waved Liam over. "You ready?" he asked.

"Yeah!" said Liam.

I could see this had taken his mind off a lot of what had happened. Another good bonus. Maybe it gave him the feeling he was taking his future into his own hands. Independence feels good, once you recognize it. Makes you feel like you're fighting back.

Roxy got up and kinda ambled over to where I stood, like she was embarrassed and dreading the whole exercise.

We had a couple more feet behind us, but we started about ten feet from the targets. I'd already filled four magazines and the Henry, so I said, "Danny, you go first. Show Liam your form."

Danny knelt down. "Liam, see this lever? That's how you get ready to shoot again. You might remember the Terminator using a gun like this from his motorcycle in T-2."

"I don't know what a T-2 is," said Liam. "But that's cool," he said, holding out his hand.

"Nothin' cool about it," said Danny, his tone firm. "This is a weapon, and not only can it kill those zombies out there, it can kill you or anyone on this boat, or anywhere else. Now, when I hand it to you, you take it by the stock. That's this part right here," he said, patting it. "Support the rest of it with your left hand, on the bottom side of the barrel."

Danny gave it to him and I saw right away he did just as he was told.

"Good. No bullets in there right now, so get used to it. How it feels. Put that stock against your right shoulder and hold it up so the gun's straight out, like an arrow."

"I used to shoot a bow and arrow in Boy Scouts."

"Good, then you know it's gotta be true to hit your target. Were you any good?"

Liam shrugged. I'd seen enough. Danny had that under control.

"Your turn," I said, and Roxy gave me a smile.

"Okay, I guess."

"Like I told Liam, this is just a .22, but it looks more badass than it is. You hear everything I said before, and what Danny told Liam?"

She nodded, her face still frozen in a look of apprehension. "I'm ready, I think."

"Good. Now, this is really more of a pistol, and you're not supposed to use the bipod as a forward grip, but I don't think the ATF is patrollin' right now, so don't worry about that."

"Okay, I won't," she said, giving me a slight smile.

"No sights on this weapon, but it's got a nice little red dot mounted on the top rail." I pushed the button, turning it on. "You just look through that little window there, and you'll see a red circle dancin' over your target. Point, look and shoot."

She leaned over and looked through. "Oh, that's neat. Just make sure it's over what you want to shoot."

"Exactly. Be sure to turn it off when you're not usin' it so you don't wear out the battery. This one has a tactical brace installed, so it'll butt up against your shoulder. You want me to go first?"

I fully expected her to tell me yeah, but she didn't.

"I'm ready." She held out her hands.

I shrugged and glanced over at Georgie, who gave me a wink and shrugged back.

"Here you go."

She took the gun easily in hand. Just as I was about to show her how to charge it, she did it herself.

"Okay, that was pretty impressive, I gotta say. Now, the red dot –"

I never got to finish. She'd already powered it up, had the stock to her shoulder and her eye level with the sight. With three quick trigger pulls, she put three clean holes almost dead center in the top of the life preserver.

She lowered the barrel to the deck and looked at me. "This is easy."

I looked at Georgie. "Y'all punked me, didn't ya?"

"Her father took her to the range *a lot*. He used red dot sights, too. So, yes."

"And y'all thought it might be funny to mess with me."

"We weren't wrong," said Roxy, a smile on her face.

We saw Liam pull the lever and raise the rifle slowly, and everyone shut up. He aimed for a long time.

"Now squeeze that trigger like you're just bending your finger," whispered Danny. "Got one of those dots in your sights?"

Liam nodded and fired. A hole appeared near the top of the life preserver, just to the right of the right-side circle I'd made with the marker.

"Good job!" I said. "Like you been doin' it all your life."

He lowered the barrel and looked at me, and I automatically checked his finger. Off the trigger, just like I'd told him. "I played a lot of shooting video games," he said. "Xbox. This sight's kinda like the one on my video gun."

"I didn't have the luxury when I was growin' up," I said. "But that said, I did start with a real gun when I was a helluva lot younger than you."

"I guess so," he said. "Can I shoot more?"

"Hell yes," said Danny. "One lucky shot doesn't a marksman make."

As he continued to shoot, even improving on his first shot, Roxy called Terry over and gave him a nice long lesson on the Ruger. By the time it was over, there were tired trigger fingers and satisfaction that in a pinch, everyone could defend themselves.

Ω

There were some canned string beans in the cupboard, along with some corn, and we had that crapload of tamales, which was what I chose to eat again. They were damned good, and I didn't think I'd get tired of 'em anytime soon.

The moon was partial but bright. After dinner, I bummed a smoke off Lilly, who was down to a single pack of Marlboros. She reluctantly agreed to give me one, and I slipped up on the bow, sitting crosslegged just behind the rail, staring out at the dark Gulf, wondering how we'd all make out.

"Sleeping quarters are getting tighter now," came a voice behind me.

I turned to see Georgie. Everyone else was still in the salon. I was glad. "Come on over and sit. I'll scoot over."

"You'd better slide back first, or we'll be fishing you out with that boat hook back there."

I smiled, slid back, and patted the gelcoat. She eased down, crosslegged like me. "It's nice tonight."

"You come up here to talk about the weather?"

She shook her head. "You come out to hide and smoke?"

"Busted," I said. "Don't like smokin' in front of doctors."

She reached down, her two fingers extended, and I raised my eyebrows, giving her the smoke. She hit it good, breathed it in, and exhaled.

"Better be ready to steady me," she said. "It's been a while since I've had any nicotine buzzing around in this brain."

"I learn somethin' new about you every day."

"Every nurse I knew smoked," she said. "I bummed off them. Never bought a pack for fear I'd get hooked."

"It eases tension for me," I said. "You really pulled one over on me with Roxy. I felt like an idiot."

Georgie laughed. "It was all in good fun. She's a great shot. Far better than me."

"Don't believe a word you say anymore."

She took another hit and gave the smoke back to me. "Let's talk sleeping arrangements. I want to sleep in your cabin if you don't mind."

At first, I didn't know what to say. No way was I gonna turn her down, but now all sorts of questions jumped into my head. "You mean, in the same bed?"

"That would be most comfortable, yes."

"And I still get to sleep in the bed?"

"It's your cabin, I think."

"Hell, I stole this boat. It's as much yours as mine. I just needed the biggest bed to handle my size."

I swear I saw Georgie blush. She saw me see, and blushed some more, then shook her head, smiling. Her eyes met mine. "I'm glad you found me."

"I'm glad, too," I said. "And before you change your mind, two things."

"Yes?"

"I sleep in the nude. Only way I can. Second, I'm a cuddler."

"Do you have someone you normally cuddle with?"

"I don't have a girlfriend if that's what you're askin'," I said. "Last breakup was a bitch. Literally. Red Rover lost a windshield on that one."

"You must've instilled passion."

"It wasn't passion. It was crazy got instilled in her, and I didn't do it."

She leaned back on her arms, her hands planted on the deck behind her. She filled her lungs with air, and my eyes went right to her tits, like steel to a magnet.

Two big, round magnets.

C'mon, at least I'm honest. Plus, she knew. I know she knew what she was doing, because once my eyes fell there, she cracked her eyes open, looking straight at me.

Plus, she was smiling.

"Sorry," I said, jerking my eyes away. "I'm still just a man, even durin' a zombie apocalypse, if that's what this is. Plus, your shirt's about two sizes too small."

She laughed, and it was a nice sound to my ears. "We can cuddle," she said, resting her hand on my leg.

"What about Roxy?"

"She's used to sleeping with Terry. Plenty of those benches out there turn into beds. Plus, I don't think I'd want her to share your bed."

"Never gave it a first thought," I said.

I flicked the smoke out into the water and she scooted closer to me, hooked her arm around mine, and leaned her head on my shoulder. I rested my head atop hers.

"Georgie," I said.

"Yes?"

"I don't know. Nothin' to say, just … this is nice, that's all. Best night I've had in a long time."

Without skipping a beat, she said, "Cole Baxter, the night's far from over."

She turned her face up to me, and I could see the moisture from her freshly licked lips glistening in the moonlight. I lowered my head, parted my lips and kissed her.

Next thing I knew, her hand was on the back of my head, and she breathed through her nose as we made out in the warm summer air.

I didn't know about her, but I was really looking forward to bedtime.

The morning? Not so much.

Ω

We all settled in early. That night, in a fit of passion and what felt like a mutual desperation to feel normal again, Georgie and I made love.

I gotta call it that, because while we may not actually be *in* love yet, it was tender and passionate at the same time. Wherever our bodies touched, it was like an electrical charge, sending goosebumps up and down our spines that each one of us could feel on the other.

I hadn't done it three times in one night for at least five or six years. Didn't know for sure I still had it in me.

Guess it comes down to the partner. Georgina Lake had the moves, she had the body, and she had everything else. Needless to say, I was penciling her in on my mental calendar for more of the same, ASAP.

But it was morning, and we had some important shit to do. Before we called it a night, Danny and I figured out our next stop if this went well. Figured another 225 miles or so north from Steinhatchee would get us near Fort Walton Beach, along the panhandle.

I still didn't like the sound of Deadman Bay. We'd have to get through that first.

She spooned me on my left side, my arm around her shoulders, her knee bent over my legs. I liked the feel of her breath coming out of her nostrils, blowing across my chest. It just felt good.

I rubbed her shoulder. "Hey, Doc. Rise and shine."

Before she opened her eyes, she smiled and stretched. "What time is it?"

I checked my watch. "Already 7:22. Half the day's gone."

"I don't think you did any airboat tours at night," she said, opening her eyes and looking at me. "I was the one on nights, remember?"

"You got me there."

"So, we just get up and go?" asked Georgie, sitting up and leaning on one hand.

"Me and Danny can do it," I said. "No sense in riskin' everyone."

She smiled and slowly shook her head. "Nope."

"Nope?"

"This messed up world is all of ours now. Every one of us needs to learn how to face down the challenges, as well as our fears. Do you know how hard it was to actually cut into a living human being the first time? Even with all the book knowledge and cadaver work we'd done before?"

I thought about her question. While I know very well that cuts heal, they do leave scars. Like cutting paper and taping it back together. It might be stronger than before, but that cut leaves its mark, and nothing can ever undo it.

"Good point. Even Liam?"

"You and Danny are good teachers. He's old enough." She looked down at me and smiled again.

"Come down here, wouldya? I'm strainin' my neck lookin' up."

She smiled, and I loved the lines that formed at the sides of her mouth. She plopped back down beside me, and I pulled her in close again. "I know. Liam's more than old enough, but today's kids are kinda soft. Southern boys not so much, but it feels like they're guilting the manliness out of 'em these days. Like if they have masculine tendencies, they're the exception rather than the rule."

"The boys are definitely more feminine," said Georgie. "Sensitive, too. Not sure how that plays out for the world. Not sure it even matters anymore."

I knew what she meant without asking. What did it matter what boys grew up to be if the dead were walking the earth?

I took a deep breath and let out a big sigh. "Might as well get this show on the road," I said, sitting up. "But Georgie?"

She looked up at me. "Yeah?"

"Thank you."

She smiled. "Thank *you*."

There was more I could've said, but we both knew all of it without any words. I think we'd known it from the shower I took outside Baxter's that day.

"Get your butt dressed. Time to get our zombie-killin' crew through Deadman Bay and into Steinhatchee, Florida – whatever the hell that is."

"If it's got something other than tamales and string beans, I'm all in."

Ω

The DP-12 shotgun strapped over my shoulder and the Glock on my waist, I was ready. I let Liam handle the

Henry, 'cause he liked the classic design and he felt pretty comfortable with it.

Roxy knew how to handle the Ruger like a champ, and she chose a good equivalent for Terry, who'd really come along the evening before.

I gathered everyone on the rear deck. "Okay. It's still up to you whether you leave the boat or not. You're all welcome to come along, but you gotta keep your eyes open. Just like with goddamned terrorists, you see somethin', you yell somethin'. Call out and we'll all come runnin'. This is a team right here, and nobody's less important than anyone else. Got it?"

They all nodded.

Danny said, "When I get off, my job's to find a small skiff we can tow behind us. I need a volunteer. Who wants to come with me?"

Liam raised his hand. "I will!" he offered.

I'd seen Lilly's shoulder twitch, but Liam was too fast. I knew my sister, and I saw the disappointment in her eyes.

"That's good. You watch my back out there, and I'll watch yours. Agreed?"

"Agreed," said Liam, tossing his red hair from his eyes.

"You do the honors," I said, nodding toward the flybridge helm. "You're still a better boater than me."

"I saw you mannin' those thrusters," said Danny. "Saved my ass. You pilot. I'll be beside you."

I shrugged. "Good enough."

We went up top and Danny called back down, "Y'all get ready to switch the bumpers if we need you to. Depends on where we dock."

The Sea Ray's motors were reliable; the big diesels fired immediately. Once they settled into a smooth idle, I called for Lilly, who was crouched near the bow rail. She powered up the anchor winch.

She gave me a thumbs-up a few seconds later, and I waited for her to scramble back to the port rail before moving the throttle forward, turning the wheel right to point our nose from Deadman Bay into the Steinhatchee River.

As we approached, I felt the hairs standing up on the back of my neck. The smell of fire got stronger again, which made me scan well beyond the inlet before us. Sure enough, black smoke still billowed in the morning light, reminding me again how everything had changed.

We had a good distance to navigate down the canal leading to the filling station before we'd get there.

"Lookie there," said Danny, pointing at the large and small boats adrift all around us. Most had either hit shore and gotten tucked between overhanging mangroves, or they'd floated into other boats and gotten hung up.

We heard the thump of feet behind us and we turned to see Terry emerge. "Hey," he said. "Just so you know, lots of bodies in the water. Here and there. I know you had trouble with their clothes getting caught in the propellers."

"Thanks, Terry," I said. He disappeared down the steps again.

"There's one. Crank to port," said Danny.

I did, and saw the deadhead's arm come up outta the water like he was at a Christian music concert.

"Why the hell don't I know how to sail?" I asked. "I could avoid refuelin'."

"You see old Floki on Vikings, man?" asked Danny. "Bastard was stuck on the water for days, no wind to be had."

"Yeah, yeah. Unlikely on the Gulf of Mexico, but I get your point. Plus, need to get away from those floaters when they get too close."

"Ain't that the problem," groaned Danny. "Just 'cause they're floatin' don't mean they're true dead."

True dead, I thought. Words we'd never thought to put together before.

We both looked down and saw a body in the middle of a roll from front to back. As the dead woman's face rotated into view, she clawed at the sky and was taken under by the wake of the Sea Ray.

"Hard to get used to," said Danny. "Man."

The canal was wild on the south side, all mangroves and other natural canals feeding off it. On the left side, it was seawalls and boat slips. Ahead I saw the fueling dock and the red and green pumps. Figures were moving on the dock, but it was still too far away to tell if they were alive or dead.

I said, "The more people get off this boat, the more worried I'm gonna be while we try to get refueled. You wanna jump out first and give it a scout beforehand?"

Danny looked ahead. "Yep, those are those dead things up there. Lookit how they're shufflin'."

I did, and no response was necessary. "Just take 'em out fast. Not a whole lot of activity."

"Nope, if what you said about the fireworks is true, we fire a couple times and they'll come from everywhere."

"Yeah, I'd rather shove 'em into the water than fire the gun. If you can, give 'em a trip."

We motored closer to the fuel docks. Unlike our last experience, there was no boat occupying the closest slip. I was able to swing it toward starboard and back straight in, bouncing off the 10-inch thick layer of slit tires they'd stacked up and mounted to the seawall as bumpers.

He tied us off, then ran back up. I cut the engines.

As I reached the bottom of the steps, Roxy, Terry, Georgie, Liam, and Lilly were all there.

And they were all staring at me.

"Where's Nokosi?" I asked.

"We shut her in the big bedroom," said Georgina. "She was on the bed last I saw."

"Good," I said. "Don't need her jumpin' off the boat or anything. Anyway, y'all see how vulnerable that swim step is? Once those dead bastards make it up on there, they're on the boat. It's as easy as fallin' off the seawall."

"Get to the point, CB," said Lilly.

"My point is, we need someone to stay on the boat and shoot anything that comes aboard that ain't us. Otherwise, we could come back to an infestation."

"I'll stay here if nobody minds," said Terry. "I'd rather, anyway."

"Alone?" asked Roxy. "You sure?"

Terry nodded. "Nokosi's here, and the sun's up nice. I'll relax on the rear bench, catch some early morning rays."

"Leave the dog in the cabin. She might be trained to run toward gunfire or something. And Terry, don't fall asleep," said Georgina. "You hear me?"

"Yes, yes. Thank you. I have my trusty firearm." He held up the long gun and flashed her what I'd call a Marilyn Monroe smile, complete with a wink.

"Me, too!" said Liam, his barrel pointed toward the deck and his finger well off the trigger. I know, because I checked.

"Lilly, you said you, Roxy and Georgie were gonna check the store and grab anything we could use. Lighters, batteries, flashlights, food, whatever. If we get the tanks filled pretty fast, we'll come over and help."

"Keep your eyes open," said Lilly. "Liam, you're coming with us, so that applies to you, too."

"I wanted to go with Danny and CB!" he said.

I walked over to him and put a hand on his shoulder. "Buddy, you're about to pass up goin' into a store and bein' able to grab all the candy you want. Free. It's your call. What's it gonna be?"

A crooked smile touched his mouth. "I'll go with the girls. Hope they have Sour Patch Kids!"

"Okay," said Danny. "Terry, be alert man. Everyone else, check your pockets for spare magazines and let's go."

Ω

CHAPTER TEN

Danny and I led the group off the dock, onto the captain's walk that led to the pumps and the small marine store.

"Whoa," I said, stopping short and holding up my hand. I'd seen a lot already, but what lay on the dock in front of me sent my stomach into flip-flops. It was a child; a girl no more than ten years old.

"What's that?" called Liam, from the rear.

"Y'all turn him away for a minute."

I looked back to make sure they had, and saw Lilly and Georgie, hands on Liam's shoulders. He faced away from us. Roxy saw why we'd stopped and knelt down to say something to the boy.

"Help me with her, would ya?" I asked Danny.

"Yeah," was all he said.

The girl had been dismembered. The job looked clean enough, like someone had taken a mightily sharp blade and swung it with both hands. I could see where after chopping off her arms, the blade had sliced a nice wedge into her rib cage, just a few inches below the armpits on both sides.

"What kind of sick fucker gets off chopping up little kids?" I asked.

Danny just shook his head. Wrapped around the girl's torso and severed limbs was a fishing net; she'd been caught in it when the blade fell, 'cause her arms and legs were still there, laying beside the body. Her messed-up face pushed against the net as her perfect young teeth snapped together.

"Let's just push her off into the water," I said.

"We should finish her off first," said Danny. "Don't seem right to leave her like this."

I closed my eyes and prayed he'd take it on. It was early, and the last way I wanted to start my day was by shooting a kid in the head.

Even a zombie kid.

To my relief, Danny pulled a small .380 from his belt holster and bent down. He pushed the barrel against her forehead as her strange growling grew more intense.

He fired once, and her eyes stared skyward, sightless.

"What was that?" asked Liam, still turned around.

"C'mon," I said, and grabbed the net up by her head. Danny caught hold of it by her severed left leg, and we dragged her body a foot or so to the edge of the dock. With a grunt, we rolled her over the ledge into the water, where she hit the jagged rip-rap and flipped face down into the canal.

We watched as she floated there for a couple of seconds, then sank down, disappearing beneath the surface.

"It's one thing to kill 'em," I said. "It's another to chop up a little kid. Didn't even kill her, for Christ's sake."

"Can I turn around now?" asked Liam, his tone impatient.

I looked back, caught Georgie's eye, and nodded. The girl's body was out of sight now.

When we turned again, there were three people, all coming at us from different directions. They walked in that shambling way I'd grown used to, and seeing them made me look for gators and crocs, too.

"Think my gun drew them to us?" asked Danny.

"We know they can hear still," I said. "Maybe we need to get some spears or something."

"Or knives," said Lilly.

I turned. "You really wanna get that close? Plus, it's easy to pierce a skull with a bullet. Not so much with a blade."

"Let's get this done," said Danny. "All of a sudden, I'm feeling pretty exposed."

A gunshot rang out from behind us, and everyone spun around.

Except Liam. He was already facing behind us, his Henry's barrel lowering by the time we all saw.

He'd shot a rotter that was about five feet behind him. I hadn't seen it, and he didn't call out or anything.

It was strange; we all just stared at the thing's body, waiting for it to move. It didn't, which told us all that Liam's shot had been accurate.

I almost yelled at him to call out – you know, the old 'see something, say something' requirement. Instead, I called, "Nice work, kid. Good job."

I saw both Lilly and Georgie smile at me. I responded with a nod and turned back, seeing the other three were much closer now, but still moving slowly.

There was a NO PARKING sign leaning at about a 15-degree angle to my right. It was mounted on a square, galvanized steel tube, about 2"x2". I went to it, pushed it and pulled it a few times, and yanked straight up. It pulled out of the ground.

"Perfect," I said. The end was pointed for easy penetration into the earth. "We'll do this quieter. You guys keep walkin' and keep your eyes out for more."

I trudged across the grass toward the older man in a red tee shirt. When I got to within about ten feet, his staggering pace seemed to increase, and his growling took on a more fevered pitch.

I started to wonder about their eyesight. I knew their eyes were clouded from early on, but beyond wondering how they could see at all, I hadn't given it much thought.

Now I figured they only saw blurry images from more than about 10 feet away. As close as we were now, either my smell or his eyes told him I was food.

He moved toward me, and I planted my feet, my gun tucked away and the pointed signpost in my hands like a javelin. When he was about four feet away, I jabbed forward, hard.

The crack of the bone was sickening. My post sank through the broken skull about four inches, and I gave it a little twist.

His legs buckled at the knees and as I yanked backward, he fell forward, face down and dead.

The women were harder for me; I'd always seen myself as a man who'd stand up for any woman in distress, and it was hard to argue these women weren't.

It was just too fucking late for them.

Based on the bikini she wore, she'd been on the beach when she'd been bitten. I saw the teeth marks clearly on her right thigh, and I could also figure out that she jerked her leg away, because the skin was torn and hanging down toward her foot.

Now she came at me. This time I figured I'd come up under her chin. I held the post in my hands, letting it hang down about hip level.

"Hey, you! Right here!" I called, trying to keep my voice low enough that she could hear me, but I didn't draw any more of them in my direction.

I heard a sharp sound off to my right and jerked my head to see the small market's door bouncing off the frame. I didn't like that they'd let it shut like that. I knew they were probably inside, cursing themselves for the error, too.

At my initial call, the girl had turned toward me, but at the sound of the door slamming, she instinctually turned toward the market. Shaking my head, I jogged around, stopping a couple feet in front of her.

"That's right," I said. "Just a little closer, sweetheart."

At that moment, the clear sight of her captivated me; guess I hadn't really looked at details before.

The bite, pronounced on her leg, had blood-red maggots burrowing in, giving her wounds a shimmering effect. Her throat vibrated a new growl, and her ugly-ass tongue poked out, licking away another couple of maggots that had settled into a pustule on her face.

Oh, hell no. That was all I could take. My head got light and I felt that goddamned vomit coming, but if I wanted to stay alive, I had to act, right then. I know for a fact – you know, from my younger days – that you can't puke with your eyes open.

At least I can't. And I wasn't closing my eyes right then, or stopping the barf.

I pulled the post back like a battering ram, then swung it in an upward arc, the point piercing her neck just below her chin. As it hit, her lower jaw slammed into her upper jaw, sending broken teeth shooting toward me, just before my instrument of death jammed straight up into her rotten brain.

I'll admit, I turned my head by the time the steel post broke through the top of her skull.

She fell backward and took the post with her. I felt it pulling from my hands and let it go before the tweaked edges of the sign amputated one of my fingers.

I heard a low whistle and turned to see Danny standing by the kiosk. He threw me a thumbs-up, and then he pointed at the last walking zombie, nodding his head.

I knew him so damned well. The first motion said he got the pumps powered on. The second asked if I needed help.

I shot back a reciprocal thumbs-up in response and walked forward to yank my post from the girl's neck. The last zombie was moving toward our boat as the signpost pulled out with a nasty, wet sucking sound.

The damned post now felt like it weighed a ton. I stopped for a second and leaned on it while I analyzed the scene.

I spotted Terry sitting on the deck, but he didn't see me, because his head was back. The dude looked like he was on vacation.

"Terry!" I called, but that only confirmed what I already knew; the motherfucker was wearing ear buds or something. I was starting to be sorry we'd shut Nokosi in the salon, 'cause she'd have warned him for sure.

I started running toward the boat. I would easily make it there before the deadhead, but with Terry listening to goddamned headphones, he'd have no idea of the danger approaching.

I started to slow down, easing back into a walk. The man, wearing blue jean shorts and a Corona Especial tee shirt, had just stepped down onto the dock. He might or might not make it onto the boat, but I hoped he did.

Terry started fucking with something in his hand, and I realized he was looking at whatever device he was using to play his music. I was sure when he was done he'd look up and scan the area around him, but nope.

He leaned back, his arm thrown over the bench cushions beside him, his rifle laying across his lap. I couldn't see it, but I was sure his foot was tapping.

Without me, he would be lucky to have his foot in a few minutes.

Or skin. *Or* eyes.

I stepped down onto the wood planks of the dock and gained on the rotter fast. As he reached the boat, now shuffling just seven feet or so from where Terry sat, I watched as the thing tried to navigate the step from the dock to the boat.

If I'm being honest, I gave him a little help. I snuck up behind him and put my post against the small of his back and assisted the stinker with a little push.

You see, it's hard for me to pass up a teachable moment, much as I hate the fuck outta that term. Teachable moments could be fun, and after killing bikini girl, I needed a little fun.

The dead son-of-a-bitch staggered onto the Sea Ray's deck as I watched. I secured my grip on the post again, two-handing it. I then stepped aboard, staying just a couple feet behind it.

Terry now leaned back against the bench seat, his face angling toward the rising sun, his eyes closed. I swear he looked so at peace, I envied him right then. I was never a sun worshipper, but I recognized bliss when I saw it.

I think the fucking zombie was a little taken aback, too. It was like he didn't quite know what to do if his food wasn't running from him. He and I stood just three feet from where Terry sat, oblivious.

I kept one eye on the thing and turned my head to see Danny standing on the grass, the fuel nozzle in his hand. My buddy was smiling at me. He knew what I was up to.

The man-monster in the Corona shirt reached out its arms toward Terry, ready to fall forward. In one motion I sidestepped the rotter, kicked Terry in the left knee with my boot and jabbed out with the post as hard as I could.

The cracking skull I'd heard and felt with the first one I'd killed that morning was nothing compared to this one. I swear, it caved in half the guy's head before it plunged into his brain. It fell forward, bouncing off Terry's legs before he had a chance to jerk them back. His eyes got as wide as saucers, as the scream erupted from his throat and kept on coming. Before I knew it, he'd scrambled backward so fast, he flipped over the edge of the boat.

"Oh, shit," I said. The splash I heard sent chills through my spine.

Not so much for what happened to Terry; for the shit I was gonna get from the girls.

Danny's laughter bellowed as he held the pump out and showed me he had power by squeezing the nozzle and squirting diesel onto the ground.

He walked it over to the boat while I grabbed the longest boat hook and hurried to the rail. Terry was already splashing toward the ladder mounted on the dock faster than I'd seen him move since we ran outta Hemingway's house.

"You tiresome, backwoods asshole!" he yelled, splashing more water than moving himself forward. "That how you get your goddamned kicks? What about the crocs? You know they're in the water!"

"I didn't know you'd *jump* in the water!" I said, trying to keep from busting out laughing again. "I was just tryin' to teach you a lesson. You serious, man? Headphones? With damned zombies around? And I'd recommend less splashin', too. Draws the crocs."

He immediately moved to a quiet dog paddle, his eyes darting side-to-side, his face frantic. I didn't really care the kid called me backwoods, but I did notice. Hell,

I'd run into a thousand college students over the years working at Baxter's, and just from my manner of speaking, most of 'em just assumed I didn't have a college education. Might've been my imagination, but they treated me accordingly; talked slower and used simple words.

They were right about me, of course, though I did know a whole slew of four-syllable words.

Or is that *four-letter* words?

Anyway, I made my assumptions about them college boys, too. I assumed those squishy soft fuckers couldn't change a tire to save their lives, couldn't fix a leaky pipe, couldn't prime a carburetor *or* build a shed from scratch.

So, our initial, less-than-stellar impressions of one another were both correct. I figured he'd prove himself to me in time, and I'd do the same to him. That process was called getting past your preconceived notions and being proved wrong. I'd done that on a regular basis most of my life.

Terry had gotten to the ladder and climbed it with gusto. A few seconds later, he reached the top and stepped onto the dock.

He just stood there staring at me, like he expected I'd have a big pre-heated beach towel to wrap him in.

"You don't have to worry about the headphones or the player anymore," he spat, pulling the waterlogged device from his pocket and tossing it in the water.

I guess the headphones got lost when he fell in.

"I never worried about *them*, Terry," I said. "I worried about *you*. You needed a quick lesson in survival, and that's what you got. Now, get inside and change into some dry clothes."

"I'm not going anywhere near that boat until you get that … that thing out of there!"

163

Damon Novak

I curled my index finger toward me two or three times. "Then come here and give me a hand, buddy. You're the reason he got on the goddamned boat in the first place."

I didn't need to fill him in on my zombie assist.

He looked at me, confused. "What do you mean?"

"He spotted you, man. He was on his way to eat you for breakfast, and when I saw you takin' in the mornin' rays and listenin' to whatever you were listenin' to, I decided to keep ya from dyin'."

Terry, looking like a drowned rat, nodded, pressing his lips together. "Thanks, CB," he said. "Now I kinda feel stupid."

"Better'n feelin' dead."

He nodded. "Way better. I'll help you with him. Like you said, he's my fault."

I nodded. He said, "Will you get up by his head, though?"

"Hell yeah, I will."

We slipped past Danny who'd made his way to us by that point. "You get things sorted out?" he asked.

I patted him on the shoulder and turned. Our winks were simultaneous. By the time Terry looked at me again, my smile had vacated my face.

"Okay, on three."

We bent down and lifted the dead rotter up, swinging him over the side. He landed in the water with a splash.

"Feel like goin' to the store? They might have another music player."

Terry held up his hands, palms out. "I'm swearing off Madonna until this thing is over."

Ω

164

"Okay, you owe $762.94. You wanna put that on a card?" asked Danny, putting the nozzle back in the pump.

"Put it on my tab. How the girls comin'?"

"No screaming from in there. Place must be stocked, though. They been in there for twenty, twenty-five minutes."

I quickened my step. "Come on, man."

Danny turned and fell in beside me. "Wish like hell I coulda seen that kid's face," he said, squeezing my shoulder with a laugh and a shake of his head.

We got to the small bait, convenience and marine supply shop and I pulled the door open.

"Hey," said Georgina. Her voice was muffled, and I noticed everyone had novelty tee shirts tied over their mouths and noses.

I didn't have to ask why. The live shrimp had all died and gone to rot. Danny'd gotten the generator running to power the fuel pump, but it couldn't save all the frozen bait in the now open chest freezers.

It was eye-watering.

"Shirts!" I called out.

Georgie pointed. "Over there!" came her muffled voice. There were several plastic bags sitting on the checkout counter, all filled with supplies.

"There's tons of cookies and chips!" said Liam, his eyes excited as they peeked out from over his tee shirt mask.

"That's because fishermen have a long-standin' and well-known reputation for lovin' junk food 'n beer."

"Yeah, there's lots of beer, too."

"How's Terry?" asked Roxy.

"Funny you should ask.. He's fine and still on the boat," I said.

"Why is that funny?" she asked, smiling.

"Scared him but good, actually," I said, eying Georgie, who was already shaking her head at me. I guess she'd gotten to know me over the last few days. Had a feel for when I'd been up to something.

Made me feel a little exposed, or something. It'd been a while since I'd really cared too much what anyone thought of me. I sure did care when it came to her.

"He's fine, promise," I said. "I'll let him tell ya the rest. He might even laugh about it later, but I doubt it."

We finished ransacking the store. Everybody got a good hat to protect 'em from the sun, and we stocked up on everything from batteries to sunblock. We took the best rods, both for inshore and offshore fishing, and dozens of lures.

They had flatbed carts for coolers and stuff, so we loaded everything onto three of 'em and rolled 'em back to the boat, satisfied we'd gotten enough.

We got to the boat and the black-red muck still remained on the deck of the boat where we'd killed the deadhead.

"My God!" said Roxy. "Terry!" she called.

"I said he's fine!" I said, jumping onto the boat and taking the stuff as they passed it to me. In five minutes, our booty was on board, and I was helping the others on, keeping an eye out for more stinkers.

Danny bypassed me and helped Lilly get on. "CB, start talking," she said. "Now. What happened here?"

I knew I was in trouble then. "We killed a goddamned zombie, Lilly, that's all. Nobody's hurt. Hell, Roxy, you should thank me for savin' the kid."

"He's right, sorta," said Danny, a smirk on his face. "And Terry's fine."

"I'm damned right. Just step past the sticky shit and I'll hose it down once we get underway."

"He ain't *that* right," said Danny, laughing.

"You get the hose, *old pal*. I did the killin', so you do the cleanup. We'll talk about your duties as my best friend in the whole goddamned world later on."

"Hopefully over tequila shots," he said.

Danny helped Lilly, Georgie, and Roxy around the gummy shit on the boat deck, and Liam just cleared it in a standing broad jump.

I was somewhat impressed. I used to be able to jump like that.

As Danny passed me, he punched me in the arm and laughed. "You don't get away with nothin'."

"Never have," I said. "Especially when my best buddy tosses me under the bus."

Ω

True to his word, while I hauled all our supplies into the salon for the others to stow, Danny cleaned the dead zombie's bloody chunks from the Sea Ray's deck. Afterward, he said, "Now hold on. In case you forgot my other job here, I didn't."

"What?"

"The fuckin' skiff, man. I saw a cool wood boat with an outboard back there. I can get it started for sure."

"Okay, don't dick around," I said. "We'll drift out to the middle and wait to make sure you get it goin'."

"Good enough," he said.

He jumped off and we threw the lines. Once I got back to the flybridge, I bumped the motor to float us just between the docks and the mangroves to the south.

Floaters clawed at the bow of the Sea Ray near the waterline, but none made purchase. There were a couple of highly polished oars mounted on the wall of the salon – very retro stuff a rich boater probably loved – and Lilly unscrewed one from the wall and took it to the back of the boat. Until we got into deeper water, she was there to hammer the floaters off the swim step.

I heard two thumps before I realized the skiff was approaching, Danny waving from behind the center console. It was a weird-looking little 15-footer with an electric motor, but it was moving pretty good.

He flipped the dock line and pushed off with an oar of his own, and next thing I knew, he gave me a finger in the air, telling me, "Let's go!"

I would've gone, but with all the bodies in the water, I wasn't sure he'd be able to plow through, so I waited.

Sure enough, he zigged and zagged, shoved some of them away with his oar, and finally gave it enough juice to lift the bow up a bit and slide into open water.

I pushed my throttle forward and followed.

The water was crystal clear, so I guess he had a better view than me, because before I knew it, he was out of the channel and back in Deadman Bay. I opened it up and started plowing half-steam through all the floaters in the Steinhatchee River.

We entered Deadman Bay behind Danny, continuing on for another half mile before I pulled back on the throttle. As I stood on the flybridge, watching Danny at the center console helm of the little skiff, I took note that the wind was calm, the sun was fully visible, and the water was mostly flat.

I motioned to him that I was dropping anchor. He threw me a thumbs-up. The man had a smile on his face, and I knew he was in his element. He preferred boats that put him right down low on the water; he liked to feel saltwater spray in his face.

I called Georgie up to help with the anchor, then asked her to hang up on the flybridge while I went down for a few minutes.

I made my way down the short staircase and turned into the salon. I spotted Terry, storing away canned goods. The store had mostly pull-top cans of Vienna sausages, pork-n-beans, and other low-end stuff fishermen could open easily and eat cold.

I spotted the Coors Light on the counter and got a little twinge. There'd be time for that later. I looked at Terry. "Hey, man. You got a minute?"

He looked worried. "What did I do now?"

I smiled and shook my head. "Nothin', man. It's me needs to apologize to you."

"Hey, it's okay –"

"No, it's not," I interrupted. "It'll just take a minute."

I glanced over and saw all three ladies had smiles on their mouths. I guessed he'd told 'em all what happened.

We got outside. "Have a seat," I said.

We sat together on the stern bench seats.

"Terry, you know what I did for a livin' before all this started, right?"

He nodded. "You ran an airboat tour company."

"Yep," I said. "In the Everglades. You know what we got a lot of in the Everglades?"

"I know," he said. "Alligators."

"Yep. The ones with the big teeth and powerful jaws. You know the only thing that kept me alive out there?"

He sighed, and I knew he already got it. But I'd spent so much time working it over in my head, he was gonna hear every goddamned word.

"You were careful," he said.

"That, plus I was properly scared of 'em. That's what it takes. The bein' scared part is the respect part. You gotta respect what they can do to you. And you gotta know they'll do it anytime they get the chance. Anytime you let your guard down it can be all over."

Terry nodded, and I knew he felt stupid. Good. I needed the kid to feel stupid. That way I could get to know him better, 'cause he'd be around a good long time.

"I get it, and you're right," he said. "When it all started, we were in that house, safe on the second floor. Yes, it was frightening, but I didn't have to face any of them. Never had to kill any."

"Still haven't, right?"

"Right."

"We gotta pop your zombie cherry."

The kid nodded. A smile touched his lips. "I wasn't aware I had one."

I smiled back. "Neither was I, until recently. Just remember, Terry. Respect what they can do and what drives 'em, and it'll keep you alive. Roxy's gonna feel a whole lot better about this world if you're still in it."

"Thanks, CB. I plan to learn a lot from you."

"I've got a feelin' we're all gonna learn a lot from each other over the comin' days. Come on up to the flybridge. First lesson is drivin' the boat."

His face went white.

I turned to hide my smirk and climbed the steps back up top. "Don't worry. For now, we'll just get you familiar with the controls."

$$\Omega$$

CHAPTER ELEVEN

Micky Rode

The road's either clogged with the new monsters of the earth, or it's empty. I haven't seen any other conditions since we took off from Buckingham.

The glass is either full to overflowing, or it's got calcium deposits on the bottom, bone dry.

This is Micky Rode. I figured I should start documenting this and writing things down on this journey, rather than just broadcasting. I don't know how many people are hearing me, but it's cathartic for me anyway. If I'm up and around, it's question after question from a lot of people who've come along with us, but the only problem is, I know as much as anyone else.

Or as little. Yeah, they think I know more because I'm the one who first raised suspicions about the Indian, Wattana.

I have good reason. It's not just what I saw. It's more than that; it's a feeling, really. He was lying. He *is* alive.

To recap what's going on, I was a DJ, working at a classic rock radio station on the FM dial. The call letters were WJAM, and they let me play pretty much whatever I wanted.

The last day, all I did was play warnings. The boss was dead-but-not-dead by that time, and I wasn't listening

171

Damon Novak

to him anymore. Especially when I saw his wife eating him through the glass in his office. Imagine my relief when I realized she no longer had the mental capacity to remember how to get out.

My producer, Glenn Hewitt, was stuck in the building with me, but everyone else had abandoned the studio. Earlier, when the rain had started, he'd been outside having a smoke while I played *Green Grass and High Tides* by The Outlaws. Since it's almost a ten-minute song, he had plenty of time to get doused by that black rain.

Seems smokers will do almost anything to get in those last couple of hits. I remember him coming back in, his white tee shirt peppered with black spots, and him wiping the crap off his head with black-stained paper towels.

"What the fuck happened to you?" I asked, when he came back in.

"It's weird, man! It's raining! Out of the blue – and I mean totally out of the blue!"

"Wasn't in the forecast," I said. "I mean, it's always in the forecast, but not until tonight."

"Smells, too," he said. "And it's black."

"Black?"

"Like ink."

I pulled out my cell phone and dialed my wife's cell number. It rang, and I drummed my fingers on the desk until she answered.

"Hello?" she said. "Mick?"

"Hey, Heather," I said. "Everything okay there? Is Pete in the house?"

"Not yet," she said. She seemed out of breath. "He's still over at Matt's house. Honey, did you see that rain? Petey said he and Matt were outside when it started, running around in it, jumping in those black puddles. They ran to his house afterward."

"It smells, right? That's what Glenn said."

"Yeah, like industrial waste or something."

"Get him home and make him take a shower right away," I said. "You too, if you got it on you."

"I did. Honey, you coming home?"

"No, why?"

"The news is saying stuff. Weird stuff. *Can* you come home?"

"Baby, I don't know what's up yet. You two get cleaned up. You both feel okay?"

"Yes, so far. Okay. We'll call you when we're done."

"The minute you're cleaned up, okay?"

"Yeah. Love you, Mick."

"You too, H."

I hung up and reached over to grab the remote, turning on the television mounted on the wall.

"She alright?" asked Glenn.

"Yeah," I said, flipping channels. "Sounds okay. Let's find something about this rain shit."

"It's gotta be there," said Glenn. "People were stopping their cars in the street. That was the last thing I saw before I couldn't see anything. Shit turned day into night."

There were no windows in my studio, and the insulation was effective, by design. I couldn't see outside or hear a damned thing in there.

As I flipped the TV stations around, Glenn pulled off his shirt, wiping his underarms.

"You mind, man?" I asked.

"Fuck off," he said. "Gotta get this shit off me. I smell like a sludgebucket."

"You're telling me," I said. I hit a station where they were showing a reporter standing outside in the black rain, a yellow raincoat covering her. Her hands were exposed, and the ebony water ran off of them in rivulets.

The picture then cut to an anchor in the studio and I put the sound up. Glenn dropped down in the chair in front of my desk, and the chair groaned in protest.

Now, if I were to describe Glenn, you'd probably think I was drawing a picture of John Candy. He's almost a body double for him, and his hair's never been much tamer than Candy's.

I'd gotten him to come down from North Dakota when I took the job at WJAM. I'd taken radio broadcasting and communications courses at the University of Central Florida, and Glenn was in most of my classes. After we both graduated, he headed back to Grand Forks, North Dakota to try to get a job in the third largest radio market in the state. It was a tough market, and he never found anything.

We'd kept in touch, though. That's why he jumped when I called him to come work with me at WJAM.

I don't need to get into what we saw on those first few news broadcasts. They announced they were going to show Wattana's video, and I had the wherewithal to hit the record button.

I had an odd feeling I'd want to see it again. People were already coughing in the background of the news report. I knew that meant the fits came on suddenly, because in broadcasting, there's always a button marked COUGH beside it. If you've got some throat-clearing or farting to do, that's the button you hit before you do it.

I watched that recording with Glenn the first time, and he's the one who looked at the screen and said, "Hey! There's a cut!"

"Yeah," I said. "I thought I saw something."

"Not just thought. That thing was edited. They bill it as live?"

"They said it was broadcast live, so unless they clipped it for some reason, it should've been exactly what Wattana put out."

"Back it up."

I did. I played it again.

"Stop!" yelled Glenn.

"What?" I asked.

"The clo- "

He was interrupted by a fit of coughing. "Jesus, Micky. Give me your trash can," he choked.

I did, but I didn't want to.

He cleared his throat – I mean, he worked up a man-sized lugey – and coughed it into my trashcan.

"Shit. Blood," he said.

"You sure, man?"

Glenn nodded. "Kinda black, but I see blood."

I picked up the phone.

"What're you doing?" he protested.

"Calling 911, you idiot. You're coughing blood and … whatever that is. You need –" I stopped talking when it started ringing. "Hold on."

I waited. And waited.

"What's going on?" he asked, wiping at his mouth with his bare arm.

I pulled the phone from my ear, then hung it up. "Can you drive?" I asked.

"I'm fine, man. Put your attention back on the video. Look at the clock behind his head."

I shook my head but did as Glenn suggested.

"Definitely a splice," he said. "Can't see the minute hand, so it could only be several seconds, or it could be a whole minute or more."

"I see that now. What are you thinking?"

"No idea. I'd need more time to review it on my Roland Vidmixer to see what's been done."

I was still obligated to play music, so I stuck on the live version of *Freebird* by Lynyrd Skynyrd to burn another thirteen-plus minutes.

"If I weren't sitting here with you, I'd rip on you for playing two ridiculously long songs in a row."

"Shh," I said, pointing up at the screen. "It's the governor." I turned it up.

"Wonder what that dick's got to sa- –"

Glenn doubled over in another coughing fit before he finished his smart-assed comment.

Governor Watkins began: "I'm asking that everyone, all Floridians within the sound of my voice, stay in your homes and let emergency services carry out their responsibilities on roads that are as clear as possible. If you were out in the black rain, we suggest you get to a shower and rinse it off you as quickly as possible, but do not leave your current location."

I was relieved I asked Heather to get Petey rinsed and clean herself up. They were heavily on my mind, though.

"If all you have at your disposal is a garden hose, then use that. If you have neither option, use moist towelettes, anything. The doctors with whom we've consulted have advised us that the element that turned the water black has not been identified and is not a known toxin. This means that whatever it may be, it *is* potentially poisonous, so we don't recommend any of you take any chances."

"Hose me off," said Glenn. "Outside, okay?" When he turned to me, his eyes looked partially clouded.

"You feel okay?" I asked.

"Little lightheaded," he said.

"Your eyes are … I don't know." I tried 911 again, only to get a constant, sharp beeping. I'd never gotten that on my phone before. It was like it wasn't even connected to any service.

Suddenly, Glenn stood up, teetered side-to-side, and fell hard to his right. I was on my feet, but too late. His head smacked my desk so hard my computer monitor jumped.

I ran around, kneeling beside him. "Glenn! You okay, man?"

"Fuck no," he groaned.

A crash came from the other room that shook the walls of my studio.

"What the hell is going on around here?" I yelled, but nobody came over the intercom to answer my inquiry. There were still about five minutes remaining on *Freebird*, and the second I logged that in my head I wondered what the hell was wrong with me.

I knew what it was; I worked hard for years to get my gig, and I was so close to a national syndication deal that I didn't want to mess up my chances by on-air fuckups.

My mind went right to the Woodstock performance of *I'm Going Home* by Ten Years After. I ran around my desk to get it queued up. After that, I put Grand Funk Railroad's *I'm Your Captain* in line, followed by Iron Butterfly's *In-A-Gadda-Da-Vida*, which would kill almost twenty minutes. Last, I put The Doors' song, *The End* in line, which seemed appropriate. Once I set it to continuous play, I ran to the door and yanked it open. "Hose yourself off, man. I gotta get home. I queued up over an hour of tunes."

"You coming back?" yelled a groggy Glenn, as I ignored him and charged out to the parking lot and got on my imaginary Harley. I fired it and powered into the street, turning toward home.

I only lived five minutes away, which is why this was a perfect gig for me.

Ω

I tell everyone on air that I ride a Harley, which is why I call it my imaginary Harley. I pretty much lie to my fans because a lot of my classic rock listeners are American purists, and they love their Harley Davidsons.

In truth, I ride a Kawasaki. It's a crotch-rocket, and right now, I was glad. I fired it and tore out of the parking lot, holding onto those handlebars with all I had.

I found the road slick with the black stuff that coated everything within sight. Slowing more than I wanted to, I still got to my house in just under four minutes, and that was when the dogs caught my attention.

The first one I saw might've been a Dalmatian. It was the right body type, but it was so coated in black muck that I couldn't identify it for sure. If it was, then it was Pongo, named after the 101 Dalmatians hero. He was the only Dalmatian on our street and he was owned by a kid named Brandon.

I only know that because while Brandon was always outside calling Pongo, his mother – whose name I don't know – was always out calling Brandon.

The presumed Pongo was staggering, barely staying on his spindly legs. When I passed him, his four extremities crumpled beneath him and he fell.

Fear gripped me. I didn't stop; I wanted to, and on any other day I would've, but my family was just down the street and I had to get to them.

I noted the absence of Brandon's voice, echoing through the neighborhood as he searched for his dog. That made me notice the absence of any cars or people on the street except me and my bike.

I gunned it to get clear of the dying Dalmatian, and my rear tire broke free, causing me to fishtail just before I reached my driveway. I managed to get it back under control and bounced over the raised concrete slab at the foot of my drive that had been slowly lifting over the years; the victim of a tree root.

We lived in the shittiest house on the street; while I was negotiating national syndication, I wasn't there yet, and my pay reflected what a mediocre deal I was, radio air-wise.

I screeched to a stop, cut the motor, and kicked the stand down. Jumping off, I headed toward the door.

I didn't see Petey out there, and Heather wasn't out calling for him, so I assumed she'd convinced him to stay inside after his shower.

When I saw the door standing open and black crap in the form of handprints smeared on the jamb, I ran.

I heard sobbing as I hurried through the foyer and into the hallway, instinctively following the sound. I knew it was my wife. When I got to the bathroom, I saw Heather kneeling beside the bathtub, and my boy's arm hanging limp outside of it.

"Heather!" I shouted, dropping down and nudging her out of the way. She was hysterical, and when I had clear view of my son, I knew why.

His head was jerking back and forth, and black spittle flew from his mouth. While his face was spattered with the black stuff, the water was like ink, so I couldn't see through it. I reached down and pulled the plug. The gurgling of the water sounded as the tiny vortex spun over the drain.

"Baby, what's wrong with him?"

"I don't know, babe. Glenn got sick from the rain, maybe that's it. Here. Stand up."

She did, and I grabbed a handful of the shower curtain and yanked it down, rod and all. I wadded it and tossed it into the hallway beyond the door.

"What are you doing?" Heather screamed.

"Getting that crap out of our way!" I yelled back and was immediately sorry.

"I'm sorry, H. I'm just –"

"It's okay. Me, too. It's Peter."

When the water had almost drained completely, I saw my son's arms and legs were convulsing. Reaching over, I turned the water on and adjusted it closer to the red than the blue. Then I pulled the knob on the tub spout. The shower rained down.

Standing, I aimed the spray at Petey, rinsing every last bit of blackness from him. Face, hair, everything.

Then I saw it; the bite on his inner left forearm. I aimed the water away and turned his arm. "Heather, did you see this? This looks like a human bite!"

She shook her head. "He didn't say anything about it and I didn't see it under all that black stuff," she said, her voice shaking. "He was lethargic when he got here, and all I could think of was getting that stuff off him!"

I turned off the water and reached down, scooping him into my arms.

"Petey!" I yelled. When he failed to acknowledge me, I tried, "Peter Rode! Do you hear me?" I lay him on the floor and slapped his face several times, trying to elicit some response.

Nothing.

"Micky!" cried Heather. "We have to take him to the hospital!"

"Did you call 911?" I asked.

"No, this got really bad just before before you came in, and –"

"Call them now!" I shouted. I picked Petey up again, nudged past her, and carried him into his bedroom. I rested him on his bed, but he immediately began twisting around, tangling in the sheets beneath him.

"Hurry!" I called. Peter had never been sick in his life; just a healthy kid all the time. I'd never had to face losing him.

I heard something drop from the other room. I was opening my mouth to call out to Heather to ask what happened when all of a sudden, my 8-year-old son's body stiffened. He sat bolt upright so that he was bent at a 90-degree angle at the waist.

His legs were as stiff as steel posts; hands planted on the mattress with eyes wide open, staring past me, blank.

The moment I reached out to take his shoulders, he screamed.

Not like a boy. Not like anything human. His raw cry was both similar and dissimilar to any number of Hollywood-conjured creatures I'd watched over the years in a thousand horror movies.

He howled like a child possessed.

The fact is, I still can't describe that sound, and it still sends chills up my spine.

Hearing it made me wonder what had changed inside my boy to give him the capacity to produce the sound.

"Heather!" I called.

I looked at Petey. He was still stiff as a board, staring straight ahead. No more sounds came from him. It was as though he were struggling against himself. I could practically look into his strange eyes and see that little boy fighting with what he … was becoming.

Damon Novak

"Goddamnit, Heather!" I shouted again. "Are you okay?"

This time I heard a whimper. I jumped up, glancing back one time to see him still sitting there, taking no notice of my departure. I ran down the hall, rounded the corner to the kitchen and saw my Heather on the floor.

"Heather!" I shouted, dropping down to help her.

Black red smears were everywhere, like a finger-painting done with bodily fluids on the kitchen floor all around her. Heather lay on her stomach amidst the mess, still reaching for the phone, but now just slapping at it. It was as though she had some idea she needed the phone, but no idea what to do with it now.

Like she'd lost her mind at lightning speed, and a tiny part of her still clung to the knowledge that caused her to drop to the floor.

I didn't think. I bent down, grabbed her arms, and dragged her from that mess into the living room, laying her to rest on the carpet. The moment I released her arms, she rolled over and clawed at the floor again.

Clinging to her sane intentions. I started crying then, everything was so overwhelming. I didn't normally cry at all, and I haven't cried since. Part of the reason I never found a need to cry before was that I had no goddamned reason to. I had the best girl and son in the world.

Now both of them were being torn away from me by a mysterious, dog-killing, human-ravaging disease.

Jumping up, I ran to the counter where Heather always dropped her purse. I fished around inside and found her keys. She drove a Toyota Highlander that stayed in the garage. It was silver, and the paint was like it was when it was new, in 2008.

As I got her keys, I saw the phone in the muck again. It looked active, and the numbers on the screen said 911.

182

Trying to stay out of the blood and vomit slick, I leaned down and two-fingered it. Wiping it on my jeans, I put it to my ear.

And heard the *circuits busy* message, playing over and over. *Please try your call later.*

I wasn't sure there *would* be a later.

A scraping noise came from the porch, where'd I'd obviously left the front door open, just as I was ending the call to 911. I looked up to see a woman standing there, screaming. "Bandon! Bandon! Andon!"

It went on. The words became less intelligible with each passing second. Worse, I knew who it was.

It was Brandon's mom. She might've been pretty once. Blonde hair, nice figure. Not very attractive with the sludge running down her chin and chest, though.

Her eyes looked like Pete's. Vacant, staring toward me but not at me.

I hadn't seen Heather's eyes yet, and you have to remember that at that time, I didn't know Brandon's mother was a danger. I turned my back on her and bent down, slid my hands beneath Heather's spasming body, and carried her to the sofa.

I rested her on her back, but just like Petey had done, she jerked and twitched and clawed at the cushions, but never settled. Her eyes were open, but darted side-to-side, clouding with what looked like yellowed cataracts.

I felt my entire world slipping away as those tears ran down my face.

Suddenly, I felt hands on my shoulders and a growl beside my ear, accompanied by a rank odor. I jerked my upper body away as Brandon's mother's teeth snapped closed on the material of my shirt. Allowing my momentum to carry me over the back of the sofa, I landed on the hard tile on my hands and knees and scrambled to my feet.

She came after me. I ran to my bedroom, flinging the door closed behind me, but not hard enough to cause it to latch. Reaching my nightstand in seconds, I yanked the door open, grabbed the lockbox from the middle drawer, and cradled it against my waist as I tried to dial in the 4-number combo and make it into the bathroom.

I glanced up to see my delirious neighbor staggering in front of our king-sized bed, heading for me with hands reaching, mouth open with her teeth bared.

I got into the bathroom and slid the pocket door closed. She slammed into it and kept on slamming.

I fumbled with the lock wheels and finally got 1-7-9-1 dialed in. The latch popped, and I put the box on the counter, pulling out the 9mm and the ankle holster that went with it. Bending down, trying to ignore my crazy neighbor about to make mincemeat out of my bathroom door, I secured the Velcro holster straps around my ankle. Then I pulled all four magazines out of the small metal box. All full.

Putting three magazines in my pockets, snapping one in the gun. I took two deep breaths and reached out, putting my fingers into the handle of the slider.

"Your son isn't here!" I yelled. "My boy's sick. If you don't get out of my house I'm going to shoot you."

Another slam, and the door fell from its upper track.

"Goddamnit." I tried to pull the door, but it tweaked at an angle and caught. "Fuck!"

I was frantic. I got back four steps and ran at the door, my right foot raised. My Nike hit it dead center, and I was shocked to find how easily the door broke in two as the fractured halves folded into the bedroom, knocking Brandon's mom backward.

As my momentum carried me through, I two-handed the gun and walked backward toward the door to our bedroom. She was only stunned, but clawed at the bed and dropped back onto her feet on the floor.

My hands held the gun out, but I couldn't fire. I'd never shot anyone before. Something in my mind clicked, and I just backed up two more steps and yanked the door all the way closed.

She hit it. It wasn't a slider, though. It opened in, so she was up against a solid wood frame and jamb.

Still, I watched that door for another thirty seconds or so, just to make sure she couldn't get out. Before I was certain, a figure moved into my peripheral vision.

It was Petey. His face was nearly white, as were his entirely clouded eyes. The black pupils were still visible beneath the cataract-like film, enormous.

Like a dead person.

With the kid's mom in the bedroom scratching and throwing herself at the door, and Heather now trying to get to her feet, I didn't know what to do.

Then, after teetering there and staring blankly at me, Petey started staggering toward me. His mouth was open, and he was emitting the same growl as Brandon's mother. He was as detached from the world around him as the other two.

I needed more information. I could see if I grabbed Petey, he'd never acknowledge it. Heather was up and moving behind him, both of their strange, alien-like faces facing me. I needed two straitjackets if I wanted to make sure they didn't hurt me or anyone else.

Of course, I didn't have any straitjackets. I ran around the kitchen island and slammed the front door closed. The front was now secure, and the rear sliders were closed. They couldn't go anywhere, and I couldn't see how they could hurt themselves any worse than they had.

I charged through the kitchen again, hit the hallway, and ran into my office. Neither had seen me after I disappeared around the wall leading into the kitchen.

I eased the door closed before they happened upon me and dropped down into my office chair. I woke up my computer and put on a news site.

SUSPECTED VIRUS CAUSING CANNIBALISM AMONG INFECTED was the headline.

I stared at it for a moment, then my eyes went to the door. My wife and son hadn't yet figured out where I'd gone, because they weren't at the door. I just heard the odd thump from the living room where I'd left them.

I'm no speedreader, but my eyes ate up the words on that website. Emergency Services had been overwhelmed, but now it just seemed they were out of business. People were posting on Twitter, Facebook, on blogs, posting horrible pictures on Instagram; you name it.

It was the same everywhere. Family and friends getting sick, presumably from the black rain, and attacking everyone. Others were getting sick from being bitten or scratched by the rain-infected. It was vicious. Deadly.

Cannibals. It was like bath salts rained from the sky, driving everyone mad.

But I knew right away it wasn't that. The bath salts seemed to supercharge people, like adrenaline was surging through them, tapping the most violent parts of their brains.

These things were slow and deliberate; they'd eventually do the same things to you as the bath salts people.

Only slower.

You know how people say their minds were running at a mile a minute? So many thoughts passing through that reaching a decision was impossible?

It's where *I* was. It was the only place I *could* be. I couldn't get any help. I couldn't leave my family there like that, but I also couldn't contain them in any meaningful way.

They began to stream live video. It was what looked like a doctor on the screen. He stood before a monitor that appeared to show the top of a man's head. I glanced toward the door again before looking back at the screen.

Opening the right-hand drawer, I located my ear buds. I grabbed them and jammed them into my ears, plugging them into my laptop's headphone jack.

Across the screen, the previous message was replaced with GRAPHIC VIDEO TO FOLLOW.

"… you will see, when I remove this crown, what has occurred. This is one of the earliest victims brought into the ER. He died minutes after being admitted and by the time we wheeled him down to the morgue, he'd already begun to … well, I can only use the term, reanimate. Granted, we're only a few hours into this black rain phenomenon, but it's an incredibly fast transformation, and we've had to make some serious on-the-spot decisions.

"Now, I have draped off his face so that only the top of his head is visible. When I remove this crown, you will see what has become of what should be a healthy, pink brain."

I felt my lip start to quiver. It was then I realized my whole body was shaking.

He fitted a filter mask over his face. When he turned the cap and lifted it off the man's head, it separated with a sound like a vacuum releasing. The black goo stretched from the main reservoir – if that's what it could be called –

to the crown of the man's skull the doctor now held in his hand.

The many squiggly crevices that made up the brain were filled with a black, tar-like goop. Every indentation was a small river of ink.

"What you see is common among several we have captured. We are beyond all tenets of medicine. What we do now we do in the name of saving mankind, if it is even possible. What you will see next may convince you of what I know to be true."

As I stared, unable to turn away, he unwrapped the head as the camera pulled back, revealing the man's face.

His eyes were like Petey's and Heather's. His mouth gnashed, and he snapped his teeth as he let out a low growl.

When they'd pulled the camera farther back, I saw a clamp around the man's neck that appeared to come right out of the chair. Then I realized it was a restraint.

The doctor began turning the clamp counter-clockwise, loosening it. When it fell away, the man with clouded eyes and infected brain threw his body side-to-side, fighting to get out of the chair and at the people in the room.

He was belted to the chair at the waist. Nobody appeared to be at risk from the doctor's actions.

Suddenly the doctor stood. He said, "I did not ask permission to do this, but you must know. All of you. What you are seeing here is irreversible. I will prove it now."

The doctor produced a handgun from behind him somewhere. Suddenly, a panicked voice sounded from the distance, joined by several others. The camera jerked, then pointed at the studio lights, showing nothing but glare.

"Damnit!" came the doctor's voice, and the next thing I saw, the camera was moved hastily back into position.

The doctor walked by, held out the gun and fired once into the man's chest. Then again, right at his heart. And a third time. And a fourth. With his fifth shot into the man's chest, he stood aside and pointed. "See?"

Nothing had changed about the thing. It wasn't dead. It still struggled side-to-side, trying to escape.

"You see they do not die. Not that way. But this."

He jammed the gun straight down against the black brain and fired a single round.

The body went limp.

"They are already dead. I cannot explain it. I also cannot deny it. One last thing I would like to point out; some of the patients in the hospital were bitten or scratched by the infected. This leads me to the conclusion that any contact with an infected individual could potentially result in transmission of the virus.

"I suggest you gather up anyone who is not infected and go to an isolated location nearby. Perhaps the government can get this under control. Your infected loved ones will never be cured. Save yourselves if you want to save humanity."

With that, the doctor stepped out of the camera's view, leaving me to stare at the dead monster.

Just like the monsters on the other side of that door.

The monsters that I had once loved.

I checked my gun. Ejected a round, just to make sure. Checked the magazine.

I didn't know I was about to do what I did until it was done. I leaned forward and reached for the doorknob. Turning it, I pulled and swung it toward the wall, leaning back in my office chair.

"Heather, Petey," I said, slapping my hand repeatedly on my desk.

Like obedient pets, they came.

Heather came in first. I'd never kill her son in front of her. I held up my shaking hand and put a bullet right between her eyes.

My tears began to flow again, so many of them that my vision became blurred, and I struggled to blink them away as my son, Peter Rode, staggered into the room.

As his dead mother collapsed to the carpet, he never even looked down at her.

I held the gun out with both trembling hands, squeezed my eyes closed, and fired.

I didn't open them until I heard the thump of his body hitting the floor. I had prayed he would fall face down, but the shots had knocked his tiny frame backward, and he lay in the hallway, propped against the wall.

I'd put two in his head. I choked back the vomit that rose in my throat as I jumped over Heather and turned my face away from my dead boy as I moved past his now motionless body.

Leaving Brandon's mother to claw at our bedroom door, I hurried back to my motorcycle on weak legs.

I went back to the only place I knew to go. The radio station.

Ω

CHAPTER TWELVE

The sun was just sinking when Pa's ham radio crackled to life, then shut up again. All I caught was, "Sixteen meters – 17.48-17.90 Mhz is supposed to be best for day and night –"

"CB! Was that the DJ dude?"

"Hell yeah. Fuckin' thing's still on frequency scan."

I flipped the dial back to fixed frequency and locked in on the one the DJ had just mentioned. I made a mental note to keep it there from now on.

Micky Rode's voice came back on.

"Things have taken a turn people," he said, his voice conspiratorially low. "I told you we were trying to avoid big cities, but we were on the outskirts of St. Louis and I guess there was an amphitheater I wasn't aware of. The road was supposed to be rural, but not when this thing hit.

"I guess it was an all-day charity fundraiser or something, with ZZ Top as the main draw. Unfortunately, it's an open-air venue, and I'm guessing when that black rain fell, everyone got doused. I mean, rain wasn't even in the forecast as far as I've been able to research.

"Anyway, the street we were caravanning down was dark and empty, and if someone would've asked me to rank how good our choice of a route was, I'd have said it was the best. I was dead wrong. Literally."

"Wonder if he lost anyone," said Danny.

"Sounds upset," said Georgie, sitting on the bench seat beside me. We'd anchored the Sea Ray, all ready for

191

some rest and time to plot our course for fuel and our final port of entry.

Speaking of ports of entry, I could feel Georgina Lake beside me, and occasionally, her arm would brush mine.

It was like electricity. I really don't know what's gotten into me lately, but this whole zombie apocalypse has turned on my horny switch. Hell, maybe it's a side-effect of the black rain, but all I can think about is that doctor laying in my bed, those warm breasts against my chest.

"CB!" shouted Danny. "You hear that?"

I startled back to the present, feeling embarrassed, but I'm not sure why. Nobody knew what was on my mind.

"No, sorry, man! Spacin' out. What'd he say?"

"Fucker lost thirteen people in his damned party!"

"Jesus," I said, opening my ears again.

Rode continued, only this time I was listening.

"... didn't know them very well, but all of them were willing to come along and help. I feel like I let them down; led them right to their deaths. Yeah, I told everyone to keep their windows up and don't get out of their vehicles for any reason, but I guess some survivors were hiding in the trees alongside the road, and when they saw us coming, they ran out to ... well, to see if we'd save their lives.

"All we did was lose some of ours. Not one of those people made it. Four of the cars opened their doors to save those people, and everyone was overrun with zombies. We jumped the median and drove back around to see if anyone could be saved, but all we could see in the stopped cars and SUVs was blood smearing the windows."

Lilly had come in with Terry and Liam. She sat, Nokosi at her feet, and intertwined her fingers as she listened. Roxy was still mad at me for the joke I'd played on Terry, so I understood why she didn't want to be around me right then. She was sleeping in her small berth.

Liam yawned and closed his eyes after settling down on the couch. The kid was exhausted. I guess it had all caught up with him. When I heard what Rode said next, I was glad he'd conked out.

"But there was something else," said Rode, his voice shaky. "They're strong. Really strong. Ever tried to take a big steak and just tear it in half with your bare hands? Well, it's meat. Just like we are. Those monsters tore arms off. Maybe chewed through them first, but they ripped arms from bodies. Bone snapped and everything. I guess I'm going on about it because I was shocked today."

"I see why," said Lilly. "All the more reason to shoot them from a distance."

"Remember what it was like before we knew what was really happening," said Danny. "People changin' out of the blue, and you didn't expect someone you love to try to kill you. I bet lots of folks were surprised and ended up dead."

"If they were lucky," I said. "I keep thinkin' of poor Sonya. Talk about bein' taken by surprise."

Rode interrupted me, and I shut up.

"So, you have to be careful out here, and realize there's no police or military presence that I've seen. Nobody who's joined us has, either. What this means is our little mission, whether it's genius or foolishness, is still valid. I don't know if anyone else out there has a plan, but if they do, I haven't caught wind of anything on my radio."

"He's been the only voice we've come across, as crazy as that sounds," I said.

Everyone nodded in agreement. They all looked a little more worried than before, and I got why. Rode may not even be aware of the crocodilian problem, which I have to assume affected not only gators and crocs, but caymans and a shit-ton of other creatures in the same family.

"Our destination hasn't changed," said Rode. "For now, set your GPS to Lebanon, Kansas, and be careful. All we've got to go on still goes back to that video, but we've watched it more times than anyone else, I'm guessing. We know he manipulated that broadcast, and we're going to find him.

"Worst case scenario, we get to the Henomawi Reservation and find out it's the same as everywhere else. If that's the case, and we can verify the Indian is dead, we'll just make a new plan. Don't bother asking me what that is. I have no idea. Stay safe. We'll see you in Lebanon."

That was it. I turned to everyone else. "Well, that ain't good."

Lilly glanced at Liam, and I knew she was making sure he was asleep. She whispered, "You mean the part about them being able to rip body parts off with their hands and teeth?"

Everyone nodded.

"Are we sure we're not better off just finding somewhere safe and hunkering down?" asked Georgina. "I almost lost Roxy once. And it's not just the people, it's the crocs and gators, too. I wonder if Rode does know that."

"All the more reason to get outta gator country," I said. "Gulf states don't seem like the best option these days."

"We need to inventory our ammo and keep our guns in good workin' order," said Danny. "I know y'all have a good amount, but with what that Rode dude said, we could go through what we got fast."

"He's right," said Lilly. "We've got time on our hands. Let's spend this evening doing that. Maybe on our next stop we can resupply ammo, get more weapons, too."

I got up and looked off to the east, at the Florida shoreline. "Anchor seems to be holdin'. Thank God for calm waters. Let's get all the guns and do it in the salon. I'll set up the table."

"So, we're still planning on following the DJ?" asked Terry. "Wonder if they're hearing him in Lebanon."

"For now let's stick to the plan. If somethin' better comes along the way, we'll exercise our democracy and make a decision together. Nothin' holdin' us to anything."

Everyone agreed with me. I didn't see that we had much choice anyway.

Ω

We had too many guns to clean, and a few of 'em that none of us knew exactly how to break down. Don't get me wrong; I can take nearly anything apart and put it back together, and I'll take pictures of it if I'm not sure I'll remember. But that kinda stuff takes time, and I didn't want to disable a weapon that was in good working order, just because I was an idiot.

Some of 'em were self-explanatory to break down. I could figure out any of the regular shotguns or handguns, and Georgie even had a good handle on a couple I didn't.

But if none of us felt comfortable breaking a weapon down, we cleaned what parts we could get to. I mean, there's nothing worse than a spring or a little rod popping out and rolling under a table, leaving us with a useless weapon. I did manage to figure out the DP-12, though. I wanted that puppy to work, so I was just careful.

We did the inventory, too. We had a good amount of ammo for most of the guns, but if what Rode said was true, anything we had left in stock when we got to Lebanon would be put to good use.

More 12-gauge shells, 9mm rounds and .45 rounds were top on the menu. We had a lot of the .22, and with only Liam and Terry, and maybe Roxy shooting that ammo, it would last a while.

I was glad we were well-stocked, but I wanted way more. Nobody ever complained about having too much ammo. The worst words you can yell in the English language when you're under attack are "I'm out!"

Liam looked comfortable when we'd headed down to get started on the guns, so we left him on the flybridge bench seat, sleeping. He'd need to know some of this stuff, but we could teach him in good time. For now, I'd prefer he stay a kid, as much as possible.

A kid who listens, but a kid just the same.

"So, up and at 'em early?" I asked. "Danny, how far to Fort Walton?"

"We got about 95 miles to go," he said. "If conditions hold, maybe three, four hours in the mornin'."

"Help me set up the beds and let's turn in," I said. "It's been a day."

We all moved the seat cushions from the table, and I pushed the button that lowered it to the bench level. Once we pulled out the extension and put the cushions back on, it was a decent, comfortable full-sized bed. It was where Liam and Terry slept.

Georgina and I retreated to the main cabin. I was still surprised Lilly didn't demand a switch. The bed she was sharing with Danny was a cot compared to the one we had.

I slid the door closed while Georgie crawled into what I guess had become our bed. I can't say I was bothered by that at all.

"Made it through another day," she said, sitting up, propping herself up on an elbow.

"Thanks to everyone."

"Except Terry, right?"

"He'll learn," I said, pulling off my pants and shirt. I sat on the edge of the bed and pulled off my underwear and crawled in.

"Generator on tonight?" asked Georgie.

"Yeah. Plenty of fuel to get to Fort Walton," I said. "Danny said so, and he knows his shit. I think he's read that damned Sea Ray manual from front to back."

I slid beneath the light sheet and blanket and put my arm over Georgie's shoulder. She snuggled in, and I snuggled back.

Her head on my chest, she said, "Have you had any bouts of hopelessness yet?"

I stroked her hair without really realizing I was doing it. "Hard to feel hopeless with you right here."

"It's hard to know if what we're doing is the right thing," she whispered, as though afraid somehow her daughter would hear her voice her fears.

"Nobody's ever faced anything like this before," I said. "Believe me, this is a trail I'd rather not blaze."

She was quiet for so long I was sure she'd fallen asleep. Then: "I want to get medical supplies. Any one of us could get hurt. Butterfly bandages, rubbing alcohol, suture materials, needles. Scalpels, too. Maybe some portable lights, in case something happens that requires more extensive procedures."

"You're right," I said. There were a thousand ways to get injured, and the more medical supplies she had, the better for all of us. "Make a list tomorrow when we get underway. A hospital or clinic run should be on our schedule."

Now it was my turn to think. A few seconds later, I said, "You get bit, you change, right? Like with Clay."

"We still don't know if that was a delayed result of the black rain," she said. "Yes, Tanner bit him, but that might've had nothing to do with it."

"Don't even say that," I said. "Man, I don't want to believe any one of us could change anytime."

"It's been long enough now that I'd think we'd be exhibiting some symptoms. I have no idea why we aren't affected, but I'm not looking that gift horse in the mouth."

We didn't do anything that night but sleep. I didn't mind; when I woke up in the morning, around 5:45, Georgie was already in the shower in the corner bathroom.

I joined her. It was tight in there.

The shower, I mean. It was a small shower.

She didn't complain. Neither did I.

Ω

We'd anchored in about twenty feet of water, and it was calm. Before anyone else got up, I snuck around the kitchenette and made coffee, trying not to wake Terry and Liam, then prepped my cup and headed out to stand on the bow.

Looking out at the shoreline, smoking another of Lilly's Marlboros and watching the sun begin to peek over the eastern horizon, I noted there weren't as many raging fires burning. Maybe they'd burned themselves out.

I considered the causes of the fires in my head, but it could've been anything; people setting fire to buildings crammed with the living dead, or errant lightning strikes

198

that no longer had any opposition from the local fire departments.

It was nice before the sun came up and really started blazing. I wouldn't call it cool at 78 degrees, but it was nice.

I flicked the butt over the edge, 99% sure some damned sea turtle would get it caught in his fucking eye – if goddamned Greenpeace was right. I figured all the sea life was gonna have it so good with most of humanity no longer consuming goods and generating trash, I had to ease them into the apocalypse with my own contribution.

I pulled the anchor myself. There was no danger of drifting into anything, 'cause there wasn't anything out there to drift into. Then I trotted up to the flybridge, half a cup of coffee in hand, and fired the engine.

That's what probably woke everyone else up.

Everyone but the kid eventually dragged their asses up to say good morning, but it was muggy, so they all retreated back into the air conditioning. I could've gone down and piloted the boat from the cool of the salon, but I liked being higher up, 'cause it gave me a feeling of security.

There was pancake mix in the cupboard, and it was the kind where you just had to add water and a little vegetable oil, and we had both. Georgina brought me a 3-stack of pancakes and a full cup of coffee to refresh mine.

She didn't leave, and eventually, Lilly and Danny came up.

"Couple hours to Fort Walton?" asked Danny.

"Yep, almost exactly. I'm keepin' it to 30 miles an hour, and it's about 64 miles from here."

"How will we find gun stores?" asked Lilly.

"We need to be careful as hell," said Danny. "Fort Walton Beach is a tourist town, so even this time of year, I'm sure they had their visitors."

"Yeah," I said, "luckily most of the snowbirds went home after Easter."

"Which leaves the idiots who thought vacationing in Florida in summertime was a good idea," said Lilly.

"Idiots make the worst zombies," said Georgina, without cracking a smile.

We all looked at her. She turned her head and said, "What?"

"Was that a joke, Georgina?" asked Danny.

She smiled. "Stream-of-consciousness. It was the first thing that came to mind."

"If they shuffle how they drive, we're in for a reckonin'," laughed Danny.

We all got a good chuckle out of that. I finished my pancakes and put the plate aside. "How's the kid doin'?" I asked, changin' the subject. "Terry's gotten pretty close to him."

"Liam's good," said Georgina. "I was having a look at his bruising, and he's clearing up fine. He was responsive when I asked questions. Doesn't seem too down, but he still won't really talk about his family. I haven't learned anything other than what he first shared."

"Does he still seem stable enough to handle the responsibility of a weapon?" asked Lilly. "I know he seemed okay yesterday when he shot the one on the dock, but he is still just a kid."

"He seems to be a typical boy," said Georgina. "I'm no psychologist, but nothing alarmed me about his demeanor. I suggest we all watch for any signs that he's struggling anyway. Things could turn on a dime."

"Good call," I said. "Sadly, I don't have a lot of faith in the backbone of today's youth, 'specially when they're raised up north. Anti-gun, anti-this, anti-that. I got no idea what those folks are for, I only know what they're against."

"No matter," said Danny. "Once that zombie apocalypse smacked 'em in the face, I guaran-damn-tee you, they're all for guns now."

"Seems they're all red states now," said Lilly. "Unfortunately, they're dyed in blood."

I turned to her. "Fuckin' Debbie Downer. I was waiting for the *waa waa waaaa* sound effect."

"Drive the boat and shut up," said Lilly, getting up and slapping me on the back of the head. "I'm going down to wake Liam up. He needs to eat, then help me with the dishes."

"Paper plates at the next stop," said Georgina. "We need the fresh water, and we've got enough to do without dishes."

"A girl after my own heart," said Lilly. Danny followed her.

"Thanks for hangin' out with me," I said.

"My pleasure," said Georgina.

"Any ideas on how we'll find a gun store in Fort Walton?" I asked.

"Believe it or not, something's still working, because when Roxy tells Google to navigate on her phone, it does."

I considered the satellites flying high over the planet and figured there's no reason they shouldn't still be working. "Will it find points of interest?"

"It might suggest options from a database or something. I don't really know how it all works."

"Nobody does," I said. "Maybe they did once, but now it's a tangle of technology. Kinda like modern cars."

"You miss Red Rover?"

I laughed, but only half-heartedly. "Hard to believe I'll never see her again."

Georgie squeezed my shoulder. "Well, she sure saved us. Maybe you can make a run back to Key West when this is all over."

"Hell, by then, some rainbow-haired freak will be livin' in it."

Georgina laughed, and I loved the sound.

The time crept by and before long, the fuel gauge was down to a quarter tank and the shoreline to our north was in full view. It was the Florida panhandle, and our destination. The boat's GPS showed we were about a twenty-minute run to reach it.

We all stood up on the flybridge, including Liam, and stared out at the dozens of hotels that lined the beach. They looked to me like giant Lego buildings, all designed in the same rectangular block shape.

"Are those people on the beach?" asked Danny.

I turned, and Lilly was already reaching for the binoculars. She scanned the coastline.

"Not people," she said, her voice like ice. "Not unless they're drunk."

"What do you mean?" asked Roxy.

"They're … staggering. And they seem to be all moving toward one another."

"Lemme see," I said.

She handed them over. I raised the glasses to my eyes and noticed right away what she meant. Like steel to a magnet, they all appeared to drift toward one another. Once they met, they just wandered the exact same way, but together.

"They're pushin' together," I said. "Like they're drawn to one another."

"Maybe it's the motion," said Georgina. "But when it involves cancer cells, we call it clustering."

"They are a cancer," said Danny, his voice low. "As deadly to us."

"Only much more quickly," said Georgina.

"Are we going over there?" asked Liam. His voice sounded small, and I knew he was beginning to understand that his family was just the start.

"You don't have to go," said Terry. "Right? I'm not sure I want to go."

"I think we'll make this excursion voluntary," I said. "But we'd better pick our entry point, and that ain't it."

I swear I heard sighs of relief behind me. Georgie wasn't one of them. I glanced up at her, and her eyes met mine. "You don't have to go either," I said.

As we motored closer to the shore, she said, "I want to help, Cole. It's just that I'm not sure I'm ready to face them again."

"Me and CB'll go," said Danny. "We'll be faster with just two of us."

I was about to concur, when Danny said, "Is that a marina over there?" He squinted his eyes and pointed northwest, and we all followed his finger. "If it is, there's a couple miles of pretty empty beach between there and that herd of dead cannibals. Give us a little buffer."

"Looks like it," I said, looking through the binocs.

"Who's up for a quick lesson drivin' this boat?" I asked. "Danny's gonna hold some quick lessons. We got a lot of daylight ahead, so we've got the time."

"I will," said Terry. "You showed me the controls the other day, so I'm the logical choice. Like I said, I worked on my dad's sailboats, so I have a good feel for wind and current conditions."

"Perfect," I said. "Danny?" I got out of the captain's chair and motioned toward Terry. "Take a seat, Ter."

He sat down and examined the helm. "Okay," he said with a sigh.

"First off, we're anchorin' and takin' the skiff out, but if we get in trouble and can't get back to where it's docked, you might need to motor this thing to where we end up," said Danny.

Terry nodded his understanding. "Okay, what's the first lesson?"

"Backing up," said Danny. "Then we'll go over the thrusters, just in case you need 'em."

The lesson went really well, and before long, Terry was changing from forward to reverse, stabilizing the boat and engaging the thrusters. We used a channel buoy as his target, and after two failed attempts, he was successful the next four tries, bringing the boat's port side right up against it.

Then, just to fuck with him, we had him come up on it from the south side, which reversed the wind conditions. He still got it twice in a row.

"You think you're ready?" asked Danny.

"As ready as I'll ever be."

"Okay, like I said, we'll take the skiff to the dock, but if somethin' goes wrong and we can't get back to it, you might have to bring it up to another dock. Lilly knows a bit about drivin' boats, too, so she'll be your co-captain."

"So, I'm not driving now?" asked Terry.

"No need," said Danny. "But things change. We'll let you know by radio if we need you to save our asses."

I called, "Hey, Lil? Could you grab a couple of those handhelds?"

Danny shook his head, smiling. "Just one'll do, CB, 'cause I ain't leavin' your side. Thought you were dead once, and that ain't happenin' again."

"Likewise, but some of those deadheads might come between us, and both of us need to be able to get hold of the boat if we have to."

"Point taken," he said, hoisting a nice AR-15. I grabbed the DP-12 and a Glock 22. We had a good amount of the .40 caliber ammo, and it was good and deadly.

"Take a handgun, too," I said. "There's a few nice nine millimeters in there."

I hadn't noticed Lilly leave, but when she came back, she had two bright-colored fanny packs, straight out of the 1980s. "Here," she said. "Radios are inside. They may be a little gay, but they'll hold –" Suddenly she stopped and looked at Terry. "I'm sorry. I didn't mean anything by –"

Terry burst out laughing, and almost doubled over trying to control himself. Pretty soon, we were all laughing along with him.

I'd never heard the kid laugh before, and it was infectious – this time in a good way.

Roxy wiped the tears from her eyes and said, "You don't even know how often I joke about how flamboyant Terry is. If you'd ever seen him dressed up for a night out in Key West, you'd get it. It's like a glitter explosion."

"Even I wouldn't wear that sissy pack," Terry said. "But in the 80s? I imagine I'd have rocked that thing!"

"Well, crank the disco, 'cause it's a good idea," I said. "Let's load up and get our asses to shore. Roxy, see if that phone GPS of yours can find us a close gun store. Also, make yourselves a list of shit we need to get, and we'll do our best to accommodate."

"What about fuel?" asked Georgina.

"Let's see," said Danny, taking the binoculars from me again and scanning the dock he'd spotted. "Damn.

There's no fuel station on that dock, but there's bound to be somethin' for the larger vessels nearby. They get some big boats comin' in here, which means there should be some pumps on docks that extend out into deeper water."

"Either way, we're just under a quarter tank now," Lilly said. "It's enough to do what we need to for now."

"Terry," I said, "You can practice with the forward, reverse and thrusters while we're gone, but don't let it get below an 1/8th tank. If we find fuel pumps and clear 'em, we're going to need you to motor in, maybe test those thrustin' skills of yours."

He just looked at me and smiled.

I knew I'd messed up and opened a door.

"I've been thrusting since I was sixteen," he quipped.

I know I blushed, and I ain't a big blusher.

"This is gonna be a regular thing with you, ain't it?" I asked.

"If I like you, yes," he said. "And so far, I still like you." He batted his eyes.

"Smokes are on the list," said Lilly. "But please don't kill yourselves trying to get them."

"Yeah, right," I said. "You'd kill us if we didn't."

"We'll head down to the skiff," said Danny. "See the T dock with the red boat on the right? You stay in at least 20' of water until we get back."

"Shit," said Lilly.

"What?" I said.

Lilly shook her head. "Can't do it," she said, looking up at me and Danny. "I'm going. I have to."

"Lilly, like I said, we'll be faster if –"

"And if you end up dead, I'll never forgive myself. I shoot better than both of you."

"I shoot better than Danny," I said. "There's that."

Danny looked around. "I ... yeah, I shoot better than Liam."

Lilly and I shook our heads. "Nice. You taught him," said Lilly.

"Then I'm going, too," said Georgina. "I'm a better shot than I'll ever admit. I can help, plus I know what kind of medical supplies to get if we come across a clinic."

"You ever heard of makin' a list?" I asked, staring at her. "Georgie, you don't have to do this. Neither do you, Lil."

"CB, you know it's not a matter of *having* to do anything. I made the decision. Terry, drop anchor. We're heading out."

"What am I going to do if you guys can't get back to the little boat?" asked Terry, his eyes panicked.

"It's called a skiff, and don't drop anchor yet," said Lilly. "Practice like they said, then anchor. Keep the radio on and loud."

"Okay," he nodded, but I knew he wasn't convinced he was ready. I knew he was.

"C'mon, Georgina," said Lil. "Let's go get some guns."

"We'll meet you out there," said Georgie, following my stubborn sister down the steps to the main deck.

Now, another thing about me; I don't dictate to women. Never have. I don't think I've ever told a woman what to wear or how to do her hair, even when I had opinions about it. Call it male intuition. That's what I call the ability to shut the fuck up when it's the prudent thing to do.

I had mixed feelings about Georgie going, of course. I found myself wanting to spend every second with her, and just being on the boat wasn't enough. I swear, I wanted her right beside me. I felt goddamned lovesick, if y'all wanna know the truth.

That ain't me and I suppose it could just be the situation, but the more my mind turns to her when she's not with me, the surer I am that I'm kinda hooked on Georgie.

So, while I'm too smart to actually say it out loud, I will be playing the part of protector on behalf of Dr. Georgina Lake once we step off this boat and into the danger zone.

And it ain't my choice, either; it's just built inside me from the time I was a little boy, watching out for Lilly. I was taught that boys never hit girls and boys and men took care of what they once called the *fairer sex*.

I don't know what's wrong with that. I mean, femininity ain't a bad word, right? Hell, I know I can bench press more than Lilly and Georgie combined, but that don't mean I'm better'n either one of 'em.

I'm more capable in some areas, and those two women are more capable in others. Most of this shit is common sense, but I'll just finish with this: Whether Georgina wants me to do it or not, and whether or not she even figures out I got one eye on her, that's the way it is.

I'm looking out for my girlfriend.

That's kinda strange. I didn't even want a girlfriend until the zombie apocalypse.

Ω

CHAPTER THIRTEEN

Climbing Fox Wattana
Henomawi Indian Reservation

Wattana sat up in his bed, his body drenched in cold sweat. He glanced quickly toward the window, seeing beams of bright sunlight filtering in through the blinds.

How long had he lain here? What had awakened him?

He swung his legs off the bed and put his feet on the faded wood floor. Eyeing the shotgun leaning against the headboard, he stood.

The blinds were drawn, but a shadow passed by one curtained window, then another. He took a quiet step toward the gun and curled his fingers around it.

The stock against his shoulder, he walked softly into the living room and saw the shadow again, pass by the south window. Wattana raised the gun.

As he reached the sliding glass door, Dancing Rain ran into view, her eyes panicked. He rushed forward to flip the lock lever and slide the door open, but as Wattana reached it, several figures emerged from the distance. His hand froze in place. As the things moved toward Dancing Rain, he staggered backward and fell against the wall opposite the door.

"Mundunugu!" she cried, pounding on the thick glass. "Help me! Let me in!"

Her face was bright red, her eyes wide with panic. Behind her, two filthy men and a woman, all with ravaged, pustuled skin, staggered ever closer behind her.

Do I have time to help her? Will they reach the house before I can let her in? Even as the desperate thoughts passed through his mind, Wattana didn't move toward the door. He couldn't.

The questions he had asked himself were nothing more than stalling; giving him an excuse for later, after the things killed her.

His weakness prevented him from taking action to save the terrified girl; he knew that in his heart. He felt his own paralysis, brought on by the realization that the ceremony he had conducted from the ancient texts had somehow borne fruit.

Putrid, tainted fruit.

Frozen with fear, he knew he would never open that door. He had a clear view straight ahead, but no way of knowing what might be approaching from the left or right of her, and as the only human being alive who had any hope of reversing the curse, he could not be killed.

If only he knew what to do about any of it! If he were being honest with himself, he'd admit that before the ceremony, he had lost much of his faith in the ancient spirits. While the old text had been intriguing, he really hadn't thought it would work.

In his mind, it had been a way of bringing his people together. Maybe that's all he ever thought it would be; something to inspire the young people in his tribe to actually *do* something besides waste away on the reservation.

Even as he'd gone through the ancient blood-curse in front of his entire tribe, he'd felt a bit foolish. But that feeling was nothing compared to the guilt that burdened him now.

One of the monsters reached the girl, his splotchy, peeling arms extended out before him. The filthy fingers caught and tangled in Dancing Rain's long, black hair, and she spun around, screaming.

She clawed at the thing's face, her badly bitten nails tearing its rotting skin away, peeling down bloody tatters, exposing rotting muscle and sinew beneath. Climbing Fox wanted only to fire his shotgun through the glass door and stop everything from happening, but if he did, he would be their next victim.

Wanting to close his eyes but finding he could not, Wattana watched the other two skinwalkers converge on Dancing Rain, and she spun back around to stare through the glass at him, accusations of betrayal clearly visible in her terrified eyes.

Her mouth opened wide as she let out a shrill scream that only died when two of the creatures converged on her, tearing out both sides of her throat. As her dark eyes rolled back in her head, she collapsed, and the feast began in earnest; the creatures fell upon her, and with hands and mouths, bit and clawed, gripped and tore her limbs from her body until she was only a macabre torso.

Others came now, from all around the house, as though the melee had drawn them, either by smell or instinct.

The skinwalkers did not leave after they finished devouring Dancing Rain's body. They gathered at the sliding door, at least seven or eight of them now, pressing in, their disgusting tongues lapping at the glass, their blood-covered bodies pressed against it as they sought his flesh.

Are these my people? he wondered for the first time. He allowed his eyes to drift from one horrid face to the next. Despite the horrific changes in their features,

Wattana soon concluded that he did not recognize any of the skinwalkers.

This meant the curse had been cast as the text said it would be; anyone with the blood of the land in them was safe.

The door did not appear at risk of caving in, so he scooted away, then stood and approached it from the side, drawing the blinds. He did the same in the other room until the interior of his house was shrouded in shadows.

Wattana hurried into the darkened bedroom, closing himself inside. He dropped down on his bed and hung his head.

Climbing Fox cried as he reached beneath the bed for the book Dancing Rain had brought to him.

He had betrayed her. She had suffered a horrific death because of him.

He opened the book. He had to stop it. He had to try.

Hands shaking, ravaged by guilt, and with Dancing Rain's terrified screams ringing in his ears, he scoured the ancient text for some way to stop what he had set upon the land.

Ω

The Florida Panhandle

The skiff we had picked up was a strange little boat that appeared to be either custom built or made by a small manufacturer. It was called a *Peeler Skiff,* and it was around fifteen feet long with a weird-ass electric trolling motor on it called a *Torqueedo.* It was only a 15-horsepower motor, but it pushed that skiff along real good at around 14 knots – with four people.

It had a small center console, and the seats were basically wooden benches that curved around the inside perimeter of the craft. The boat was made of wood, too, with teak oars mounted to the inside rails – which told me it was definitely a small, artisan boatmaker.

We reached shore in no time, cutting the engine before we reached the dock and using the paddles from there. We rowed into position behind a larger boat where we could disembark without being seen.

Georgina said, "I think it might be a good idea to minimize our time out here. So, I suggest we pair off and hit the grocery store and the gun shop. Thoughts?"

"If we're doin' pairs, then you're with me, Dr. Lake," I said. "Danny, you mind gettin' bogged down with this dead weight?" I nodded toward Lilly, who held up her middle finger on her right hand.

"Bite me, CB."

"We're good," Danny said. "And quit with the smack, man. You get cocky, shit goes wrong. Hell, CB, that's been our motto since high school."

"Yeah, I know, but she's my sis, so it's okay. God forgives that shit. Let's prep. Check your weapons and don't get separated."

"Here," said Georgie, handing me a piece of paper with scrawled handwriting on it. "Directions to the Publix grocery store and the bait shop. Roxy said it looks like they're on the same block."

Danny stared at me, then jerked his head toward Georgina, then at Lilly. "After all this shit, I'm just goin' food shoppin'?"

"Necessities come in many shapes and sizes," said Lilly. "Don't worry. I'm sure they have charcoal briquettes, or something manly like that you can throw over your shoulder. Maybe a big bag of dog food for Nokosi."

"Don't cry," I said. "You're hittin' the bait shop, too."

"Hope the power's still on or the emergency generators kicked in and kept the bait frozen."

"You know how to toss a cast net," I said. "Bait's the least of our worries. Get some fishin' rods, nets, stuff you lost."

"Let's do this," said Lilly.

We got out as Danny tied the boat to the cleats mounted to the dock. The large boat that blocked anyone on shore from seeing us was a Sunseeker 86. The thing looked brand new, and it started me thinking.

"Let's have a look at that monster when we get back here," I said. "We're a little tight on that Sea Ray now."

Danny let out a low whistle. "You're puttin' a lot of faith in me if you see me drivin' that beast."

"Yep," I said. "Now get shoppin'. Georgie, lead the way."

We all peered out from behind the big Sunseeker like a bunch of cartoon detectives. There was a big sign that read: *Summer Palms Marina – Fuel Docks.* There was an arrow pointing to the west, which was the opposite direction from the earlier horde we'd seen. Nobody was visible.

"Looks clear," I said. "Let's move."

Georgina headed out and I tucked in behind her. To keep from thumping along the dock, we didn't run, but walked slowly until we hit the sand. Exposed, it was then we started to move steadily faster.

The small marina had a bait shop, which Lilly and Danny immediately angled toward. Georgie had her directions back in hand and went straight, between two buildings. I saw a pretty big boulevard beyond the structures.

"How far is it?" I said, then reached down for my radio. I pushed the button.

"It's about a half-mile," said Georgie, as I said into the radio, "Danny, Lil? Y'all read?"

"We do," said a voice I recognized as Roxy. "Loud and clear."

"So do we," said Lilly. "Now, only use it when we have to."

Afraid my sis would bite my dang head off if I said, "Roger that!" or anything else at all, I just clipped it back on my belt. I wasn't sure acknowledging her instructions qualified as "having to use the radio."

"Shit," I said, as we rounded a corner. A pretty sizable group of the deadheads were milling around but hadn't yet caught sight of us.

"C'mon," I said, spotting a bunch of colorful scooters in a rack. There was a sign that said, "Scooter, Golf Cart & Jet Ski Rentals."

She jogged behind me as we put another building between us and the crazies. "Good," she said. "The estimate appears to be off a bit. We're probably about three miles from H & H Firearms."

"Guess we docked at a different spot than Rox figured."

"There's a kiosk there," said Georgie. We both jogged toward it, our heads on a swivel. There were a couple people staggering around to the east of us, and another six or so to the west. None were close enough to worry about, but by the time we got to the small tiki-style building, they were moving in our direction.

"Number and color, please?" I asked.

She glanced over at the scooters. "Seafoam green. Number 18."

"I'll take 22 black. My lucky Roulette combo."

"We need all the luck we can get," she said.

The kiosk had a thatch roof and a hatch that flipped up and became a shade top while people signed the rental contracts, while the proprietor stood inside. There was room for like two people, but it looked empty.

I leaned over the counter to lift the keys off the clips.

"Watch out, Cole!" shouted Georgina, but it was too late. A blistered, ragged arm shot up from below my field of vision, and the hand attached to the end snagged my wrist.

Maybe the guy running the booth had been clawing at the floor or whatever, but I didn't see him, and he wasn't making any noise before I reached inside.

I instinctively jerked backward, but the fingers gripped tight. Just as I heard the sharp crack of the bone, the dead thing had made it to its feet, and I saw both its face and the shiny barrel of Georgie's favorite handgun passing my eyes. She fired into its forehead two times in rapid succession.

Black spattered the back wall of the kiosk, covering the dozens of swim masks and snorkels with the putrid-smelling gunk.

The fingers relaxed and slid from my arm, and a thud sounded as the dead monster collapsed in a heap at the bottom of the kiosk. I leaned over, just to be sure it wasn't moving. My eyes now adjusted to the shadowy area inside, I watched the black ooze running from its fatal wounds.

"You have to be more careful, Cole," she said, touching my shoulder. Her voice was shaky.

"Thanks for savin' my ass," I said. "Never saw him."

She leaned past me and lifted keys 18 and 22 from the hooks. As she did so, she looked down. "Cole, there are cigarettes underneath the counter."

"Marlboro reds?" I asked.

"Four cartons."

"Grab 'em. Get a bag, too."

I turned back to watch the approaching mini-hordes from both directions, but they still weren't a threat.

Georgie came up with a plastic bag containing the four rectangular boxes. She tied a knot in the top and turned. "Let's mount up."

I shook my head. "You have nerves of steel, Georgie."

"You experience a patient's heart stopping on the operating table and try to keep your cool. It happens, and I wasn't exactly Dr. Smooth the first time."

She passed me the smokes and I opened the seat of my scooter and tucked them inside. We both put our keys in the ignition switches and turned them a click. The scooters had been refueled, and both tanks read full.

"On three, hit the starter," I said.

"Okay," said Georgie. "One, two … three."

We pushed the buttons, and as one, they cranked and started.

"You ever ride one before?" I asked.

"Yes," she said. "They're automatic shift, so just gas on the right and use the foot brake to stop."

"Sweet," I said. "You know where the gun shop is, so head out."

As we drove away from the kiosk, the crazies were only within thirty yards or so.

I really hoped our luck held.

Ω

"I swear, we're like goddamned fireflies in pitch dark!" I said, yelling so Georgie could hear me as I rode beside her.

"Yes, they do angle toward the noise when we pass. Hope the path back isn't clogged with them."

"What the hell?" I said.   It had begun to smell strongly of charred wood.

Georgie raised her hand and pointed to a parking lot. We both pulled in front of a pile of blackened rubble and stopped.

"Cut the motor," she said.   I did, and she did the same.

"This is the address," she said. "That must be the gun shop."

"Shit!" I said. "Ammo would've all gone off from the flames."

"Yes," she said. "Luckily, Rox gave me a second address."

"Yeah?" I said.

"Yes, it's Ranger Firearms & Mercantile, but it's about another three miles north of here."

"Got scooters, so that's not a big deal," I said. "Let's stay tight, though."   We counted three again, fired the scooters, and took off.

As we pulled away, I saw American Legion Post 235 next door to the gun shop, the marquis announcing a fundraiser that would never happen.   An old U.S. Army tank stood in front, a monument to past wars.

I secretly wished that sucker would fire up. I'd feel a lot manlier – and a hell of a lot more secure – driving that thing.   Instead, I putted on my scooter alongside my new girlfriend toward Ranger Firearms.

We reached Memorial Parkway and turned right, heading east, past a cemetery.

I swerved toward the curb, stopped the scooter and turned it off, putting put my feet down.

"What are you doing?" asked Georgie, pulling up beside me.

"Shh. I'm just checkin'."

"For what?" She cut her motor.

I looked at Georgie. "You've seen the damned movies. If we both agree these things are dead, then who's to say they can't … I don't know, wake up?"

"You really did watch too many horror movies, Cole," said Georgie. "Most people are embalmed, and the ones that aren't were likely eaten away by every creepy crawler living in the dirt. There's no coming back from that."

"If you say so," I said, but still scanned from grave to grave, looking for any signs of movement. As I watched, a breeze swirled past us, creating a whirling dervish of leaves that definitely would've turned into a monster and chased me down the street when I was 10 years old.

But there were no zombies crawling from their graves. I was satisfied, but had to justify my fears. I turned to Georgie.

"What's happened so far is impossible," I said. "So it's up to everyone to keep an eye out for other impossible shit. I'm satisfied."

"Good. I was never worried," said Georgie.

"But I reserve the right to think they might just be havin' a tough time crawlin' out, so ask that you withhold judgement for now."

"Whatever you say." She smiled. "C'mon. We don't have all day to assuage your childhood fears."

"Assuage?

"Not a swamp word?"

I laughed. "If I can't spell it, I try not to say it."

We fired the small, efficient engines and made a left on Beal Parkway NW.

As I rode, I pulled the radio off my belt and held it to my mouth. "Lil, Danny? You guys on?"

"What you need, CB?" came Danny's voice.

"Nothin'," I said. "Just checkin' on you."

"We're in the bait shop. Smells to high heaven. They have all the shit snacks fishermen take out on boats. They got boat carts too, so we're fillin' up a couple. Takin' anything we could use."

"Run into any trouble on the way in?"

"Not bad. Still kinda queasy, though. Killin' things that look human fucks with your head."

"Then we'll all be fuckheads before long, 'cause this don't seem to be endin' anytime soon. Be careful and grab some beer."

"Already in my little wagon."

"Good man. First gun shop was burned out. Headin' to another, a little farther inland."

"Stay safe, man."

"I will."

I clipped the radio back on my belt.

Beside me, Georgie said, "Everything okay there?"

"Right as rain," I said, as we rounded the corner onto Lewis Turner Boulevard.

At first, I was too shocked to react. When Georgina hit her brakes full on, I did the same, and we both skidded to a stop.

If I wouldn't have looked like a giant pussy, I would've used my feet to push myself around and haul ass in the opposite direction. Instead I stared at the crazy scene.

It was inexplicable.

First, there were alligators. Not just a few. There had to have been twenty of 'em, all up on their legs how they do when they're on land. Betwixt and between 'em were zombies of all shapes, genders and sizes, paying not one bit of attention to 'em. I couldn't see the end of the procession with the naked eye and had no idea if there were another few hundred zombie gators mixed in with the main horde.

They walked along together like they'd been on a goddamned hayride and the tractor broke down. A motherfucker of a tractor pulling two dozen hay-hauling, daisychained flatbeds.

Now, gators don't normally walk around with their mouths open unless they're looking to eat something. This congregation was different; as they moved toward us, not a hell of a lot faster than the clustering deadheads they were with, their mouths opened wide and snapped closed, repeatedly.

I listened for the deep croak that told me they were nearby, and believed I heard it … only different.

I walked my scooter to the side of the road slowly, motioning for Georgie to do the same. She followed me and we both cut our motors.

"If there was any doubt," said Georgie. "We now know they are both afflicted with the same … disease, curse, whatever this is."

"They don't act like they saw us," I said.

"Their eyes are filmed over, such as a cataract might cloud the pupil," said Georgina. "I would imagine this condition carries to any affected species. Their vision would naturally be very poor at a distance."

"We got the wind with us, too," I said. "But that said, you smell that rot?"

"It's like the morgue on steroids. Let's go back and detour on a side road. I'll feel more comfortable when we're away from them."

"You keep on preachin' to the choir," I said. "And I'll keep on singin' your tune."

We pushed the scooters until we faced southwest, then rolled until we were out of sight of the massive horde. Georgie had her hand on the starter button when I said, "Wait."

She looked at me. "What?"

I nodded toward the CVS Pharmacy. "You said that gun store's just up at the next street. That other side road's still too close for comfort. Judging from the size of that herd, they'll still be pouring down the street when we get there."

"Got it," she said. We both started the scooters and drove into the CVS parking lot, then drove around to the front doors.

"Bound to be somebody in there who wants to eat us," I said.

"Better than a thousand of them," she said.

It was a hard point to argue.

We parked the bikes, double-checked our weapons, and headed toward the entrance.

Reaching the door, a raggedy dude wearing the blue CVS shirt with the red collar and nametag slammed into the glass front, his mouth open, then bounced off it and landed on his dead ass. Thankfully he hadn't hit the door square, or he'd have pushed it open and run right into us.

Georgie and I hadn't seen him coming, 'cause the lights in the store were out and the sun was pretty much straight up overhead by then, letting the shadows be. We both jumped back and nearly fell ourselves.

When his face smashed the door he was in full-on bite mode, so most of his front teeth either shattered or got knocked out of his rotting head. What was left were only jagged remnants that might actually work better on us than the originals.

"I'm already tired of this outing," sighed Georgina.

"Can't go back now," I said. "We've come too far."

She nodded. "How do you want to do this?"

I searched the parking lot for a nice rock. I didn't want to fire my gun with the horde as close as they were. No rock, but I did find some loose bricks arranged around a planter. I grabbed one and showed it to Georgie.

She just stared at me.

I felt a need to explain. "Okay, we'll wait until he comes at the door again, then be ready. I'll yank it open fast and when he comes stumblin' out, you trip him and bash his head in with this brick."

She folded her arms. "Or *you* can just rush in and bash his head in with the brick," she said.

"And I'm doin' the bashin' because?" I asked.

"Hippocratic Oath," she said. "*Do no harm.* Now, go get 'em, cowboy."

I turned and shook my head. "Re-write. Now the new oath is just *Harm*." I went to use my brick.

Ω

CHAPTER FOURTEEN

Climbing Fox Wattana
Henomawi Indian Reservation

Wattana tried to ignore the scraping and slapping at the outside of his house. He knew what they were, and now faced the horrifying reality that *he* had created them.

If he had any courage, he'd just open the door and let them kill him. But one thing he'd learned as he watched Dancing Rain die in front of him; he was a coward.

A coward who had doomed his own people in a fit of revenge, driven by hubris and doubt.

Yes, he thought. *Doubt is what led me to do it. I never believed the ceremony would do anything.*

Of course, he'd been raised to believe in the gods and in the power of the spirits, as all Henomawi had. However, with the passage of time, advancing technology and the encroaching influences of the outside world, many of his people had begun to doubt the legitimacy of the old ways and beliefs.

As had he.

Wattana crept around the corner, the old text in his hands, making sure the blinds were drawn so that he would not draw their attention. He put the book on the kitchen table and slid open a drawer, removing a candle.

Lighting the candle, he placed it in a holder in the center of the table. The soft glow should not attract them.

Opening the book to the incantation he had used at the fateful ceremony, he read the words again. When he went through them a second, and a third time, he noticed something.

Writing. Faded, and in red ink. He looked at the words, digging deep in his memory. *What did they mean?*

Then, it struck him. He carefully turned all of the pages, coming to the end of the book. There, in the same red ink, was a paragraph.

It was not the language with which he was familiar; it was not Henomawan. There were two separate paragraphs, each scrawled in a shaky script, and Climbing Fox did not recognize even one of the elaborate symbols.

His cell phone rang in his pocket. Wattana quickly closed the book as though leaving it open may unleash a new curse, perhaps worse than the one he had brought to bear.

Pulling the phone out, he saw it was Magi Silver Bolt. He slid the button to accept the call, and before he got it to his ear, he heard, "Mundunugu! It's Magi! Have you seen Anji?"

Wattana's head felt cloudy. He dug in his memory. "Anji?" he asked.

"Anjeni! *Dancing Rain*! I can't find her anywhere! Is she there?"

The younger people disrespected the Henomawi traditions by shortening their names to sound more like American names, and it always irritated him. Now he didn't care; he just wanted them all to be alive.

"I have not seen her," he lied. "You say you could not find her. Have you gone outside?"

"Yes! It's dangerous, Mundunugu. The skinwalkers are everywhere. When I left my house this morning, I did not see them, so I got on my bicycle to ride to her house. I would have taken my car, but the noise draws them, so I –"

"She is probably in her house, hiding. How did you get through?"

"I'm sorry, Mundunugu. What do you mean?"

"On the cell phone! How did you get through? They have not been working!"

"I don't know! I didn't think of it. I just couldn't find her, and I decided to call you to –"

"Do not come here. The creatures are outside my home and I am trapped here. I am trying to find a way to reverse what I have done."

In a low voice, Magi said, "They move together, Mundunugu. When I was out, I saw one stumbling down Sequoyah Street, so I stayed on the sidewalk and followed him. When I reached the corner by the tire store, I stopped and peeked around the corner. There had to have been a hundred or more!"

"You did not see Dancing Rain among them?" asked Mundunugu, knowing the answer.

"No. I watched for as long as I felt safe, but they began to move toward where I was hiding, so I hurried back home."

Silver Bolt hesitated for a moment, then asked, "Why would I ask if she was at your house if I had seen her there? Is everything okay, Mundunugu?"

Ignoring his question, Wattana said, "I am going through the texts now. I have found something in the back, but I do not recognize the language. It is referenced by a small marking in the middle of the ceremonial text I used."

"I may be familiar with the language," he said. "You're sure it's not Henomawi?"

"Positive," said Wattana, irritated at being questioned in such a manner. "I do not recognize it."

"Can you take a picture of it and text it to me?"

Magi was excellent with languages, and Henomawi and English were not his only skills. Wattana did not know how many languages he spoke, but there was a chance he knew this one.

"I think so. Hang up and I will try to send it."

"Okay. Mundunugu, if you see Dancing Rain, bring her in and make her stay there, okay? I'm so afraid something has already happened to her."

"Of course, I will. As I would do for any of my people."

"Thank you, Mundunugu."

"I'll send the text right away."

He disconnected the call, crying as he held the camera over the book, took the photograph, and attached it to a text. He hit the SEND button.

Having done so, he moved to the bed again and sat on the edge of the mattress, wishing he could drown out the sounds of the skinwalkers outside his home.

He wanted so desperately to appeal to the gods, but he refrained. Climbing Fox Wattana no longer believed it wise to pray to spirits that could unleash such evil on the world.

Ω

Florida Panhandle

We left the dead rotter laying just inside the door, which had been unlocked. The brick was highly effective; so much so, I had to choke down puke the minute it cracked the guy's skull.

Seemed wrong somehow, killing a dude in CVS, when people come in there to buy stuff made to heal things.

The door was a pull, so I was a little surprised the dead guy hadn't found his way out, just by accident. They did tend to crash into glass, being clear and all. I was confused about the ones trapped in cars at first, wondering why they just slammed their faces into the glass, but then it hit me.

Like glass in the face.

They can't see the shit with their cloudy eyes and figure they're moving in for a bite. Like me and my buds used to say: *Psych!*

The door pushing outward from inside probably explained why we didn't run into another soul, dead, alive, or both, inside the store. Any other sick customers or employees that had been there must've shambled their way around the inside perimeter and when the door opened, they kept walking.

It's what they fucking do, right?

"I'm going to grab some of those cloth shopping bags and fill them with antibiotics and pain meds," said Georgina. "I'll top it off with gauze, Band-Aids, ace bandages, topical ointments, and other things. Lots of anti-bacterial hand cleaner, too."

"You sound like a damn doctor," I said. "Get Tylenol, too. And don't forget the Xanax. Things get nuts, we might all need that."

"I plan to take all they have of everything we may need. That includes condoms and birth control. I can't see any one of us dealing with a pregnancy in this world."

"Cood call," I said. "You're a thinker."

Georgie smiled. "Luckily, there's a pharmacy on every corner in Florida, so I'm not worried about leaving someone else in the lurch."

"Yeah, get cholesterol meds for sure. I take 'em. Simvastatin, Pravastatin, whatever. They've switched me around a couple times."

"You take baby aspirin every day?" asked Georgie.

"I was, until this. Just as a precaution."

"We'll load up on that, too," said Georgina. "Do you know what medications Danny and your sister take?"

I shook my head. "Danny doesn't take anything so far as I know. As for Lilly, we've really never talked about it. I know she's called in some prescriptions in the shop before, but I never listened. We tend to mind our own."

"I'll bet she could name your medications."

"Bet you're right."

"I'll just get the most common things people take."

"Sounds good," I said. Then: "Hell, wait a minute. We're bein' stupid. Let me just radio and ask her." I grabbed the radio off my belt, preparing to call, but then something in the background perked my ears.

A sound slowly increased in volume, and to me it sounded like static. I held my hand up. "Georgie, you hear that?"

She was still for a few moments. "It sounds like a hundred straw brooms sweeping over asphalt."

"Oh, shit," I whispered. I moved over to the door, crouched down, and looked through. The giant horde had reached the bend in the road and were now pouring down Beal Street. The hiss-scrape sound that Georgie had likened to the sound of a broom sweeping was actually dragging limbs.

Watching them pass, it struck me they moved like a lava flow. It was because they moved steadily, and they were damned sure unstoppable. And like molten lava, they *would* destroy anything in their path.

Now, you know me and gators go way back; I'd been watching their behavior and harvesting the prehistoric bastards since the Bee Gees were popular, or thereabouts.

These dangerous crocodillians didn't notice the staggering dead men, women and children beside 'em. Might as well've been other gators. Once in a while one of the rotters would step on the gator and tumble to the ground, tripping others behind 'em.

It was kinda nice nobody yelled at anyone when that happened. Maybe the zombie world was the most compatible world. The end of arguing and fighting over stuff. They all dropped down on a single corpse and ate until the food was gone, then moved on. I didn't recall ever seeing one of 'em push another, at least on purpose.

Ironic as hell. We have to die before we can play nice.

"Are we good?" asked Georgie, and I turned.

"Yeah, sorry. Got a little mesmerized by 'em."

"Are they moving by us?"

"Slowly but surely," I said in an instinctive whisper. "Good call comin' in here. You go on and hit the pharmacy. Since Lil and Danny are doin' the food thing, I'll focus on apocalypse essentials. Batteries, lights, portable radios, anything else I can think of."

She walked up to me and stared into my eyes. "Let's find a car and drive back, okay? In fact, might be best to get the car before we go to the gun shop."

I held up a finger. That means I had an idea.

I walked over to brickhead and knelt down, reaching for his pockets. "What are you doing?"

I looked up at Georgie and saw her face all scrunched up. I had to laugh. "I'm checkin' for keys."

"Oh!" she said. "Good idea."

I felt a lump in his left pocket, and pulled the jean pocket outward to slide my hand in. They were keys. I plucked them out and saw there was a Toyota key fob.

"I'm bettin' it's that red pickup out there," I said. "Get movin'. Now we can haul whatever we want."

We didn't hurry with the herd of deadheads working their way past us, but we didn't dawdle either, and I know my gun hand was twitching with every out-of-place noise I heard.

When all was said and done, we had about eight bags stuffed with shit to carry to the truck.

"That was exhilarating!" said Georgina. "I've never stolen anything before."

"I know," I said. "Feels like it, huh? Shit would go bad if nobody took it."

"I found something interesting back there. Sample packs of dicarba insulin. I first heard about it around 2010, but it was developed by a Monash University chemist. It was just in FDA approval the last I heard."

"What's special about it?" I asked.

"It survives heat for several years. It doesn't need refrigeration."

"How much did you get?"

"There were twenty packs. I took them all. Nobody's mentioned diabetes, but we still may encounter someone who could benefit from it."

I looked outside and said, "In a world like this one, somethin' like that could even serve as currency."

She didn't say anything. I looked at her. "What?"

"I wouldn't ever hold medicine hostage in a barter, Cole."

I thought about it for a sec. She was right. "That's a good point. I know you wouldn't."

The street was mostly empty now. The enormous horde had moved passed us, and only stragglers and draggers passed now. I keyed my radio, but still spoke low. "Danny? Lil?"

A second or two passed, and Danny came on. "Yeah, CB. What's up?"

"You know what Rode said about clusterin'?"

"You mean the zombies?"

"No, fuckin' peanuts."

"Peanut clusters?"

"Yeah, the zombies. Must've been a couple hundred passed us just now, headin' south."

"Y'all safe?"

"Yeah, inside a CVS. Got a bunch of bandages, meds, batteries, good stuff. Anyone there need any specific meds before we get outta here?"

"Hold on a sec."

I held on.

He came back on. "Lil says get some Pravastatin or Simvastatin. Any cholesterol stuff. I'm good, and so is everyone else."

"Just keep your eyes open, then."

"Thanks for the heads up. We're makin' a good haul, too. Got some good fishin' gear at the bait shop. We hit the Dollar General instead of the Publix. Easier to clear. Had to take out four of those nasty things."

"You both alright? We only had one in the pharmacy," I said.

"We're good," said Danny. "How long you gonna be?"

"We still gotta hit the gun shop, so maybe an hour, maybe less. Depends on whether the Toyota pickup in the parkin' lot starts up."

"Should we hang out?"

"No, y'all head back to the skiff if you want. Make a run back to the boat."

"Good call. Sounds like you'll have a good load, too. We'll do that."

"Be safe. Talk at ya later."

I clipped the radio back on my belt and went to the door, stepping around brickhead again. I pushed the door open slightly and leaned out.

The horde was completely out of view, and like a static-charged cloth, they seemed to have picked up every random deadhead along the way; the streets were clear, save for what I'd come to notice more and more; tufts of hair.

The hair, which I'm pretty sure was falling out of thousands of zombie heads, seemed to blow together and cling, making bigger and bigger balls. Almost everywhere you looked, they rolled down the streets like tumbleweeds in an old western movie.

The more I thought about it, the more disgusting it was.

I pushed it outta my head and grabbed four of the bags, threading my arm through the handles. "I'm gonna see if that Toyota will start."

"Don't you want to wait until you try it before taking that stuff?"

"This is what you call positive thinkin'," I said, pushing outside. I was relieved to see Georgie move to the door, pull out her pistol, and scan in all directions.

She was looking out for me, and it was becoming second nature. That made me feel better.

The pickup was parked right at the front curb, just about fifteen feet from the door. I hustled down the sidewalk and jumped off the curb next to the red truck.

Setting the bags in the bed, I decided not to use the remote, to avoid any double-chirps when it unlocked. I put the key in and unlocked it, then pulled the door open.

Once inside, I put the key into the ignition. When I turned it, the fuel gauge jumped to a half-tank, and all the dash lights came on bright. I didn't bother turning the motor. Toyotas were known to be dependable, and this one was maybe six, seven years old. That's infancy for a Toyota.

I got back out, leaving the door open, running for the pharmacy.

"Okay, good to go. Let's pack."

"That's great."

Together, we had the truck loaded up in under five minutes, leaving room for whatever we grabbed at the gun shop. When we were all done, we both sat in the extended cab and I looked over at her. "Wish us luck."

She smiled and wiped a straggling lock of hair away from her eyes. "Luck to us," she said.

Oh, I read a lot more into that than there probably was. I turned the key all the way.

I swear, the starter barely cranked when that motor fired and settled into a smooth idle.

"Thank you," I said to myself, then pulled the shifter down into reverse. I cranked the wheel and drove out the rear driveway, turning east onto Mar Walt Drive.

"Make your next left," said Georgie.

The street was clearly in a depressed neighborhood, with flat-roofed, cinderblock homes that looked to be in major disrepair. The grass was growing out of control everywhere, making the whole world look abandoned.

Beside CVS was a home for the developmentally disabled, and I couldn't help but wonder what kind of madhouse existed inside there.

Part of me asked the question, *what if they're immune? What if the innocence of not being in control of your own actions exempted them from this bug?*

Then I mentally slapped myself. I ain't that smart and should never start thinking above my pay grade.

We drove on. In a few more seconds, it became clear. The neighborhood, once past the few run-down residential homes, was a satellite of the Fort Walton Beach Medical Center. There were drug treatment centers, physical therapy businesses, and every other associated medical facility imaginable.

Now I was real glad the moving horde had picked up stragglers. It gave us what appeared to be a clear path from here.

"God, seeing a hospital," said Georgie. "Makes me feel guilty I can't help these people."

I reached down and patted her leg. "Maybe you'll help 'em by learnin' more about what changed 'em. Give it time."

She nodded and said, "Turn here, I think."

She was right. I turned and drove past a neuroscience center and some other specialty medical offices. Once that stuff was history, the neighborhood returned to run-down homes and dilapidated trailers, surrounded by junk cars.

We saw the occasional deadhead stumbling along, clearly having missed the earlier parade, but by the time they turned to see us, we were already gone.

We finally got past all the trailers and reached the T-intersection where Hospital Drive hit Lewis Turner Boulevard, and I saw a tattered sign standing in the parking lot of the gun shop. It professed its website to be rangerfirearms.com, and below that, the letters spelled out, "CCP   ASSES AVAILABLE."

Clearly a few letters had blown off at some point.

"Too small to have a gun range. Your existin' skills'll have to do," I said.

"I'm good enough," she said. "Let's get this over with. I'm ready to be back on that boat."

We pulled right up alongside the door that faced Hospital Drive and I cut the engine. We both got out, each carryin' only our handguns.

"How do you feel?" she asked.

"I feel fine," I said. "Let's get some ammo."

I walked up to the single door with bars across the window and tried it.

Locked.

"Damn," I said. "Oh, shit." I pointed to the sign, which couldn't have been any bigger. It read ENTER IN FRONT, with an arrow pointing toward the big boulevard.

Georgie shook her head and took off. I followed, but as she rounded the corner, she stopped so suddenly, I ran into her back. "Whoa!" I said. "What –"

I didn't need to finish my sentence. We both stared at the thing, our mouths hanging open.

The gator had to have been a 9-footer. It stood there, just outside the door to the firearms and mercantile store, its mouth open, and some sort of metal contraption curved around its neck and part of its head.

It didn't respond to us, but that didn't make me feel any better about getting closer. "What the fuck?" I asked.

"I second that. Think the owner's inside?"

"Not sure of the point otherwise," I said. "I'm gonna get closer."

"Cole," she said, her voice tinged with apprehension. "Maybe we should go somewhere else."

"Right now, nobody owns shit," I said. "Unless that thing is owned by the proprietor of this store, we got as much right as anyone else to stock up."

When I walked, Georgie came with me. We got to within ten feet or so. It wasn't tied up or chained that I could see.

My gun in hand I stayed back, but looked it over more carefully, now that my shock had worn off and I could take a moment. Whoever had built the armor plate over the gator's natural armor had taken time to do it. It looked like metal, but it had been painted almost an army green that blended with the gator's natural coloring.

The harness – 'cause that's what it was, pretty much – had been custom bent and welded, sitting atop its neck and head, with some sort of hinges, just six inches or so behind its eyes. A loop had been welded on top, where a chain was connected.

The chain was bunched up beside it, not secured or being held by anyone. There was a metal plate blocking the creature's vision, too, and I saw it had something to do with the hinged piece.

The main piece seemed to perfectly conform to the gator's shape, and it curved underneath the big bastard and appeared to be connected with something. A cotter pin, maybe, running through a hasp.

The piece had been finished off with dozens of what appeared to be razor-sharp spikes, giving the gator the look of a prehistoric dinosaur of sorts. Either that or an 80s punk chick wearing a collar.

Its mouth was unnaturally wide open, like those we'd seen walking.

The door behind it pushed open and we both jerked our guns up fast. Before the person came into view, we heard, "You ain't plannin' on killin' Chester here, are ya?"

I looked up to see the owner of the voice. He was a skinny white dude with long, straggly blond hair. He stumbled out the door of Ranger Firearms & Mercantile, wearing overalls over his shirtless chest.

He was smoking a cigarette as he held a four-foot-long rod with the tip bent into a hook. The man reached down and hooked it through a plate over the gator's eyes. Then he bent down and picked up a length of chain, wrapping it around his fist.

I shook my head. Little did I know, this wasn't the worst it would get.

Ω

CHAPTER FIFTEEN

I glanced at Georgie and held my arms up, one hand open palm out, the other with my gun pointing skyward. "Never considered hurtin' your gator, friend."

"I pull this and let go this chain and you're toast. Even if you shoot it, *friend*, you won't kill it," he sneered.

"You don't know what I know about gators," I said. "I'm Cole Baxter and this is Georgina Lake."

"I don't give a rat's patootie who ya are," he said. "Neither does Chester and neither does Billie Jo."

I looked around. "Who's Billie Jo?"

The door pushed open fast and wide, knocking into the man who was taunting us. He lost his balance and took a small jump off the porch, landing in the gravel to the right of the open door.

Now that he was on the ground, I could see he was maybe five-feet-five-inches tall. Goddamned Napoleon complexes. I hate that shit, and never saw the point. I guess that's because I'm well over six feet tall.

"Garland, who you talkin' to?" the girl asked, then lifted her head to look me square in the eyes. "Oh," she said. "I see. Who are you, sweetie?" Her voice had gone sultry. She looked directly at me. She never looked at or acknowledged Georgina at all.

Georgie stepped forward, holsterin' her gun. "Like he told your friend, he's Cole Baxter, and I'm Georgina

Lake.   Garland, Billie Jo, we came here to get some ammunition. I'm sure there's plenty to go around."

When the gun fired and the dirt from the parkin' lot blew toward us, pepperin' our legs and arms with rock fragments and dirt, I realized I didn't even notice she'd been holdin' a gun.

When I actually looked down and saw the gun, I was amazed I'd missed it. It was some kinda long-barreled revolver. She never raised her hand to fire it at us, which was somehow worse than if she had. Just pointin' it in our general direction, she could've hit either one of us in the leg, messin' us up good.

Billie Jo laughed hard, but now her eyes were on us, and the gun *was* raised.

I raised both my hands toward her, palms out. "The other store's gone, or we'd head back there. We don't wanna cause any trouble."

"You're here, ain't ya?" she sneered.

The woman was probably twenty-four or twenty-five, thin with flamin' red hair tied in a ponytail. She wore a white tank top with the word BITCH emblazoned on it in some kinda sequins, and I could readily tell she didn't have a bra on.

Her shorts were the color of an orange Dreamsicle, and they were real short, letting her ass cheeks hang out. Her shoes were bright blue high-tops.

To be fair and perfectly honest, she *was* cute, but her bangs were cut real short and straight across her forehead, and that was my first indication of a nutso chick. That's why I've always called 'em *crazy bangs.*

"Gimme that rod, Garland," she said, chewing what had to be a huge wad of gum. Her southern accent was easily as strong as Garland's, even through the mouthful.

The man gave it to her after a brief hesitation. She hooked the end through the receivin' hole on the eye plate.

"I pull this, and Chester sees you. I think he can get to you faster than you can find the sweet spot to kill him."

Lookin' at the contraption on the gator's head, I knew she was right. It looked like whoever'd designed the armor plate had left a wedge of metal that extended down between the gator's eyes. Even if the plate that blinded it was pivoted up – like she was threatenin' to do – I wouldn't be able to put a bullet under the plate.

"You're right. Y'all got the upper hand. What I'm strugglin' with right now is why you'd sic your gator on us at all. We're not here to mess with anyone. Just need some ammo. Like I said, the gun shop farther south's burned out." I pointed toward the Gulf of Mexico.

"Where y'all headin' anyways?" Garland asked.

"Don't matter where they're headin' 'cause they ain't goin' nowhere once I pull this rod." Billie Jo smiled at us and smacked her gum. Just as I was about to make an appeal to her, she yanked the steel rod.

The blinders pivoted up and that gator was up on its legs full height, and pullin' hard toward us.

We both staggered back about three steps as Garland two-fisted the chain, leanin' back and holdin' onto the porch railin'

"Billie Jo, put it back down!" he shouted.

The gator pulled to the end of the eight-foot chain now, its feet in the gravel and kickin' plenty of it behind it as it struggled against its restraint. We moved back some more.

"You're no fun!" she said, takin' two steps forward and pushin' the rod downward. The blinders dropped back into place and she unhooked the rod as the alligator settled back down.

I wanted to kill this crazy bitch for that bullshit stunt, but the gun still dangled at the end of her hand and somethin' in her eyes warned me to play nice. At least for the moment. I'd be keepin' my eye on her, though, that was for damn sure. This self-proclaimed bitch was totally off her rocker.

I steeled my nerves and acted like her little stunt hadn't rankled me. In fact, I was playin' the cool cucumber, even though I was sweatin' like a pickle just out of the jar.

"Thanks," I said, walkin' forward, my hand extended toward Garland. He walked toward us, his hand out to meet mine.

I shook it, and immediately observed his grip was like a wilted celery stalk. "Nice to meet you, Garland."

I squeezed extra hard, like my grip was a goddamned juicer. I let go after three pumps.

"What did you say your names are?" he asked, shakin' his hand as he tried to get the blood back in it.

"I'm Cole and this here's Georgina. She's a surgeon, and I used to run Baxter's Airboat Tours & Gator Park."

Georgina stepped forward, holdin' out her hand to Garland. To his credit, Garland shook it, but not before glancin' back at Billie Jo, who still had her hand off the gator's blinder rod.

"Nice to meet you," said Georgie.

Billie Jo jumped off the side of the porch, and I figured it was to avoid bein' anywhere near Chester's gapin' mouthful of teeth. She bounced toward us.

When she reached us, she stood beside Garland, looked Georgie up and down, then said, "You are sure pretty." Her words and her tone didn't match one bit.

"Thank you," said Georgina, holdin' out her hand to Billie Jo.

"No, I'm a hugger," said Billie Jo, movin' in and wrappin' her long arms around Georgina. She put her mouth beside Georgie's ear and whispered somethin' I couldn't hear.

"It's deodorant," said Georgina, with a strange look on her face. Then she added, "And no, of course not. I'm with Cole."

"I see why," said Billie Jo, once more lookin' me up and down, from head to toe. "He's a big boy, and handsome."

"Where y'all from?" I asked.

"Come here from Destin."

"You friends before?" I asked.

"Me and Billie Jo here? Nope. Met her while I was wranglin' Chester here."

"Where'd you get him at?" I asked.

"Fudpuckers," he said. "Heard of it?"

I had. *Fudpuckers* was the highly advanced version of Baxter's, with full shows, a pettin' zoo, restaurant, airboat tours and pictures with gators. I'd seen their tee shirts for years.

"Yeah, they have a couple of the albinos," I said.

"Too small, or that's what I'd have," said Garland. They was all changed, all crazy-like. Tossed a big beach towel at one and settled it right down. Once I figured out they go quiet when you cover their eyes, I got this idea. I'm a welder/fabricator by trade."

"May I?" I asked, pointin' at Chester.

As Billie Jo smucked her gum, fingered her gun, and stared at Georgina, Garland said, "Sure, have a gander."

I glanced back at Georgie, who smiled and nodded. She said, "Billie Jo, what kind of ammunition is left inside?"

"It was locked and barred before we got here," she said. "So, lots. We ain't worked a deal out with you yet, though."

I checked out of that conversation and joined Garland beside Chester. When I got right up beside the gator, I saw how clean and perfect the welds were. The quality was clear even under the coat of paint.

I knelt down, and he joined me. "Damned nice job, man," I said. "I can weld, but my skills are mainly limited to motors of all kinds. I tend to stick the rods and make ugly work."

"Amateur mistake, easy to learn past," said Garland. "Built this one for protection. People see a man with a gator on a leash, and they tend to take an earlier turn outta my way."

"Y'all headed anywhere in particular?" I asked.

Garland shook his head. He had six piercins' in his left ear and another ten or so in his right. A stud ran through his nose and another in his chin, and in each eyebrow he had four silver bars, or pins, or whatever the hell they call 'em.

It was all topped off by a scraggly mustache that didn't quite connect to his billygoat chin beard. I forced myself not to study the overall picture or stare at the individual parts.

"Not goin' anywhere," he said. "We're just havin' fun, takin' all the free shit. Never been a time I could afford anything I wanted, even workin' hard. Hell, I've already wrecked a Lamborghini, a Porsche, and a Vette since I hooked up with Billie Jo. Just for fun!"

I laughed, but inside I was cursin' my luck. I wanted to get the shit and get out, but Garland and Billie Jo stood in our way. I wouldn't have cared so much if they'd seemed rational, but I felt like I was dealin' with the main characters from that movie, *Natural Born Killers.*

"Look, Garland. We're usin' a boat to get as far west as we can. Right now, there are seven of us, and we're headin' for Lebanon, Kansas."

"Where the fuckin' towelheads live?"

I had to fight an eye roll. "No, Kansas. It's called Lebanon, but it's here in the USA."

"Got room for us?"

The goddamned question I prayed he didn't ask. I decided to try and play his woman against him. "Hold on," I said.

Walking over to where Georgina and Billie Jo stood talking, I prepared my reverse psychology.

"Billie Jo," I said, "you and Garland should come with us. We're headin' to Kansas to prepare for a fight with the Indian."

"A fight?" asked the young woman, her voice rising two octaves. "What Indian?"

"Hell, I wanna kill me some injuns!" cackled Garland.

Dang. I didn't expect either of 'em to look so excited, and now I felt like a jackass. Georgina caught my eye and furrowed her brow.

"Climbing Fox Wattana," I almost sighed. "He claims he started this shit with the black rain, a curse or somethin'. Anyway, I understand if you don't wanna come. We're puttin' together an army and it's gonna be hard work –"

"Hell, yes we'll come," she said. "I wouldn't mind hangin' out with you gorgeous hunk of man meat. Shoot, maybe I'll just take a turn with ya, Garland won't mind." She eyed me up and down, and just a bit sideways. I felt like turnin' around, 'cause her eyes were square on my crotch.

"Did I make it clear that we're together?" asked Georgina, her eyes flashing at Billie Jo. "Plus, there are several other people with us who need to decide whether it's alright. I know Cole means well, but they all have a say, so I'd recommend being on your best behavior if we get that far."

I gritted my teeth at that, but kinda turned away so Georgie wouldn't think I was judgin' her. She said what I was thinkin'.

Billy Jo took a deep breath and let out a long, moanin' sigh. When she finally mumbled, "Come on inside. They got tons of stuff," I was relieved, big time. Until she followed with, "This is my *only* behavior, girly. *Real*."

I saw Georgie wanted to counter that, but wisely, she said nothin' in return. She saw just how unstable the girl was as well. Her jaw muscles were workin' though, because she was grindin' her teeth.

"Don't mind Chester," said Garland, as we mounted the porch behind the gator.

I looked down again, analyzin' the design. "Why doesn't he go after y'all when you take off the blinders?"

"'Cause we still block his side vision, plus if there's nobody standin' in front of him, we hang rotten meat a couple inches away from his mouth to get him walkin'. That keeps him from lookin' behind him, too. See it there?" He pointed.

I followed his finger and I'm still not sure how I missed it. There was a bent steel rod with an apple-sized chunk of rotted beef or somethin', run through with a large, chrome hook. The chunk of meat was stuffed into a square compartment welded to the side of the gator's harness. I saw a cylindrical tube where the end of the rod could be inserted to dangle the meat in front of the gator's mouth.

I shook my head in wonder and we all went inside.

They'd already begun ransackin' the place, so not all the handguns were still in the front case. I looked to my right and saw another four cases, each containing roughly 90 guns or more.

They could have 'em. We were there for ammo, holsters, and other accessories.

"Hey, Garland. You and Billie Jo come across any silencers?" I woulda asked for suppressors, but I didn't want to have to explain.

Billie Jo heard me say her name and she stopped and smiled at me, doin' somethin' with her eyebrows that I guess was supposed to be sexy. "You like it quiet, do ya?"

Her voice was soft, but if I had to add a description to that, I'd say it was menacin'. Somethin' in her tone said she was about one stoplight away from crazytown.

"Matter-of-fact, there's about twelve of 'em in that case. For all calibers."

"We could use a few of 'em," I said. "If you ain't put dibs on 'em yet."

The truth is, if they stood in our way one too many times, I was prepared to put a hurtin' on both of 'em if I got the chance. It might not be in my nature, but I can only get pushed so far before decorum gets shoved aside, too.

"We'll split 'em," said Garland. "Right, Billie Jo?"

"They should have to trade us," she said.

"Trade for what?" asked Georgie.

With a smack of her gum, Billie Jo raised that long barrel up, pointin' it right at Georgie. She closed one eye.

I held my breath as my heart slammed in my ears.

"A ride on your boat," she said, smackin' her gum and lowerin' the barrel again with a girlish laugh, tinged with evil.

"What the hell is your problem?" I yelled. "You point that fuckin' barrel at her or me one more time, and somebody here's gonna die."

"I was just playin', stupid," she said.

I let out my breath and went to Georgie, puttin' my arm around her. Her breath was comin' fast, but she was calmin' down.

"She's fine," said Garland. "Billie Jo wouldn't hurt her. Anyway, so yeah. We'll go with y'all."

"We're not even sure it's our final destination," said Georgie, her voice flat. She pulled away from me, and I saw her hand relax near her holster. "Plus, the boat's full. Nowhere else to sleep."

"Why ain't y'all just drivin' anyway?" asked Billie Jo.

I glanced over at Georgie, who wasn't lookin' at me, but was shakin' her head back and forth. I read her message: *short answers.*

Before I could figure out somethin' to say that wouldn't piss Georgie off, she spoke up. "We're just staying offshore to minimize contact with those … things. And like I said, we might not go to Kansas at all. I suppose we're really just biding our time until the government gets control of this problem."

"That ain't true," said Garland. "When we were outside, Cole here told me y'all were headin' there for sure."

"It's a plan under development," I said. "Subject to changin' on short notice. Situation kinda demands flexibility."

"Ain't no government I seen," said Billie Jo. "No planes, no helicopters. Nobody gunnin' them zombies down from the sky."

Garland nodded. "Damned straight. Whatcha say, Billie Jo? Wanna join up with these folks in *Lebanon, Kansas*? They seem nice enough." He looked between me and Georgie, then tapped his temple with his index finger. "And don't worry. I know how to make a fine first impression."

248

I don't think Billie Jo caught any of it. "Can Chester come?" she asked, looking directly at Georgina. "I wanna bring Chester. He'd like to see more of you with his blinders off, Miss Priss."

Georgina's jaw was set and I could see she was still grindin' her teeth. "You were just pointing a loaded firearm at my head less than three minutes ago," she said, her voice icy.

My ire was increasin' with each dig directed at Georgie, but I talked myself down each time. I also didn't want to tell 'em the gator they were walkin' around was likely a female. She was a big girl, at right around 9 feet, but her body was narrower than a male that size. So was her snout. They just seemed too batshit crazy to take news of that kind very well.

"I'm afraid we've got a kid on the boat," I said. "And while I trust Chester here just fine, I'm not sure about Liam. He might dance with danger if he sees her."

"Her?" Garland and Billie Jo said in unison.

I fucked up. I didn't wanna get into it. "Uh, him. Sorry."

"That's what I thought," said Garland. "Okay, I suppose we can pick up another gator somewhere. I'll take the harness."

Right then, my radio crackled, and Danny's voice sounded. He said, "How are you makin' out, CB? Kansas ain't gonna come to us."

I cringed and closed my eyes, hopin' upon hope that neither one understood him.

"Thought you said your plans were subject to change," said Billie Jo, twirlin' a revolver on her finger as she walked toward me.

I hoped it wasn't loaded, because her finger was sure to be pushin' on that trigger the way she was handlin' it.

"They are. At the moment, our group is potentially headin' to Kansas. Look, no offense," I said. "But just because the world's gone to shit doesn't mean we're all on the same team. Me and Georgie are lookin' out for our own, just like you are."

"Is it pretty there?" asked Billie Jo.

I was startin' to wonder if she had a whole lot of the A-D-D goin' on.

"If you prefer nothin' but farmland for miles around and you like sippin' iced tea instead of beer or whisky," I said. "I spent three days there once and it felt like three weeks."

Georgina tried backin' me up again. She softened her voice and spoke directly to Billie Jo. I think we'd both figured out she was the puppetmaster here.

"Like Cole said, Kansas is where we intend to go, but if something presents itself along the way, we may give up on the idea and settle in somewhere else.

"Plus," she continued, "Kansas could just be a way point. It's right in the middle of the country, so we thought if we got there and the plans to confront the Indian fell through, we could choose another destination then."

It seemed like a lot of words for the two it was directed at to comprehend. Especially when I knew Georgie really just wanted to scream, *My daughter's on that boat, and you'll never even see it, much less step foot on it you crazy bitch!*

"Hmm," the strange girl said, a strange smile on her face to match. Then Billie Jo reached into her pocket and pulled out a piece of Bazooka bubblegum. She unwrapped it, readin' the cartoon on the inside of the wrapper as she popped the gum in her mouth, addin' it to the wad she was already chewin'.

A second later, she tossed her head back and laughed so hard I thought she might have a stroke. "Y'all won't believe this! Listen to this joke!"

"Billie Jo, we really have to be on –"

"This one guy says to the other one, 'Joe, what in your opinion is the height of stupidity?', and the other guy, who I guess is Joe, says, 'I don't know, how tall are you?' That's real funny, right?"

Right then, Garland started laughin' so hard I thought his head might explode. Billie Jo joined him, and before long, I was starin' at Georgie's expression.

Right then, I felt like me and Georgie were trapped in a cage full of monkeys. Two crazies, laughin' like they were at the Redneck Comedy Stand-Up Hour, and poor Georgina Lake, M.D., starin' at 'em, wonderin' how she got there. I couldn't take it. I busted out laughin', and when Georgie caught my eye, she let loose, too.

Now we were all bustin' our guts, and I'm sure the others thought we were just as entertained by Bazooka Joe as they were.

An idea struck me then. It came fast, and I knew it might be our only chance. While his eyes were closed, tears runnin' down his cheeks, I ran toward him, takin' full advantage of my long strides.

My gun was already in my hand and raised high when he opened his eyes and said, "What the fu –"

I clobbered Garland but good, bringin' the grip right down on the back of his head. He dropped like a sack of taters.

Georgie had stopped laughin' just a second before Billie Jo, and when I looked up from Garland's motionless body, Dr. Lake had her gun pointed at the girl's head, her left hand supportin' her wrist, and her hand steady as steel.

"Move and it'll be the last thing you do," she growled, in a tone I'd never heard from her before.

Billie Jo never stopped chewin' her gum. Lookin' between Georgie and me, she said, "Would y'all look at that. You beat me to it by half a second. I was gonna shoot your girl here," she said, flippin' her chin toward Georgie.

"I think you know you're lucky you didn't," I said.

She sighed, overdramatically. "Oh well, Garland better be all right. And mark my words, y'all are gonna pay for this."

Her voice was steady and soft, way more controlled than I expected, but the menace was still under the surface – and I don't just mean in the words she spoke.

"He'll be fine," I said. "But y'all need to figure your shit out. If you wanna make it in this world, you're gonna need more friends."

"It's a zombie apocalypse, asshole!" she screamed, and before I knew it, Georgina hauled her fist back and punched the girl in the face, knockin' her sideways into a display table. By the time Billie Jo looked back up at her, Georgina had the gun barrel in her face.

"Jesus shit," mumbled the girl, layin' on her side, rubbin' her red face with her hand.

Georgina Lake wasn't done. "We're here to get what we need and move on, and there's plenty for everyone. Cole, I've got her covered. You find something to tie her up with, and let's get what we came for. I want to get back and leave these two behind."

I ran in the back room and found some boxes bound with nylon twine. Usin' a box cutter to slice off four good lengths, I carried 'em out front. "This'll do it," I said.

"Get down on your knees, slowly," said Georgina. The girl put her hands behind her head and followed her instructions. Judgin' from her expertise at assumin' the proper position, I figured she'd done it a time or two for the cops.

I handed Georgina the twine, and she tied the girl's wrists together behind her back.

I knelt beside Garland and slid his boots together. Wrappin' the twine around 'em three times, I tied a helluva knot. It was tight enough that it crimped his boots, so he wouldn't be able to just slide 'em off.

When I stood, I said, "That'll keep him from chasin' us if he wakes up before we're out of the parkin' lot."

"What about me?" asked crazy girl. She was still on her knees and Georgie was tyin' her bare ankles together just above her weird blue hightops. I took note that she wasn't goin' easy on the girl. The twine dug into her skin, it was so tight.

I was seein' all kinds of Georgie I hadn't before. Goddamned mama bear, for sure.

I said, "After Garland wakes up and falls down once or twice, he'll figure out why, untie his feet, and free you," I said. "I didn't wanna do any of this, but y'all made it an us or you proposition."

"You ain't seen the last of us," she taunted.

The second Georgie finished tyin' her and stepped back, she tried pullin' out of the bonds – which I fully expected her to.

"Garland!" she yelled. "Garland, wake up!

I ran over and slapped my hand over her mouth. "You wake him up, we gotta put him back to sleep, so shut your ass up and we'll be outta here that much sooner," I said, tryin' to keep my voice low. "Georgie, would you grab me one of those holster belts?" Billie Jo tried to bite my hand, but I stiffened it to make sure she couldn't. With her, it wasn't just the zombie virus I worried about.

Georgina brought back one of the belts made to appeal to women; it was a light blue belt with a silver buckle. I had Georgie position it, then I yanked my hand away.

"Garland –" she started, but we had the belt over her mouth in a split-second, silencin' her.

I went to Garland and took his gun from his holster. It was a Glock 22 with one in the chamber.

There were lots of guns in the store, but they weren't loaded, and it would take a bit for him to wake up, recover, untie himself, realize his gun was gone, and get another to load.

"9mm, .45, .22 and 12-gauge ammo for now."

We got to work while Billie Jo struggled to free herself between muffled screams. There were little plastic shoppin' baskets, and we both grabbed one and got loadin'.

I ran out to stock the shit in the truck while Georgina stayed inside, makin' sure everything was status quo. We did that three times. In the ten minutes it took, Garland was still conked out, and the crazy bitch hadn't made any headway with her bonds as of yet. We were done.

At the door, I said, "He'll wake up in a few, and untie you. Next time try playin' nice. You'll get farther."

Muffled anger spewing out behind us, we stepped around Chester the Zombie Gator and headed for the truck.

$$\Omega$$

CHAPTER SIXTEEN

I spun gravel outta that parkin' lot as I floored the Toyota and bounced onto the street. Georgina held on for all she was worth when I cranked it left on Beal again.

"Watch for that horde," she said, her voice jigglin' with the bouncin' of the pickup. Apparently, our CVS employee didn't fuckin' realize he needed new shocks.

"Yeah, I thought about that. I hope we can skirt around 'em."

"Oh, shit. They're right up there, about a quarter mile."

"That's them?" I asked, squintin'. After a moment, the enormous herd of dead humanity came into the proper perspective in my brain. For a moment, it had just looked confusin', like one of those magic eye posters from a few years back. Now I could see every shiftin' body, as well as the human debris they were leavin' in a macabre trail behind them; rotted, severed arms, hands and always the blowin' tufts of hair.

"Hell, you're right," I said. "Must be a thousand of 'em."

"Left here!" she said.

I cranked it left and swung the Toyota onto a street called Fetting Avenue and floored it. There were a few dead-eyed people along the sides of the road, but by the time their ink-black brains realized there was a noise, we were already past 'em. I figured lots of 'em hooked up with the southbound horde.

"Get on the radio, would you, Georgie? See where they are."

Georgina Lake keyed the radio. "Lilly? Danny? Are you there?"

"Mom!" It was Roxy's voice.

"Yes, baby!" said Georgie. "Is everything okay?"

"Yes, but Danny and Lilly have already made two runs to the boat with the skiff. They're waiting at the dock for you now. Where are you?"

"We had a little trouble," said Georgie. "We're driving back down now. Had to go a little farther than we hoped."

"Did you get what you went for?"

"Yes. We got it. How long, Cole?"

"We'll be back at the dock in ten minutes if we can get past that horde," I said.

"Ten minutes, sweetheart," said Georgina.

"I caught that," came Danny's voice. "Y'all okay?"

I held out my hand and Georgie gave me the radio. "Hey, Danny."

"CB. All good?" He sounded winded.

"That horde is huge," I said. "And they're probably pickin' up more stragglers along the way, so they might be fillin' out from the front. That means they may get to you faster than we do. Just keep an eye out to the north."

"Don't worry about me sleepin' on the job, man," he said. "Put on some steam, though. We still need to find a place to get fueled up."

I cranked it right on Hazel Road, but that soon ran out and I had another choice to make. "Damn! Wish I had a GPS in this damned thing!"

We were stopped at the T-intersection at Yancy Street. To our left, it was a dead end, just two blocks up.

To the right, we could see the massive horde flowin' down Beal. I looked straight ahead to where Hazel continued south just as Georgie pointed.

We didn't have a choice. I drove across Yancy, drivin' as fast as I dared to now. In under a minute, we hit another T-intersection at Clifford Street. I looked to my right and saw the very first rotters comin' down Beal.

"Look! They're just gettin' there now. We might be able to beat 'em."

"Are you sure?" Georgie's voice gave away that she wasn't sure I was right. "Can we go further?"

"Hell if I know," I admitted. "Fuck it." I cranked it left on Clifford and immediately came to another north-south street called Trowbridge. I turned right and floored it.

"When we dead end again, we'll head over," I said. Sure enough, in seconds, we hit Lewis Street, and I saw no other options to continue south. "It's now or never," I said. I turned right.

Beal was clear. Feelin' encouraged, I pressed the Toyota pickup to its limits. When I got to the corner of Lewis and Beal, I looked right, seein' the horde a block back.

"Yeah!" I screamed, turnin' left. In minutes, I was back on Memorial Parkway, then back on Highway 98. I turned left and made my way back to the dock.

To my surprise, the Sea Ray was docked along the end. Everyone was out of the boat, and they were moving supplies onto the dock.

"What the hell are they doin'?" I asked.

"Maybe something's wrong with the boat?" said Georgie, a question in her voice.

Danny saw us and waved. He then pointed at a boat I couldn't see from where we were and gave a thumbs-up.

I drove as far out onto the dock as I could, then stopped and put the pickup in park.

"I think we got a new ride," I said. "I'm bettin' it's got more beds."

"I *was* feeling a little guilty," said Georgie, grabbing a bag of ammo from the back of the pickup. "Especially since Danny joined us."

"Hold on. They have dock carts." I walked over and upended a big, green plastic cart. The mold-covered ice chest that had been inside slid onto the dock.

Rolling it back to the Toyota, we began filling it with ammo and the things we'd gotten from CVS.

"This should only take a couple runs," I said. "Let's go see this new ride."

Ω

I swear the boat was more of a ship. I whistled when I saw it floating there, the huge radar thingy on the top spinnin', the deck so far above the dock that I couldn't even see it.

"Is that a fuckin' hotel or a boat?" I asked.

"Glad y'all made it," said Danny. "Looks like a good haul."

"Got what we went for, plus a little more from the drug store," I said. "What the hell is this beast?"

"This, my friend," said Danny, proudly, "is a Dreamliner 26. Four guest cabins, plus crew cabins, and a flying bridge, which I know you love."

Georgie and I stood starin' up at the nautical behemoth. "How's the fuel? Can you start it?" I quickly realized I wasn't givin' him time to answer anything.

"Funny you should ask," said Danny. "Harbormaster's office is right over there, and they had a key for it. Turns out for the big boats they do that in case of emergency and they have to move it without the owner around."

"Fuel?"

"Full," said Danny. "Topped off and ready to roll."

"Ready to float!" yelled Liam. I looked up to see him standing on the bow, wavin'.

"What's up, kid?" I asked.

"I'm sleeping in the crew cabin!" he said, then ran off.

I whistled and turned back to Danny. "*Crew cabin*? We may not want to get off this thing. What's the range?"

"You're gonna shit."

"Try me. But I didn't get adult diapers from CVS, so if you're serious." I turned. "Did we, Georgie?"

"Maybe in a few years," she said. "Not now."

"1,400 nautical miles," he said. "We've made our last stop for fuel 'til we get to where we're going."

"Good," I said. "We won't have to hug the coast if we don't want to. Great job, y'all."

Lilly walked up. "This crap isn't gonna load itself, so enough with the chit-chat."

"You warm the cockles of my heart, sis," I said.

"Look!" said Terry, who I hadn't noticed. He was standin' north of us in the center of the dock, pointin'.

"That the goddamned horde you mentioned?" asked Danny.

"Yes," Georgina almost whispered. "Oh, my God. They're walking right into the water."

She was right. Though they were probably about a quarter mile away, every face was pointed directly at us. Unable to look away from their food source, they stumbled over the foot-high curb and tumbled into the riprap at the base of the seawall.

It was almost sick, watchin' things shaped like humans walkin' off the edge like a bunch of lemmings. One after the other they tripped and plummeted, some hittin' their heads on the rocks and layin' still; others managin' to crawl back to their feet, only to get washed away by the poundin' surf, startin' to kick up from some distant storm we had no way of knowin' about.

"Shit, we need to hurry. We also got sweet Billie Jo and the ever-handsome Garland, along with their pet zombiegator Chester to worry about," I said. "I'm sure he's awake and pissed off by now."

"The gator?" asked Danny.

I shook my head. "Garland. Had to knock him out to get our ammo and suppressors."

"I want details."

"Once we're safe, you got it."

Ω

With the wind pickin' up, takin' that monster off the dock was a challenge. As Danny said, it was just over 85 feet long and had just short of a 22-foot beam. It was easily 10 feet wider than any other boat I'd driven before.

We managed to master the thrusters, and before we knew it, we were cruisin' west, keepin' a mile offshore.

Just before castin' off, and right after pickin' our sleepin' cabins, which were about as luxurious as any high-end hotel I've ever seen pictures of, we all went up to the flybridge. When I walked up there, I whistled.

"You're shittin' me," I said. "This is like drivin' a beachfront, rooftop bar around."

The floor was built with teak slats, and just behind the helm, which had an enormous GPS screen, was a three-seater bar. Everything was white, which was a little prissy for me, but I still hoped we didn't have any blood sprayin' across the upholstery anytime soon.

Across from the bar, with plenty of walk-around room, was a sofa that would handle ten people without crammin' together.

Right off that sofa was a dinin' table that seated seven more people in chairs, with the rest sittin' on the sofa.

You get the drift. Seatin' for 20 people, not includin' the boat's captain.

With the weather makin' the water rough, we'd held our speed down to 20 knots. It was just that visibility got more limited as the storm drew closer, and while I knew the draft of the boat was just over six feet, I didn't know the waters and how fast the depth changed if you drifted outside the marked channels.

Everyone joined us up top while Georgie and I recounted our experience in the gun store with Garland, Billie Jo, and Chester. We covered everything, from the massive horde, to the spiked harness Garland had built for the gator, how Billy Jo had threatened to shoot Georgie, have sex with me, all of it.

When we were done, they all just shook their heads. For the moment, our goal was to leave the bad behind and move on to the unknown.

Ω

We'd been drivin' two hours, and as near as I could figure, we were just off the coast of Gulf Shores, Alabama. That's when we cut the engine, dropped anchor, and heard the sound.

Danny ran up first.

"CB, we got company."

"I heard it," I said. "Just gettin' these." I held up the binoculars, then put them to my eyes to focus on the dot bouncin' along the water. It was a boat, just visible off our port side, silhouetted on the horizon.

"Looks like a cigarette boat," I said. "Lilly calls 'em dick boats. Compensation, she says, for somethin' else that's lackin'."

"Either way, it's company, and they'll be here soon," said Danny. "Gimme." He held out his hand. I handed the binoculars off.

"Closer now. Looks like a guy and a girl. Maybe your friends from Fort Walton?"

"Goddamn, I hope not," I said. "No doubt they'll be loaded for bear."

"I can't take you anywhere," said Danny.

"You can say that again," said Lilly, trailed by Georgina, Roxy, and Terry. They all settled into the seats except for Georgina, who had a bottle of Windex and a roll of paper towels in her hands. She immediately started wipin' down the brass and anything not upholstered.

"Y'all see that boat coming?" asked Lilly.

"The jury's still out, but we're thinkin' it's my friends from the gun store."

"That's not good," said Georgie, who put down the cleanin' supplies. "Everyone, grab a weapon. Preferably a rifle."

Roxy gawked at her mother. "Mom! Are you saying we should shoot them?"

"Not if we can help it," she said. "But you haven't met them."

"It's really bouncin' now," said Danny. He lowered the glasses. "They're hittin' the waves like people who don't know how to drive a boat."

I turned, and now I could see the boat pretty clearly.

262

"The guy wearin' overalls?" I asked. "And the girl. She wearin' a tank top with the word BITCH on it in shiny letters?"

"Bingo," said Danny.

"Georgina's right," I said. "Arm up, if only to drive 'em away."

Georgina sighed. "They're resourceful. You have to give them that."

We'd brought several long guns up to the flybridge, so everyone now had one in hand. Liam was on the television downstairs, 'cause there was an Xbox, and he took to it like a bee to honey.

Playin' Xbox in a world of zombies. Nuts.

"Hey, the girl's standin' up and he's still haulin' ass! Wait. What the fuck? She just dropped!"

"Dropped where?" I asked. "Gimme those."

He gave me the binoculars. Now I could see Garland very clearly, standin' at the helm. Danny was right; I didn't see Billie Jo at all.

Suddenly a huge wave formed just off their port side. "He better slow that thing down!" I said. But I could see Garland was focused on what was happenin' directly behind him, inside the boat. He didn't even see the swell comin'.

"They take that wave broadside, they're fucked!" I said. I leaned on my horn. It blared across the Gulf of Mexico, but I didn't know how it would help. I just felt like I had to do somethin'.

Had Garland let off the throttle, I think they would've made it. But if anything, it appeared he even accelerated. I turned just as the wave reached it. Just as I put the binoculars to my eyes again, the wave slammed into the Formula and it went airborne.

As the big outboard whined at full RPM, and the cigarette boat rolled to starboard, the inside of the boat came into view; that goddamned gator was there, and a dark red color coated the inside of the deck. I just caught a glimpse of Billie Jo, slidin' across the deck with Chester.

That explained the blood.

Next thing we knew, the boat was upside down.

"Jesus!" shouted Lilly. "CB, pull anchor. We gotta help them!"

"Help 'em?" I shouted. "I'm pretty sure they'd have killed me and Georgina."

"We're not them, and we never will be," she said. "Pull the anchor!"

"Goddamnit, Lilly!" I shouted, but I did what she said.

When the anchor was seated, I let Danny motor us over to where the boat was. The storm had now darkened the skies above us, and the waves were kickin' up beyond what I was comfortable with.

We got to the overturned boat just as the rain began peltin' the boat with huge drops.

I ran out to the stern of the Dreamliner. There were some controls I wasn't familiar with, so I looked 'em over and started fuckin' with 'em.

The first switch I found lowered a set of steps that had been straight up, like a ladder. When it seated at the bottom of its travel, it became an elevated dive platform with a little teak landin' at the top.

"This'll work!" I shouted, as Lilly stood behind me.

"I saw a boat hook back there," she said, runnin' off. A couple of seconds later, she was back, standin' beside me. I looked behind me and saw Roxy, Terry, and Georgie, all with rifles in hand.

I was glad they took me seriously, even with those two in the water. I didn't have any doubt that if Garland had a gun in his pants when he went into the drink, that he'd pull it out and try to fire on us.

"There's someone!" shouted Lilly, pointin'. "It's the guy!"

"Something's floating just ten yards or so behind him!" called Georgina.

"Yell at Danny to throw it in reverse!" I called. I don't know who relayed the message, but in thirty seconds, Danny was plowin' backwards.

The motor cut out just as we drew to within fifteen feet of the sinkin' boat.

The big Dreamliner's momentum carried us right up to Garland, who was too busy splashin' and screamin' to even think about a gun. "Swim toward us!" I shouted.

As though he wasn't even aware we were there, he looked up, then started paddlin' frantically toward us. I extended the boat hook and caught the shoulder strap of his overalls.

Pullin' with all my might, I dragged him from the water to the rear step. He threw his tired arms on the deck and Lilly reached down to grab his arms as I dropped the boat hook and hurried over to help her.

We got him out of the water, and he flopped over on his back where he sputtered out saltwater and coughed like a smoker with black lung disease.

"Help … Billie Jo!" he managed.

I was already searchin' the water for her. Suddenly, somethin' surfaced five feet from the rear deck.

It was fuckin' Chester. The spiked collar jutted from the water, and his goddamned toothy mouth was still wide open. The hinged, metal plate was down over his eyes, so I didn't have a clear shot. I raised the 30.06 and fired anyway.

The first shot rang off the steel harness, and that's when I got worried about a ricochet. "Bring me a shotgun!" I yelled and heard feet across the deck. A few seconds later, Terry stood behind me. "Here!" he shouted.

Now the rain was pourin' down. "Keep a gun on him!" I yelled, because Garland was sittin' up, and I didn't trust him as far as I could throw his ass.

"There!" shouted Georgina. "She's right there!"

I was focused on the gator. I raised the shotgun just as it managed to bump the rear of the boat with its snout. I aimed right at its nose and fired.

Black-red juice flooded into the water as its jaws blew apart. The tail started whippin' back and forth, so I raised the barrel and fired twice more at his legs, then two more shots at its tail, which provided all its forward momentum.

With a hiss that cut off midstream, it sank from view.

"Okay, where is she?" I yelled.

"There, at 10:00!" said Georgie.

I wasn't sure whether she meant mine or hers, but when I looked, I saw Billie Jo's motionless body, bobbin' in the waves. Against my better judgement, I dropped the shotgun and dove off the step into the water.

"CB!" came behind me, and I knew it was Lilly. Too late. I was pumpin' my arms and swimmin' as hard as I could toward the girl, who was face down in the water.

I fought through the churnin' water, the big yacht risin' and fallin' like an ocean hammer behind me. I finally reached the girl, who was unconscious.

Managin' to get my arms around her, I rolled her over onto her back and started kickin', pullin' her back to the boat. I got tired faster than I expected, and the boat was driftin' farther and farther away, the harder I swam.

"Stay back, CB!" shouted Lilly, and at first, I didn't know why. Next thing I heard was the motor crankin' up, and white foam churned behind the huge yacht.

Danny was circlin' around. Now I knew that big screen on the helm was also a rear camera. As I treaded water, he turned the boat in a big arc, movin' farther away from me than I was comfortable with.

To be honest, the whole time I was out there I was thinkin' to myself, *I wonder what other animals besides gators changed. Sure hope it ain't sharks.*

Wouldn't that be my luck. Tryin' to save a couple of snakes, I get eaten by a big, zombiefied bull shark.

When he'd made his circle, clearly monitorin' the current, he cut the motor again and the rear of the Dreamline was driftin' toward me.

Terry, Lilly, and Georgie were standin' on the rear platform. Lilly had the boat hook and held it out. I managed to grab it with one hand and hang on for dear life.

When we got close enough, I let go and threw an arm up on the deck, grabbin' hold of a large cleat. Terry and Georgie dragged the woman from my arm and onto the deck.

"Oh, God!" shouted Terry, as her entire body came out of the water and rested on the deck.

Well. Not her entire body. Her left leg was torn away, and I knew from what.

Their buddy Chester. That's what all the red was about on the deck of their boat. He must've gotten her.

Both arms free now, I timed the rise and fall of the rear deck and managed to kick hard, pushin' myself up far enough to drag my body aboard.

I struggled to call out, "Keep that gun on him, Roxy!"

"He's not moving a muscle," said Roxy. I opened my eyes to see her standin' there, her eyes filled with determination, the barrel pointed squarely at Garland's head.

"Billie Jo's leg's gone!" the waterlogged man screamed. "Help her!"

Georgina was already runnin' toward the salon door, and I forced myself to my feet, steadyin' myself against the portside rail. My heart was poundin' in my chest so hard, I was sure I was seconds from a premature heart attack.

Georgie was back in seconds, a length of rope in her hands. She quickly dropped down beside the unconscious girl and wrapped the rope around her upper thigh, cinchin' it tight. She tied it off, and I saw the blood flow almost stop immediately.

"I have to cauterize that wound!" she shouted. "I'm not sure how I'm going to do that."

Danny ran down. "Guys, it's clear to the west. I'm firing it up and I'm gonna burn some fuel. Hang on. It's gonna be rough." He looked down at the woman. "She gonna make it?" he added.

"Not if I don't act fast!" said Georgie.

Danny ran off, and I hurried over to where Billie Jo lay. I bent down and scooped her up. "Where, Georgie?"

"On this cushion," she said, pullin' it off a lounge chair with the sound of Velcro detachin'. She lay it on the deck, just under the rear overhang and out of the poundin' rain.

Just as she put it down, I had the girl's body on it. I ran over to Roxy and took the gun from her. "Help your mom," I said, turnin' the barrel toward Garland again. His eyes were on Billie Jo, and it occurred to me that while they weren't good people, it didn't mean he didn't care about his partner in crime. Hell, maybe he even loved her.

"They'll do what they can to save her," I breathed, still tryin' to catch my wind. "Once we do that, we're droppin' you two off."

"I can't take care of her like that!" he protested. "Her leg's bit off!"

"You're the idiot who had to bring a zombie gator aboard your boat," I said. "Now shut the fuck up."

His eyes were glued on his crazy girlfriend as he panted and huffed, tryin' to catch his breath from the ordeal.

In the back of my mind, and deep in my heart, I hoped she'd die. I mighta only been in her company for a little while, but I knew who she was. There's plenty enough bad juju out there without sadistic bitches like her runnin' around, addin' to the fear.

Yep. In my humble opinion, we had us enough trouble to face without worryin' about a post-apocalyptic Bonnie and Clyde.

Ω

CHAPTER SEVENTEEN

After we'd plucked Garland from the water, I searched him before he'd fully recovered. Findin' a knife and a 9mm on him, I was relieved I'd thought of it. I tossed the Taurus over the side of the boat and pocketed the knife, sheath and all. We had plenty of guns, and every one of 'em was way better than what dickwad had picked out.

The waterproof cushions on the deck furniture were highly resistant to anything soakin' into 'em, and that included blood. Georgie told Roxy and Terry to lay 'em out on the dinin' table in the salon, and while her partner was still squirmin' on the deck sputterin' out water like a boilin' kettle, we carried Billie Jo's limp body inside and rested her on 'em.

The recessed lighting in there was good, and Georgie said it would do fine.

Despite me sayin' I didn't give a shit if he was hurt or not, our resident doctor insisted on givin' him a quick once-over before turnin' her attention to Billie Jo. Aside from some badly bitten nails and some nasty teeth, Garland was uninjured, and the examination only lasted five minutes or so.

The girl was a different story. Once Dr. Lake turned her attention fully on Billie Jo, her demeanor changed. I could tell she'd turned fully to surgeon mode.

"I don't need to operate," she said. "The hard work of amputating the leg was done by that alligator."

"Danny!" I called, standin' over Garland. He came runnin' over from somewhere.

"You got zip ties, right? You pulled out a pack you got from somewhere right after we left Fort Walton Beach."

"Yeah. They're for him, right?" he said, noddin' toward Garland.

"Yeah. Not lettin' him run free, that's for sure."

"Y'all can't keep me in chains the whole time!" he protested, his voice whiny and nasally. "You're the goddamned violent ones! You clocked me in that dang gun shop!"

"Blame your goddamned woman for that," I said. "Or yourself. You never tried to settle her down. It's obvious she's batshit crazy."

"You saw her!" he said, as though incredulous. "There ain't no settlin' her down!"

"Then you should've picked better company to keep," I said. "Danny, the zip ties?"

"Nooo, I got sensitive wrists!" moaned Garland.

Danny actually laughed. "Sensitive wrists. I swear. Anyway, CB, they're the long thick ones. Got 'em at the marina. Should hold him fine."

As I stood over the skinny longhair, Danny ran up to the flybridge to retrieve the zip ties. I was just outside the salon door, on the aft deck, but I could see the folks inside, and hear 'em just fine.

Without really directing it toward anyone, Georgie said, "I need to cauterize that leg wound. The tourniquet can do more harm than good if it's left on too long."

"I think we're gonna be real happy to have you –"

My words were cut off when I felt a punch to my stomach. I looked down at Garland, who'd propped

271

himself up on one hand and had his other arm drawn back, like he was ready to throw another weak-ass punch.

"Did you fuckin' hit me?"

"Not hard enough I guess," he said.

"No, you're right. *This* is hard enough. Maybe a little too hard."

"Huh?" he said, a quizzical look on his face as he sat staring up at me, still propped up on his extended arm.

I balled my fist – which I gotta admit is pretty enormous – and punched him in the face, hard. *Real* hard. My knuckles were practically ringing from the impact, and as I followed through, his head slammed the deck and his body went about as limp as a noodle. I'd opened a sizable cut above his left eyebrow, and the blood ran down the side of his face.

Turning away from Garland again, I said, "Sorry, Georgie. Cauterize it? With what? Like … fire?" I asked.

"Is he okay?' asked Georgie.

"You examined him just a minute ago."

Georgie shook her head, and I saw her smile, even if nobody else noticed it. She hurried inside and came back out with a cloth. She knelt down and pressed it against the cut on Garland's brow, stopping the flow of blood.

"You don't cauterize with open flame," she said. "I need something flat and heated until it's red hot. Rox, would you grab that white canvas bag in our bedroom closet?"

At the '*our bedroom*' reference, I noticed Roxy glance at me, then at her mom. Must take some getting used to, seeing your mom with someone else.

I guess in the long and the short run, I'd have preferred to see my Ma with anyone else than my Pa, rather than being dead.

Roxy got past it quick, running off to do what her mama said. When she came back about forty-five seconds later, she had the bag, and set it down beside Georgie. Danny was right behind her.

"Find the Fentanyl patches," said Georgina. "It won't do anything for her now, but she's going to need them by the time she wakes up. I have syringes in there, too, but no liquid pain meds, so we'll have to dissolve some of this Oxycodone and handle it that way."

"Where do you want the Fentanyl patch?" asked Roxy.

"On her arm is fine," she said. "Anywhere, really."

"Okay, I'll do the patch and you do the oxycodone."

"Whoa," said Danny, leaning over to look at the unconscious Garland's face. "What happened to his eye?"

"He hit me, so I hit him back."

Danny nodded. "Remind me not to piss you off, but good job. Now I can zip him up easy as you please."

He set to work, so I went in to see if my doctor girlfriend needed any help. I thought about that. It took a goddamned zombie apocalypse caused by a crazy Indian medicine man for me to find a hot doc that wanted to go out with me.

There's something to be said about slim pickins'. Suddenly, a big boy from the swamp looks pretty damned good.

"Need help?"

"Yes, thanks. I've got the pain meds handled, but I still need a solution for cauterizing her stump."

"Shit. Stump," I said.

"No better term for it," she said, tying on one of the aprons from the kitchen pantry. It was the type that loops over your neck, covers your chest, and ties in back.

"Anyway, see what you can do. It needs to be steel, and it needs to be flat."

I went right into the galley and started opening drawers. In no time, I found just the tool. It was a solid, stainless steel spatula with a teak wood handle.

I pulled it out of the drawer, turned around and held it up. "This do?"

She looked up. "Yes," she said. "I believe it will. Do we have a torch, so it can be heated?"

"Stove won't work?"

"I just assumed it would be electric," she said. "If it's gas, yes, it will work. It will take longer than a torch, but it will do the job. Don't heat it yet. I've got to sedate her and trim the wound before I get that far."

I looked over to see Danny dragging Garland toward the starboard rail with one hand. Danny was huge compared to Garland, and even being dead weight was no match for his strength.

I put the spatula down and walked out to see what he had in mind.

"Gonna zip this guy to the railin' here," he said.

"Sturdy rail," I said.

With one last pull, he got him there. He raised the unconscious man's arms and threaded the zip tie inside the stainless-steel tube, then secured it around both his wrists.

When he laid him back down, he lay flat on his back with just his arms extended. It was the perfect height. Danny set to work zipping his ankles together, too.

When he was done, he stood upright. "Hope they finish with her fast," he said. "I'd like to take advantage of this daylight."

"Not comfortable runnin' this sucker at night?"

"I ain't driven a yacht before," he said. "Thing's like three times as long as the houseboat I drove years ago, out at the Lake of the Ozarks."

I patted him on the shoulder. "Thanks for the help. I'll hang with you a bit once I see if Georgie needs anything."

As I got back inside, the good doctor was holding a fillet knife in her hands, cleaning it with rubbing alcohol she'd pilfered from CVS. She looked up and offered me a slight smile. "Well, here goes nothing. I just injected her with the Oxycodone, so she might stay out through it."

"Hell, she might have brain damage," I said. "See any marks on her head? Bumps or anything?"

"That boat did fly into the air pretty high," she said, leaning forward, running her gloved hand over Billie Jo's head. Her face scrunched up, and she looked even cuter.

"I feel a small bump on her crown, but no goose eggs. If the amputation's successful, none of her other injuries should kill her. Thank God we stocked up on antibiotics."

I could tell Dr. Lake had once again embraced her Hippocratic oath. I didn't like the girl she was working on one bit, but I respected Georgie that much more.

"Makes sense," I said. "Infection from gator bites can put you down fast. You need help?"

"If she wakes up, we may need you and Danny to hold her down while I finish."

I unclipped the radio I'd put on my belt. "He's on my channel. I'll have him down here lickity-split."

"Roxy, hold this please." She held out the clean fillet knife and her daughter took it. "Mom, this is the first time I've seen you work in person."

"It is, isn't it?" said Georgina. "I'm glad you're my assistant. Now keep that blade clean while I change my gloves and find a pin."

"A pen?" I asked. "Takin' notes?"

"No, a pin. I want to stick her foot and see if she stirs."

"Hell, use the damned syringe."

Georgie closed her eyes, and I could see her chastising herself. "Duh," she said.

I laughed. "Never heard you say that before."

"Consider that a good thing," she said, pulling her dirty gloves off and snapping on a new pair. She held out her hand to Roxy, who gave her the knife.

"Okay, I need to clean up these dangling tendons. The leg is torn badly, and it's very uneven, so after I cut away the excess tissue, I'll attempt to use the large skin flap to cover the wound once I finish cauterization."

"Just remember who she was before you pulled the gun on her ass," I said. "Unless you're swappin' out her brain, that part ain't gonna change. If anything, she'll just be more pissed. Probably blame the whole goddamned thing on us."

"I will invite her to file a malpractice suit against me," she said with a wink. She turned to her daughter. "Ready Rox?"

"And steady," said Roxy.

"I'll be up with Danny," said Terry.

"Take fuckin' Liam with you," I said. "Kid's been fuckin' around with that Xbox long enough. Tell Danny to figure out some bait and y'all put some of that fishin' gear to use."

Terry saluted facetiously. "Aye Aye, Captain!" he said, and marched off, turning back with a smile and a wink.

Everyone seemed to be having a great time in the apocalypse. That being the case, I decided to take the credit for it.

At least in my mind. Nobody else needed to know.

While the medication was kicking in, Georgie found an extensive sewing kit with a bunch of different needles. She picked out a big one, then had Danny bring her the lightest test fishing line he had. She was able to thread the needle with it, and it now sat on a cookie sheet on the table beside her.

"Here goes nothing," she said. "Get those lights, would you Cole?"

I turned 'em on and the table holding Billie Jo was highly illuminated.

"Turn away if you can't handle it," said Georgie. "Once I start, even flying vomit won't stop me."

I couldn't. Georgie picked up the syringe and held it at the girl's foot. She poked near the heel.

Nothing.

She poked a couple of toes, nice and hard.

More nothing. I was guessing the girl was either dead or out like a light.

"Hope you gave her a lot of that shit," I said. "From the looks of her, she mighta built a tolerance for several kinds of drugs."

"I took that into consideration. What I gave her would knock you and me out for the night."

She looked at Roxy. "Let's get this over with. Cole, start heating those steak knives. The ones with the wood handles."

I turned on the burner and rested four steak knives, so the blades were dead in the flame. Within a minute, they were all red hot.

"Be ready," she said.

"Okay, they're glowin' red," I said.

"Bring one over now."

As I approached, I saw her use the fillet knife to cut a long, dangling something or other away and toss it into a stainless wastebasket. "Knife," she said. I gave it to her.

She used it to cauterize the tendon or whatever she'd just cut.

"Okay, cool, clean, and reheat. Get me another hot knife now."

I brought it over and gave it to her. She immediately used it to cut several other jagged areas away, and I noticed how there was no blood after she'd sliced through. The hot knives were doing their part.

"Okay, bring me the hot spatula so I can hit the rest of these bleeders, then I'll ligate the femoral nerve," she said, explaining to Roxy as she worked. "If I screw that up, she'll die no matter what. Get ready to hand me the needle."

Roxy did, and she set to work again. Roxy held a small LED flashlight, so Georgie could see what she was doing. I was glad I couldn't.

I was happy to stay on knife duty.

She tapped the flat part of the glowing spatula to several veins and tendons. When she was done, she set it aside, took the needle and fishing line and began to stitch part of the wound. She worked for a bit, then pulled the nylon line tight and knotted it. "Scissors," she said, but Roxy didn't hand them to her; she leaned in and clipped the line herself.

"Nice," said Georgie, smiling at her kid. "Cole, I need two more knives, fast."

I picked both of 'em up from the flame and scooted over to her. She took one and cauterized some shit or other, then took the other one and did some more.

When she was done with each one, she gave it back.

"Clean and reheat?" I asked.

"No," she said, shaking her head. "Just have to rasp the bone to get rid of the sharp edges, then I can suture the fascia. I have to do it from the inside out."

"No argument here," I said, feeling the first flutter in my stomach at the thought of filing down bones.

I watched as she picked up a fine file we'd pulled from a toolbox in the engine compartment and started filing away on the bone.

My stomach rumbled, and I ran outside, nearly stomped on Garland as I leaned over the rail to lose my lunch.

I'd seen some shit, but that took the cake.

By the time I recovered, Georgie was working the needle and thread. She started deep and worked her way toward the surface of the leg. When she was satisfied, she pulled the two big skin flaps together and poked her big needle through both pieces, drawing the two together along the length of the leg's diameter.

After Roxy clipped the last bit of line, Georgie leaned forward to examine the work. About thirty seconds later, she stood up and pulled her gloves off, dropping them into the trash.

"Now for the real test," she said, leaning forward and removing the tourniquet slowly. As she did, I saw the extremity turn pink-ish again. We all waited for it to explode or something.

At least that's what *I* was waiting for. At car races, I'm waiting for a crash. At hockey games I'm waiting for a fight. It's just kinda who I am.

"That went very well," she said. "And she was a better patient than she is a human being. Now I'm ready for a drink."

"A fine suggestion," I said. "Should we move her somewhere first?"

279

"Don't bother," said Georgie. "She'll be out a couple more hours with what I gave her."

I swept my hand toward the door, and she walked ahead of me. She turned and smiled. "That was exhilarating."

"Oh, for me, too," I said. "Feel like I just went on a roller coaster."

"You threw up, didn't you? When I filed the bone?"

"Maybe," I said sheepishly.

We walked upstairs where Danny was sitting in the captain's chair. He had a beer sitting in the helm cupholder, and a cooler by his feet. When we walked up, he reached down and pulled out two bottles of Corona.

"No lime?" I asked.

"I got that RealLime shit," he said. "Better'n nothin'."

I nodded toward Georgie. "Lime?"

"Always," she said. "Otherwise, why drink Corona?"

A girl after my own heart.

Ω

The clock on the helm said it was 6:30 PM. I was amazed at how the time had flown, because the intense task of the surgery seemed to erase time; it was all about the task at hand and nothing else.

We told Danny how it went, and before we were done, he and Lilly were cuddled up on the long, white sofa, looking like a couple from fucking Yacht Fancy magazine. All they needed was a fluffy, white dog and a goddamned gold-leafed captain's cap.

Nokosi was sitting right by where we'd tied up Garland. That dog was used to being around folks in restraints and seemed to know the dude needed watching.

280

Garland had woken up a long time ago, but every time he tried to get our attention by yelling, Nokosi would start barking like a junkyard dog, just four inches from his face.

Garland would shut right up, a scowl on his face. I supposed he deserved an update on his girlfriend, so I made a mental note to remind myself to get around to that eventually.

"Guys," said Danny. "Been studyin' that GPS. It's a marine model, but it has settings for land, too. Anyway, I see us settin' ashore around Beaumont, Texas. Port Arthur, really. There's a refinery there where they ship raw crude, so we can take the boat in as far as we can go. There's bound to be some nice trucks in the employee parking lot at the refinery."

"It's Texas. Pickups everywhere. Sounds good. Where's that take us through?" I asked.

Georgie looked at the map on the screen. "Not Dallas."

"Nope," said Danny. "I figure we grab one or two SUVs and hit Highway 96. That takes us in the right direction still, but away from Houston. Dumps us back onto Interstate 35 north of Dallas. I just hope it's far enough away."

"What's the drive to Lebanon?" asked Lilly.

"About 13 to 15 hours, depending on what we run into," said Danny. "Not bad. Feels like we'll be home free once we hit terra firma."

"Hope that don't end up in a famous last words book," I said.

"From your lips to God's ears," said Danny.

I looked at everyone. "We're all pretty lucky, you know that?" I said.

"Why's that?" asked Roxy, appearing at the top of the steps with Liam and Terry in tow.

"Look at all of you," I said. "I could be out there all alone. Instead, I have Lilly and I found all of you. What's more, you're all good people."

"Lower deck guests excluded," said Georgina. "But yes, I feel lucky, despite them."

"Let's get drunk. We're docked for the night."

"I'm gettin' into some night fishin', young man," said Danny. "You up for it?"

"Can I get drunk too?" Liam asked.

"I might give you a beer," he said.

"Will that get me drunk?" asked the red-headed boy.

"If you chug it, maybe."

"Deal!" said Liam.

Nobody objected. It was a new America.

$$\Omega$$

CHAPTER EIGHTEEN

Danny, with Terry, Roxy, and Liam, hung out on the stern with two lines in the water. He'd taken several mesh bags of chum and hung 'em in the water around the boat, and that was enough to get some baitfish close enough to use the cast net on.

One line was on the bottom, and he was freelining the other. Nothing happening so far.

Garland was awake and staring down Nokosi. I was glad the dog freaked him out, but that didn't stop him from bitching the entire time, practically from the time his eyes cracked open.

Guess I couldn't blame him, but it was his fault, as I see it. His pussy punch to my gut was ill-timed and ill-conceived. Mine was well-aimed and solid.

"Nokosi, come here," I said.

The German Shepherd looked at Garland, then me, and obeyed. She laid down at my feet.

"How's Billie Jo?" he asked, taking a break from his whining.

As the words left his lips, Georgina emerged from the salon and said, "She's actually just waking up. A little groggy still, and in some pain, but she's awake."

"Yeah?" I asked. "She loopy, or makin' sense?"

"Not saying much of anything yet," said Georgie.

"Why ain't she comin' out?" asked Garland.

Georgie, to her credit, pulled a chair from under some bungee straps and unfolded it, placing it beside him. She sat. "How are you feeling? I heard the blow from inside the salon."

"What saloon?" he asked. "There's a saloon? I could use a drink."

Georgie laughed, despite herself. "Not like that, but I understand some people call them saloons. It's the social area of a yacht. Like the living room."

"First time on a yacht, and I'm sittin' on the deck cuffed to a rail," he groaned.

I walked over and grabbed another chair, unfolding it beside Georgie's. I sat. "You didn't need to follow us. That was your choice, bud."

"Somebody with Billie Jo?" he asked.

"We put her in a bed in one of the crew cabins," said Georgie. "She's in and out. I check on her every fifteen minutes or so."

"Why ain't she out here?"

"She underwent a serious procedure," said Georgie. "I had to clean up her left leg and suture it."

He shifted, twisting his body and flexing his arms. "It ain't broke, right?" he asked.

I threw a quick glance at Georgina, then back at him. "Dude, your goddamned gator ripped her leg off. So yeah, I guess you could say it's broke."

His eyes went wide. "Chester? He here?" he looked around.

"Well it's good to see who you're more worried about," I said. "And fuck no. He's real dead now. The bastard managed to swim up to the stern, even with that damned spiked harness you made. I unloaded a shotgun into it's goddamned head. It's on the bottom of the Gulf right now."

"You prick!" he shouted

"Yeah, yeah," I said, shaking my head. I had to smile.

Just then the line at the rear of the boat started zinging. I jumped up and ran back. Danny held a big deep-sea rig, the rod bent in a smooth arc down toward the water.

"What the hell you got there?" I asked.

"Gotta … be a shark or … maybe a grouper or somethin'!" grunted Danny.

"You need help?" I asked.

"I'll let you know," he said, pulling up with all his might. He reeled back down to the water and pulled up again.

The line started running again, and it sounded like that fish must've gotten another fifty yards from the boat.

Danny didn't give up. He pulled back and reeled back down. The fish didn't fight again, and that gave me hope. It was dead weight now.

"Yeah, CB. You're up," huffed Danny.

I went over and put both hands on the middle of the rod as he slid his hand off the thick, rubber, giving me room to move in. He stepped out, and I almost lost the damned thing.

"Jesus, Danny!" I said, leaning back as far as I could. "You made this shit look easy!"

"What is it?" asked Liam. "A dinosaur?"

"Feels like one!" I shouted, reeling down to the water again and pulling up.

"I'm gonna and run grab that fightin' belt I got at the marina store!" said Danny. "Didn't think to put the damned thing on!"

"That's 'cause you never catch shit!" I yelled back.

He ran off, but I felt like my arms would pull out of the sockets. "Hurry!" I called after him.

"You okay over there?" called Georgie.

"Not so much!" I answered.

Georgie got up and walked over to stand beside me. Liam sat there, his red hair blowing in his eyes, staring down at the water like fucking Jaws was gonna come flying out.

It was like pulling up the Titanic, I swear. Just as I was ready to fold in two, I felt Danny's hands putting the belt around my waist.

"Move the rod!" he said.

It was digging into my midsection pretty good, but I managed to hold it out about four inches, which gave him room to slide the belt under it. Before he even had the Velcro straps secured, I had the rod in it, and now I could use my whole body instead of my arms.

"I bet it's a freakin' whale!" shouted Liam. "Hurry up! Pull it in!"

I shot a couple knives from my eyes at the kid, but I was making headway now. Lowering the rod tip as I reeled in, leaning back as far as I could to pull that beast up.

"I see it!" said Danny, standing to my left. Everybody was out there now, all gathered around me, and they were all goddamned screaming, cheering me on.

One last lean back, and I saw it, too.

A motherhunker of a red grouper if I'd ever seen one. Thing had to weigh close to 50 pounds.

"I got it, I got it. Move over," said Danny, sliding past Liam and kneeling on the back step. He reached down and stuck both his hands in the fish's open mouth, yanking it outta the water just in time for me to collapse onto my ass, trying to catch my breath.

From behind us, we heard Garland scream. I think we all spun around at the same time.

"What the hell's wrong now, Garland?" I asked, between breaths. I couldn't see him because I was sitting on the swim step.

"Billie Jo!" he screamed, and I forced myself to my feet.

"What's wrong with her?" Liam said, his eyes wide.

Billie Jo was just crawling up the steps from the crew cabins, her mouth open and snarling, her stump leaking blood through the sutures.

She snapped her jaws together like a hungry gator, and I think we were all in a trance for a second, trying to process what we were seeing.

We all knew what she had become, because she looked just like the masses of walking dead out there. Where we'd fucked up bad was not really thinking about the cause of her injury.

A zombiefied gator.

Of course, Billie Jo was gonna turn, no matter how good a job Georgie did fixing her leg; I saw that with Clay, after Tanner bit him. We could've saved Dr. Lake a lot of time and effort.

I tried to get over the stern rail, but my legs were still jelly from fighting the grouper.

Danny clearly didn't want to lose our catch, 'cause he yanked that fish with one big pull, hoisting it over the rail to the rear deck, where it flopped into poor Garland.

Two words I never thought I'd put together; *poor* and *Garland*.

"Get that fuckin' sea monster away from me!" he screamed.

"That goddamned fish isn't your biggest problem right now!" Lilly screamed, pulling out a .45 she'd taken to.

We were all damned lucky that girl had lost her leg, 'cause she was moving pretty fast toward her partner in crime, just pulling herself forward with her hands, pushing with her one good leg and her bloody stump.

"Don't let her bite me!" Garland screamed.

She was now about a foot from his legs, so Garland did his best to twist his body sideways and tuck them beneath him. "Hurry!"

She was getting awful close. It was a movie I could watch all day, so long as it wasn't happening to anyone I cared about.

It wasn't.

"I'm sorry I didn't close the door!" said Georgie. "I thought if she woke up and called out or something –"

"Don't worry about it," said Danny. "Lilly, what you waitin' for? Kill her already, baby."

She looked back at Liam and shook her head.

Georgie went to the boy and took his head, pulling his face against her stomach. She nodded hurriedly as he struggled to pull away and witness the execution.

Georgie held her own. Terry gawked, open-mouthed, at the entire scene. His face was white as a sheet.

Lilly sidestepped around Garland. Just as Billie Jo's reanimated corpse reached out and dragged her dead fingers across Garland's, knee, him screaming like a college co-ed in a slasher film, Lilly pressed the barrel against her forehead and fired.

As the first splatter of blackened brain tissue hit the deck, Billie Jo's off-kilter body flopped sideways, and Lilly stood over her, firing two more shots between her eyes as the black juice ran in dark rivers onto the gleaming white deck around her head.

She stared at the dead girl for a moment or two, then turned around, nodding. "Let him go, Georgina. Liam, don't look at her."

"I saw my mom a lot, and she was just like her!" said Liam. "I'm not a damned baby, so stop treating me like one!"

He ran past the huge grouper that was losing some of its steam, skirted past Lilly, and jumped clean over the dead zombie. When he ran into the salon, I knew what was up.

"Xbox cures the worst ills for a kid that age," I said. "Shit. Thanks, sis."

My heart was starting to slow, but it was still beating twice as hard as what it was in the middle of my fight with the grouper.

"There's some good news, some bad news and some more good news right there," said Danny.

The sun was sinking low on the horizon now, and I took a look at my watch. It was 8:40. Danny saw me look and nodded before he finished talking. We'd both had a little beer buzz going on before the bullshit started. I dare say we were both stone cold sober then.

That would not stand.

"Good news is we got about 50 pounds of good-eatin' red grouper fish," said Danny. "The bad news is, we now know a zombie gator can turn a person into one of those things, which means anything that can get infected probably can, too."

"What's the other good news?" asked Terry, who had pressed himself into one of the conforming bench seats on the port side of the Dreamliner Yacht.

"The second bit of good news is this didn't happen when we were all asleep."

Everyone nodded. Even Garland.

"What are you gonna do with her?" he asked. "Give her a proper burial?"

I ignored him and nodded to Danny. Old friends like us don't need words sometimes.

We both moved toward the dead girl and stood there, watching the black sludge oozing from her head wounds.

Georgie came up behind us and looked down. "That blood changed fast. It was bright red while I was working on her."

"Yeah, don't remind me. You don't need her for anything, do you?" I asked.

Georgina shook her head.

"Ready bud?" I asked, turning to Danny.

He sighed. "Let's do it."

We picked her up and hoisted her unceremoniously over the side, and she sank into the Gulf of Mexico like a stone.

When I thought about that later, it made sense. After all, there wasn't any goddamned air in her dead-ass lungs.

Ω

Magi Silver Bolt
Henomawi Indian Reservation

He had not wanted his precious Dancing Rain to leave, but she had insisted she must help those she could. She was an excellent runner, with amazing endurance, and the skinwalkers were slow; feeble-footed creatures.

They have numbers. They can surprise you.

The words shattered his attempts to rationalize the fact that he had not insisted she stay with him.

When Anjeni Dancing Rain wanted something, she was a master manipulator. He could never be angry with her when she used her talents on him.

She'll be fine. She's smart.

Magi looked back at the words he had scrawled. The translation had been easier than Magi had expected, and the information contained within the short passage was very valuable.

It had the potential to save the lives of the rest of his people.

It was a recipe of sorts, and there could be no time wasted in testing it. Any risk would be worth the reward if this potentially powerful compound worked.

Magi's home was simple; it was a traditional, adobe-style structure, though more modern than the older clay and straw structures built by his people.

Standing at the window, he parted the blinds to peer out. On his front lawn were four of the monsters, who would move toward one another, cluster for a moment, then spread out again, only to repeat it a few moments later.

Silver Bolt went into the kitchen and grabbed a chair. Placing it by the window again, he got a note pad and a pencil, then sat down. He parted the blinds enough to see out without making it obvious. Now his hands were free to write down his observations.

Some of the single-minded creatures on his lawn were not from the reservation, but others he recognized. If he were to capture one of them, it would have to be a stranger, for what he had to do, he could not do to the body of a past friend or acquaintance.

Studying them for a time, Silver Bolt thought he finally understood. He wrote:

If they see a shape moving, they investigate to determine whether or not it is a food source. If it is not, they resume wandering, but seem to quickly forget about their previous assertion and are drawn together again.

If one or two wander off, others will follow. Watching them for over an hour, I have seen several small groups push together to investigate noises I could not hear from where I am.

Silver Bolt got up and went to his Winchester .30-30, picking it up. He slid it out of his back rifle scabbard and inspected it.

He hadn't been to the range in a long time, and hadn't been deer hunting in far longer, but he had always been a good shot.

Watching out the window again, he made his decision. Putting the scabbard down, he took the rifle with him as he ran out to his two-car garage and right up to the roll-up door. He pounded on it with his fists for a full minute, hoping that would be enough.

Silver Bolt hurried out of the garage and to the living room, where reached down and slid the window open. There was a screen, but that would not deflect his bullet or hinder him in any way. He could see the front of the garage from this location, and it appeared his pounding had worked.

Standing in front of his garage door were six of them, split evenly between men and women. As he stared at them, he wondered how so many of his own people had changed; the curse written in the ancient text had suggested that people native to the land would not turn.

They had made so many miscalculations.

He raised the rifle, peering through the small scope. Seeing something on the arm of the first female he sighted, he had a thought. Moving to the next one – a male – he saw the same thing.

The crescent-shaped indicators of a bite, surrounded by more heavily rotted skin, as though it had become immediately infected. One on the wrist, another on the inside forearm. He suspected he would see the same on all of them.

Perhaps Wattana had been right, and the curse was limited to non-native Americans. The bites are what had turned them into skinwalkers.

He realized the name was not truly what they were; the term *skinwalker* was borrowed from the Navajo people long ago. The Henomawi people had used it to describe any human possessed by a demon, or otherwise transformed by evil forces.

Silver Bolt trained his sights on a creature milling about closest to the garage door. When its head was centered in his scope, he pulled the trigger.

As the explosion cracked the silence of the day, the female's knees folded beneath her, and for a moment, she landed on them and teetered there, as though offering a macabre prayer to an unseen god. Then, gravity overcoming the balancing act, she finally fell forward, arms at her sides.

The others ignored her death, having all turned toward the house at the sound of the gunshot. Silver

Bolt slid the window quickly down and closed the blinds again.

Moving back into the other room, he looked through the window again, waiting for further confirmation of his short-memory theory.

Without any other noise or visual stimulation, they never even made it to the window before again drifting apart and wandering aimlessly.

They did not return to the garage door, so Silver Bolt ran there. The remote on his keychain in his hand, he crouched down just inside the garage door and pushed the button. The door lifted.

As he saw the feet of the motionless skinwalker, he hit the remote, stopping the door. He reached out and took the dead monster by its ankles and dragged it inside, immediately pressing the remote again once the head and arms were clear.

Turning to look at his wheelbarrow, sitting full of dirt and now dead weeds he had pulled from his garden several weeks earlier, he was glad he was a procrastinator; now he wouldn't have to go outside.

Pulling out his phone, he brought up his messages. There was a new one he hadn't seen. It was a group text, to both him and to Chief Climbing Fox.

His heart began to race. It was from Anjeni Dancing Rain.

His Anji.

I AM COMING TO CHECK ON YOU MUNDUNUGU. MAGI, THAT IS WHERE I WILL BE.

Magi Silver Bolt stared at the words. Mundunugu had said he did not know where Anji was.

Perhaps she had never made it there, thought Magi. If the note scrawled in the book was true, no time could be wasted.

He stared down at the skinwalker he had killed, dreading the steps to come. It was barbaric, and it was horrifying, but if it would allow him passage among the monsters, that would ensure that he could search for Anji without fear.

Hurrying to the cabinet beside the door leading into the house, he first removed a box of thick latex gloves. After snapping a pair on, he next removed a 5-foot long box from the lower section of the cabinet, placing it on the floor. He knelt down and removed the pieces from it and began assembling it.

When he was done, a 9-foot high tripod stood in the empty side of the two-car garage, beside his Fathom Blue, 1970 Chevy El Camino. The car had been a gift from his grandfather when he graduated from high school; he had bought it new, and it only had about 47,000 miles on it.

The classic car with unpitted, bright chrome trim looked like it just rolled off the assembly line, thanks to maybe a hundred coats of Meguiar's Wax and lots of Armor All.

It was covered. No worries about getting anything on it.

Magi stared absent-mindedly at the corpse on the floor, lowering the game gambrel to the floor. Then, Silver Bolt took two short bungee cords from his toolbox drawer and placed them on the concrete floor.

He didn't think he would have it in him to poke the gambrel through the ankles of his kill. Not yet. Best secure it with the bungees.

Preparations were done. It was time to hoist the skinwalker. He moved toward the dead woman and lifted her feet. With multiple grunts, he dragged her until her feet were in front of the gambrel.

He removed her blood-coated tennis shoes, again thankful that he did not know the woman in her former life. Using the bungee cords, he secured her ankles to the game gambrel, making sure each was tight.

He stood, walking around to the hand crank. With a ratcheting noise, he cranked the handle at a steady speed. As the cable tightened, the gambrel began to lift from the floor, bringing the skinwalker's ankles with it. When the gambrel reached the top, he stopped.

The sight almost sickened him; it was a woman hanging from the very piece of equipment he used out in the field when deer hunting. Only now, it looked like some medieval torture device. She was just over five feet tall, though, so even extended as her arms were, her fingertips did not touch the floor.

Closing his eyes for a long moment, his mind immediately going to Dancing Rain, he regained his resolve. She was out there now, and she might need him.

Using a box cutter, he sliced the clothing from the gently swinging form, pulling it down and allowing the pieces to fall into a nasty pile just beneath it. When she was entirely nude, he got a lawn and leaf bag and scooped up the clothing. When it was inside the garbage bag, he tied it closed and tossed it to the side.

Moving to the rack where he stored his hunting gear, he pulled out a hard, plastic case and rested it on his worktable. Popping the tabs, he opened it, turning to examine the skinwalker.

He'd never done this before – not on a human being. The mere thought that he had to learn – and learn fast – was sending his stomach into fluttering fits.

Taking a deep breath, holding it for a few seconds, then releasing the air from his lungs, he lifted the SB-10 Skinner from the case of knives.

He walked over and held up the knife. Steadying the body, Silver Bolt cut around each ankle, meeting his first cut as he rounded it. Pointing the knife tip downward into the slit, he pulled it outward, cutting down at the same time.

The skin peeled down about three-quarters of an inch, and he continued tugging on it as he sliced with small, yet precise cuts. Soon, the meat was stripped below the knee, and sliding down the thigh.

Finding he was holding his breath, Magi worked, beginning to believe that he was only field dressing a deer, or an elk. Meat was meat when you looked at it, and if he didn't become obsessed with the pile of hairless skin he was accumulating, he could continue lying to himself.

Magi Silver Bolt worked fast; he did not want to drag it out. When the last hollow tube of skin pulled down from the female's left hand, he cut it away, dropping the knife on the floor.

The smell was putrid. He had not noticed until it was all over with, probably because the entire idea of what he had to do was so repulsive, the smell was the last thing on his mind.

Removing his gloves and snapping on a fresh pair, he put the pile of skin into a 13-gallon trash bag and carried it to the kitchen.

He stared at the blender, the bag resting on the tiled countertop. "I could never prepare food in here again," he said aloud.

With a sigh, he went to the blender and yanked the plug from the receptacle on the wall, carrying it back out to the garage.

As it was, the blender would be going in the trash. No sense in causing the need for a kitchen remodel.

The ancient text had detailed how to make a mud of sorts. This mud, when spread across the skin of an uninfected person, would prevent a reaction from the skinwalkers.

Their skin was the key. It must be finely ground, then mixed with native soil until it was a paste. Magi plugged in the blender and set it to puree.

Reaching into the bag, he took handfuls of the skin tissue and dropped it with a *splat!* into the blender. When it was half full, he put the lid on and hit the button.

The whirring of the blender filled the garage as the skin was finely chopped. The noise helped to distract him, but when it was done, and he hit the OFF button, he immediately heard the sounds of the skinwalkers pressing against the garage door, scratching to get in.

They had clearly been drawn by the sound.

It took seven blender loads to get through all the skin. When he was done, it had the consistency of protein shake as he poured it into an Igloo ice chest.

When that was complete, he sifted the soil, which had been rife with roots, grass, and sticks, through a spare window screen, atop the pulverized skin. He continued it until the cooler was about half full.

Magi ran into the house and got a gallon of water. He poured it slowly atop the mixture, stirring it with a wooden spoon from the kitchen. It became more difficult to stir as the concoction became thicker.

Satisfied, he stared down at the contents of the cooler. He closed the lid, turning his face to the skinless girl hanging from his gambrel.

Magi removed his clothing, chanting a prayer in Henomawan as he did so. When he was fully nude, he reached into the Igloo and took a scoop of the skin-dirt paste, spreading it on his ears, cheeks, face, and the back of his neck. He then continued this until his entire body was covered with a thin layer.

Oddly enough, the odor that had been so strong while cutting the hide from the skinwalker was minimal; it now smelled like musty earth, nothing more. Perhaps with time, as the skin fragments began to deteriorate further, it would begin to reek. For now, Magi was thankful it did not.

As it dried, he felt it tighten. When it was no longer tacky, he went into the house to retrieve a pair of deerhide trousers and a long-sleeved tunic. He had made both, using the hide of a fourteen-point buck he'd taken in a previous hunt.

He strapped on shoes made from the same animal and returned to the garage to get his .30-30. Putting his head through the strap, he allowed it to hang from his body. In a pouch that hung around his neck, he put a box of rounds for the weapon.

He bent down to close the lid of the cooler and picked it up as well.

Having second thoughts, he put the gun and cooler back down, picking up a tool belt and clipping it around his waist. In it, he put several of the longer-bladed knives.

This was all still a mystery to him, and at the moment, he was operating on blind faith. He must be prepared for any encounter with the skinwalkers.

A full-length mirror that had fallen from the door of the spare bathroom leaned against the garage wall, still not re-installed due to his tendency to procrastinate.

He stood before that mirror now, his haunted white eyes staring out of the dirt-colored coating.

"I am coming, Anjeni Dancing Rain," he muttered, picking up the Igloo.

He pushed the button on the wall and the door rose.

The skinwalkers looked at him. He looked back. They moved toward him as he stepped toward them.

One of them – a male, about two inches taller than Magi, moved toward him, stopping just inches away.

Its mouth opened, and the nostrils flared. Magi remained very still, his hand clutching the grip of the knife at his side. He could smell it now; it was the ghastly aroma of death and decay, as though emanating from a deteriorated corpse whose grave had been unearthed days or weeks after its burial.

Magi needed to know if there were any vulnerabilities associated with the skin paste. He steeled his nerves and his spine as he exhaled, allowing the released breath to drift into the skinwalker's face. Involuntarily, his fingers squeezed the knife handle tighter.

Nothing.

There was no change in the creature's movements or demeanor. The strange, dead eyes, coated with the thick, opaque liquid, seemed to see him only as an obstacle to be navigated around.

In confirmation of Magi's assumption, its head rotated away from Silver Bolt, and it took a step past him. The dead thing brushed against Magi as it passed, and he felt his skin pucker with gooseflesh beneath the biological mud. Afraid to turn his head, he followed it with his eyes, releasing his breath and finally breathing normally.

Satisfied, Magi busied himself, placing the cooler in the driveway and reaching for two of the legs of the tripod. With substantial effort, he dragged it through the open door and into the driveway. The body swung wildly within the three stanchions as he cleared the garage and released it.

Walking back into the garage, he pulled a 1-gallon gas can from the shelf, dousing the skinless, dangling walker with fuel. He pulled out a Bic lighter and held it close to her, and with a quick *whoomph!,* she burst into flame.

Magi Silver Bolt went back inside and herded the five skinwalkers from the garage, then pressed the remote control. As the door slid down behind him, and the pockets of burning fat and tissue crackled, Magi walked toward the home of his love, Anjeni.

He would retrace her steps to the home of Climbing Fox Wattana.

Dancing Rain needed him.

Ω

CHAPTER NINETEEN

It was late. I ain't sure what time, exactly. When I heard Rode's voice come over Pa's ham radio, I stared at it for a long while before I kicked Danny, who'd fallen asleep maybe half an hour before.

He shook his head and blinked his eyes at me. His belly, like mine, was stuffed with fresh grouper, cooked in oil on the stove, and like any man, he needed a good snooze after a big meal.

And several shots of Jack.

"Rode," I said. "Just heard him."

"Rode what?" he mumbled, then his eyes went wide. As he scooted up into a more suitable sitting position. "Oh, hell. The DJ?"

We figured we had a right to tie one on with some Jack Daniel's. Braving the streets for supplies, wrangling a couple of crazy crooks from a boat wreck, shooting a zombie gator, landing a huge grouper, killing one said zombie criminal, and cleaning up the mess, all added up to us deserving to tie one on.

So, we did. Georgie held her own with us as long as she could, but now she was curled up on the big bed in our cabin, snoring so soft and cute I could stand there and listen to her for hours.

"The good news is, we made it to Lebanon," said Rode. "Sign that greeted us said the population was 218."

"Podunk town," said Danny.

"Just Po," I said. "No room for the dunk."

302

Rode continued: "There has to be a lot of the changed people inside the houses, but you can drive around the entire town in about 2.4 miles. The Nebraska border's less than a hundred miles north of us, so if we needed to expand out, I guess there's services on that northern route.

"It was just getting dark when we pulled into Lebanon, past the sign that said we were at the geographic center of the U.S., and we encountered about sixteen of the shufflers on our first run through town. Coming back south a different way, we hit right around seven more, took 'em all out.

"When we got here, everyone was exhausted. We came straight up Main Street on our final trip north, and at the end, there's a school. It's brick, and there are some fences around, so it seemed like our best choice for now. Can't say we won't move, but we're settled in for the night, at least.

"If you're nearby and you show up in town tonight, just head up Main Street to the very end, and you'll see the auditorium on the left side. Please, please announce yourself verbally when you get here. We shoot at stuff that makes noise but doesn't talk."

There was a pause, then we heard Micky say, "The what? Oh, yeah. Hell yeah. Hey folks," he said into the microphone again. "We've gotten reports about alligators, crocodiles, and some caymans. You know. Turning into the same thing the people are.

"I didn't see any when we were leaving Florida, but maybe that was pure luck. If you're in the southeastern United States, just be watchful. Gators with this affliction can't be good news, and I imagine they'd be hard to kill, particularly if the shot to the brain is the only way.

"Okay, now to wrap up, we don't have a count of our people yet. They're sleeping on the big cushions the wrestlers and gymnasts use. So, that translates to no survivor numbers right now. We'll try to get a good count in the morning, so you know how many of us you'll have to contend with when you arrive.

"As for weapons, you're completely welcome to carry your own in, just so long as you know how to handle them. If you don't, expect them to be taken from you very quickly. Our weapons policy is loosey goosey until somebody fucks up and we have to change it.

"I don't have a security detail; I'm just like you guys are. Every man, woman and child here is their own person with their own freewill. I'm not in charge, either, but if you're coming here, you know what my plan is, and I assume you're joining us to carry it out, for whatever it's worth.

"It's just that – *my* plan. It may be a colossal waste of time. If you have a different idea, we'll be happy to listen, but most everyone who's had some other ideas about how to tackle this thing had personal reasons; relatives lost somewhere, friends they wanted to rescue.

"I say go ahead and find your friends or relatives, then come on back here if you want. Once we have a force of a couple hundred people here, we're starting on weapons training. Immediately after, we're moving on to Northern California. Have a good night. Watch for the zombiegators and zombicrocs. Godspeed to you."

I looked at Danny. "At least he found out about the gators."

"And crocs."

"Hate those fuckers," I said.

"Town sounds small and boring," said Danny.

"Welcome to Kansas."

"All of it?"

304

I closed my eyes and nodded. "Can't blame the folks. Most of 'em never left the place from when they were kids."

"Like you and Florida?" His eyes twinkled in the moonlight as he laughed.

"Shit, at least what I did was kinda excitin'," I said. "Better'n watchin' 'em roll haybales."

Danny laughed and lifted the half-empty bottle of Jack Daniel's from the table, taking a swig. He passed it to me. "Okay, CB, here's a fictional scenario. You come to a crossroads. On one road's a zombie gator. On the other's a haybale. Which one you choose?"

"Where's the bar?" I asked, taking a drink.

Danny laughed again, a deep, sincere sound. "Down ZomGator Road."

"You with me?" I asked.

"Nope. You're alone."

"Where's Georgie?"

"At the bar."

"I start marchin' toward that goddamned gator and he better move his ass, or I'll eat him."

"You so fulla shit."

"I know," I said, my mind working. "Hey, if only a couple hundred folks lived there before the shit hit the fan, food's gonna get tight in that town. Might be smart to keep an eye out for a big supermarket on the way. See if there's an unloaded container on the loadin' dock or somethin'."

"We'd be awfully welcome, bringin' that sucker in with us."

"My thoughts exactly. Goodwill can go a long way. Considerin' we're bringin' a piece of work like Garland with us."

"We takin' his ass the whole way?"

"He's welcome to leave, but for some reason, I'm thinkin' he's gonna opt to stay."

"Let's get to bed. Don't forget to tell everyone about that Micky dude."

"Damn," I said, standing and capping the bottle of Jack. "Why do I get all the responsibility?"

"White privilege."

I laughed, flipped him off, and felt my way down stairs.

When we got to the bottom and turned toward the salon door, we heard, "Y'all leavin' me here all night?"

I jerked my head to the left. I *had* forgotten we left Garland cable tied to the rail.

I was too mellowed from the Jack to give a shit. "Yeah," I said. "You should be ready to join civilization tomorrow. If you ain't, we toss you over."

"Jesus," he muttered, but didn't say any more.

I went to bed, stripped down, and slid in beside Georgie.

Her arms slipped around me and that's the last thing I remember.

Ω

I felt the bed shaking and fought opening my eyes, 'cause the damned morning came too soon and I wasn't ready for it.

My eyes stung, my mouth was sticky, and my whole head felt like it was stuffed with cotton. I dragged myself out of bed anyway.

I brushed my teeth and splashed water on my face before dragging my ass up to the flybridge. It was deserted.

I wanted an early start, because we needed to get our asses to Port Arthur and get on the drive north through

Texas. I didn't want to miss joining Rode's caravan to northern California, and at our current pace, I was sure he'd be long gone before we got there.

Not sure why I was so damned eager to go. Maybe because I wanted to debunk Wattana as the cause of this shit. Somewhere in the back of my mind, I suspected he was a fool, and it was really the goddamned planet telling us it'd had its fill of humanity, and our time was up.

I tried to focus through my fog. We were about a mile offshore, and I trusted somebody would bring me coffee, so I pulled anchor, fired the engines, and kept my eyes on the depth finder.

I pushed that yacht up to right around 24 knots and left it there. The morning was calm and the light swells that swept beneath the big boat could barely be felt.

I finally lost my patience and was about to run down to get some coffee when I saw a blonde head coming up the steps and smelled the brew.

"Bright-eyed and bushy-tailed?" asked Georgie, a big smile on her face. "How are you feeling?"

She passed me a mug of coffee. I didn't even answer. I just drank and raised my eyebrows.

"How long until we get there?"

"Goddamned thirteen hours or so at this speed. It's about as fast as we can go, though."

"Some hurricanes move slower than that," she mused. "They always seem to get where they're going."

I sipped my coffee, savored it in my mouth, and swallowed. "That's us. I'm officially changin' the name of this boat to Hurricane Georgie."

"*Does* it have a name? I didn't notice it."

"It does."

"What's it called?"

"Monaco Skiff."

Georgie looked confused. She shrugged. "What's that mean?"

"I'm thinkin' this is a small boat in a place like Monaco."

"Better than the Sea Ray," she said, smiling. "So, Hurricane Georgie, huh? What time is it?"

I checked my watch. "Jesus. 7:40."

"So if we don't stop, we'll be there by sunset."

"Goddamnit," I said, realizing she was right. "That means another full day drivin' tomorrow, and that's if all goes well."

"I think I'll just be glad to get back on land," she said. "It's nice being away from those things, but I get antsy out here this long."

"Much as I love the swamp, I prefer dry land, too," I said. "When's breakfast?"

Before she answered, Terry stuck his head into view. "I'm making pancakes, so who's up for some?"

I raised my hand. "Tall stack, bud. Impeccable timin', by the way."

He pointed down the steps and asked, "Are we untying that man today?"

I laughed. "Damn. I walked right by his ass on my way up here and didn't even notice him. The shit you can get used to."

I grabbed the intercom microphone and pushed the button. "Danny, you up yet?"

A few seconds later, I heard him come back, "For a while now. We're just layin' in bed, watchin' the world go by. What you need, man?"

Now that I knew he was in his cabin, I found the button for direct communication and pushed it. "Take the helm inside for a bit, would ya? I gotta go deal with our criminal captive."

"Sure you don't need help?"

"I'm good. Terry's makin' pancakes, too, so you and Lilly should stop whatever lewd shit you're up to and get some before they're gone."

"You're a dick, CB," said Lilly, and I laughed. Danny said, "Okay, give me five."

About three minutes later, Danny's voice came over the intercom. "Okay, switchin' control now, CB."

I sat back, made sure he really had it, then trotted down the steps. I sipped my coffee while Garland snored, still sound asleep. His arms were raised because of the zip ties still lashing him to the railing. I kicked him in the leg as I pulled out a pocketknife.

"Damn, I'm sore," he said. "And I gotta take a piss."

"You sleep like a goddamned baby," I said.

"Figured y'all weren't gonna kill me. Even after the punch."

I wasn't sure what he meant by that, but I said, "You hit me first. Anyway, I think you mighta learned your lesson." I glanced up at Terry with a wink.

Terry eyed Garland nervously and said, "Keep an eye on him, would you? I don't trust him."

Garland eyed him but said nothing.

"Danny and I'll make sure he doesn't get outta line," I said. "Or over the rail he goes."

"I promise," he said. "I had me a moment, that's all."

"That moment passed? 'Cause it seemed to go on an awful long time."

"Definitely passed," he said, holding his wrists up to me.

I leaned forward and cut the zip ties. "Stick your legs out." He did, and I sliced through the zip ties and put the knife away. "When was your last shower?"

"I went in the ocean yesterday. You saw it."

"Not the same thing."

He shook his head. "Don't remember."

"Your next one's right now. You ain't sittin' down for pancakes with us smellin' like you do." I held my hand out and he took it. I pulled him up. "Go that way," I said, slipping the .45 from my holster. "I'm right behind you."

He walked a little stiff-like where I'd pointed, and I directed him to the bathroom. "Towels inside, and there's an electric razor you can use if you want to. Use shampoo and soap. Plenty of water so don't rush."

"I appreciate it," he said. "Like I said, I went a little crazy on shore. Kinda got the feelin' everyone was out to get me. Figured I'd get them first."

"I know that feelin'," I said. "How much did Billie Jo have to do with that?"

"You seen her. Had her hooks in me."

"Yeah, she was kinda hot for a crazy chick."

"I mighta been showin' off. I sure was when I made that harness for Chester, but I'll admit, it was fun."

"You kill anyone?" I asked.

His eyes shifted to the floor, then to the right. When they came back to me, he said, "Billy Jo did. Two people I told her weren't zombies."

"Tell me about it."

He shook his head. "I kinda don't want to."

"That wasn't a request. You want to stay on this boat with us, spill it."

"You mind?" he asked, turning away from the door and unzipping his fly as he stepped toward the toilet. I turned sideways as he started to pee and tell me the story at the same time.

"About a week ago, we were walkin' down some road, a few miles from that gun shop you found us at. We came across a woman and a boy in the middle of the street."

"Zombies?"

"No. Just a lady and, I guess, her kid."

I knew in my head it could've been anyone's kid; she may have come across him alone and offered to take care of him.

He peed for so long I almost checked my watch and sent up a flare for the Guinness Book of World Records verification team.

"Keep goin'."

"Well, we kinda came around a corner and I had Chester by that time. The minute we saw 'em, BJ grabbed that rod and pulled open his blinder. Fucker took off so fast, I lost hold of the chain. The lady and her boy started runnin', tryin' to get to an old Jeep parked cattycorner off the curb."

"They get there in time?"

He nodded, zipping up his pants. "Yeah, they got inside. Made a mistake, though."

"What was that?" I thought I knew.

"What was what?"

"The mistake they made."

"Oh, yeah," he said. "They didn't lock the door."

I nodded and stared into his eyes, gauging him. "I don't know why she was so fascinated by that gator. I think she felt like some kinda Xena Warrior Princess or somethin', with a goddamned dragon."

"So what happened?"

He stared at me, as though afraid to say. "Billie Jo ran after Chester, but he was focused on the Jeep. When she came up behind him, she used the rod to knock his blinders down again. Once he settled, Billie Jo yanked their door open. Chester was just layin' there facin' the car, and I could hear the lady screamin', beggin' for their lives."

I thought I knew the rest, but I had to hear it anyway.

"I stayed where I was, hopin' she'd just laugh, satisfied with scarin' 'em. That's when I first figured out she was crazier than I thought. It was like she forgot I was there. Then I yelled at her to just leave 'em, 'cause they weren't hurtin' us, but Billie Jo just reached down with that rod and pulled Chester's blinders up again. He let out this weird croak and jumped in that damn Jeep so fast I couldn't believe it."

My mind went to Sonya. Seeing her torn apart by those damned zombie gators had been the hardest thing to see since my brothers. Way more graphic. This was even worse.

His eyes were kinda far away at that point in his story. He said, "I was still a buncha yards back when I saw her do it. I took off runnin' toward the Jeep, but Chester was deep inside by the time I got there. His goddamned tail was whippin' left and right while he tore them up, and there wasn't nothin' I could do. Couldn't even get close to it. Blood was spurtin' all over the windows, and I knew it was over. I just doubled over and lost my lunch."

Now. I'm a good judge of character, and an even better judge of a liar. I honestly don't think anything he said was bullshit.

"Okay," I said. "Had to be hard to watch."

He looked at me, sheepishly. "That's why I was so damned tired. Since she did that, I've been afraid she'd kill me in my sleep. Slept with one eye open."

You should've beat her to it, I thought.

"Alright. Go ahead and get cleaned up."

He nodded and closed the door. The second I heard the water go on, I hurried down to the galley and snagged a plate of pancakes, wolfin' 'em down. When Garland finally came out about fifteen minutes later, I almost didn't recognize him.

The dude was actually not a bad looking guy. His hair wasn't ratty anymore, and he'd shaved, like I suggested. While his eyes were a tad shifty, he looked a helluva lot more trustworthy than before.

"Who the fuck *are* you?" I asked.

"Feel like somebody else now, that's for sure," he said, rubbing his wet hair with his hand.

"How's the eye?" I asked.

He touched it gingerly with his fingers. "Tender. I'll live."

"Hungry?" I sipped my coffee.

"Hell yeah," he said. "Coffee sounds good, too."

"Follow me."

I went back down to the salon, which was enormous. Nice as it was, I was ready to be outta there and on to our destination. Danny was up a few steps from us, driving from the interior helm.

Everybody was there, and I was surprised when Garland held up his hand and said, "Hey, y'all. Can I get your attention for a sec?"

Danny must've heard it, 'cause he came down the steps a couple seconds later, saying, "Autopilot for a bit. Wide open out there."

"Thanks," said Garland. "Anyway, I had a talk with CB here. Tried to explain about what I did. I got no excuses. Not bein' a real ladies man, when Billie Jo took a likin' to me, I tried to overlook the fact that she was batshit crazy. Seemed almost like a benefit with all this crazy zombie shit goin' on."

"Like your own pit bull," said Roxy, whose hair was also wet from a morning shower.

"Exactly. Anyway, my last name's Hunter, and I just wanna tell you I'll do what I can to make it up to y'all."

"You're gonna be on probation a while," said Danny. "Everyone watchin, and no weapons for you."

He nodded. "Fair enough." He turned to me. "Y'all are headed somewhere in Kansas, right?"

"Lebanon."

"Yeah, that's right. Billie Jo thought y'all were headin' to the Middle East."

Everybody laughed, and the memory made me chuckle, too.

"We'll tell you the story as we know it," I said. "One job you can do is man the ham radio. Let us know if you hear from a dude named Micky Rode. He's the guy orchestratin' the whole thing."

"Ain't he a classic rock DJ?" asked Garland.

"You heard of him?" I asked.

"Syndicated, I guess. Only station I listened to. Cool dude."

"Then you'll know who to listen for. Eat some pancakes. We'll tell you the plan as it stands now."

When we were done, we assigned Garland Hunter the task of cleaning the galley. He didn't complain.

$$\Omega$$

CHAPTER TWENTY

Magi Silver Bolt
Henomawi Indian Reservation

It was a strange feeling, walking down streets, deserted except for skinwalkers.

The rifle scabbard with the Winchester .30-30 on his back, Magi had searched Anjeni's home, but there was no sign she'd gone there before seeking out others in need of help. Her phone was gone as well, which made sense, based on her last text. She never went anywhere without it.

Pulling out his own phone, he started a text. He wrote, simply, 'ANJI. WHERE ARE YOU?'

The readout showed the word *SENDING*, then after a second or two, *DELIVERED*. The word *READ* never appeared.

Frustrated, he slid the phone back in his pocket. He peered through the window to see several skinwalkers roaming in the street beyond, but that didn't concern him any longer.

Magi opened the door of Dancing Rain's home, picked up the cooler containing the skin paste, and stepped onto the front porch, closing it behind him with an extra hard pull. If she were to come back here, he could not let his negligence allow a skinwalker to make its way into her house, surprising her.

Walking slowly down the path leading to the street, Magi stepped off the curb and looked around him. He had to find her; give her the mixture to put on her body. It would keep her safe until they could either work with Mundunugu to reverse the horrible thing he had done, or escape to somewhere safe.

Somewhere isolated.

But he had gone through the ancient text. There was no way to stop it that he could find; no ceremonies, incantations or potions that would cause the Great Spirit to save the changed people. If something had the power to lift these tortured souls from the hell into which they had fallen, it remained a mystery.

There have to be millions of them, thought Magi. *Perhaps billions. How far away did the black rain fall? How many lives were destroyed?*

The worst thought occurred to him: *How many monsters walk the earth?*

Walking across the street, he stepped on the sidewalk and stayed close to the overgrown hedge that ran alongside it. No sense in attracting attention.

Magi needed to stop by the home of his friend, Atian. It was between Anjeni's house and Chief Wattana's, so it wouldn't lead him off his planned course.

If he wasn't there, perhaps Anjeni had stopped and they both went to see Mundunugu together.

He turned up the walk, toward the bright blue home with pale yellow shutters. The pots on the porch, once containing brightly blooming flowers, were now obscured by the dead stems and leaves that draped over them like shrouds.

Everything had changed. Death was everywhere.

Stepping onto the porch, he put down the cooler and reached for the doorknocker, but stopped, looking behind him.

The walkway was empty, but noise drew them. Feet slamming into pavement. Screams and cries. Knocks on doors.

He moved to the opaque sidelight window, pressing his cupped hands against it as he attempted to peer through to see movement.

Light filtered through, but no motion was visible. Moving to the other sidelight, he repeated the action, straining to see.

Suddenly, a face came into view, accompanied by a horrible shriek. The thing inside slammed into the glass repeatedly, leaving bloody smears behind with each impact. It clawed at the barrier between them, backing up and ramming it over and over, pulverizing its own face as it did so.

But that close, Magi knew who it was; even through the distortion of the glass and the cloudiness, the shining eyes were familiar.

It was his friend, Atian.

He couldn't let him stay that way. He didn't believe Atian would walk away from him, had the situation been reversed. For all the horrible things he may be forced to do as the days ahead slipped by, he must do this one good thing now.

Sliding the .30-30 from its scabbard, he eased the lever downward, then up, chambering a round. Magi held the gun barrel to the glass, tapping, lightly tapping.

When Atian's face, complete with his still beautiful, opaque yet shining eyes, slammed into the blurred glass again, Magi fired the Winchester, cutting off the snarl in his friend's throat.

The thump came next as his childhood friend's body collapsed behind the door. Only then did Magi try the doorknob.

It was locked.

If Anjeni had been there, she would've come.

A thought struck him.

Unless Atian had killed or wounded her.

He backed up several steps, ran at the door and kicked it, planting his heel just beside the knob. The jamb splintered, and the door slammed into Atian's motionless body.

Running through the house, he called, "Anji! Anjeni! Are you here?"

No response came, and soon, he had been in every room. No sign of her.

His heart pounding, he forced himself to calm. He dropped down onto the bed in Atian's room and buried his face in his hands, the coating flaking away. Suddenly, determination overtook him.

He got up and ran back to the front door, focused on his last destination. Chief Climbing Fox Wattana's home.

He reached the porch, his eyes cast downward to hook his hand through the cooler's handle.

The valuable skin and mud mixture in hand, he took several steps toward the street before looking up.

Magi stopped, his muscles tense.

At least thirty skinwalkers moved up the narrow walk toward him. His eyes went to his arms. Though the palms of his hands were rubbed bare, they were still coated with the strange, disgusting mix.

Finding his legs would not move, he remained still as they reached him, parting like water over stones, drifting around him, toward the house. The gunshot. The splintering wood. The noises beckoned to them until they heeded its call and found no reward.

Then they would drift away again, seeking life.

Mere inches away. He smelled them, and believed the very air was polluted by their stench.

When the last one passed, he hurried away, turning behind the hedge, and focusing on the path ahead. As he put distance between the horde and himself, he started to run. It felt somehow that time was running out. He had been inside his own head for so long, he felt as though he were going insane.

He must find Anjeni. He may have nobody else left in the world.

Ω

One Mile Off The Louisiana Coast
Aboard The Monaco Skiff

It was past lunchtime, but I didn't feel like eating. Everyone was digging into fried grouper sandwiches, and they smelled good, but I was getting too antsy to eat.

I wanted to be ashore. I knew with the zigging and zagging we'd have to do to avoid Dallas and Oklahoma City, the trip was more like 900 miles.

It sounded like a million miles in my head; almost insurmountable.

Georgie was down in the salon with Roxy and Terry, and I was pretty sure Danny and Lilly were having a nap or a fuck.

Behind me, sprawled out on the bench seat, was Liam. He was out and had been since he polished off breakfast. He wanted to do some fishing, but we didn't have any setups for trolling, and we sure as hell weren't stopping. With that kid, it was fish, play video games, eat or sleep.

What I'd give to be a kid again and let someone else worry about all this shit.

When the galley was spic and span, according to all reports, Garland had headed up to the bow. I looked down and saw him still there, laying on the long, bench cushion, his body swaying side to side as the big yacht cut through the easy southwestern swells.

I bumped the throttle forward. Brought the beast to 26 knots.

Checking my watch, I was surprised to see it was already 2:45. I'd glanced down at the GPS every once in a while, but the weather was clear enough, so I could see the coastline the entire run. I'd seen land ahead of me for a long time, and I did what Danny and I'd talked about. I cut south to get around the tip of Louisiana. Not just a little bit, either.

New Orleans jutted out a good 60 plus miles farther south than Mississippi and it was a big time-killer, but we'd figured it into our calculations.

I took a deep breath. It was peaceful out on the water, and I was way too eager to get to land. In the back of my rational mind, I knew that peace might just blow apart like a goddamned dandelion in the wind once we set ashore.

A blood-caked dandelion.

We'd been going about nine hours. That meant we had to be around four hours from Port Arthur, Texas.

"Can I drive?"

I turned around. Liam was standing, stretching.

"It ain't a video game, buddy. Gotta be careful. You got eight lives in your hands, includin' your own."

"Right," he said with a smile. "My life. That's why I'll be careful. Fuck all you guys."

I don't know why that struck me as funny, but I goddamned laughed so hard I almost popped the button on my Levis. "Get over here, you dick."

"You're a dick," he said, looking at me sideways as he slid into the seat. "How fast we going?"

"Right there. That's how many knots."

"Dad used to talk about knots. Is that like miles an hour?"

"Nautical miles," I said. "Knots are a measure of speed, and nautical miles indicate distance."

"Huh," he said. "I never knew that."

"Now you do. Okay, repeat it back to me, what you just learned."

He squinted up at me. "Huh?"

I laughed. "Never mind."

"Okay," said Liam. "Should I turn?"

"In a boat this size, you just turn that wheel a little. She'll take a while to respond. You just watch the bow and be patient. Folks tend to oversteer boats. In a smaller boat you can look behind an inexperienced boater and see a zigzaggy wake. That's how you know."

"Seems easier than it is," said the kid, his red hair blowing behind him.

"You'll get the hang of it. Think you can handle it while I grab me a brewski?"

"Get me a Coke?"

"Aye aye, captain. Steady as she goes."

He turned. "Huh?"

I laughed and pointed. "Go that way. Remember what I said about steerin'."

We had a lot of distance between us and the closest obstacles. I'm not a total dumbass. I didn't completely trust the kid to pilot that thing on his own, so I ran down

321

the steps and busted into the salon like a gunfighter through swinging doors.

Georgie, Terry, and Roxy all stared at me.

"Who's driving the boat?" asked Georgie.

"Liam," I said. "He's got it for a sec. Need anything from the fridge?"

They all held up their own glasses of whatever. I grabbed a can of Coors and a Coke. "Under four hours to go. We'll spend the night on the boat and figure out a ride in the mornin'."

"I'm not going to remember how to walk on land that isn't moving," said Terry.

"You and me both," I said. "Longest I've been offshore in my whole life, I think." I looked toward the door. "Better go. Seems like he's doin' fine, but he might be a little freaked."

"I'll come up in a few," said Georgie.

"I'll save a seat for y'all."

I headed back up. Liam was standing in front of the wheel, the wind blowing in his face. It wasn't Grand Theft Auto, but I had a feeling it was like the best video game he'd ever played.

"Here's your Coke, Cap," I said, putting it in the cup holder on the helm.

As the afternoon slipped by along with the distant shoreline, we let Liam stay where he was. He never even asked to go to the bathroom. Before we knew it, we saw what we'd been waiting for on that GPS Map.

Port Arthur. We had about another hour to go, and that was angling northwest to line us up with the inlet leading to the refinery.

Danny moved up and tapped Liam on the shoulder as we got closer to shore. The weather was good, but the wind had picked up and the swells were building. Liam seemed relieved to give up the helm, and Danny sat down, nursing his own beer.

"I'm goin' down to organize stuff," I said.

"I'll join you," said Georgie.

She followed me down to our cabin, and when we got inside, I walked to the closet where we'd stacked three bags full of guns and ammo.

"Leave that for a bit," said Georgina.

I turned. "Yeah?"

She moved toward me and slipped her arms around my waist. Tiptoeing, she still couldn't reach me, so I leaned forward and planted a good kiss on her.

"I'm horny," she said.

"Why, Doctor Lake," I said. "Is that a medical term?"

"It's actually from the late 18th century, derived from the original, *'having the horn'*," said Georgie, kissing me again. "I learned that in college."

"Shit," I said. "Knew I missed out by skippin' college."

She reached down and gave me a squeeze. "Oh, you're getting the hang of it."

Y'all don't need to know any more. This is a chronicle, not porno.

Ω

Georgie and I were well finished and almost nodding off when I felt the boat slow. Before I got my pants on, I heard the anchor chain feeding out.

"We're here," I said. "Guess we'd better scramble to make it look like we were workin'."

"I was working," she said. "Why else would I be exhausted?"

I smiled and slapped her butt. "Get some clothes on." I pulled my pants and shirt on. "I ain't gonna sleep much tonight."

"I doubt any of us will."

I pulled the gun bags out and stacked 'em on the floor. The bedroom was huge for a boat, and there was plenty of room. I'd stashed 'em because I still had reservations about Garland, though he could've grabbed any number of guns along the way and he hadn't.

I hoped we'd made the right call about him.

After we organized everything we'd want to haul along with us, we called a meeting in the salon. The seas were choppy, but the anchor was holding us in place. We were anchored about a quarter mile from the inlet leading into the Motiva Refinery, the name that was showing on the GPS screen.

Apparently, big-ass yachts had fancy-ass GPS units in 'em.

"What about him?" asked Danny, raising his chin toward Garland.

I shrugged. "Garland? You're a grownup. You're either in one hundred percent or you head off your own way when we hit shore. What's your call?"

He flashed a nervous smile as he fidgeted with his long blonde hair. "I told y'all before. I know I fucked up at the start, but I didn't kill no one. I'm a hell of a fabricator and a welder, so if there's a need to fortify any vehicles or somethin', I'll be a good guy to have around."

I looked at every face, and they were all nodding. "Good enough, then. Trust him with a weapon?"

This time the nods came slower, but eventually, everyone was in.

"He cleans a good kitchen," said Roxy. She looked at him, then asked, "Do you mind if I ask how old you are?"

"Me?" asked Garland. "I'm twenty-eight. Why?"

Roxy smiled, and I was glad to see she was more like her mother than I'd realized when we'd first met. Kind, and willing to offer the benefit of the doubt – like her mother did for me and my brothers.

"Now that you're showered and clean," she said, "It's not as prominent as before, but you have one of those faces that could either belong to a weathered 22-year-old or a well-preserved 35-year-old."

"I'll take that as a compliment," he said.

Still ain't sure why. It kinda meant he looked his age.

After a little more planning, we all took off in opposite directions, gathering supplies and parking everything near where we'd get off the behemoth boat. At the crack of dawn we'd be pulling into Sabine Pass.

Ω

I thought I was the first one up, but when I felt my way to the Keurig, I heard it spitting out the last drops of Danny's first cup of coffee.

"Hey, CB," came from behind me, and I turned to see Lilly, fully dressed, sitting in the salon. Danny stirred cream and sugar into his coffee.

"Afternoon," he said, smiling.

"Yeah, right. Sun ain't even up yet."

"Will be," said Lilly. "Noticed somethin' on that GPS this mornin'."

"What?" I asked.

"That pass goes seven or eight miles right through two wildlife refuges. One in Texas, the other in Louisiana."

"Lovely," I said. "Glad it's a big boat then."

"We should be fine," said Danny. "Some big damned ships go through there, I'm bettin'. Oil transports and the like. Can't tell how wide it is from the GPS, but it's damned sure wide enough, and deep."

"We're gonna need two big trucks or SUVs," I said. "To haul the eight of us and the gear."

"I don't know any oil men," said Lilly, "but if I were guessing what kind of vehicles they drove, that's exactly what I'd figure."

Danny walked to the window and looked out. Light was filtering through the curtains. He turned back to us. "Let's pull anchor. Come hell or high water, I wanna pull into Lebanon, Kansas tonight."

"Come zombies most likely, bud," I said. "But yeah. Let's go."

Ω

CHAPTER TWENTY-ONE

The Rendezvous Point
Lebanon, Kansas

Micky sat up on his mat and leaned against the wall, pushing the hair from his eyes as he stared out at the people spread across the gymnasium floor.

At each entry door was an armed man or woman, having taken watch shifts throughout the night. On Micky's watch, nobody had stirred; each day was exhausting.

Fear could do that to a person.

He stood, stretched, and walked over to the northeast door. The woman guarding the entrance was of Indian heritage, and though he knew he'd heard her name, he did not remember it.

"Morning," he said, his voice just above a whisper. "I'm sorry, but I forgot your name."

"It's Nayana Joshi, Mr. Rode," she said. "Naya for short."

"Thanks, Naya. Call me Micky, please. Any trouble on your shift?"

"I peeked out a few times," she said. "Saw a few just to the south of us, but they never got close."

"How many, you remember?"

She said, "Five. None for the last hour. The clearing we did before settling here gave us some breathing room, I guess."

"We needed a good night's rest after that trip. Where did you come from?"

"New York," she said. "Not the city. I wouldn't imagine too many people made it out of there. Had to have become a glass and steel killing ground."

"Glad you made it, Naya. You get out with someone?"

She nodded and smiled as she pointed to a little boy, still sleeping on a mat just ten feet to her side. "Yamir. He's eight. Very shy, but bold."

Micky nodded. "I'm glad you and your son got to us. What about –"

"We are alone," she said, her tone indicating it was just the two of them, and there was no need to inquire further.

"Okay. You handle that weapon like you know how to use it."

"I was a correctional officer at Fish Kill," she said. "Near the Pennsylvania state line. When the rain started, I didn't stay. I could only think of Yamir. The way it smelled. How it stained everything. I didn't ask; I abandoned my post and went to my son."

"Where was he?"

"I had found a place nearby where I would drop him off for daycare. School was still out. I left work and went to him. People began to get sick soon afterwards, and I've always been prepared for emergencies, living in close proximity to New York City. I had a portable ham radio in the trunk of my car."

"Smart," said Micky. "Heard my broadcast?"

She nodded. "Not right away. I just wanted to get as far away from heavily populated areas as possible. It just seemed wise."

She had jet-black hair tied up on her head, and her face was thin and free of lines. She stood around 5'8", with square shoulders and erect posture. Her brown eyes were big and alert.

"Glad you made it to us," he said, reaching out to squeeze her on the shoulder. "You both okay? No injuries on the way?"

Her eyes changed. "No. I can't say that for so many we saw on the way to your caravan. Also on your caravan. I'm just relieved we're here. I'll do whatever I can to help."

Micky thought for a moment. "We're going to want to fortify at least a portion of the town, maybe making barricades with cars, or whatever. Once everyone gets up, if you could help me sort out who might help with that, I'd appreciate it."

"Anything. I want to keep Yamir safe. He's a smart boy, so needless to say he's scared."

"Being afraid can keep you alive. Thank you, Naya."

"Thank you, Micky."

He walked away from the woman, hoping nothing he did would let her down.

The conversation had bolstered Micky's hope about the other people who had joined them, and of those still on the way. If the majority of people who answered the call to confront Climbing Fox Wattana were even close to the same mettle as Naya Joshi, their chances for success were great.

Ω

Henomawi Indian Reservation
The Home of Climbing Fox Wattana

Magi sat on the floor of the small nook, staring in the direction of the carcass lying just outside the sliding glass door, its bones nearly picked clean. He could see it only intermittently, for at the heavy sliding glass door were six of the blood-soaked skinwalkers, scratching at the glass, their moans and snarls muffled from the thick slider.

"I did not mean for her to be hurt," came the weak voice across the room from him.

Magi turned his gaze from the skinwalkers to Climbing Fox, who leaned against the opposite wall, his eye blackened and swollen, his cheek badly bruised; dried blood caked down his chin.

"You already said that a dozen times," said Magi Silver Bolt. He stood and walked toward his former spiritual guide and chief.

Wattana crossed his arms in front of his face and cowered.

Magi had arrived the evening before, after leaving the home of Atian Shining Eyes, having found his friend dead, and no trace of his Dancing Rain; his Anjeni.

And so, as he had planned, he came here, the place she said she was going.

Wattana had lied to him. Magi asked him if Anjeni had arrived, and Mundunugu had sworn he had no idea where she was.

But as he had answered, his eyes darted toward the sliding doors leading to his back yard. Had he not been watching him intently, Magi might have missed it. Panic. Guilt.

Chief Wattana may as well have stood up and pointed, saying, "She's out there."

Silver Bolt had charged to the door and thrown open the vertical blinds, immediately noticing the shoes and identifying the shredded clothing on the ravaged, bloody corpse sprawled out on the patio.

At that time, many of her bones were exposed, but three of the savage creatures still clawed deep into the cavities of her body, feasting on the remainders.

With a primal scream, Magi had turned on his Mundunugu, ripped the rifle from the old man's hands, and pummeled him in the face until he fell unconscious.

Magi, exhausted from grief and anger, had collapsed onto the floor across from the man he'd beaten, numb.

He had remained there, staring through the glass, immobilized by depression, to where his betrothed lay dead. He did not know whether sleep had taken him at all.

Now, Wattana's swollen eyes turned to follow Magi as he walked past him and into the kitchen. Sliding a knife from the butcher block on the counter, he turned.

"Please do not kill me!" he begged. "I would not have known of the text had it not been for her!"

The words burned in Magi's mind. Was the old man blaming Anjeni for his carelessness? Closing his eyes, Silver Bolt took a deep breath, raising his eyes again to the skinwalkers outside the glass door.

Their numbers had not grown.

He stepped over the bent legs of Wattana and walked to the door. As he reached for the handle to pull it open, the old man screamed, "No! Do not open it! They will kill us!"

He pulled. The skinwalkers turned toward him. Magi gripped the butcher knife in both hands and jabbed upward, into the soft neck and chin of the first one, a female with multi-colored ceramic beads woven in her gray-black hair, driving it up into her brain.

"You did this!" screamed Magi, shoving the dead one aside. With a scream that originated from deep in his shattered soul, he gripped the knife with both hands and drew it across the neck of the next creature, just a foot away.

Nearly decapitated, black goop oozed down its bare chest as it tripped on the dead female and dropped to its knees before Magi. Gripping it by the hair, he cut its gurgling growls off by jabbing the blade into its ear, all the way to the hilt.

It too, crumpled to the ground.

He shoved the third one backward, and it staggered and tripped over the bones of his beloved Anjeni. Kneeling down, Magi placed the knife on the ground and reached down to unclasp a silver necklace from around his late fiancée's ravaged neck.

The skinwalker, ignoring him, had moved toward the open slider. Magi, clutching the necklace in his fist, picked up the knife again and stood.

He walked behind the monster. It stumbled toward Mundunugu.

"No! Nooooo!" cried the chief, his eyes closed, terror on his face. He squirmed, trying to press himself into the cabinets against which he leaned, but still, the skinwalker advanced.

When it got to within six inches of him, Magi charged forward and stabbed the knife in at the base of its skull, letting it fall on the frightened elder.

He walked back to close the door, opening his palm to look at the bloody necklace.

Wattana's eyes were wide with fear and confusion. "How … why didn't they … they …" he trailed off. He tried to crawl out from beneath the weight of the dead skinwalker, grunting. His hands slipped in the putrid liquid running down his chest and pooling around him.

To Magi, he sounded weak. A useless man in any society, and no use to most of the Henomawi people now.

Climbing Fox Wattana had only one value remaining, if it was even possible.

Magi walked over and put the knife on the counter, then slipped the fine, silver chain over his head. He looked at Wattana.

"You'll die when I say it's time. Now get up and bring me the book."

Sabine Pass, Port Arthur, Texas
Aboard The Monaco Skiff

Liam stood beside me, holding onto Nokosi's collar with his right hand, his left gripping a stainless-steel handhold for all he was worth.

Nokosi was on her hind legs, barking up a storm. She had good reason.

The goddamned water was teeming with croaking, jaw-snapping gators, and the sons-of-bitches weren't shy. They crawled over one another, tried to bite the sides of the yacht, and generally defined the word *relentless*.

Their mouths open – all of 'em – and I swore every ugly eye was on us.

The fresh meat.

We all stared back, and I know that I was hoping there wasn't any shit out there we hadn't seen yet. Hell, we knew these killers existed, and I think I was more freaked out right then than I'd been back at Baxter's.

And that was no picnic in the swamp.

Some of the gators had body parts in their chops, and I'm only talking of the human variety.   Arms, legs,

Damon Novak

headless torsos, and every other goddamned combo you could come up with.

The dead floaters were mostly of the zombie variety; I could tell from the pitch-black staining on the edges of the severed limbs.

But when the bow of the Monaco Skiff hit an overturned life raft, a torso that still had its head attached slipped from beneath the yellow rubber, rolling onto its back.

The dead eyes stared upward, like a promise of what was to come. There was a bullet hole in the center of its forehead.

"God," said Roxy, turning away. "That's horrible." Terry put an arm around her and joined his friend on the bench, out of view of the melee below.

The second the gators saw the untainted meat, it was like a frantic starburst pattern of slashing teeth and swishing, armored tails, falling away from our boat as they stopped swimming and fed.

The water-logged torso quickly became a dozen separate pieces, bitten and ripped apart by a handful of the crazed zombie gators.

"Wow," mumbled Liam, his face gone pale. "I'm going downstairs." He let go of the handhold and pulled the police canine back down the steps with him. He'd begun to use pieces of cereal to coax Nokosi into following him around.

Nokosi was good with the boy. She let him pull her along. Maybe she couldn't stand seeing the only species besides her own that ever befriended her being ripped to pieces.

I stepped sideways and pushed the throttle forward, bringing us up to 10 knots. There was a lot of debris in the inlet, but I figured even if I did breach the hull, we'd make it to the dock well before she sank.

"Hey!" said Lilly, down on the bow, pointing. "Parking lot! Lots of trucks!"

I spied the dock. There was one huge platform supply vessel docked further up on it, and another several large ships free-floating just off it, but there was room to bring in the 80-plus footer safely.

"Danny! You're up man."

He knew what I was saying, so I didn't bother pointing to the thruster controls. We'd only get one shot at it. I was more likely to bounce us off the dock and into one of the other loose boats.

"Y'all ready to hit the highway?" he said, spinning the wheel to port as he reduced speed. The big yacht responded, and he started turning it back to starboard about twenty feet off the dock.

"This boat's nice, but I wanna plant these boots on terra firma," said Garland. "And this might sound crazy comin' from me, but I never wanna see another gator in my goddang life."

I chuckled to myself, but kept watching Danny's hands on the controls, trying to guess what he'd do next.

I was right. He kept pulling the throttle, all the way back into reverse. When he'd countered the forward momentum, we sat perfectly still.

Danny engaged the thrusters as I eyed the approaching dock. It was pretty high outta the water, and no gators had made their way up onto it.

I looked off to the left and saw the refinery had put up a helluva fence on the south edge of the parking lot. They probably did it to keep their employees safe from whatever normally roamed the wildlife preserve on the Texas side of the pass.

I let out a breath. My increase in speed had left almost all of the undead gators behind, too, so we were in the clear.

"CB!" called Lilly. I looked down at her, holding the bowline in the air. "Quit daydreamin' and get the stern line!"

"Oh, shit," I said, turning to run down the step. Georgie was sitting beside Roxy and Terry, and she shook her head with a smile. I smiled back.

We got the boat tied off without incident. When it was secure, Danny came clomping down the steps. "Should be a boarding ramp stashed somewhere, CB."

"I didn't see it. We got on at the stern."

He opened a large hatch. "Got it," he said. "We did it the hard way. Give me a hand."

I headed to where he crouched, and we lifted it out and laid it flat on the deck. After pivoting the handrails up into their locked position, we lifted it over the low rail and spanned the gap.

"Like a goddamned glove," I said.

Everything was already stacked on the rear of the boat. We were ready to start unloading once we found vehicles to unload into.

Everyone made their way to the stern. I turned and said, "Y'all give the boat another once over if you want. If you wanna help us find transportation, grab the gun of your choice and follow us. We're lookin' for a quad cab truck and an SUV."

We jumped the rail and crossed the ramp. "Heads up," I said, pointing. I saw several figures staggering between the cars and trucks in the half-full parking lot.

"Gotcha," said Danny. Just then, Lilly and Terry came running up behind us. I didn't give my sister a second thought. I looked at Terry and said, "You sure, man?"

He nodded and raised the barrel of his shotgun. "They won't get anywhere near me."

I nodded at him. "Welcome to the jungle." I liked the kid a lot. So did Roxy, and he was a good-looking guy. I figured if he didn't wear the other team's jersey, she'd be all over him.

We stopped and scanned the parking lot.

"Two over there," I said, pointing. "Same overalls. Employees, I'm guessin'."

Terry punched me in the arm, and I jerked my head toward him. "Yeah?" I rubbed my arm. I think the kid frogged me.

"Keys," he said. "They were in the parking lot, right?" He pointed toward a footbridge leading over the waterway. "They have to go through a security gate to get over there, so maybe they just got back from lunch or something."

"Pretty damned good thinkin'," said Danny. "Hey," he said, pointing to the south side of the lot. "Couple more over there. Let's split up."

I reached over and frogged Terry on the arm, my middle knuckle extended.

"Ouch!" he said, rubbing it.

"Turnabout's fair play. Whatever the fuck that means. Anyway, we ain't splittin' up Hansel and Gretel there, so let's you and me be … umm … Starsky and Hutch."

"*Who*?" he said, looking at me like I had sixteen heads.

"C'mon," I said. "Find me a red Gran Torino with a white stripe and I'll kiss ya." I took off and heard him following.

When I turned to look at Danny, he was smiling big, shaking his head. Hell, we needed a little fun. It'd been a long-ass boat ride and I was still swaying a bit.

As we approached the first rotter, Terry's steps slowed. "I know it was my idea," said Terry. "But … maybe you do the honors?"

I shook my head. I was serious. "Nope."

"What?" he asked, and I saw the color drain from his face.

"Terry, I'm doin' you no favors if I handle this for you. You pump a round into that gun yet?" I asked, looking at the 12-gauge.

"I don't think so," he said.

"You're tense and it's makin' ya forget stuff ya already learned. Now, hold it steady, and push that pump forward, and you're ready to go. The second it seats toward the front, you pull that trigger. You can shoot as fast as you can slam it home. They call it slam firin'."

"Okay," he said, kinda tentatively. "There's only two, and you're taking one, right?"

"You can do it. There's a term called keepin' your head on a swivel. Be aware of your surroundin's and be prepared for anything."

He took a real deep breath. "Let's go get some vehicles."

Lilly and Danny were already halfway past the first row of cars, trucks, and SUVs, and almost made it to the shambling dead things.

"Keep your eyes low, too. You saw 'em a bit at that marina in Marco, but gators and crocs can surprise you from under a car. That sucker in your hands can do some damage, maybe blow their jaws apart."

"Jesus!" he said. "Can I go back?"

"You really want to?" We were just approaching the first row of vehicles, and these had to be management's. Some nice big quad cabs, and a good lot of SUVs, too.

"I'm just nervous."

"Good. Keeps you alive." I pointed. "You got a friend," I said, nodding my head toward the first gray-faced deadeye to get to us.

"Now?"

"Yeah, now!" I said.

He raised the shotgun, the stock against this shoulder. Kid had good form.

"Raise that barrel, Ter. You shoot him in the fuckin' pocket, we'll screw up any keys he's carryin'."

Terry actually laughed and took two bold steps toward the advancing thing.

I had my eye on the other one. He'd been milling around the front row when we saw him, but he was about ten spaces over.

I heard a distant boom and looked over to see Lilly and Danny watching their first kill fall.

The next explosion was closer. It was like a water balloon filled with rancid blood exploded. It was raining reddish-black pus in Florida-sized drops.

Me and Terry both ducked down, taking the disgusting after kill on the backs of our shirts. I was wearing a baseball cap, so only a little of the shit got in my hair.

Terry's pretty hair would never be the same.

"God!" he said, standing up.

"Yeah," I said. "You let him get a little closer than I would've."

"I wanted to hit him."

"You did that. Check his pockets. I don't think he's a danger now. That other dude has some extra shit on the front of his overalls. Maybe a bigwig. Nicer car."

I marched off toward the other remnant of humanity. He was a heavy boy, buncha pens still intact in the pocket protector in his overalls. I stopped about ten feet away from him and held up the Remington 770. It was a cheaper gun, but it was it in the .30-06 Springfield caliber, and I liked the feel of it.

I raised the scope to my eye, centered the wobbly dude's head, and fired.

His head spun sideways, and his legs buckled. I could still hear the shot echoing through the enormous clearing of the parking lot when he hit the pavement.

"Cole!" shouted Terry, and as I walked toward my kill, I saw him holding up a set of keys. I threw him a thumbs-up.

I got to my guy, saw a big bulge in his right pocket, and felt it from outside. Hell yeah. It was keys. I reached in and grabbed 'em.

Chevy, complete with key fob. I stood up and pushed the button.

A double-beep sounded, but I wasn't impressed. Too high. I hit it again.

And I turned around to see a goddamned Chevy Cruze, mocking me. Hell, that car would barely haul me, Danny, and a couple guns and six-packs.

I tossed the keys on the ground and pretended to feel bad about killing a dude for his compact car.

Seeing what I'd done, Terry hit his remote. The horn that sounded in response was more like it. Kinda throaty.

I followed the noise. He'd hooked us up with a big, blue Ford Excursion. I headed over to him.

"Nice job, man! That was like Russian roulette, though. Coulda been anything."

Terry smiled. "Nice car you got," he said.

"Fuck off."

Just then, I heard an engine turn over, and saw a big red Silverado rocket out of the second aisle over. Danny whipped that big sucker around and jammed right toward us. I saw Lilly in the front seat, her teeth flashing through the glare of the windshield.

We were set. Plenty of cargo space, too. And we didn't have to hotwire shit.

"You found it, you pull it into position," I said, patting Terry on the shoulder. "Good job."

He rubbed his shoulder.

"Sore?"

"That gun has a kick."

"You're a kick. Get it lined up and get back to the boat. We got a road trip ahead of us."

$$\Omega$$

CHAPTER TWENTY-TWO

We were all pumped, I'll tell you that. Four kills netted us two vehicles. The Silverado was full of fuel, and the Ford was about three-quarters full. Both ran on gas, not diesel, which was good. It'd be tough enough refueling at all, much less searching for a station that had both fuels.

By the time we found the transportation, got unloaded, reloaded, and pulled outta that parking lot, it was just past 10:30 in the morning.

I do love an early start.

Oh, yeah. Another reason for our slightly later departure; with the Dreamliner 26 at our disposal one last time, everyone who needed a shit, shower, and a shave, got one. By the time we all loaded our butts into those two rides, we smelled like herbs, flowers, and Colgate.

I think Garland even put on some Old Spice, which is why I insisted he ride with Danny and Lilly.

Yep. We got the Silverado. Being a southern boy, I don't do Fords unless there's an apocalypse, and then only if it's my last choice. I mean, when did Bob Seger sing about a fuckin' Ford, anyway?

Like a goddamned rock.

Georgina offered to drive, and I didn't argue. Nokosi rode with Liam and Garland in the back seat of the Excursion, and obviously, we took Roxy and Terry with us. Hell, if we'd had that damned dog with us, it woulda felt like a family outing. Minus the dead folks walking around.

I liked that Georgina wanted to drive, because being a passenger's underrated. Lets a man take in the scenery.

And there was a fuck-ton of scenery.

We planned our route by plugging in the towns along the way that would keep us off the main highways, and away from the big cities. That was our original idea, and we never wavered from it.

We passed through smaller cities and towns mostly, but the first scary place we got to was Beaumont. From the GPS, it looked like the biggest city we'd pass through, and what it looked like was true.

You ever get driving through mud or deep water, where you know if you stop – or even slow down – you'll get stuck in a hurry?

Damn, I felt bad for Georgie. Fucking zombies and crashed cars were everywhere. Danny had taken the lead, but she stayed on the ass-end of that Excursion like a greyhound on a rabbit.

"You're doin' good, girl," I said, holding that *holy shit* handle for all it was worth, right along with everybody else. At one point, I thought Terry and Roxy were bawling, but when I turned my head to calm 'em down, I saw big smiles on their faces. They busted out laughing, and Georgie yelled, "What is so funny?"

That got me going, too. This was Mr Toad's Wild Ride on steroids. That's a Disney ride, just in case they've turned it into something less bone-jarring and you've never heard of it.

The deadheads came at us from every side. We must've been the only passersby in quite a while, 'cause they were ill-prepared to get to us in time, but it was like playing fucking vehicle pachinko, and we rocked from side to side. All that was missing were the dang bells.

Yeah, we dented a couple fenders, bouncing our way through that mess. Then the road narrowed out to about two lanes with some turn lanes, and the towns got smaller. When poor Georgina Lake finally got a chance to slow down, I knew she was done for a while. That's okay. I took the wheel.

We drove on, and while we saw a good number of the staggering freaks turning their heads toward us as we zipped by, the plan was working out nicely; we got through.

Until we didn't.

A sign announcing we'd arrived in Nacogdoches, Texas appeared on the side of the road, the familiar Lone Star Flag emblazoned on it. That was when we started seeing the dead zombies sprawled everywhere.

Now, Nacogdoches wasn't exactly New York City, but it did have almost 39,000 folks living there, according to that sign.

"This is interestin'," I said. I grabbed the handheld. "Danny, y'all seein' this?"

Lilly came back. "Somebody's taking them out."

Lilly, Danny and company were trailing us right then in the Excursion, but we'd switched off a few times, with them taking the lead. That didn't mean all that much, considering Georgina's ordeal and the beating our truck took as the trailing vehicle.

"Keep a sharp eye out, and your heads down," I said. "Don't need whoever's shootin' them poppin' one of us."

We drove on. We'd only been on the road about two-and-a-half hours, but to me, it felt like ten. We'd only gone a mile past the sign when we came to a roadblock. I felt my muscles involuntarily tense as I said, "Everyone, grab a gun."

When I glanced beside me, I saw Georgie already had hers in her hand. I pulled to a stop just before the blockade of cars, leaving enough room to spin it around if I had to. I hadn't noticed before, but now that I looked, there were pairs of cars and trucks blocking off the side streets, too.

No way out except the way we'd come.

In my rearview mirror, I saw Danny had also left enough room between us to get out if he had to.

Brilliant minds thinking alike? Hell, no. Just common sense.

I put it in park and looked around. The radio blurped out Danny's voice: "Wanna get out?"

I pushed the button. "Sure. Armed?"

"Hell yeah," he said. "But let's put our hands up in case whoever set this shit up is watchin'."

"Okay, go."

I looked at Georgie, then at Terry and Roxy. "Stay put. Be ready. Georgie, slide over. I'm leavin' it runnin'. Anything goes wrong, drop it in gear and get the hell outta here."

"Uh huh," said Roxy, from behind me. "Mom's not leaving you."

"You do what you think's best to stay alive then," I said. "Remember that's your daughter back there."

"Excuse me?" said Terry. "Gay lives matter." He held the DP-12 over the top of the seat with both hands. "Two in the chamber and twelve on standby," he said.

I took it. "Hell yeah you matter," I said, opening my door. "Now you matter just a little more. Hang tight."

I got out, the shotgun in my right hand, holding it in the air. I turned to see Danny, who watched me. We both closed the doors easy and walked toward the roadblock.

It didn't take long to meet who had put it in place.

"Hey," came a man's voice. "You've got about 32 gun barrels pointed at you right now, and every one of the people behind 'em can shoot."

"Fair enough," called Danny. "We ain't plannin' to shoot. Least not first."

"Keep 'em raised," the voice said. Directly in front of us, on the other side of the blockade of cars and trucks, a man stood. He was about six feet tall with brown skin, and his hair was cropped short, dark except where it was sprinkled with gray.

"I'm Jimmy Sanchez," he said, his Texas accent strong. "We're not blockin' you for long. Just tryin' to figure out what's goin' on."

"I'm Cole Baxter, and this gentleman here's Danny Williams," I said. "Came up from Florida. Headin' north."

The man's eyes scrunched up for a sec, then he asked, "Where in the north you headed?"

"Why you wanna know?"

"Because if you came from Florida, ain't no way you'd be passin' through Nacogdoches, Texas."

"Depends on whether we got to Port Arthur on a boat from Key West, don't it?"

Jimmy Sanchez smiled, and I knew he was a savvy dude. It immediately made sense to him.

"Fair enough. Y'all ready for some chow?"

I looked at Danny and raised my eyebrows. He shrugged and said, "Sure. I could eat."

I turned back to Sanchez. "Yeah, thanks. Need to make it a quick stop, though. We got some miles ahead of us, and I ain't big on the dark anymore."

He nodded and turned his head to the sides. With a quick lift of his chin, I'd estimate about thirty men, women and children stood. They all held rifles identical to the one Jimmy Sanchez held; they were lever-action .22 calibers as

The Zombie War Chronicles: Convergence

far as I could figure. The one Liam was using was similar, but these guns looked well-used.

Some of the kids were probably as young as six, but they held the rifles with a level of confidence I wouldn't necessarily expect from children their age.

"Quite a crew you got there, Mr. Sanchez."

"It's all we have left," he said. "You?"

"We're a total of eight, plus a police K-9."

A whistle came from somewhere in the group standing in front of us, and I heard two quick pops right after.

When I spotted the gun barrels responsible, I jerked my head in time to see two emaciated zombies about fifteen yards away, both in in mid-collapse. They'd just gotten through the west blockade of vehicles.

Clean head shots I guess, 'cause they hit the ground and stayed put. Little bullets make little holes, but ask JFK about that shit.

That's right. You can't.

I looked back. Both the shooters were girls. One had to be twelve or so. The other, her hair in pigtails, couldn't have been older than nine.

I was impressed.

Ω

"These children are remarkably mature," said Georgina. "There must be a story behind that." She'd just returned to the long picnic table where we sat with Jimmy Sanchez and a woman named Carla Solis.

She was a handsome woman in her forties, maybe, with jet-black hair pulled back in a short ponytail. Her eyes were intense and dark, almost black, and her features were sharp and soft at the same time.

347

Georgie had been moving among the ten or so tables, paying particular attention to the kids. I saw both Jimmy and Carla watching her as she examined almost all of 'em, obvious gratitude in their eyes.

When Georgina sat, she said, "I hope you don't mind. I'm a doctor, and I feel obligated to do what I can."

"We don't have a doctor among us," said Carla. "We appreciate it."

Georgina smiled. "We have quite a few medications in the vehicles, antibiotics, that sort of thing, but nobody needs it right now that I can see."

"We also have everything we could take from the pharmacies in the area. Just in case."

"Well, everyone appears to be healthy," said Georgie, with a smile. "That's impressive, considering everything."

Both of 'em nodded, like they already knew what Georgie'd told 'em, but I also saw relief in their eyes.

"Thank you," they said together.

The food was grilled chicken and mashed potatoes, and there was lots of it. The minute they led us through the 8-foot chain link fence and into the large, brown tent, the smell smacked me in the kisser.

I almost had a foodgasm.

"How are there so many of you?" asked Terry. "And what's with those cute rifles?" Roxy's best friend leaned forward and bit into a drumstick, turning his eyes back to Carla and Jimmy, who both smiled.

"They're a tradition with our people," said Jimmy. "Nostalgia, mostly. At least before that black rain turned everyone. Now it's necessity."

"Who's your people?" asked Danny, his mouth full of mashed potatoes.

348

"We are fairly diluted now," said Carla. "But everyone you see here is from the original Nacogdoche Tribe, at least somewhere down the line."

"Heard of the town," I said. "Never knew about the tribe."

"It's not surprisin'. Never got granted a reservation or anything. We were down to about 110 purebloods way back in 1809, evenly split between men, women, and kids. Eventually, our people were just absorbed into the general population of the area."

"So how'd you all end up together now?" asked Roxy, sitting between her mom and Terry.

I saw a little sadness touch Carla's eyes. She said, "Long before all this, I knew about my heritage, but not necessarily my relatives. My husband, Michael, gave me a DNA kit for my birthday. I did the test and sent it in. When it came back, it didn't tell me too much I didn't know before, but it did identify others in Nacogdoches and nearby towns as relatives. That was about six years ago. We started a club, collected dues, and started becoming a tribe again. At least a little."

"Carla's and my family had been friends before," said Jimmy. "My wife, Anna, and our kids, Tommy and Will." He pointed to another table, and I saw a pretty woman wave, a boy and girl on either side of her.

"My parents died when I was young, and my grandparents were already dead when I was born. I had no idea I was part of the tribe until I did the test. Unfortunately, Anna didn't have any Nacogdoche blood in her."

I took his comment as sorta strange, but Terry glanced at the woman again and asked, "Why do you say unfortunately?" He dabbed at his mouth with a napkin. "She looks fine from here."

"That's not my Anna," said Jimmy, a touch of sadness in his eyes. "Just a family friend."

"My husband wasn't of our tribe either," said Carla. "Michael and Anna both changed after the rain."

I was understanding. But at the same time, I was confused. I said, "You're sayin' you think Native American blood is what kept you from … changin'?"

"Look around you," said Carla. "Of all the people who became sick after the rain, not one person in our resurrected tribe turned."

"Interesting word choice," said Roxy.

Carla smiled. "Unintentional, but yes. We were only twenty-four strong. Some died in attacks by the dead. Others in town who didn't know their bloodline joined us. In the end we are what you see now."

"And you're tellin' me there's nobody here right now who isn't Native American?"

This time Jimmy spoke up. "I was surprised, too. We've been over it again and again. Of the thirty-eight people here, inside this fence, more than 80% are known to be of Nacogdoche heritage. It may be higher than that. Not everyone's been tested."

Inside my head, my brain was twisting around the information. What she was saying seemed to point to Indian blood – at least Nacogdoche blood – as the factor in preventing the transformation from human to zombie.

But that couldn't be right. I didn't change, but my brothers did.

"Much as your numbers seem to buck the next words that are gonna come outta my mouth, your bloodline can't have anything to do with it," I said. "The whole Indian thing. I'm not an Indian. Neither's Lilly. My brothers both changed, and we didn't."

Jimmy looked at Carla before turning back to me. "How did they change?" he asked. "From scratches or bites, or … from the rain?"

I stared at him for a sec, but my mind was working a hundred miles an hour. I thought about it. "Tanner changed from the rain. He bit Clay later, and a little while later, he changed. But that doesn't explain me and Lilly."

"Everyone known to me to be of Nacogdoche heritage did not change from the rain," said Carla. "Granted, there are unknowns. But what you see here can't be coincidence. The bites and scratches will still change any of us. We know this to be true from the ones we lost."

I looked at Lilly, and she turned away from me. I wasn't really sure at first, but a few seconds later, when I turned back, she was staring at me again, either fear or sadness in her eyes.

Now, I know my little sister. I know every expression, 'cause I've seen 'em all. I said, "What is it, Lil?"

Right then, a tear slid down her cheek, and it surprised me. I'd seen her cry recently, but this was deeper somehow. It wasn't just grief … it was something I couldn't put my finger on.

Just then, two more whistles came from outside the tent. I heard a double click, a pop, a double click, and another pop.

"It's protocol," said Carla. "Before shooting the dead, we alert everyone, so they expect what comes next. They also know it is not aggression from within our group."

"CB?" said Lilly, standing up. I turned to her again, and she flipped her chin toward the flap of the tent as she walked. I didn't have to ask. I got up and followed her.

As I walked up behind her, she said, "You got the keys to the truck?"

I pulled 'em out, and they jingled. Some kids opened the flap to let us out, and I noticed two of 'em fell in behind us, both armed with what I now saw were .22 caliber Henrys.

I was real impressed with their internal rules. Lilly and I'd both left our guns in the tent, so I guess they were bodyguards.

I got to the truck and unlocked the doors. Lilly and I got into the front seat.

"Shit must be serious," I said.

She looked up at me, wiping away another flood of tears. "I'm sorry."

"What are you sorry about, Lil?"

She took a deep breath and let it out with her eyes closed. "It's about Tanner."

"What about him?" What could she say about the brother I'd known all my life? That we'd both known?

"He … wasn't … wasn't …" her voice trailed off and she turned her head out the window.

"He wasn't what, Lil?"

"Our brother. Not by blood."

I stared at her, not believing my ears. "What the hell are you talkin' about?"

"CB, Tanner was adopted."

"How can that be right? Lil, it was Tanner!"

She turned in her seat to look me in the eyes. "When I was ten years old, you, Clay and Tanner went off on a weekend trip with Pa. Camping and fishing. Mom had her friend over for dinner that night. Enid Devereaux, I think it was.

"They got to drinking wine, and Ma started telling her a story, and they didn't know I was …"

She hesitated, like she was considering not telling me any more. I said, "Yeah, Lil? What was the fuckin' story?"

She reached out and took my hand. "CB, she miscarried before she had Clay. The doctor told her she wouldn't be able to have any kids after that. It was pretty late in her pregnancy, I think she said she was like five months along. But then, four months later, she got pregnant again, with Clay.

"It was a hard pregnancy and delivery, and after he was born, a different doctor told her she would never be able to have any more kids. She believed him. Ma and Pa wanted a bigger family, so they went to a private adoption agency and found a boy, just a month old. Clay was so young he never knew."

I stared at her. What she was saying was beginning to muffle in my ears, like it was some dream I was waking up from and the words weren't going away. When she squeezed my hand and said, "CB?" I stared at her.

"They were going to leave it at the two boys, but next thing she knew, she was pregnant with you. You were an easy pregnancy, and then I came along. I never told any of you because I was so afraid of our family getting torn apart. I was really afraid Tanner would feel like he didn't belong."

I stared at Lilly for the longest time, then turned forward and fell back into the seat. I let my mind chew on it all for as long as I needed, and Lilly didn't interrupt me. I looked outside and saw the two Nacogdoche kids on sentry with their Henrys.

Taking a deep breath, I said, "I never felt it for a second. Never gave it a thought."

"Why would you?" she said, no answer expected.

I looked at her, understanding beginning to take hold. "So. If what they say is true, we've got Native American blood in us. Tanner obviously didn't, and neither did Pa, since he changed. Ma must've been the Indian."

She stared at me. "So, Georgie and Roxy?"

"And Garland and Terry," I said. "That also explains Liam's family changin', but not him. And anyone and everyone else we meet."

We both sat in silence a long time, staring outta the front windshield at the empty streets all around us. I finally nodded, turning to look at her. "I'm sorry you had to keep that to yourself all these years. Had to be hard."

"It was. But you understand why I did?"

"Yeah. I get the feelin' Ma was gonna tell me a few times. Somethin' in her eyes. She never did, though."

"Tan was our brother, CB. Every bit as much as any one of us, he was a Baxter."

"Hell yeah, he was. Maybe more a Baxter, 'cause he was chosen."

A whistle, muffled from the closed windows, sounded beyond. It was followed by three pops.

"Let's get back inside so those kids can relax. I guess we got some shit to share."

Ω

CHAPTER TWENTY-THREE

We'd kept our promise to ourselves, having learned a lot about our predicament and that of the rest of the world.

I guess I'd always kinda accepted that Climbing Fox Wattana had started all this shit, at least to some degree. Now it was driven home that it could well be that only people long of this land – of the North American continent – had survived this.

But being born here wasn't enough; you also had to carry the blood of the original inhabitants.

American Indians. Least that's what we used to call 'em. Funny, even they'd mostly accepted it. Indian Casinos, Indian Bingo. Not a one of 'em from India.

But my mind came back to the reality of it, meaning the bloodline thing. Somehow that really hit me.

Soldiers and Marines in Afghanistan and Iraq, Syria, and the *real* Lebanon. All over the world. If they had Native American blood in 'em, they were there, wherever they were, far from home and surrounded by thousands who didn't carry the protective plasma in their veins.

Thousands of the walking dead. Hungry as hell and looking to them for sustenance.

Did it extend to others? Could it? I didn't see how. Aboriginals in Australia? Remote African tribes?

I pushed the thoughts away for right then. I'd have plenty of time to roll that shit over in my head, pointless as it was.

Garland was quiet as we left the tent. He walked with his shoulders slumped, like he didn't have a friend in the world. As the thought hit me, I realized it was true.

He didn't.

A procession of kids and adults, all with their .22 rifles, walked alongside us as we made our way to the vehicles. In the distance, I saw small pickups kicking up dust as others of their tribe stayed busy, doing what they did before we got there.

Sure, we had our guns, but still the kids walked diligently beside us. It was their way, and I, for one, appreciated it.

I stopped Garland, taking him by the shoulder, pulling him aside. After everyone else got inside our two vehicles, I stared at his face.

"What's up, man?" he asked, obviously uncomfortable.

"Just gotta ask you somethin'."

His eyes met mine. "Shoot."

I nodded, took a breath, and said, "Garland, are you a good guy?" I closed my right hand and rapped my knuckles on my chest. "In here, I mean. You a good person in here?"

He stared at my fist and got it. "I am," he said.

"Before all this shit I mean."

Nodding, he said, "Pretty harmless. Did some stupid shit when I was younger, didn't hurt no one but me, but I got my shit together. Kept my head down, got machinin' work, kept an apartment."

"Good," I said. "Then we're your family now. All of us. If you want it to be that way."

"I do," he said, nodding fast.

"That means you gotta look out for us, and we'll do the same."

A whistle came from behind us somewhere. Four rifle pops. Me 'n Garland looked around. Crack shots had taken out the threat again.

"I will, CB," said Garland. "Thanks for draggin' me out of the water. Savin' me from that crazy bitch."

"Between you, me and the lamppost, I'm glad it was her turned zombie, not you." I held out my hand and he shook it.

Without another word, we got in our respective vehicles. As I closed the door, Jimmy came up and knocked on the glass. I hit the button to roll it down.

"We'll head up tomorrow. Need to spend today to gather everything we plan to bring."

"Even though you know what they're plannin'?"

"Yeah."

"Folks may hold some grudges against Injuns, you know," I said, smiling.

"If they're still alive, they shouldn't," he said. "That *Injun* blood saved 'em."

"Good point."

"See you there."

I reached a hand out and he took it. "Godspeed, man," I said.

"Same," said Jimmy.

I raised the window again and looked around the cab. "Wagons, ho."

"Huh?" asked Roxy and Terry at the same time.

"Never fuckin' mind," I mumbled, and dropped it in gear. "Y'all wouldn't know a good western if it sat on your face."

Ω

The next four hours, I gripped that steering wheel, dodging past every dead son and daughter of a bitch we came across. Hit a few, dodged more. Luckily we'd decided to stay well east of Dallas, and we did our best to skirt away from any town bigger'n Nacogdoches.

I can tell ya, when we crossed the Red River and saw that sign that said 'Now Entering Oklahoma', I felt like cheering.

"What's it feel like to be outta Texas?" I said.

"Feels just like being in Texas," said Roxy.

"Is that a store up there?" asked Georgina, pointing.

I squinted. "Yep. And they have a gas pump. Grab the radio, tell Danny to pull over."

Georgie did, and my buddy swung the Excursion into the store's lot, which was gravel and empty, except for one dust-covered pickup. A sign said COLD BEER TO GO, and I think I started salivating when I saw it.

The old building was built to look like any general store in any old western town, with a faded wood façade and a straight wood porch running the length of it. The windows were plastered with so many beer posters and blacked out neon signs that we could see nothing in the darkness beyond.

We both backed our rides in on either side of the pump and everyone got out, weapons of choice in hand. Nokosi leapt out, too, landing on the dusty surface and shook, then took a nice bow, getting a good stretch.

Every time I looked at that dog I thought of Sonja. I missed her a lot.

As I stared, I felt Georgie's hand take mine. "C'mon. I've been craving a moon pie, and this is just the sort of place I'll find it."

"Doctors should know better," I said. "That said, I could down a couple."

358

"There's a shed over there," called Danny. "Power's out, just like everywhere. Maybe a hand pump or somethin' in there." He held up the radio. "Me n' Garland'll check it out. We'll radio if we need you to find a key."

"Be careful," I said.

He held up his gun. "Every second of every day, nowadays." They started toward the shed as the rest of us grouped together, ten feet from the front of the store.

"It's quiet," said Lilly. "CB, let's you, me and Georgina go in first, make sure it's clear."

"I can do it!" shouted Liam, his .22 rifle in hand.

I turned to him. "No yellin', man," I said, using a loud whisper to get my point across. "It's the first rule of stealth."

He looked embarrassed and upset. I reached out and squeezed his shoulder, kneeling beside him. "Until you know what's behind a door, you can't give away your position. Can you see in those windows?"

He shook his head.

"Right, neither can I. But I guarantee you, if somebody's in there, they can see out. Understand?"

A nod this time.

"Alright, kid. You see what you're doin' right now?"

He looked confused. "Huh?"

"You're holdin' that rifle just right. Barrel at the ground. Finger off the trigger. You know more than you think you do, but you still got some stuff to learn. Good job. Now, stay sharp."

Patting him on the shoulder, I stood. Georgina was looking at me like I was Father DoGood from the neighborhood parish. I winked at her.

359

I heard something metallic and felt everyone around me bristle. We all scanned the length of the building.

Around the south corner, I could see a big pasture behind it, enclosed by a split-rail fence. It was several acres, from what I could tell. The grass was dead but tall, and I still thought I spotted the ribcages of a couple horses laying out toward the middle.

As everyone followed my gaze, two dead men came into view, their ravaged faces turned toward us as they hit the fence and reached over, clawing the air in our direction.

I keyed my radio. "Heads up, we got zombies."

"Roger that, man," came Garland's voice. "Danny's almost got this lock pried off."

A driveway led between the store and the shed, heading out of view on the north side. Between the two structures, I could see the split rail fence continued off in the distance, so it was a big-ass pasture.

I wondered how many horses had been in there, and how many more of the walking dead had feasted on 'em while they were alive.

A loud metallic pop echoed across the distance, followed by a man's surprised scream, off in the direction of the shed. I knew it wasn't Danny, so it had to be Garland.

Three gunshots, followed by footfalls, and next thing I knew, Danny, yanking Garland along by his shirt, came charging around the corner. Garland still had his gun in his hand, but he was barely able to keep up with the huge stride of my old friend, and he was being dragged, more than walking.

"Shed full of zombies!" yelled Danny, his voice higher than normal, charged by adrenaline. He waved his hand for us to run, but nobody was willing to do that until he was safe.

He finally let go of Garland as they left the grass and hit the gravel, and just when I thought they were in the clear, Garland's feet slid out from under him. He went down hard, sliding a good two feet before his body started rolling, his gun four feet behind him, outta reach.

The sound of breaking glass and splintering wood came almost at the same time; everyone except Garland turned their heads to see the double doors of the old store burst wide open.

Rotted zombies of every size, gender and level of deterioration poured out of that old store like water, hitting the faded wood porch in droves. They scrambled toward us like goddamned Europeans at a Nutella sale.

"Back, back!" I screamed, but Danny hadn't seen Garland fall. I only watched the skinny dude for a split-second before deciding he was hurt bad enough to need help to his feet.

I told him we'd be his family, and I didn't let my family get mauled by a horde of the rotten dead.

I hauled ass toward him and Danny stared at me like I'd gone nuts. I guess he turned to see what I was doing, because the next second he was charging right behind me, gun raised and firing round after round past Garland's writhing body.

I joined him, firing the DP-12 about head-height as I ran, missing with half my shots. Thank God the buckshot spread wide, 'cause the peppering they got was more than adequate to take half their faces off and drop 'em to terra firma.

More gunfire erupted behind us, and I jerked my head over to see the larger horde from the store twitching and jerking as well-aimed lead blew their heads, chests and extremities into bloody mincemeat.

Danny angled toward Garland's rifle and scooped it up.

"Danny!" I yelled, and he tossed it perfectly, allowing me to snag it in mid-air.

I finally got to the skinny newcomer to our group. I put his rifle on the ground and slung the DP-12's strap over my shoulder as I held out a hand that Garland took. I jerked him up and he hopped on one leg, wincing.

"Do you need me to carry you?" I almost screamed, I was so worried about Georgie, Lilly, and the others. I saw more deadheads making their way out of the store, and Danny was still working on the shed rotters.

"Cover me a sec!" he said, hopping on his left leg while he bent down and did this sick little twist-snap to his right knee. I dropped the DP-12 back into my hands and along with Danny, we finished off the shed deadheads.

Behind me, even above the gunfire, I heard the loud *POP!* as Garland's knee snapped back into its socket. Almost made me sicker than the zombie brains and guts.

The next thing I knew, he put both feet down, flexed once, and snatched his gun off the ground. A second later he had it up and shooting as he ran sideways, firing on the larger horde.

"Spread out!" yelled Lilly, and hearing her voice made me feel good. "Liam, stay with me!"

Georgie was damned good with her 9mm, and I watched her fire it, then assess. Fire. Assess. She was surgical in her approach, and hell yeah, I'm using a pun.

One of Dr. Georgina Lake's eyes was on her daughter and her friend, and as one of the jerking freaks began to move in too close for her liking, she put a 9mm round through its head.

Terry, for his part, had learned his lesson well on the boat that day, and while he wasn't getting any closer to the advancing horde, he wasn't running away, either.

Roxy was right beside him, her face flushed white with terror, but exhilaration was there, too. She had a bit of her mama in her.

"Keep slidin' around!" I yelled, because whether we realized it or not, we were surrounding them in a semi-circle. "Space evenly and keep firin'!"

Instinct pulled the dead walkers straight toward each of us, and our arc was flat, so there wasn't much risk of shooting one another. When the rounds passed through the gelatinous flesh of the formerly living, it embedded into the well-worn wood of the storefront.

They'd stopped pouring out of the store now. Bunches of 'em had blown-apart legs, now clawing at the black blood-stained gravel to get to the fresh meat that was busy annihilating 'em into even smaller pieces.

As the horde crumpled to the ground, it was as though our entire group was moving in like a single organism, our little half-oval getting tighter and tighter until they almost lay at our feet.

Lilly held up her hand and we all quit firing. As we stood there, surveying the mess of half-rotted humanity, Liam raised his gun.

We all just watched the boy as he sighted in and fired once. He moved his barrel and fired again. Scanning the pile of dead for another five seconds, he raised it again and took out a single stinker, standing in the door of the store.

Late to the party and unwelcomed.

Suddenly, from behind us, we heard what sounded like a thousand whistles, followed by one loud gunshot.

We all spun around to see a line of Toyota pickups, men, women, and children standing in the back, strange straps around their legs, every .22 barrel pointing in the air, smoking.

It was the Nacogdoche Tribe. They were all smiling. Looks like they got 'em a head start on tomorrow.

$$\Omega$$

"To be honest," said Jimmy, "Carla and I kinda thought you all was ... let's say, a little helpless. It's why we thought to head out early. In case y'all got in trouble."

Lilly walked forward, smiling. "It could've gone much worse. It's nice to know you were behind us, even if we didn't know a few minutes ago."

"Not sure why you thought we'd get in trouble," said Danny. "I mean, don't we exude confidence and ability?" He was still breathin' hard from the fight, but flashed his bright, white teeth in a big, facetious smile.

"You said you were on the water for the last part of your trip," said Carla. "In the Gulf. That's like being on an island, and it sounds safe. We've been on land from the outset, fighting the dead. We've learned they never tire and they never sleep."

"We weren't so sure your time on that boat didn't allow you to forget how bad it can be out here," said Jimmy. "We followed early just in case."

"Good point," I said. "But we fought our share of 'em in the Florida swamp and on land before we got aboard the first boat in Key West. Some along the way, too. Like we told you at your tent, zombiegators and zombiecrocs, too. It's not somethin' anyone ever forgets."

"You're worthy traveling companions," said Carla, lifting her chin toward the store. "Think anything in there is untainted?"

"Well, Moon Pies ain't on a zombie's diet, far as I know," I said. "And this lady here?" I indicated toward

Georgina, who stood beside Roxy, a look of relief on her face. "She wants a Moon Pie."

Suddenly, in the distance, we heard the sound of a motor cranking. It caught and sounded like a lawnmower.

Two bells rang at the gas pump, a dim light flickering to life above it.

As we stared at it, Garland, who'd disappeared without anyone noticing, came running up. He huffed, "Saw the gen between them zombie legs when we opened the shed door. Went to check it out, and she fired right up."

"Good goin', Garland!" I said. "Let's hit that store, fill up our tanks, and get back on the road. We got ourselves a real caravan now."

Ω

Liam was turning into a little warrior. He had that .22 rifle on his shoulder like a little soldier marching off to war, and he was first stepping over the piles of reeking dead to get to the store entrance.

I could see the door had been latched, 'cause the top crossbar, made of weathered wood like the rest of the place, was splintered outward. Not strong enough for the weight of the dozens of undead.

The reek in that store was about the worst I'd ever smelled I my life; rotted body parts that had fallen off their owners – legs, fingers, feet, among other less-identifiable parts – littered the smeared linoleum floor.

I wanted to clear the store first, so me and Garland tried to open the east door behind the checkout counter, but it was locked. We searched behind the counter, opening drawers and looking for key racks, but found nothing.

Everyone else who'd come in grabbed grocery sacks and stepped over the nastiness as they grabbed stuff that didn't appear to be moldy or ruined in some unspeakable way by the walking dead.

Carla and Jimmy came in, but the other adults in their group and about half the kids stayed outside on sentry; it was their way, and it felt like we had armed guards at our service. I'd never complain about that.

Our search fruitless so far, Garland finally pulled out a sizable pocketknife and jimmied the cash register drawer open. Sure enough, a brass key sat in an empty coin compartment. He snagged it, proud of himself.

"Nice work," I said. "Do the honors."

We walked to the storeroom door and he slid the key in the lock. It turned. To his credit, before opening it, Garland put his ear to it, knocked on it, and listened.

"It's quiet," he said. I nodded.

We went in. There were extra stocks of pristine product. Chips, candies, cases of sodas and beer. Nothing real perishable, but we'd have to get used to that, I figured. There was even some Tostitos Cheese Dip.

We reached another door, the sunlight from outside shining around the edges, and he pushed the center bar. It swung outward.

About forty cars and trucks were parked in the middle of the pasture. The gate was closed which is why the horses hadn't been able to escape the hungry dead.

"That sure explains a lot," said Garland.

"Wonder whose bright idea it was to keep that door locked," I said.

"Yeah," said Garland. "Maybe they started to turn in the night or somethin'. Couldn't figure out the front lock in a panic, and the back door … shit." His voice trailed off, and I could tell he was picturing what might've happened in there.

"What's done is done," I said. "Now, didn't I see a case of Moon Pies in that storage?"

"Fucking vanilla ones, but yeah," he said.

I patted him on the back. "We're gonna get along just fine."

Ω

CHAPTER TWENTY-FOUR

The Toyota Tacoma pickups the Nacogdoche drove north in our caravan all had good winches mounted on 'em, which is more than I could say for either the Chevy or the Ford.

Jimmy, Carla, and the rest of their tribe had more handheld radios – turns out the whistles weren't the only way they communicated – and they made sure we were all on the same channel. 23.

Two of the other adults, Liza, and Phillip, drove ahead of the rest of us, their Tacomas designed more for clearing traffic obstructions in our way than hauling people.

"I don't like that they have most of the children riding in the beds of the trucks," said Georgie. "If they overturn …"

I looked over. What they'd done was kinda ingenious. The bed of each truck had six chairs mounted in back. They looked like movie theater chairs in rows of two, where the seats flipped up when you weren't sitting in 'em.

Behind each chair, probably welded or U-bolted to the back of 'em and then to the truck bed, were steel posts, about six feet high.

The first time I saw how the setup worked, I actually laughed, 'cause this group had their shit together. Even through my window and the sound of the motors running, I heard 'em whistle.

All six of the kids in back of that truck stood up, .22 Henrys in position. Harnesses they wore secured 'em to that center pole, and the chair spun with 'em as they spun in any direction they wanted, firing on zombies.

This shit was super handy when we hit towns occupied by good numbers of the deadheads. I tell ya, we had to fire nary a shot. Those kids were disciplined, trained, and unafraid.

Made me sad a bit, thinking how they'd lost their youth.

When they'd cleared the threat, they spun their seats back around facing forward and dropped back into 'em. Hell, all they needed was popcorn.

Back to Liza and Phillip's Tacomas. They accommodated just two kids in back, both with the same setups. Danny had checked 'em out, noticing they were different, and he said they had a bunch of dumbbell weights layered on the bottom, spot-welded together for weight.

Not a whole lot, but enough to allow them to pull larger vehicles out of the way with their big winches. That's why they went first – to clear a path. Half the time they were so far ahead of us they were out of sight.

All in all, we got damned lucky to run into 'em.

Night fell, but we kept driving. Nobody wanted to stop before we got to Lebanon, Kansas. It had been a long run north, but we were so close, stopping could only spell disaster.

Idle hands may well be the devil's workshop, but idle caravans draw soulless corpses. I'd keep these hands on the Chevy steering wheel until we passed the sign for Lebanon.

Ω

That happened just after 3:30 in the morning.

I don't know why such a wave of relief washed over me, seeing that sign. I pretty much knew life wouldn't get much easier from that point on, but somehow, the forty-six people and the single German Shepherd in our group gave me hope.

Now we had to hope Micky Rode wasn't a fucking kookaloo, and that his plan made some kinda sense. Not that I really thought any of those deadheads could be brought back to life; I didn't. I didn't wanna think of what kind of life it would be, even if it were possible.

Neither did anyone else, far as I knew. But maybe – just maybe – Wattana had a way to drop the monsters he'd created with that black rain. If he did it once with his dark curse, impossible as it seemed, maybe he had one piece of good magic left up his sleeve.

I couldn't believe one without having some hope of the other.

We stopped when we got to Phillip and Liza's vehicles, which had parked in the middle of the street, lights on. The kids in the back of the beds were on alert, scanning the area around us.

We all parked and got out, meeting in the middle.

"No sentries," said Carla. "I'm a bit surprised."

"They just got here a couple of days ago, right?" asked Terry, who looked exhausted. "Maybe they needed some rest before they secure the place."

"Can't secure anything when you're dead," said Jimmy. "There should at least be some folks with radios at the main roads into town."

A fucked-up thought struck me. I looked at Georgie and took her hand before I whispered it. "Maybe they were overrun already. We haven't had the ham up, but silence is silence, and you're right. No guards."

Roxy shook her head, which meant I whispered like I can dance – like shit. "They're not military, right?" she said. "So they might not know the best things to do to stay safe. I didn't know anything about that before this, and Terry screwed around that time and almost got himself killed."

"I *wasn't* gonna let him get killed," I moaned. "Had that rotten bastard in my sights the whole time."

"Whatever," said Roxy. "Rode's just a damned disc jockey and the rest of his people are probably just survivors, like us. It's not like we're a trained army. These guys are as close to that as anyone we've come across." She indicated to Carla and Jimmy.

"Good point," said Carla, 'cause apparently the whispering attempts were over. "I say we circle the vehicles, create a barrier, and set up in this intersection for the night. No sense in approaching them in the dark."

"And sleep on what?" asked Liam.

"We've got banana loungers, beach chairs, director's chairs. Enough for everyone," said Carla. "We'll build a fire and settle in right here until morning. It'll be light in three or four hours. Then we can get everyone fed and go see who is at the school."

Everyone looked at everyone else, and I think we all admitted at once that it sounded like a good plan. Hell, I could've laid down on a pile of rocks and it'd feel good. I was tired.

"I got some Jack Daniel's," said Danny. "Anyone wants a little comfort, head over to my spot."

I guess I didn't mention how many Tacoma pickups there were – No Tundras to speak of. Guess they were a bit too big, drinking that much more fuel.

A lot of the kids drove, too. You'd have no way of telling whether it was an adult or a child who drove a given vehicle, 'cause if they were at the wheel, they could drive as well as they could shoot.

I could tell everything had been practiced; the vehicles started tailgating one another, all turning left around the intersection, with another pulling behind, then another, and finally, with the vehicles in a perfect circle, a whistle sounded and they all braked at once.

Duffle bags were removed and tossed down to cover all the gaps beneath the pickups, and only then did everyone pull the chairs out and set up camp. The fire was started and burned low in the center of the intersection.

The .22 rifles were there beside all of 'em. I had my Remington 770, and of course Georgie, sitting on my left, had her 9mm.

I stared at the fire a long time. Danny was to my right, and every once in a while, I'd hear the liquid splash in the whiskey bottle and turn my head. I wasn't sure it was a good idea, but I *did* want it.

Finally, when I turned again, Jimmy smiled and said, "Go ahead, friend. We've got your back tonight."

I nodded, smiled, and squeezed Georgina's hand. She, in turn, patted Nokosi, who sat at her feet, head on her paws, eyes closed. I held out my hand and Danny gave me the bottle. I tilted it to my lips, and the liquid ran warm down my throat. My eyes closed, I felt Georgie take it from me. I thought I might just love that woman.

Ω
Micky Rode
Lebanon, Kansas – North End

Micky couldn't sleep. Not only because he didn't have any faith in the people standing watch, but because he had begun to question everything.

Even his own motivation.

Because it seemed he would need a better selection of people before even considering heading out for California, he'd used his ham radio setup to broadcast again the night before. He announced he had arrived in Lebanon and had reiterated the plan. The cloud cover over the area had been as thick as a blanket, and he was not sure the message had even broadcast successfully – or if it had, clearly.

So, as expected, he'd wasted another day. Sure, he'd gathered a fair number of people along the way, but the rag-tag group spread out over the floor of the gymnasium wasn't equipped for either a road trip or battle.

It seemed like most of them thought this was their final stop; that Lebanon, Kansas was their final destination.

Micky never indicated that. Every broadcast, he'd said what the plan was. Most of the people who'd joined his little procession of survivors seemed to be looking for someone to protect them.

He'd done it, up until now, along with three or four capable men and women. But now, he needed them to step up, learn how to fight if need be, and be ready to go after Climbing Fox Wattana.

But in the roughly 48 hours he'd been in Lebanon, he'd even begun to wonder if his initial plan wasn't a fool's errand, borne out of anger and revenge.

Did he really want to force the shaman to reverse what he'd done, or was his true intention to kill him outright for wiping out those he loved?

Rode struggled with the answer. Was the former even possible? In any manner? The more of the undead

Micky came across, the less he believed anything could be done. They were dead; they were deteriorating, day by day.

The world was being polluted by their decomposing flesh, and it was getting worse, not better.

And still they walked. Still they hunted down the living, putting terror in their hearts, sapping their will to fight, and in many cases, their will to live.

In places that hadn't seen any true rainfall since this started, the rank, black residue from the ungodly black rain still stained the fields, streets, and buildings. Only time would rinse it away, and then, to where? Its inky pitch would seep into the crust of the planet, poisoning the soil, perhaps.

Maybe even food grown in it would change people into monsters.

Just in the two days they'd been in Lebanon, a woman and her son had committed suicide. She had taken a six-shooter and fired it into her nine-year-old boy's temple, then put the same gun to her own.

She was careful to hit both their brains, so they would not come back. Somehow, that touched Micky even more than the act itself; in ending her fear, she had protected the ones left to carry on.

It was very quiet in the auditorium as the word got around. Nobody had known or befriended them; perhaps that was the problem.

One woman was pregnant, ready to pop any moment. She said she believed her due date had passed already. Micky dreaded that ordeal – for that's what it would be. They would have to find soft blankets, formula, a crib, and everything else necessary to care for an infant.

Worse, maybe, was that the baby would remind him of his own loss, of the early days of his marriage when his son was born.

It wasn't the mother's fault, he often reminded himself. What was her name, anyway? Micky thought it was Carrie.

He hoped by the time that baby was born, he would be on his way to the Henomawi Nation Reservation.

Standing to walk the floor once more, he stepped over several bundled shapes and made his way to the edge of the crowd. He had asked them to stay in the middle; leave room for the sentries guarding them. At least they had listened to that.

Nobody who was supposed to be awake was sleeping. At least he had some he could rely upon.

He nodded at the guard and pushed outside. He lit a stale cigarette, looked at the still streets in the clouded moonlight, and said a prayer for all of them.

Snuffing the smoke out on the black-stained ground, he moved toward the door when somebody pushed through and hurried toward him. He reached for his pistol and had the .45 out before the person reached him.

"Whoa!" came a female voice. He did not recognize it, so assumed they'd never had a conversation.

"Mr. Rode, it's Carrie. The pregnant woman. She's gone into labor."

"Damnit," said Rode. He was seeing everything get more and more complicated.

"What?" asked the woman, perplexed. "Without babies, this world will die out … if you're in charge, you should realize that much."

"I know, I know. I'm just feeling like I've gotten myself – maybe everyone – into more than we bargained for. Do you know if there are any doctors here?"

The woman said, "No, not that I've heard."

"Alright," he said, sliding sideways past her, into he building.

A lantern had been lit, and several people stood around Carrie, who was on her back, resting against a pillow.

He reached her and did what they all expected him to do. He knelt down and took her hand. "How are you?" he asked. The woman looked to be in her late twenties.

"It's time," she moaned. "I'm … really cramping."

"Don't worry, I'm sure you have lots of time," said Rode. "You can be in labor for hours. We just have to try to keep it down as much as we can. Sound carries at night."

She shook her head. "No," she whispered through her pain. "It's my third delivery. I feel the baby crowning now."

Micky Rode suddenly felt dizzy.

Ω

Magi Silver Bolt & Climbing Fox Wattana
Henomawi Nation Reservation

Silver Bolt stirred from a fitful sleep; one in which he had nightmares of Anjeni Dancing Rain, ripped apart by a horde of skinwalkers.

Anger turning his blood cold, he looked over at the bound shaman. He was still as he had been when Silver Bolt had looked earlier; seated in the chair, his wrists tied, the ropes crisscrossing beneath the chair before wrapping around his mid-section several times.

He was not going anywhere.

Silver Bolt stood. Fingers squeaked along the blood-smeared glass of the sliding door, the sound accompanied by muffled snarls and moans. The creatures there were not giving up their pursuit of blood-filled flesh.

Their presence teased Magi; tempted him to sacrifice the old man to their hunger – the ultimate punishment for what he had taken from him.

His mind went again to the brief transmission he'd heard last night on the ham radio; the compact one the shaman had kept for emergencies. The person identified himself through the static, saying something about a road. Nicky, or Ricky, maybe. There was no such street in or around the reservation.

Still, the broadcaster's intention was clear. He was coming for Climbing Fox Wattana. He did not believe their new chief was dead; he was convinced the video was faked, as it had been.

He knew. Mundunugu had called them over as soon as he had the idea, and he, Dancing Rain and Shining Eyes had helped the old fool carry out the plan.

They would not just kill him. This group of angry white people would wipe out any of the Henomawi who had survived.

They would not get the chance, though.

He stormed over to Mundunugu, kicking him in the shin.

The old man moaned, then jerked his head up. "I'm awake!" he said angrily.

Magi retrieved a pocketknife from his pants and leaned down to slice the ropes securing the old man. "Stand up. You must prepare."

"What do you mean, prepare?" he mumbled.

Magi stormed across the room and retrieved the Igloo cooler. He carried it to where the old man sat, gingerly untying the remaining ropes from his wrists and ankles. Magi dropped the cooler on the floor and opened it.

The smell permeated the room immediately. It had not been pungent at all when he'd first mixed it; now it was a horrific smell, like that of death itself.

Choking back a gag, Silver Bolt reached inside the Igloo and took a handful. He smeared it on his own forehead, cheeks, and chin. "Put this on all the exposed parts of your body. When you are done, we will allow it to dry while the sun rises."

Climbing Fox stared at him, his eyes wide and frightened. "It's … putrid!"

"I don't care!"

Wattana reached in, scooping a little onto his shaking fingers. He looked up at Magi Silver Bolt. "What then?" he asked.

"We go out to each home on the reservation and find all who survived. We must form an army of the living – and the undead."

"Why? How?"

"Obey me!" screamed Magi, his fists clenched, dripping the ripe compound from his fingers to the floor.

"But I am the chief of the Henomawi Nation now!" shouted Climbing Fox Wattana. "I alone may command our people!"

Without warning, Magi Silver Bolt dipped his fingers into the bucket of skin and earth. He drew his hand back and slapped it into the old shaman's face, knocking him backward out of the chair.

"You are *no* Standing Rock! You are *no* chief!"

Magi's hands trembled and he clenched them into fists. Leaning close to Wattana, he growled, "You live only by my will, and only long enough to stop this evil you have set upon our land and all people! The moment I am convinced you cannot do that, is the moment you take your last breath."

Magi's heart slammed in his ears. His breathing was shallow and fast. He tried to calm himself.

Magi stood again, looking down at the man he once respected. "If this group *is* coming to kill you, it is my duty to protect you until you do what must be done."

Wattana turned his eyes upward toward Magi, but remained silent and motionless.

"Now" said the young man. "Do what I said."

Ω

EPILOGUE

Through a very short night filled with sharp whistles, the tiny pops of .22 caliber rifles, and silent gaps, all of us were safe.

Nokosi chuffed a bunch of times in the night when the whistles sounded, because she was smart enough to figure out what they were and what they meant.

I'd open my eyes, too, and over Georgina's shape beside me, I saw the German Shepherd's ears pricked.

After the shots, they'd stay that way for about five seconds, then go down again.

When I sat up and stretched, the sun was higher in the sky than I could believe, and the Nacogdoche Tribe was like a well-oiled machine once again.

Bowls of oatmeal, Malt-O-Meal, or pre-packaged granola bars were on the menu, and there was enough for everyone. I downed a bowl of the Malt-o-Meal and snagged two granola bars. I only took the Malt-O-Meal 'cause I hadn't even heard of it since I was a kid.

Tasted like shit, but it brought back memories.

When I finally got outta my banana lounger and moseyed around, I spotted about sixteen prone deadheads spread all around our little peaceful circle of solitude, taken out by our Indian friends.

I sat back down as my girl stirred in her uncomfortable lounger, noticing that Nokosi had wandered off somewhere. "Morning," she said, just cracking her eyes open. "What's that?"

"Let's just call it slop. Want it with brown sugar or not?"

"Coffee. One of those granola bars."

I handed her my cup. "Looks like they're ready to straighten out this circle of trucks and head to the school. I'll make you a cup when we get there. How's that?"

"What time is it?"

I checked the old Timex. "Man. 7:45. We slept in."

She reached her arms up in a stretch and yawned. "I did, at least."

Lilly, Roxy, Terry, and Danny all walked up, looking fresh and ready to move. "Where's Liam and Garland?"

"They took Nokosi. On patrol," said Lilly.

"Kid's a little fighter," said Terry. "I guess we should've known when we saw him on that boat with his mother."

"We should keep an eye on him," said Georgina. "Trauma can hide in the young."

"I am, mom," said Roxy. "I talk to him a lot."

The whoops and whistles told us it was time to get moving. I didn't mind someone else taking over. I felt like a huge journey had just ended, but I accepted that another was about to begin.

Ω

When we guided our caravan north up Main Street, like Rode had instructed, we saw the school before we got to it. It was, as Rode had said, the largest structure in the town, and appeared to be the most solid.

So as not to alarm our hosts, Carla, Jimmy and the other Nacogdoche elders told the kids to only take out immediate threats to our caravan.

There weren't any. I guessed Rode's people had done a bit of clearing themselves.

In the lead, Jimmy and Carla stopped their truck about 100 yards from the school. They banged on the horns three times fast, just to offer a few chirps of greeting.

It didn't take long for the big auditorium doors to open. People came out, each one gripping their weapons just a little tighter. Then another dude came out.

Long hair, little overweight, but not much. He threw us a wave.

We all waved back with our free hands. We all smiled too. We'd discussed it. A smile goes a long way with a stranger.

He handed his rifle off to another man, who nodded at him. Micky Rode made his way toward us, walking briskly and like a man with a new energy in his step.

When he got close enough, he called, "Welcome to Lebanon!" His eyes scanned our numbers, everyone with a gun of some kind in hand. "I can't tell you how I've been waiting for you."

He was smiling, too.

Ω

We got oriented and evaluated, analyzed, and scrutinized, and we did our share of the same to them.

Being the one who convinced my group of eight-and-a-dog to head to Lebanon in the first place, I invited Mr. Rode to sit with us for a bit and talk in private.

Carla and Jimmy let us have our audience with the disc jockey.

"So, Micky. We've caught a few of your broadcasts. Not all of 'em. Your plan the same?"

He looked at each one of us, smiled and nodded. "Had my doubts for a bit. Until you guys showed up."

"What do you mean?" asked Danny.

"You see the people in that gymnasium?"

We all nodded.

"Okay," he said. "I'm no badass. I'll grant you that. But I know how to fire a handgun and I know how to fire a rifle. I can count the others with some skill on one hand."

"So you couldn't head to California with no militia to speak of," said Garland.

"Right," said Rode. "I offered to help train them, but they seemed content just to be here. My last option was to threaten them with expulsion or something, but I'm not a damned tyrant. I know they're tired and scared."

"We all are," said Georgina. "Any medical issues with the group? I'm a doctor, and we have some medications here."

"No medical issues ... not really. Just a concern."

His eyes shifted, and I saw trouble there.

"What's up, Micky? Somethin' wrong in there? If we're part of this thing, you need to share."

He turned his eyes to us, and they were troubled. "I'd started to question why I was doing this in the first place. I wondered if I was just telling everyone I wanted to find this lying son-of-a-bitch Wattana and make him fix this mess, when I really wanted to kill him for what he did to my family."

"We all want to kill his ass, my friend," said Danny. "But if any of us was killers, we wouldn't be in this group. We're just survivors, good people. I'm sure we all understand how you feel, though."

He shrugged. "Doesn't matter now. I changed my mind. Before you showed up. I'd have gone by myself if I had to."

We all glanced at one another. Terry scratched Nokosi's ear. "What changed your mind?" asked Liam.

Mickey knelt down and put a hand on Liam's shoulder. "What changed my mind, I don't think you should see, but I'll tell you what. There's lots of kids here. Why don't you head on in and meet some of them."

He picked up his rifle and I reached out and put a hand on it. "Leave the gun for now, Liam. We're safe enough here. Got a few guards around us."

The kid looked like he was going to argue, but in a sudden burst of common sense, he didn't. "Okay. See you guys," he said.

"Follow me," said Rode, standing and looking squarely at Georgie. "You might find this especially interesting, Doc."

We all got up and fell in behind Rode. He went to a door set into the brick side of the building. He opened it, and I saw brooms, rakes, shovels, and other supplies. He leaned in and pulled out a large ice chest, setting it down.

Looking up at us, he said, "If you've got a weak stomach, better turn away."

Terry and Roxy turned away. After another second, Garland did the same. Me, Lilly, Danny, and Georgina looked on.

He opened the lid.

I almost puked but turned away before it came up. The others stared in horror.

Rode reached in and lifted the blanket, the dead baby staring sightless up at the sky. Its eyes were open but covered by a gray film. Its mouth was open, too. Its skin was mottled and vein-ridden, and black stains ran down the sides of its dead face.

I knew what it was. He said it anyway.

"One of our survivors, Carrie. She was full-term when we got here. This little guy was delivered last night. Healthy. Pink. Then … this. Two hours later, it started coughing, choking, spitting black."

He turned it sideways. "I had to do this. Nobody else could."

The puncture was clearly from a knife blade. The zombie baby had been bald, and you could see where the black had leaked out from its infected brain.

"This changed my mind," he said, returning the baby to the cooler. "If this is still happening, and if it's going to continue to happen, we need that bastard alive. So, I trust myself now. I won't kill him. He needs to fix this."

I took a deep breath and took Georgina's hand in mine. I also met the eyes of my sister and my best friend.

Before I could say anything, Lilly Baxter reached out, rested her hand on Micky Rode's shoulder and asked, "Mr. Rode, exactly when do we leave for California?"

Ω

LOOK FOR BOOK 3 IN THE ZOMBIE WAR CHRONICLES COMING EARLY 2019!

MEANWHILE, LEAVE A REVIEW ON AMAZON.COM AND LET OTHER READERS KNOW WHAT YOU THINK!

Made in the USA
Middletown, DE
20 September 2019